PRAISE FOR KARLA SORENSEN

"If Karla writes it . . . I'm reading it."

—Devney Perry, #1 *New York Times* bestselling author

"Karla Sorensen's books are pure magic!"

—Penny Reid, *New York Times* bestselling author

"An expert at her craft, no one writes heartwarming characters with emotional depth like Karla Sorensen. She's a perfect fit for readers who love to laugh, build a found family, and fall in love."

—Kandi Steiner, *USA Today* bestselling author

"It was beautiful, heartbreaking (yet it put me back together, too), and the perfect mixture of spicy and sweet."

—Megan Reads Romance on *The Best Laid Plans*

"Sparkling tension between our main characters, a slow burn that doesn't leave you unsatisfied for too long, witty and smart banter, all blended together with romance that feels right and natural."

—Helpless Reads on *The Best Laid Plans*

"A perfect blend of raw emotion, tension, and humor, it was everything I didn't know I needed."

—All in with A on *The Best of All*

"With a torturous slow burn that finally snaps with the most electric kind of tension, a seriously swoony tortured hero, and a storyline that made my chest ache, this was even better than I expected."

—Jeeves Reads Romance on *The Best of All*

German children from hunger and despair in the aftermath of a war that Ireland had not fought.

Even from the corner, Gisela could see eyes widen as visitors took in the sight of scraggly, malnourished strays standing a little straighter, smiling a little toothier, eager for a bed and a seat at any table. She feared she and her sister would never have a turn, especially since Elisabeth had made a stink when the nuns who oversaw the children had tried to separate the two of them. Only one week before, a woman in a fine coat the color of cornflowers, with a hat and purse to match, had spotted the two of them and said she'd take Elisabeth, who was slightly smaller. Gisela had imagined the castle where Elisabeth might go to live, the hounds with silky coats, tea served from silver pots. But Elisabeth had gripped Gisela's arm, stomped her foot, and said, "No," over and over until the fine woman changed her mind and chose a quieter girl from the crowd of eager orphans. Gisela had scolded Elisabeth later.

"What were you thinking, Bit? You should have gone with her! You could have won her over then maybe she would come back for me!"

"And what if some other family took you away before I could get back? Did you think of that? Then what? Where would we be?"

Gisela had shrugged but thought again about that fine woman's castle, the long quiet corridors, silken curtains, and feasts of roasted bird, far away from war and famine and the stench of death.

The din rose as the old nun Johanna shouted names and waved children over.

"We should go closer," Elisabeth said. "So they can see how nice and sweet we are."

"These people don't want two mouths to feed," Gisela said. "Look at them." Some of the men wore coats or vests, others only suspenders and shirtsleeves. The wives were rosy and plain in their frocks and flat shoes and worried glances. "They look like they have barely enough for their own. I told you. You should have gone with the blue lady."

Johanna's deep voice boomed their names. Elisabeth gripped Gisela's hand. "I have a feeling," she said, as they made their way through clots of children.

"These are the Flanagans," Johanna said, gesturing to the sturdy couple. She thumped the woman on the chest first. "Hannie. Hannie." Then the man, "Hugh. Hugh." Words flew between the women, English words that Gisela could hardly understand. Beside her, Elisabeth had gone stiff, steeling herself, Gisela knew, for disappointment. This time, though, Johanna raised her hands then lowered them. "Easy now. You'll go together. No fears." When she said "together" and Hannie nodded, Elisabeth grinned.

She and Elisabeth were plucked like weeds from the refugee center and plopped into the Flanagans' car. "Off to your new home," the old nun said with a final wave, her marble-knuckled fingers waggling like iris stems caught on a breeze.

After hours in the jerking car, they arrived in West Cork. From the ragged back seat, Gisela caught glimpses of wild seas, rock cliffs, inlets dotted with fishing boats, villages with capped men hauling bags into stores, kegs into pubs, bustling on streets that had not been bombed. She and Elisabeth had been in Ireland for months now, this place of sun and rain and peat-smoked skies and singing birds in the trees. This place that had not seen their horrible war. Hazy purple rhododendrons bloomed on the hillside flecked white with sheep and every shade of green to the gray of stone. Gisela exhaled heavily. It had been war for so long. War and marching, war and yelling, war and worry. War and war and war. War was all she knew. It had been less than a year since the bombing, since Gisela had lain pinned in the Cologne rubble next to her sister. Her teeth and jaws and eye sockets had ached from grimacing, from calling for help, so much so she had wanted to never hear her own voice again. She had felt too young to feel so old. In the eerie quiet of the bombed-out street, leaflets and ash billowing on a sour breeze that smelt of flesh and misery, it had been a relief to give up, to wait with her sister for death, to imagine heaven.

HOW NOT TO FALL IN LOVE

DISCOVER OTHER TITLES BY KARLA SORENSEN

The Wilder Family

One and Only

Head over Heels

Promise Me This

Forever Starts Tonight

This Wild Heart

The Wolves: A Football Dynasty (second gen)

The Lie

The Plan

The Crush

The Ward Sisters

Focused

Faked

Floored

Forbidden

The Washington Wolves

The Bombshell Effect

The Ex Effect

The Marriage Effect

The Bachelors of the Ridge

Dylan

Garrett

Cole

Michael

Tristan

Three Little Words

By Your Side

Light Me Up

Tell Them Lies

Love at First Sight

Baking Me Crazy

Batter of Wits

Steal My Magnolia

Worth the Wait

The Best Men

The Best Laid Plans

The Best of All

The Kings

Lessons in Heartbreak

Single Dad Dilemma

HOW NOT TO FALL IN LOVE

KARLA SORENSEN

Published by Montlake, Seattle

www.apub.com

EU product safety contact:
Amazon Media EU S. à r.l.
38, avenue John F. Kennedy, L-1855 Luxembourg
amazonpublishing-gpsr@amazon.com

ISBN-13: 9781662536212 (paperback)
ISBN-13: 9781662536229 (digital)

Cover design by Caroline Teagle Johnson
Cover image: © Michelle Lancaster PTY LTD

Printed in the United States of America

HOW NOT TO FALL IN LOVE

PROLOGUE

Remi

If there were a headline to this ill-advised evening, it would be something like: Single Mom Forced into Wild Night by BFF, Still Plans to Be Home and in Bed by 10:30 p.m. And really, the wildest part of the entire thing was the belief in myself that I could stay awake that late.

Okay, no, that wasn't wild. It was everything else about this evening that put me squarely in the What Friggin' Universe Am I Living In category. But that was the product of an impetuous best friend and a sort-of breakup with a sort-of boyfriend.

Starting my day with laundry, a million unread texts, and copious amounts of both coffee and dry shampoo to keep me functioning was completely normal. Ending my day in the dark corridor of some overpriced bar, wearing a shirt showing entirely too much boob, was not.

"I don't know if I can wear this."

Was it too late to protest the clothing choices? Yes. But logic had fled in the wake of exposed cleavage.

Vanessa rolled her eyes, yanking down on my arms when I tried to cover myself. "You are, because you look hot and if I were into women, I'd bang you seven ways till Sunday." She stepped back, giving an appraising look. "Maybe eight. You could make someone see God with those tits."

"Thanks," I said dryly.

Ness leaned forward, slicking a fresh coat of magenta lipstick over her lips. It was a darker shade than her hair, and the effect, I'll admit, was pretty impressive. "Come on, I told Christian we'd be here thirty minutes ago."

The throb of the music was obscene. We weren't even in the main room and my bones pulsed in time with the beat. God, I'd be deaf by the time I got home. And if Ness was distracted enough by the guy who'd invited her, that would hopefully be very soon.

"Why did I say yes to this again?"

Vanessa ran her pointer finger under her eye, even though the thick black eyeliner was immaculate. "Because you are in a multiyear slump, which I thought would be broken by what's-his-name—" I gave her a sharp look, and she held up her hands. "I know, we're not talking about that train wreck."

"Just because he didn't break the slump doesn't mean I need . . ." I fumbled for words, eventually settling on a vague gesture toward my chest. "God, I must be more buzzed than I thought for agreeing to this."

She patted me consolingly on the shoulder. "It was only two drinks, sweet pea."

"Two drinks with a heavy pour," I pointed out. "I have zero tolerance, Ness."

"I know." She smiled. "You have not had a night of harmless debauchery in a decade of this single-mom gig, and this morning you said you were annoyed that the most exciting part of your life was the thirty minutes at the end of the day where you read the books I force on you. I find that unacceptable."

I rubbed my temples. "Yeah, I did say that, didn't I?"

"More than once."

"It's your fault," I accused. "You gave me that book."

"You'd think I'd be out looking for a bunch of hot brothers living on a mountain in Colorado somewhere, because"—she shivered—"I can get on board."

"You got invited to this party by a musician, Ness. I think you're doing just fine."

She smiled a devious smile. "True. And just think, if I hadn't gone backstage, we wouldn't be here right now."

I shifted uncomfortably, tugging on the straps of the black sparkly top that was draped over my upper body.

"Stop that," she admonished.

"No. If I walk into that room with nipple showing, I'd never forgive you."

"Yes, you would."

"I know," I sighed. "It's too hard to find best friends in your late twenties."

"For you," she pointed out. "Because you don't go anywhere or do anything. Hence the sexy shirt and the sexy bar." She wrapped her hands around my shoulders and turned me in the direction of the pulsing lights and too-loud music. "And hopefully, a sexy guy who will appreciate you in all your MILF glory."

"I hate you." I swatted her hands away. "I'm not sleeping with anyone tonight. There is zero chance that anyone here will fit the list."

Vanessa groaned. "That fucking list. If I thought burning it would help, I'd do it." She hooked her arm in mine and started walking toward the bar and dance floor. "I'm not saying you have to sleep with someone—"

"Oh, goodie."

"—I'm saying you just need to have some fun. Talk. Flirt. Maybe a dance or two." She dipped her head closer to mine. "It won't kill you."

"You do not know that. It might."

"Let's go, hot stuff. I've got a good feeling about tonight."

I had to slow my steps to match hers. Her legs, on a normal day, were as long as mine, both of us above-average height (she was an inch shorter than my five nine, but consistently lied and said she was five ten), but tonight, she was wearing five-inch heels.

According to her, she wanted to be able to make out with the tall, hot musician without getting a crick in her neck. Seemed logical enough, but the sight of her knifelike heels made me wince. I'd allowed for a kitten heel and that was it. The faux-leather pants and the top that flowed around my midriff, allowing glimpses of my stomach, were enough adventure for me, thank you very much.

"I can't even raise my arms too high, Ness," I shouted, the volume getting louder as we neared the dance floor.

"Why not?"

I turned and showed her. "Underboob," I cried. "I can't show underboob in public."

"Bitch, yes, you can." Her face transformed into a wide, excited smile. "I see Christian. Do you want to come meet him?"

My mouth hung open as I took in the scene in front of me.

This wasn't a normal bar on a normal Saturday night. We'd stepped into some alternate universe—glistening, beautiful people who did not exist in my normal sphere. I never paid too much attention to celebrity culture, but based on the presence of numerous security guards, and the sheer size of some of the men milling around—with cut jawlines and massive, muscular bodies—I was likely surrounded by them.

They were inked and hard-bodied. The women were stunning—all shiny hair and slinky dresses. Pink, purple, and blue lights flickered off writhing bodies on the dance floor, giving the room an intoxicating glow.

My chest tightened with nerves. "No, you go ahead. I'm going to find a seat at the bar until I feel a little bit less . . . overwhelmed by the hotness."

Ness laughed, leaning in to kiss my cheek. "I'll allow it, as long as you promise to stay for one hour." I opened my mouth, and she laid a finger over my lips. "And no, it doesn't count if you sit in one place and don't talk to anyone."

I rolled my eyes, pulling her hand away from my mouth. "Fine, what's my ticket out of here?"

She pursed her lips. "A good conversation. And a dance. You have to dance with someone."

"Vanessa."

"One dance." She adopted an innocent expression. "That's easy enough."

I snorted. "Sure, it is. Maybe for you."

She grabbed my face in both hands. "For *you.* You are a tall, gorgeous, leggy redhead with a great rack. Remi Sinclair is a grade-A hottie, even if she lives her day-to-day life in T-shirts and leggings and has forgotten her objective hotness because she thinks her entire life revolves around taking care of other people."

That was the thing, though, wasn't it? My entire life *did* revolve around that. Setting that aside for fun, for frivolity, the innocent debauchery she spoke of, was a herculean task.

Even with two drinks in my bloodstream, lowering my inhibitions enough that I'd actually shown up, I battled the discomfort of what she was trying to say. Even if it was meant with all the love in the world, admitting that you'd lost something of yourself without realizing it wasn't easy either.

Instead of admitting that, I narrowed my eyes. "Still doesn't mean I remember how to dance like"—I pointed to the dance floor—"this."

"I know what you were like in high school, Miss Sinclair, so don't act like I've never seen you do this before."

"You mean, before I got pregnant at seventeen?"

She smacked my ass. "Yup. Now, go find a seat and have another drink for courage."

Without another word, she was gone in a whirl of pink hair, and I was left standing by myself in a place where I definitely didn't belong.

If I were home, I'd be halfway through a chapter, Kindle almost falling on my face because I could hardly keep my eyes open for more than thirty minutes once I was lying in bed. That sounded nice, didn't it?

Just a quiet night for a little smutty reading and an early bedtime, where the most disquieting part of the entire process was trying to figure out why my feet were always freezing when I went to bed.

A couple women passed me, both holding expensive-looking cocktails. The brunette had boobs that defied gravity, in a shirt that was cut down to her belly button. No breastfeeding for *her*, I could almost guarantee that.

The blonde gave me a friendly smile when she caught me staring. "I like your shirt," she said.

"Thank you." I glanced down, making sure there was no nipple to be seen. "Where did you get that drink?"

She pointed to the other end of the room. "Specialty drinks are over there in the corner, at the bar with the blue lights, but the regular bar is back here." With a conspiratorial grin, she leaned closer. "The men are back by the blue lights. Definitely go to that one."

After saying thanks, I puffed out my cheeks, blowing out a slow stream of air. In order to have that pretty pink thing with the sugared rim, I'd need to trek through the writhing bodies, and I was not drunk enough for that.

I wasn't drunk at all, really. There was just enough that my head felt light and my shoulders weren't tight with tension like . . . well, like they always were.

There was another bar along the wall to my right—the regular bar, as she'd called it, which didn't look all that regular to me. The bottom half glowed white, the edge lined with a hot-pink light that reminded me of Vanessa's hair. Three beautiful bartenders flipped bottles and pulled taps and filled drinks for the equally beautiful people who waited on the long edge. But where the bar made a 90-degree angle, there were three seats, two unclaimed, and in the third—the middle—was a man's broad back in a simple white shirt.

His head was down like he was staring at something in his hands, probably his phone, and I sucked in a fortifying breath and made my way to the seat to his right, so that I could hide in the corner until I felt a bit less like I wanted to run and lock myself in a bathroom stall.

I tried to edge around his arm without making contact, but my shirt brushed against his skin as I tucked myself into the empty seat.

He glanced up sharply, and my mouth went dry at the fierce look on his face.

"I'm sorry. I should have asked first. Is this seat taken?" I asked, nerves making my fingers tingle.

His frown deepened for a moment, but it didn't change what I knew to be true.

He was beautiful—features hard and chiseled in the flashing lights of the club. The sheer breadth of his body was intimidating, rounded biceps and curved shoulders, veins roping over his forearms and hands. The air around us was thick, like standing outside as a storm rolled in, raising the hairs on my arms while I waited for him to speak. It was dark in the corner where we sat, and with the pulsating lights behind us altering my perception, it was impossible to tell what color his hair or eyes were. Gray, maybe. Or blue?

God, how long had I been staring? Like I'd never seen a jawline like his before.

I had. I'd seen lots.

Okay, maybe not *lots*. But at least three.

"I'm not trying to hit on you," I blurted out. "I'm not even trying to make conversation with anyone. I'd prefer not to, actually. You can sit here and not say a single word, for all I care, but I shouldn't have assumed you were sitting alone." His eyes narrowed slightly, and with the suspicion there, let me tell you, it didn't help stop the nervous rambling. "I don't even want to be here. My friend forced me, and I'm kind of in hell."

His brow furrowed. "No."

I blinked. "No to which part? Because I promise, I don't want to be here."

There was a glass of beer in front of him, and for a moment, he looked down at it, spinning the glass in tiny circles with his giant man hands. They were massive. Everything about him was. Eventually, he lifted his head and pinned me with another unreadable look.

"No one is sitting there."

I exhaled. "Okay, good."

He arched an eyebrow. "Doesn't mean I wanted company, though."

My stomach dropped right down into my cute kitten heels. "Oh." Then my gaze narrowed incrementally. "That doesn't mean you get to claim the entire row just because you're oversized."

His brows shot up. "Oversized?" Slowly, he turned on the barstool, his legs spread wide, one brushing mine as he faced me with an elbow braced on the bar. Being in his crosshairs made the air do that electric buzzing thing again, but this time it was the hair on the back of my neck. "I'm quite sure I should be offended, Red."

I rolled my eyes. "Oh, come on, like that isn't the most unoriginal nickname in the entire world. And you are."

"What?" He was staring at my hair now, gaze lazily trailing down to my face and then landing on my mouth. I wet my lip, more of a nervous tic than anything else, and his mouth opened slightly, like he was going to speak and then thought otherwise.

"Oversized," I repeated. "You're . . . larger than average."

"Average what?"

"Anyone. The average male is five feet, nine inches, and that's how tall I am."

He leaned back slightly, studying my legs, then dragging his gaze back up over my cleavage and to my face. "Are you?"

"Don't try to unnerve me," I said lightly. "It won't work."

He ignored that. "So you're body-shaming me."

"No. You were"—I waved my hand at his general person—"manspreading. Taking up more space than the average person would. I'm not saying you're *too* anything. I'm sure your body is very . . . nice."

"Very nice," he repeated slowly.

As I said it, my eyes locked on the cut lines of his heavily muscled arms. It wasn't just the muscles either—they were wrapped in ink, designs I couldn't make out in the dim light of the bar. Who was I *kidding*? This man was a fucking specimen.

"Perfectly fine, I'm sure."

My voice came out strangled, and that's when I realized his lips were edged up in a slight smirk.

"Perfectly fine," he echoed. He pulled the beer up to his mouth and took a long drag, the thick line of his throat moving as he swallowed. What about that was so attractive? It was swallowing, for crying out loud. But he had a very manly throat, his Adam's apple a prominent wedge of cartilage in the middle, and damn it if that wasn't really nice too.

The bartender approached. "What can I get for you?"

I hadn't been to a bar in about eighty-seven years, and my drink of choice at home was when I transitioned from coffee to Diet Coke in the afternoons, so there was nothing to be done but panic-order. Like when you're at a nice restaurant and you get the chicken tenders because you're overwhelmed by too many options.

"A lemon drop, please."

His brows furrowed. "A lemon drop?"

"Do people not order those anymore?"

"Not usually, no." He grinned, his eyes dipping briefly to my cleavage, then to my ring-free finger on my left hand. "Don't get out much, I'm assuming."

The bartender was cute. Very cute. And the guy next to me sat forward, taking up even more space, the outside of his arm coming dangerously close to my bra-free chest. "How about you make her the shot she asked for?"

Polite professionalism snapped into place at the quietly issued command. "Of course. One lemon drop, coming up."

The bartender turned to make my order, and the guy next to me withdrew from my space, and I couldn't help the scoff that escaped. "What was that?"

He took another drink of his beer. "Nothing. It's not his job to give you shit about your order. It's his job to make it."

"I think you're overreacting a bit."

"Maybe," he conceded, eyes still on the bartender as he twisted a bottle of vodka upside down, pouring with a flourish. "I have a tendency to do that on occasion."

"The people pleaser and the hothead." I sighed. "What a pair we make."

He cut me a sideways look as the bartender slid the shot in my direction.

"Twenty-five dollars."

My mouth fell open. "For a *shot*? That thing better do my laundry if it costs that much."

The bartender didn't miss a beat, his eyes lingering on mine before he answered. "Well, it's made with—"

"Put it on my tab," the man next to me said. "And go away."

Instead of getting pissed, the bartender merely smirked. "You got it."

My neck felt hot. "This is the strangest night of my life."

"I find that hard to believe."

He turned slightly and waited for me to bring the shot to my mouth. Instead of talking myself out of it, I knocked it back and waited for the alcohol's burn.

Holy shit, no wonder it was twenty-five dollars. I stared at the empty shot glass as my companion let out an amused chuckle. "Good?"

"That was the best shot I've ever had in my life," I said despondently.

"When's the last time you *had* a shot?"

Math was hard when you'd drunk what I just drank. I pinched my eyes shut. "High school?"

He laughed. "Yeah, right."

"I'm serious." I ran a hand through my hair and tipped the shot glass back again to see if there was another drop or two remaining. When there was nothing left, I pouted, setting it back down on the counter. "He was right. I don't get out much, and when this shot hits me, you'll know why. Or maybe you won't, because you don't want to be here, either, and you'll leave now."

"You think so? I didn't even say if you could sit here yet."

My gaze caught his. "If there was another seat, I'd let you get drunk in peace, but I regret to inform you that this seat is now mine."

He smirked. "I wouldn't get drunk even if you weren't here. I don't drink and drive."

Well, wasn't that an attractive personality trait. He had a lot of those, apparently.

"I'm not getting drunk either," I sighed. "Any more of those shots and I'll just get tired and sad. No one wants a weepy girl at the bar."

When he set his beer down, he leaned in, the space between us disappearing to almost nothing. Heart hammering against my ribs, I went perfectly still at the sudden nearness.

"Until about six minutes ago, I didn't want to be here either."

"No?"

"Would've given anything to leave."

"Wh-why didn't you?"

"I was invited to a birthday party, but I'm not sure they really want me here. I'm not really close to anyone I work with."

"That's too bad. I love my coworkers."

He tilted his head, eyes locked on my mouth. "You're probably nicer than me."

"Oh, I'm sure of it." I didn't even know his name and I was *flirting*. Flirting in a *bar*, with my tits practically hanging out. Were they piping pheromones into this bar? My mind raced for a subject change, even though his eyes gleamed. "Too nice, if anything," I rushed to say.

"Is that so?"

I glanced pointedly toward the dance floor. "I say yes to things like this just because I know it makes my friend happy."

He hummed. "People pleaser?"

Why did that feel like such an accusation? *People pleaser* conjured an image of a doormat who twisted themselves in knots for the approval of other people, even if they were miserable. No one ever called you a people pleaser and meant it as a compliment.

That was someone who couldn't say no. Who couldn't stand up for themselves.

I liked to please the people in my life. Make them smile. Make their lives easier. And that was not the same thing.

"No. Not really. But I like doing things that make my people happy."

"*Your* people."

It was a bit of a leading statement, and sober Remi probably wouldn't have picked it up, but this was Remi on two margaritas and the most expensive lemon drop in the world, so she felt like following the leading statements from the handsome man taking up too much space at the bar.

I held up my hand and ticked off my fingers as I answered. "My son, my grandfather, my best friend." I pursed my lips as I thought of more people, more faces. "My neighbors. My coworkers. My grandfather's neighbors."

His lips curved in a barely there smile. "Quite a list. No boyfriend."

"See, I had one for a little bit. Or I thought I did. Six dates is nothing to sneeze at, right?"

"I wouldn't know," he answered gravely. "He didn't think so?"

"He was a money pit. You know those houses that have really good bones and you think if you can just work hard enough to get it to meet its potential, it could be awesome?"

"If you say so." His brow lifted slowly. "So, the bones were good," he added pointedly.

I huffed, but his shockingly direct gaze did a number on my composure, so I just kept talking. "I don't know. We never got that far."

"Poor guy."

"Oh, please. He survived just fine with the other girl he was dating at the same time."

He grinned, teeth flashing in the dim light of the bar. "So you didn't worry about making him happy?"

"*He* wasn't one of my people."

"Ahh." His gaze was intoxicating. More potent than the alcohol making my head pleasantly fuzzy. "Did your friend tell you to take a shot?"

"No," I said, drawing out the word. "But I needed that for courage because you're very intimidating."

"Why's that?"

I snorted. "Please. You own a mirror. Plus, it doesn't make a girl feel very welcome when you give her the big scary man glare as she takes her seat."

"I did do that, didn't I?" He dipped his chin in a deferential nod. "My apologies. That was past me, who wasn't in a very good mood."

"But you're in a better mood now?"

Talk about leading statements. I couldn't even dredge up a single ounce of shame.

"Yes." His gaze dipped to my mouth again. "I find myself more inclined to stay, at the moment."

A long-neglected part of me preened. This man was flirting right back.

His eyes were locked on mine. "While we're being brutally honest," he said, voice rough and just loud enough for me to hear over the thumping music, "your body is"—he wet his lower lip and stared unashamedly down at my heaving chest—"perfectly fine too."

My nipples were probably tearing through the fucking shirt, flimsy little piece of material that it was. He smelled clean, a little bit woodsy, and my head was spinning like a top. Why was he so close? Why wasn't he closer?

"I've never minded it," I answered unsteadily. "Though I don't typically wear clothes where so much of it shows."

"A shame," he said gravely. He rested his other arm along the back of my stool, because I'd turned to face him as well, my crossed legs slotted between his. His fingertips brushed along the side of my arm, and I sucked in a trembling breath. When I didn't move away, he edged forward in his seat, dipping his mouth closer to my ear. "So if neither of us wants to be here," he said in a delicious whisper, "why don't we leave?"

My eyes fluttered shut. His nearness was intoxicating. Forget the alcohol—I was drunk off him. It was exactly the kind of interaction that terrified me, because the sheer power of chemistry like this could get you in all sorts of trouble.

Good trouble.

Very, very bad trouble. The kind I worked very hard to avoid. The kind I'd kept firmly away from the important parts of my life for years.

But tonight wasn't my life, was it? It was a pocket of time with a person who didn't know me, who had no power over my feelings, and who I'd never see again.

That kind of freedom was intoxicating, and it built, picking up speed like a snowball in one of those old cartoons, growing bigger and bigger until I was defenseless to stop it. For the first time in years, I didn't want to stop it. I wanted to let myself be the fun girl at the bar who didn't worry about paying bills or if her kid missed a test or if the air conditioner needed replacing before the summer.

I was just Remi. Flirting with a handsome stranger who made my pulse race.

And it felt *good.*

My hands fisted in my lap as he pulled back and kept his intense stare on me.

"I don't even know your name," I whispered. I wasn't sure he could hear it, not with the music. I could feel the throb of the bass between my legs.

"And I don't know yours." On Vanessa's insistence, I'd left my hair in loose waves down my back. He shifted his arm forward, letting his wrist drape over the back of my stool. For a moment, I couldn't breathe, but in the really pleasant, *I might die from sexual tension* way, simply because of how he'd so effectively caged me in. He wrapped a few tendrils around his pointer finger and tugged. "But I'm not sure it matters."

Danger!

Something screamed in the back of my head, a survival instinct that I'd be stupid to ignore. It wasn't physical danger, like he'd hurt me, but something far, far worse.

A part of me, the one that had held the reins of my self-control for the last decade, gave one last violent heave and tried to break, gasping, through the surface. But I held that bitch down and let her drown. Just for tonight.

Tomorrow, I promised. Tomorrow, she could be in control again. When everything was normal and I wasn't this fantasy version of myself.

"I can't leave," I said slowly.

Disappointment filled his eyes. "Why not?"

It was my turn to stare at his mouth. "My friend. She . . . she made me promise I had to do something before I could go."

"Then fucking do it," he growled near my ear, dragging his nose over my cheek.

I exhaled a quiet laugh, willing the thrashing of my heart to slow so I wouldn't pass out from sexual tension. "She told me I needed to dance with someone."

"What?"

I bit down on my bottom lip, and he clenched his jaw, not even attempting to hide the feral flash in his eyes when I did. "She wants me to prove that I'm trying to have a good time. I don't . . . I don't ever go out."

"Why not?"

With his eyes steady on mine, his hand was sliding underneath my hair now, calloused fingers wrapping around the back of my neck in a proprietary squeeze that almost made me groan.

"Like I said earlier, I have a son." His thumb dragged over my pulse point, and I sucked in a gasping breath. "I take care of my grandfather. And I'm always working so I can afford to do both of those things, and I can hardly do that. A twenty-five-dollar shot is not in the monthly budget, I can promise you that."

The second the truths came out of my mouth, I wondered if that was it. If the reality of my day-to-day would break the spell that hung heavy over this small corner of the bar.

But it didn't. His attention never lessened, never wavered.

He nodded slowly. "So tonight is . . . what?"

I exhaled through my nose. "A break in reality that will *never* happen again."

There was a flicker in his expression that I couldn't define, but whatever I'd said seemed to make his decision for him.

Slowly, he stood, unfolding his body from the seat, and I swear to every deity in existence, I almost came on the spot when I saw how tall he was. Easily six four. The broad expanse of his chest and shoulders was all sculpted muscle, the simple T-shirt and flickering lights making him look dangerous in a way that he hadn't when we were seated eye to eye.

He wasn't pretty. Nothing about him was sleek or refined. This was rugged, manly hotness, and I was a fan.

And it was all for me. If I wanted him.

Then he held out his hand.

A knot wedged in my throat, and I tried to swallow it down while I stared at that outstretched hand.

"Come on, Red. Let's make it count, then."

The woman who'd crawled out of bed that morning never would have said yes. Who slept like shit and worried about paying bills and whether Gavin was okay at school and if Pops took his medicine that day.

But for just a little while, I didn't want to be her. I held my breath and slid my hand into his.

His palm was big. Rough and warm and dry as his fingers wrapped around mine.

He turned and led me through the crowd of people, and they parted like the Red friggin' Sea. Some women looked at him longingly, and no small handful of men stared with their mouths hanging open.

A dangerous thought wrapped around the back of my head, latching on to my logical thinking skills and hijacking a portion of the fantasy that I'd let myself fall into. Who *was* he?

Don't ask, don't ask.

I wanted to let this moment happen without the intrusion of reality—his or mine—because I felt good and powerful and sexy. I wasn't Mommy in need of a nap. I was the version of me who I hadn't been in a very long time.

He found a corner on the far edge of the dance floor, where we'd have the illusion of privacy. He kept his grip on my hand and twirled me once. I smiled, assuming he would do the same as he tugged me into his body, but he didn't. His mouth was in a firm line, those delicious lips unsmiling as he stared down at me.

His hands settled on my lower back, fingers brushing the bare skin under my floaty shirt, rolling my hips against his with our legs slotted together. My skin was on fire, hotter than the surface of the sun, and I set my forehead against the wall of his chest, my hands lightly fisting the cotton of his T-shirt while we moved back and forth to the sultry beat.

The music was louder, but not so loud that I couldn't hear him when he brushed his lips against my ear and said, "Can she see you?"

Groggily, I lifted my head. "I don't know."

His gaze traced over my face. "Maybe I shouldn't have hidden you in the corner. Should I move us up there?" he asked, nodding toward a small stage, where a few beautiful women were grinding on each other in slow, sensuous movements of their hips. "Let everyone watch us?"

I shook my head, trying to swallow around a bone-dry throat. "N-no. Here is fine."

His hands slid lower, and his fingers were tucked beneath the waistband of my skintight pants. "Perfectly fine," he said in a ragged voice.

I could hardly breathe when he pressed his fingertips into the top of my ass and tugged my hips flush against his body.

Oh God.

He was hard. And he was huge.

He wanted me so badly that one conversation, one dance did this to him.

I did this to him.

I'd never felt this good. The head-spinning euphoria made me feel reckless.

My hands were shaking as I pushed them up his chest so I could feel the flex of muscle under my palms. He dipped his head to nose my hair away from my neck, his teeth dragging over the sensitive shell of my ear.

"You want more?" He spoke softly, a devilish edge to his already sinful voice.

I nodded, relishing in the catch of his stubble against my jaw. It would hurt if he rubbed it over my skin. And yes, *yes*, I wanted more.

More.

Everything.

My hand cupped the back of his neck, fingers digging into his thick hair. He groaned against the side of my head, one hand dipping underneath my pants, even though he could hardly move with how tight they were. The other moved up my back and fisted in my hair. The sharp edge of pain made me gasp.

"Oh God," I whimpered.

"Oh, no, Red, if I take you home, you'll be screaming my name." Then he spun me, my back pressed against his chest and his hips rolling against my ass. "This fucking body," he moaned. "You're driving me insane."

One hand locked on my hip, holding me so firmly that it almost hurt. The other slid across my stomach underneath my loose shirt. I arched back, rolling my head against his shoulder. My hand covered his on my stomach, and the thrilling jolt of energy from the music and the lights made me feel like I was suspended in midair, attached to invisible strings that he controlled.

Our fingers intertwined underneath my shirt, and I clasped his hand so hard that he chuckled darkly into my ear. "Can I touch you?"

My breath caught in my lungs.

Yes.

No.

Yes. I did want him to touch me. Whether it was good or bad or so fucking out of character, I didn't care, refused to think about how I'd ended up there.

"I don't want people to see."

Wait. What?

That wasn't what I'd meant to say.

I'd been distilled down to my baser instincts, someone driven by her screaming pulse and a need for touch and taste and release. I wanted him to snap my spine in half. Nothing else mattered.

He turned us so that I was facing the wall, and his big, warm palm immediately moved up, and his chest rumbled on an indecent groan when he realized I wasn't wearing a bra. His rough hand engulfed my breast, and my knees went weak.

"You'd taste so good, wouldn't you?"

I was mindless. He rolled his palm over the tip of my breast, then pinched, and I tried to turn to kiss him, but he held me firmly in place.

"No, not here, Red." He licked down the line of my neck, placing sucking kisses as his fingers plucked at the hard tip of my breast. "I'll take you somewhere and make tonight so good for you."

His other hand moved from my hip, deftly unbuttoning the front of my pants.

I rolled my hips against the hard line of him, and he growled, sucking at the side of my neck so hard that I'd probably have a mark.

Please, please, please, I thought with frantic, sharp panic that made my entire frame shake.

"Listen to you," he praised. "You're so sweet, aren't you?"

Had I said that out loud? I couldn't even care. I didn't care about anything except finding an end to this unbearable climb of tension. My entire body was strung tight, skin humming, pulse screaming, and if it didn't snap soon, I'd scream.

With one palm cupping my breast and the other slowly easing down the front of my pants, he pressed kisses along my jawline.

I gripped his thick wrist as he pushed underneath my underwear, my other hand shooting out to brace against the wall in front of us. My back arched, pressing my ass into his groin, and I bit out a ragged curse.

When he slid the blunt edge of his fingers between my legs and found me slick, he groaned into my ear. "I could take you right here, couldn't I, Red? Make you scream with all these people watching, and you wouldn't care."

I sagged into his embrace, the filthy words only ratcheting up my insatiable need to feel good, feel better than I had in a long time.

Would I let him?

Could I let him take me somewhere dark, somewhere private, where I would have to gather my clothes and walk home knowing that I'd done something I'd promised myself I'd never do again?

No. *No.*

My eyes flew open.

What the fuck was I doing?

My skin went cold, and my body went still.

I'd let a stranger shove his hand down my pants in a public place. A stranger with no name, who knew nothing about me except my willingness to let him touch my body. Maybe anyone could've sat next to him and he would've done the same thing.

An interchangeable vessel.

Even worse, I couldn't fight the curl of shame as I realized I'd done the same to him.

Behind me, he froze, too, instantly sensing the change in my body language.

I tugged frantically at his wrist, and he complied, stepping back so quickly that I almost fell over.

I didn't want empty or fast, even if it was mutual.

Hot, embarrassed tears blurred my vision, and I took a few jittery breaths to will them back. I'd been doing it my entire life, whenever my feelings got too big for my body. Happy tears, sad tears, and in this case, tears that sprang up when I wanted to run and hide from the consequences of my own choices.

I couldn't, though, could I? I might not see his face again, but I'd still have to make peace with the fact that I'd allowed myself to go this far.

With trembling hands, I buttoned up my pants and righted my shirt. When I finally risked a glance up, his face was unreadable, but his eyes . . .

His eyes still burned.

"Too much," he said. "My apologies if I went too far."

I shook my head. "No, it was . . . it was both of us."

He took a small step forward. "Tell me your name," he begged.

Tomorrow I'd wake up and none of this would be real. Trying to fit this into the reality of my life was absolutely futile.

"Good night," I told him instead. "I'm sure you'll find someone else to dance with soon enough."

Chapter One

Remi

One month later

If a single mom on a tight budget were hired to rule the world, we'd all be in a better situation. Shit would get done, and everyone would be taken care of. The side effect, of course, was that wasting money was the scariest thing you could possibly talk to her about.

Case in point, my normally fearless ten-year-old wavering in the hallway just outside my bedroom door, breathing loudly. He never did anything quietly, which I was grateful for most days.

"Gavin, I can hear you. What is it?"

He sighed. Did that loudly too.

Instead of waiting for him to pluck up the courage to come into the room, I merely glanced up, and when there was no sight of him, I went back to pulling the needle through the hole in his school uniform pants.

Another sigh. This one even louder.

"Did you get in trouble at school?" I asked, wincing when I almost stabbed myself in the tip of my pointer finger.

"No."

"Good start. Is someone bullying you?"

"No."

"Even better. Now, how about you stop sighing in the hallway and tell me what's on your mind."

Gavin shuffled through the open door, leaning his shoulder against the frame and staring down at the floor. No eye contact was never a good thing.

"Do you remember that really expensive present I asked for, for my birthday last year? And you said it was something I needed to take care of and respect and not, like, roll around in the dirt when I was wearing it?"

My brain was locked on my never-ending to-do list and not on past birthday presents, and I had to blink for a second while my thoughts came into focus.

"Yeah, the football thing."

Gavin rolled his eyes, a chunk of his strawberry-blond hair sticking up from his forehead like he'd been shoving his hands in it. "It's a *jersey*, Mom, not a 'football thing.'"

I did not need him reminding me what it was, because the cost of that jersey had tied my stomach into a ruthless knot for a solid week. It was a few chunks of material, for crying out loud. I could've made one for less than half the price.

But the look on his face when he'd opened his tenth-birthday present was worth it. Wide-eyed awe, the kind that couldn't be faked and appeared less and less as he got older. I'd bought it a little big because at the rate he was growing, he'd be out of that thing in six months, and that was not the most economical use of a ridiculously expensive gift.

For the first three months, he wore it to bed every single night, desperately waiting until he'd grown a little to wear it in public and the pride on his face when he wore his Archer Evans jersey to school was one of those mom moments that shouldn't make you cry but totally does. He didn't want toys anymore for birthdays and Christmas. It was getting harder and harder for him to make a list that didn't consist of video games or jerseys or . . . video games. And the day he was able to wear it in front of his friends reminded me why it was important for me to try my best to understand this shift in the tides as he grew older.

My kid was on top of the world—absolutely nothing could take him down when he was wearing that thing.

I tied a knot in the stitch, then another, and snipped off the end of the thread. "What about it?" I asked.

Gavin chewed on his bottom lip, then walked the rest of the way into my room, his hands behind his back and a sheepish look on his face. There wasn't really anywhere for him to sit. The bed was covered with laundry, which I usually shoved to the empty half before I face-planted on my hand-me-down mattress that sagged in the middle.

He sucked in a deep breath and thrust his hand out, the jersey balled up in his grip. "I don't want it anymore."

When you've lived your life in a near-constant state of chaos, something fascinating happens. Nothing—and I mean nothing—shocked me. Not even when a stranger shoved his hand down my pants in a weaker moment. I'd rolled with that little bombshell very quickly, banishing the entire evening to the dark, cobwebby parts of my brain.

Honest to God, it was my best personality trait (compartmentalization was right up there too), allowing me to show up whenever and wherever someone needed me, and somehow, I hadn't lost my mind yet.

A litter of eight puppies from out of state needs emergency foster placement because they still have to be bottle-fed? On it.

My kid comes in the door at seven p.m. and informs me that we need a scale model of the planets for school tomorrow? No problem. Happened way more frequently than I cared to admit.

The school secretary calls right in the middle of a big donor meeting and tells me that Gavin puked in math class and I need to run over to pick him up? On my way. I had a strong suspicion he was faking half the time, but honestly, I'd puke, too, if I needed to do that pointless shit on a daily basis.

(I'd gone twenty-seven-and-a-half years and not *once* had I done algebra outside of school, but please, I'd love to have them tell me again how useful it is.)

Don't even get me started on Pops and his absolute refusal to do anything to keep himself healthy because *life tastes better when your food is deep-fried*. I'd fielded no fewer than five calls that month from his nurse, reminding me that he needed better eating habits.

Yeah, no shit, he did. But the man was as stubborn as a mule, and I'd learned years ago that I couldn't make him do anything he didn't want to do.

Seriously . . . before Gavin had walked into my bedroom way too late on a school night—both of us still awake past ten because his soccer practice went long and he had homework to finish—I would've sworn on a giant stack of Bibles that nothing he said could genuinely surprise me.

But this had me sitting up straighter.

"Why don't you want it anymore?"

The rest of my question stayed locked in my throat, but it was something along the lines of *Do you have any idea how much that thing cost? You're going to wear it until it falls apart.*

It took everything in me to leave it unsaid, because four months of use was not what I'd had in mind when I dropped a hundred and forty freaking dollars on that thing.

Was I sweating? I was sweating.

But then Gavin's chin trembled, and his eyes immediately filled with tears.

"Oh, bud," I whispered, gently taking the jersey from his hands. "Talk to me."

He dashed a hand under his eyes when a few stray tears escaped. "You know that quote Pops always tell us?"

I pushed some laundry aside, making room for him. "Which one? Pops loves his inspirational quotes, doesn't he?"

More tears slipped down his cheeks, and seeing him so genuinely upset made it feel like I had concrete blocks stuck in my gut. "A-about respect. That the right to be respected is won by respecting others."

I couldn't remember exactly where it came from, but he did repeat it often, and my tenderhearted kid, who didn't have a father to teach him lessons, absorbed everything his great-grandfather said like a dried-up little sponge.

"Yeah, I remember that one." I ran my hand through his hair. "What about it?"

Gavin stared down at the jersey in my hands, looking unbearably sad.

"Remember last year, when Coach King benched Archer at the end of the season because he wasn't playing as well as he could and he wasn't . . . he wasn't being, um, a good leader in the locker room?"

Nope, not even a little. At any given time, my brain had 172 open tabs, and the local sports drama had not earned one of those spots. But my child's room was covered in posters and flags and pennants from the Buffalo teams. The Buffalo Storm was his absolute favorite. He idolized the entire roster, but the quarterback most of all.

So no doubt he'd told me. Multiple times, probably.

"Sort of," I hedged. "It's been a while. He didn't play last season either, did he?"

Gavin shook his head, his eyes locked on the jersey. The way it was lying in my lap, the number 9 was visible, as was the last name. I smoothed my hand over the letters, folding it just a little bit more neatly.

"He was supposed to have, um, an epic comeback, they said. But he tore his ACL during preseason. Carson did good as the backup, though. We went to the playoffs, and they hadn't done that in years. They still lost, though. I think they would've won if Archer was playing."

"That's too bad," I murmured, watching the flush on his cheeks fade as the tears did. He'd done that since he was a baby, his cheeks reddening instantly when he cried. Something he got from his father, no doubt, because it wasn't a trait of mine. In fact, Gavin didn't share many of his physical traits with me. Not the nose or the smile. Not his height, or his love of science, or his dimpled smile. He didn't have the light dusting of freckles across his nose like me. But I saw myself in the strawberry-blond locks and the color of his eyes.

Sometimes blue. Sometimes gray. Even green, depending on what we were wearing. Chameleon eyes, Pops called them. Those came straight from me.

"He threw for over thirty-seven hundred yards in the last season he played," Gavin continued. "Thirty touchdowns, and five of them were rushing touchdowns." He blinked up at me, his eyes dry and earnest now. "He's really strong. Stronger than most quarterbacks. Taller too."

I'd heard this before, of course. Much of it against my will, and I usually forgot it shortly after he told me. This, though, I remembered. Archer Evans stood six feet, four-and-a-half inches tall, which was taller than the average quarterback. Which, according to my stat-obsessed child, was six foot three.

"But we don't want his jersey anymore?" I asked gently.

"No." Gavin wrinkled his nose, face scrunched in deep thought. "Because DUIs are, like, bad, right?"

My eyebrows popped up. "Um, yeah. Was anyone hurt?"

"I don't think so. But he ran into the outside of a building." His fingers reached over to the jersey and touched the edge of one of the numbers along the back of the deep-red material. "I saw it online."

I narrowed my eyes. "And how did you get online?"

Gavin gave me a sheepish look. "You left your laptop out, and I googled his name."

"We'll talk about that later," I said. "But if you want to stop wearing his jersey because of this, I completely understand. Sometimes the people we admire make stupid decisions. Thoughtless ones that can hurt people, or worse."

"It said the accident was in the same neighborhood as the shelter. There was a picture of it on the article."

My brows furrowed. "Really?"

He nodded. "I didn't read very much of the article. I think I hate him now."

"Oh, honey, *hate*'s a really strong word. It's important not to judge people too quickly, and hope that he makes some changes now that he's made this really big mistake. But I don't want to hear that you *hate* anyone, okay?"

"I wanted to be him when I grew up." His eyes were so big, so sad. "Not anymore."

There was a part of me that wanted to believe my son bore no scars from not having a father around because I'd done a damn good job raising him. He knew what it meant to work hard for something important. He was kind and thoughtful, his teachers always raving about how friendly he was to all his classmates. He was loved and supported and encouraged, and it didn't matter if our house was small and worn and didn't have the most stylish furniture—I'd built us a home where he felt safe.

But sometimes, in moments like this, when I saw the absence of something in his life, my heart ached with such deep, bruising force that it was hard to breathe.

"I know, buddy. It's hard to feel disappointment, isn't it?"

"Yeah," he replied sadly. "But it's just a feeling."

"Not a fact," I added. "What else?"

"And it won't last forever," he finished.

I kissed him on the top of his head. "That's right. Now, can you hand me my phone? Maybe I can post this online and see if we can sell it."

Gavin hopped off the bed. "Where'd you leave it?"

I speared my hands through my hair and sighed. "I don't know. I think I set my purse down on the kitchen counter when we got home from soccer. It's probably still in there."

By the time he'd fished it out from the front pocket of my purse, I heard him make a small sound. "Um, Mom? Was it your night to be on for the shelter?"

"No, why?"

We'd developed a rotating system of the first on call about a year ago, and it helped give all of us a well-needed break in case something happened after hours. The shelter held regular hours, and the dogs requiring round-the-clock care were in foster homes, but if we received a call about an emergency, someone had to be the first contact. It was my week off, and as such, I often went hours without looking at my phone while I stayed busy with Gavin and Pops.

He held my phone out. "You have a lot of missed calls. And Auntie Ness used a *really* bad word in the text right at the top."

"Yeah, she does that sometimes," I muttered. At the sight of my home screen, my stomach dropped. Six missed calls and about ten texts, from both Vanessa and my boss, Muriel.

"She swears a lot more than you, doesn't she?"

"Yeah, but she doesn't have little ears at home listening to her," I said, gently tugging on his earlobe, which made him grin. His dimples flashed, and I found myself smiling in return. "Mommy only swears when it's very, very important."

"I know," he sighed. "Like when your tire exploded that one time. Or when you left the coffee machine on and it melted and the whole kitchen smelled like burned plastic for a week."

I gave him a sidelong look. "Yes, thank you, I remember that."

He hopped back up onto the bed and peered over my shoulder. "What do they want?"

I scanned the texts, but they were variations of *holy shit*, *answer your phone*, and *what the fuck are you doing that's so important*. Muriel, the founder of our shelter, was a bit more professional, but her texts became increasingly alarmed too.

My thumb tapped on the first voicemail, but it was just Muriel asking me to call. No information beyond that.

Then another text came in from Ness, and I covered Gavin's eyes because the f-word was on high display. It included a picture of the shelter and a news article.

Buffalo's Star QB Taken Into Custody After DUI

My stomach dropped when I scanned the headline, because oh baby, was my mind connecting some of the dots. Then I tapped on the picture Ness sent.

The entire side yard, the one we'd just finished renovating, was completely demolished. The chain-link fence mangled, torn away from the side of the building, and the two benches destroyed, having been dragged underneath a sleek-looking vehicle with a destroyed hood. Pops had finished those benches for me, a gift because he knew that our budget was tight. He'd kept them for three decades, something my grandma had purchased because she liked how they looked by her flowers.

Gone.

My hand rubbed at my aching chest when I thought about those benches.

I thought about how much work we'd put into that area, months and months of saving so we could do it without any extra fundraising efforts, because we tried to save that for things like food and puppy pads and all the things that actually kept our animals alive and healthy.

And in one stupid night, someone who was too rich and too self-centered to think about how his actions might hurt anyone besides himself—he ruined all of it.

My thumb kept scrolling, a mug shot coming into view.

Once the entirety of his face was visible, I dropped the phone onto my lap with a squeak, slapping my hands over my mouth.

The jawline.

The stubble.

The thick hair—a light brown in the unforgiving light of the jail.

And the *eyes*. Holy shit, his eyes. They were blue. Vivid, bright blue.

My lungs ceased functioning as I struggled to breathe, and for just a moment, I felt the ghost of his mouth over my neck.

I'd let Archer-*fucking*-Evans stick his hand down my pants.

The revelation failed to settle, and my mind whirred unceasingly. The only thing I could land on was him telling me he never really drank. That he didn't drink and drive.

How stupid I'd been. He probably said that to ten other girls over the course of a single week. He'd probably said it to someone else that same night, after I'd fled the scene of my *innocent debauchery*.

"Oh, that fucking dick," I whispered.

"Mom."

I couldn't even bring myself to apologize, because sometimes it felt really good to say the bad words that I tried not to say in front of my sweet, impressionable kid.

My hand tightened in the jersey I'd been so careful to fold up. I stared down at the letters of his last name, the cold build of rage making it hard to breathe deeply.

Then I stood up and shoved his stupid jersey right in the garbage.

Chapter Two

Archer

It shouldn't be hard to control which version of yourself you show to people.

Be nice. Be friendly. Smile and say something kind. That's what most people do, right?

Not me. Not the son of Alexander Evans.

He'd yanked those instincts out, root and stem, by the time I hit high school.

But for how much he'd molded me into something aloof and arrogant, someone who knew exactly which armor to wear in any given situation, the place where I was most comfortable controlling my reactions was with him.

To piss him off, I simply had to talk back.

By the age of ten, I'd learned that the quickest way to keep my dad happy was to stay completely silent. When perfection was the expectation, and that expectation was broken, it didn't take long for his words to increase both in volume and frequency. As one of the most successful defense attorneys in the state of New York, he was exceptionally good at both. The man loved hearing his own voice. A captive audience was his drug.

Keeping quiet might've seemed like weakness, but it wasn't. It was strategy.

We strode out of the courthouse, and I fought the urge to tip my face down, allow the brim of my hat to block my face when I spotted paparazzi across the street. My father didn't hide. He merely raised his chin—arrogant as ever—and made sure they got his best angle.

So I did the same thing.

As much as I hated it, I was his mirror image. The same jawline, the same nose, the same height and broad shoulders. I simply used my size in a different way than he did. His intimidation happened in a courtroom, mine on a football field.

He tugged at the wrist of his navy Armani suit, adjusting the sleeve before we crossed the street into the parking lot. "At least I'm dressed appropriately if they're going to put this to print," he said on an annoyed sniff. "You're in streetwear."

It was said with so much disdain that I almost laughed. Any sign of humor would probably send him into apoplexy, so I merely let out a quiet breath and kept stride with him.

I'd come from the weight room, so yes, I was in black joggers and a white Buffalo T-shirt, a black Buffalo hat covering my head.

His Range Roger was parked next to my truck—not just newer, but shinier too. Every morning, the car was washed and buffed to a gleaming finish. Not by him, of course. He'd never take the time.

Dirt from the road leading to my newly built home always seemed to cling to the lower half of my truck, and that was what my father was currently eyeing with distaste as he slowed his steps.

"I'll tell Mike to wash your car the next time you come over for dinner," he said.

The presumption that I'd want him to loosened my tongue. "It'll just get dirty again when I drive home."

His eyes narrowed slightly, the exact same shade of blue as mine. I hated how much we looked alike.

"I'm happy to learn that you are still capable of speech."

I held his gaze.

Dad sighed, sliding his hands into his pockets and glancing over his shoulder at the two cameras aimed in our direction. "I can talk to the judge again. It's ridiculous that she won't just let you pay the fine and be done with it."

My jaw locked tight, and unspent tension had the muscles along my neck rigid.

That judge hated him, which meant she probably had an impeccable radar for the humanity of each person who walked into her courtroom. I'd kept my mouth shut in there, too, on my father's instructions, allowing him to do the talking.

It would be easy, he promised.

My blood alcohol level had been .08 percent, the lowest threshold for the legal limit, and as a first-time offender, a hefty fine to cover any damage to the animal shelter should have been more than sufficient. They'd collect a check, he'd told me, and I'd be able to move forward.

Except he'd been wrong. And he was pissed.

My dad stepped closer, lowering his voice to a hard-edged whisper. "Don't you care that she's making an example out of you?" he hissed. "It's humiliating. You'll have to show up and do menial labor, for God's sake."

I tilted my head, eyes locked on his. "Of course I care. She probably thinks it'll do me some good."

"What would have been good is if you hadn't gotten behind the fucking wheel in the first place," he snapped. "Never thought a son of mine would be pathetic enough to self-sabotage."

The dry laugh burst out of my mouth before I could stop it.

"Oh, this is *funny*. I'm glad you think this is funny." The vein in his forehead was throbbing to the point that I wondered if he'd stroke out right in front of me. "I don't know what the hell has gotten into you since you got drafted. I thought keeping you in school for your master's would mean you'd walk right into that locker room and establish a dynasty. Except you dick around your first two years in the pros, that know-it-all coach benches you in some pissing match meant to humble you—" His eyes flashed. "I still think he should've been fired for that stunt."

Heat built in my chest, a defense for Coach King making my tongue tingle as I slicked it over the front of my teeth to keep myself quiet. When I regained control of my emotions, I said, "Obviously he thought I *needed* humbling."

He scoffed, tugging on the wrist of his sleeve again. "Evanses don't humble themselves, Archer. You know that."

Evanses don't humble themselves. I'd heard that my entire life. Who fed that to a child as words to live by?

I hadn't been taught to be kind or selfless. I hadn't been taught to treat everyone with respect, because in his mind, unless they'd earned his respect, they were beneath his notice. I hadn't been taught how to be a good human. Alexander Evans had taught me the same thing his father had taught him—to be the best and do it in a way that was so indisputable you became untouchable.

The only way I'd learned to fill in the gaps was by watching other people in my life.

Friends in school. Teammates. Coaches.

The pursuit of perfection was a dangerous thing because it was a moving target. Something that could never be satisfied.

I'd tried. I'd *tried* to satisfy what he wanted from me. His notice had been heady when I was younger. A clap on the shoulder and a proud nod were sickening in their effectiveness. I'd done everything for that tiny glimpse of affection from him, turning myself in knots all through high school and college to keep his focus on how good I was, until I realized he'd never actually be happy with anything I'd done, because I could always be better.

As I stood there in the bright sun, I wished I could tell him exactly when and why I'd stopped trying. Stopped caring. And how that decision had brought us to the point we were at now. If I thought he might care, I would do exactly that.

"Are we done here?" I asked flatly.

His eyebrows bent over a cold expression. "That's it? You don't have anything to say?"

I tucked my hands in my pockets and rocked back on my heels, pursing my lips briefly like I was contemplating his question. Then I shook my head slowly. "Nope."

"You make me sick, do you know that?"

He spoke so quietly, so evenly, that the impact of his words didn't land right away. Four years ago, they would've rocked me to my core. And now it was nothing. Less than nothing.

The only reaction I gave him was a ghost of a smile that faded after a few seconds.

He hated it. He might have even hated me, but I really didn't care about that either.

"Don't you want to know why?" he asked.

I let out a slow breath and then shook my head again. "Nope."

"Fucking waste," he muttered. "I thought you could turn all this around. I thought I'd raised you to be stronger than this, you know? Your first chance at retaking your team last season and you were reckless on that field. You shouldn't have even been playing in preseason—if you hadn't been, you wouldn't have torn your ACL." He stepped closer, and I fought to keep my face even, like the impulse to shove him backward might be stamped all over my face. "Another year on the bench. Wasted. Sitting back and watching that hack of a backup start for your team."

This time I didn't bite my tongue. "He's a good man, and he played well when I couldn't."

"That's exactly right. You couldn't play, and your team—the one paying all that money—has done just fine without you." His eyes were cold. "And the second chance you get to turn your pathetic career around, you pull this shit." He shook his head. "That's why you make me sick."

I pushed my tongue into the side of my cheek. "You know . . . I think I can sleep at night knowing that."

The flash in his eyes was so gratifying that I almost grinned, but I managed to tamp it down.

"Figure out a way to make this community service benefit you. The worst thing you can do is have a bunch of holier-than-thou do-gooders take advantage of this. They're all martyrs who think they're better than everyone. Better than you." He poked me in the chest. Hard. "But you're an Evans. Don't fucking forget that."

"As if I could."

His eyes glinted, and for a moment, I thought I'd gone too far.

But in the end, he let out an annoyed puff of air and yanked open the door of his vehicle, disappearing without another word. As the engine roared to life and he took off, I could finally breathe again. Space from him always had that effect. Like someone had unlocked an iron band around my lungs.

The guys with the cameras had left at some point during the exchange, and I pulled myself into my truck and leaned my head back with a sigh, closing my eyes for a few moments while I untangled how fucked up this had gotten so quickly. I unfolded the piece of paper that explained my sentencing.

Fifty hours of community service at Second Leash Animal Sanctuary.

A provisional license to go back and forth between work and community service, for three months.

And a fine of $5,000 to cover the damage to the building.

To be honest, I'd gotten off easy. A suspended license was what I'd expected, but that was the one battle my father had won for me.

I pinched the bridge of my nose and tried to breathe through the weight pressing on my chest, but it simply kept getting heavier and heavier.

Three beers, slick roads, and the shadow of a dog darting across the street. With my eyes closed, I could still hear my sister's frantic shriek when the car jumped the curb and plowed through the fencing.

The muscles in my neck were tense again, and I tried to roll them out. Maybe some extra time in the treatment room after workouts the next day.

"The rescue will be expecting you," the judge had told me, peering over her wire-rimmed glasses with a steely glint in her brown eyes. "Take this as the opportunity it's meant to be, Mr. Evans. Do you understand me?"

Understanding was fine. Application was something else entirely.

According to my dad, Evanses weren't meant to humble themselves, but as I turned the truck on and entered the address to the rescue, I couldn't help but wonder what would happen when they were forced to. Like shoving an elephant through the eye of a fucking needle.

The drive from the courthouse to the rescue took about twenty minutes, and in that time, I thought about the disappointment I'd faced from different people in my life over the last couple years. Some, like my father, hardly registered. Others, like Coach King, hurt more.

Even worse was that Coach hadn't even had to tell me he was disappointed the first time I came into the facilities after the DUI. It was all over his face. My teammates' faces too.

I'd hardly spoken to any of them since.

I got there early, did what I needed to do, and left with as few words exchanged as possible.

What was I supposed to say? *Sorry you thought I'd changed? That you thought I'd turned into something different?*

It was better not to expect anyone to think well of me at all. If I could just find a way to do my job free of the burden of those expectations . . .

To be a good man. To lead the team by example. All the things they wanted from me.

I didn't know *how*.

For the first time in a week, a flash of pretty eyes and red hair went through my mind. She'd been disappointed in me too. Whenever the opportunity to do the right thing was in front of me, I always ended up veering sharply to the left of what that was. My moral compass was skewed so fucking badly that I didn't know how to correct it.

All their individual reactions still sat heavy in my gut, like a rock that kept tumbling around in my stomach. Something impossible to break down. Eventually it would have to, though, right?

Frustration built and built under my skin, a low hum of energy that I couldn't expel. Frustration with myself. With my dad. The judge who was using me to make a point.

Like I needed anything to make me feel worse.

My hands tightened on the steering wheel as an uneasy feeling turned my stomach into knots.

I just needed to get it over with. Feed some puppies or take some pictures or whatever the fuck they wanted me to do.

The sunny-yellow building came into view, a large white-and-blue-and-yellow sign on the black shingles. Something I hadn't noticed the other night when it was rainy and dark and the flashing lights of the police car distorted everything in sight.

Someone had cleaned up the damage done from the car, but I could still see the mangled fence and the wooden bench that had hooked on to the front bumper. The parking lot was empty, save for two cars parked in the back corner underneath tall, thick trees that shaded the entire space.

Just behind them, I saw a woman crouched on the ground with her hand outstretched. Her hair caught my notice first—red and curly and tied on top of her head in a messy knot.

The air punched from my lungs so fast, like someone had taken a baseball bat to my chest.

It couldn't be.

A black dog was in the tree line, eyeing her warily, and I sat up in my seat as I turned the truck into a parking spot.

It was the same dog that had darted across the road the night of the accident.

His attention turned to me, and I let out a deep, aggravated breath before hopping out of the truck. The door got away from me, and it slammed more loudly than I'd expected.

At the noise, the dog was gone in the blink of an eye, only some rustling leaves left behind. The woman deflated, dropping her arm with a groan.

"Sorry," I said.

"It's okay," she answered, standing from the crouched position, her focus on the tree line. Tall. She was tall. I drank in the sight of her body, now covered with a baggy T-shirt and black leggings. It *had* to be her. "He's been cagey all week."

In the seconds it took her to turn around, my mind spun in a million different directions.

She was here.

Oh fuck, she was *here*. That meant she worked at the shelter.

She was either going to punch me, or we'd have a great fucking laugh about how small of a world this was. I really, really hoped it would be option two.

What color were her eyes?

Then she shook her head and swept her hands briskly down the front of her leggings before turning toward me with a friendly smile on her face.

God, it sounded cheesy, but she was so fucking beautiful, my lungs stalled for an agonizing second.

When I finally pulled in a breath and thought maybe, just maybe, this community service thing wouldn't be so terrible, her smile disappeared and her eyes—big and green and thickly lined—went just as cold as my father's.

Before she even opened her mouth, that gorgeous, kissable mouth I'd fantasized about no fewer than a dozen times in the days since I'd seen her, I felt a sick twist in my gut.

"You *asshole*."

Option one. She was definitely going for option one.

Chapter Three

Remi

The words were out of my mouth before I could stop them, something that never happened. My ability to stay calm was legend.

So when I started mouthing off, I was either on the cusp of my period, when things like verbal filters were for cowards, or I needed about fifteen straight hours of sleep.

Unfortunately for the giant, muscled meathead with poor decision-making skills, it was a dangerous combination of both.

I don't know what I'd expected from Archer Evans in the harsh light of day, but it wasn't this. It was probably a healthy dose of self-preservation that had me fully believing he'd be less gorgeous and less intimidating outside of our weird little fantasy bubble that never should have existed.

A snide narrator's voice popped into my head: *He was, in fact, not less gorgeous.*

My stomach fluttered with nerves as he tried to respond to my less-than-friendly greeting.

The length of his legs, the intimidating breadth of his shoulders, were just shy of stupid, because every inch of him made me feel like a shrimp, and I was no petite, tiny thing. I had to tilt my chin to look him in the face, that prick.

For a moment, his stubble-covered jaw worked back and forth, and I braced myself for some asshole response that would trigger my *I will slap the shit out of you* instinct, which had never been triggered in twenty-seven-and-a-half years on this earth. But for this guy—driving his drunk ass into the building I loved so much—I'd break that streak in a heartbeat.

But then his chest expanded on a deep breath, and he leveled his electric-blue eyes right onto mine. "I am."

That's it.

Two words, spoken in a deep, low tone that flipped the pit of my belly upside down. It was brutal.

I crossed my arms. "What are you doing here?"

He glanced sideways to where the dog had disappeared, and blinked a few times before shifting his attention back to me. Whatever genetic lottery had given this man his bone structure should not be out procreating all willy-nilly, because I was fairly certain he was the most attractive man I'd ever shared space with.

That also made me want to slap the shit out of him.

"In the neighborhood. Thought I'd drop by to say hi."

"Is that supposed to be a joke? I don't want to talk to you unless you're coming to write me a fat fucking check for what you did."

His smile was tight. "Don't worry, Red, that'll come too."

My pulse skipped at the nickname, a traitorous little bitch of a skip.

"Do not call me *Red*," I said hotly. "I have a name, and if I'm forced to talk to you, I'd prefer you use that."

He raised an eyebrow. "If I knew what it was, I'd consider it."

My lips rolled together as I tried to decide if I wanted to meet this asshole step for step. Unfortunately, I had a conscience, and being bitchy took more energy than I'd been blessed with that day. "Remi. Remi Sinclair. Now you know my name, and now you can leave."

"Unfortunately, I can't."

"Why not?"

"You're stuck with me. Or weren't you aware?"

Oh God, my fingers were tingling as my hands lowered to my sides. "What?"

His eyes flickered. "My fifty hours of community service. The judge made it sound like you knew."

"No fucking way," I breathed.

Archer's gaze narrowed. "Believe me, this is the last thing I'd lie about."

The apology for not believing him sprang to the tip of my tongue—decades of ingrained behavior rearing its ugly head. We apologized for everything, didn't we?

I'm sorry I'm late.

I'm sorry I'm bothering you.

I'm sorry I need help.

I'm sorry I can't do this on my own.

I'm sorry I had a human moment.

Even Mother Teresa must have had a moment where she was ready to snap, right? There were a lot of amazing people in this world. Helpful and kind and lovely. But boy, oh boy, there were a lot of dicks too. And I didn't much feel like apologizing to this particular dick, or at least not until he did a little apologizing of his own.

"I need to talk to my boss," I said, marching toward the building.

Mondays were a quiet day for us. We only had open visiting hours the second half of the day, and until Vanessa came in for her shift, it was just me and Muriel.

"I thought this was your building."

With my hand on the door handle, I froze in place and sent him a scathing look over my shoulder. "Buddy, in all the ways that matter, I promise you it is. That's why I take particular offense at all the shit you ruined."

His cheeks flushed the slightest bit pink, but his eye contact never wavered.

"See, now, this would be a perfect time to apologize," I said, slowly and methodically, like I was speaking to a child. Or someone who'd likely sustained multiple concussions and had poor people skills. "In case you were wondering how to proceed."

"Would you believe me if I did?"

That stopped me short, and that nervous flutter erupted in my stomach again. I thought about lying, just to be polite. I was *always* polite. In fact, I'd never been less polite in my entire life than I had been to this guy.

"No."

"See? Being honest is fun, isn't it? I don't apologize often, Remi Sinclair, and if I do, I'm gonna make it count."

My hand balled up in a fist as I wondered if I could swing hard enough to break his nose.

"For instance, if I wanted to apologize to you, I could start with: I'm sorry I played with your absolutely glorious tits in public."

A shocked gust of air burst from my mouth.

"You wouldn't believe that either, though, would you? Or I'm sorry for sticking my hand between your legs, getting just enough of a taste that I've thought about you for fucking days. You want me to apologize for that, Red?"

"That entire night was a mistake I narrowly avoided making." Angry tears swelled in the back of my throat. "Thank God I didn't go home with you."

His features were practically carved in stone. "Like you said, it doesn't take me long to find someone else, if that's what I want. You just happened to fall right in my lap," he said, brow furrowing like he couldn't believe his luck. "You made it so easy. Maybe you *are* the good girl who never gets out—but when you do, Red, you're a lot of fucking fun."

The crack of my hand across his cheek rang through the parking lot. My palm stung as I cradled it against my chest, mind reeling. I'd slapped him. I'd *slapped* him.

Archer gaped, gently laying his fingers over the reddened mark on his face. "You hit me," he said, tone incredulous.

Anger like this was brutal. The blood rushing through my veins felt undeniably hot, like I'd emit steam if someone doused me in cold water. I clenched my teeth so tight that my molars creaked. Something indefinable flashed through his eyes. I wanted to believe it was regret, but I'd never be so stupid as to give him the benefit of the doubt.

Even though my legs were quaking and my stomach trembled, I stepped right into his space. "If you ever speak to me that way again, I will castrate you with a smile on my face."

His blue eyes narrowed, his mouth firming into an unforgiving line.

"Is that clear?" I asked slowly. "Or do you need me to use smaller words? I'm sure you've had your fair share of head injuries."

Archer studied my face with a tilt of his head, like he was weighing the strength of my threat.

"Crystal clear," he said after a moment.

My chest was heaving, adrenaline screaming through my system after that slap.

I needed a nap. And a pound of chocolate. And a safe place to go cry for an hour.

If anyone wondered why my ideal-partner list looked the way it did, I'd like to enter Archer Evans into consideration—the primary exhibit as to why I wanted safe and quiet and normal and average.

These egotistical pricks who thought the world revolved around their cocks were the last thing I wanted in my life, and he'd just reminded me exactly why a ruggedly handsome face and honed muscles were severely overrated.

"Stay here," I commanded.

I turned and disappeared into the building, praying to any deity who would listen that he would keep his ass outside while I had a PMS-y meltdown to Muriel.

Her office was right next to mine, and because she was in the process of reducing her hours now that she'd turned sixty-eight, it was usually used to meet with families while they completed paperwork.

A few days earlier, she'd effectively handed me the reins of the shelter while she prepared for a two-week trip to Europe.

Day one of being in charge and I'd *slapped* our newest court-mandated volunteer.

It was going great.

The sound of clicking keyboard keys filtered through the cracked door, which was why I only gave a cursory knock before pushing it open.

The sight of whatever expression was on my face caused her to slowly arch an eyebrow. "Oh dear."

"Did you know?"

Her face was all innocent patience, but I didn't believe it for one freaking second. "Know what?"

"That he was coming here."

"Ahh. That." She folded her hands on her desk and studied me carefully. "How did you find out?"

"He's out in the parking lot," I answered through a tight jaw. "It's hard enough to find volunteers, and those are people who are passionate about rescue work. He's here as punishment. All he'll do is get in my way and bitch and moan when I give him work to do."

Her smile was brief. "You don't know that."

"Muriel, the man is a professional football player who's not exactly winning any congeniality awards. They paid him millions of dollars last year to sit on a bench. You think he cares about how clean our kennels are?"

"He will if he wants us to sign off on his hours to satisfy the courts."

I scoffed. "This is going to be awful."

Muriel gave me an appraising look. "Then it's a perfect challenge for the interim director, isn't it?"

With a groan, I sank into the empty chair tucked into the corner of her office. On the end table set between it and a second, identical chair was a little vase of wildflowers and a business card holder with the rescue's contact information. I plucked one out of the case and fiddled with the edges.

"Can't we just ask the judge for a check and make him go away?"

"No," she said around an amused smirk.

"Ugh. We need the money more than we need him lurking around."

"Will he lurk?"

"Yes," I answered emphatically. "Someone of his size can't help it. Wait until you see him. It's ridiculous."

"I've never known you to be so judgmental right off the bat."

"I'm not usually, but come on—it's completely fair to judge him off what I know, and nothing I know speaks well of him. And that was before the DUI. And before he opened his asshole mouth."

Muriel crossed her legs and let out a slow breath. "People make lots of mistakes. I have. You have," she said gently. "But hopefully, we're not always viewed with those mistakes as the standard for who we are."

"Well, if you're going to be rational about it . . ." I grumbled. For a moment, I closed my eyes and let my head rest against the wall. "What would you do? If you were in charge of him?"

Probably not get into a situation where he finger-banged her in a club, but that was not a point I felt moved to make.

"Hold him to the same level of accountability you expect from employees or volunteers. You're the boss, and you need to act like it." When I opened my eyes, she was watching me carefully. "This is a big test for you, Remi. I expect you to set aside whatever distrust you might have and be a professional."

I nodded slowly. "So no more hormone-induced temper tantrums? Even when he's awful?"

It wasn't like I could tell her what had happened out in the parking lot. That would trigger way too many questions, and I'd prefer to take that entire experience to my grave, where it belonged. Even Ness didn't know what had happened at the club. I'd told her I danced with someone hot, we flirted, and I went home while she was busy sucking face with Christian.

"How do you know he's going to be awful?" Muriel asked with a smile.

"Believe me. I know."

She laughed at my ominous tone.

"As long as you do it in your office where no one can see, have at it." She pulled open the bottom drawer of her desk. "Why do you think I stashed chocolate in here?"

"I think I need some. Maybe the whole bag."

She pulled something out of a crinkly plastic bag. I reached forward, and she set two foil-covered pieces of chocolate in my outstretched palm. I arched a wry brow but didn't argue. As I unwrapped one, she selected another for herself, and for a moment we both ate our chocolate in peace.

The burst of rich, sugary sweetness had me sighing. I eyed the second one and unwrapped that too.

Muriel finished first, balling up the foil and tossing it into the garbage underneath the desk. "I want to remove the *interim* off your title as much as you do, Remi. And if you can manage this situation well—use it as a tool to generate something positive out of an unfortunate situation—I think we'll do exactly that."

I wanted the *interim* gone too. Removing it came with more stable hours and even better pay, which I desperately needed.

"Has the shelter ever had court-mandated community service volunteers before?"

"Nope. But we'll treat it exactly as we do any of our other nonpaid employees. Work with him on his schedule. If he's willing to come in for three to four hours at a time, it won't take terribly long to get through his community service."

"So I need the patience of a saint and can't step a toe out of line with Mr. Football."

She grinned. "Easy enough, right?" I gave her a look, and as she laughed, I stood to leave the office. Muriel held up her hand and then tossed me another piece of chocolate. "Just in case."

Chocolate had the powerful ability to grant delusions.

With chocolate, I was calm and centered again. I didn't need a nap and a double-shampoo shower. With chocolate, I wasn't on the edge of snapping whenever I saw the chiseled jaw and inked biceps.

Unfortunately for Archer, every time I looked at him, I'd be reminded of my very worst impulses, swinging wildly between both ends of the spectrum.

The Remi who still craved wild affection and unbridled lust—who wanted to be wanted, even if it didn't make sense . . . She needed to take several fucking seats.

And the Remi who occasionally had violent outbursts at the slightest sign of disrespect to either me or my loved ones . . . She needed anger management.

Unfortunately, my chocolate was gone by the time I turned the corner into the lobby, and the object of my ire was standing by the front desk, studying the pictures on the walls—a record of successful adoptions over the last year. We were closer to the side of the building with the kennels now, and the sharp barks of our current guests punctuated the thick silence as I stared at Archer.

He was *totally* going to lurk. It wasn't like he could help it. Even standing there like he was, hands tucked into the pockets of his joggers—muscles flexing every which way—Archer filled the space like no one I'd ever seen before. Maybe it was always like that for guys like him. Larger than life and intimidating just by existing.

But even with all that, he was just a guy who'd fucked up and was now paying the price. I thought about my son's face when I'd tossed that jersey into the garbage. Mistakes always came with consequences, didn't they? We might not see the dominoes topple right away, but they always did.

"You were supposed to wait outside."

"I'm not great at being told what to do," he said easily, eyes still on the wall. "What's the easiest job you can give me for you to sign off on these hours? Take some pictures with some dogs? Cuddle a puppy or something?"

"Easy," I mused. "That's what you want out of this?"

He squared his shoulders in my direction. "Yes. And after this, I'm guessing you want me out of your hair just as badly."

"I'm quite used to not getting what I want."

Archer gave me a speaking glance at that unfortunate admission, because between the two of us, that could mean a whole lot of things.

"Come on," I told him. "I'll show you around."

We walked through the kennels first, and I pulled bits of hot dog out of the bag in my pocket to feed some of the pups. The room was big, and loud, so we didn't do much talking. When I stopped to feed some treats to Scout—a sweet, sad-eyed hound dog missing his back right leg—Archer paused to read the sign affixed to his kennel's fencing.

He kept moving without asking a single question.

The sign outside each kennel described the dog's temperament and what we knew of their story. How long they'd been with us. Scout was our longest resident: He'd been with us for more than a year. The missing leg and the shy personality didn't do him any favors when there were almost always friendlier, more energetic options. There were twelve kennels on each side of the long room, twenty-four in total, and all but one was filled. Each dog had a bed elevated off the concrete floor, food and water bowls attached to the cinder block walls, a soft blanket, and a stuffed animal or toy for them to play with.

"The door at the end leads out to the first of two yards," I told him, keeping my focus on Scout, who leaned into my hand as I reached through the fence to scratch the back of his head. "We rotate the dogs as best we can through the day. Scout and a couple of the others can be left out for longer periods of time together because they get along really well, but they still need supervision when they're in the yard together. Most of the dogs go outside by themselves."

No response from the walking Neanderthal. Probably because he didn't care.

My phone buzzed in my pocket, and when I checked the screen, it was the school. "This is Remi."

"Mom?"

"What's up, buddy? Are you okay?"

"My stomach hurts. Can I come home?"

I glanced briefly at Archer, who was watching me with unreadable eyes underneath the brim of his hat. "When did it start hurting? You were fine this morning."

"Uhhh . . ."

He paused just long enough that I rolled my eyes. "Is this because of your math test? Be honest, dude."

Gavin let out a dramatic sigh. "What if I *fail*?"

"You won't fail the test. But just because you're nervous about it doesn't mean you can skip school. If you puke in class, I promise I'll come get you."

"Thanks a lot."

"Always here to help," I said magnanimously. "Take a deep breath and do your best. That's all I'll ever ask of you—you know that, right?"

"And if my best is a C?"

"If your best is a C, then I'll be the proudest mom in the world."

"Fine."

I smiled, tucking my chin down to my chest when he sighed. "Love you, bud."

"Love you more."

"Impossible."

Archer was still watching me when I tucked my phone into my pocket. "My son," I said briskly. "He's ten and hates math tests. Not that I needed to tell you that or anything."

God, it would have been so much better if he'd nodded or made some inane comment to put me out of my rambling misery, but instead he simply watched, those blue eyes taking in every inch of my face, which was currently holding all the blood in my entire body as it rushed to my cheeks.

Curse my fair skin.

I cleared my throat. "Anyway."

I gave Scout one final pat and moved on to Daisy, across the aisle. She was a six-year-old shepherd mix with fluffy golden hair and droopy ears. When my hand went back into my pocket, she started dancing in circles, front paws immediately going up on the fence as she waited for her treat.

"Hey, Daisy girl," I said. "You're going out next, don't worry. I know you need some exercise."

The back of my neck tingled, the weight of Archer's gaze heavy as he stood behind me and watched. We walked down the rest of the aisle, and he never reached through to pet any of the dogs.

I swear, I didn't want to judge him, but if someone didn't like dogs, I totally judged.

Wordlessly, Archer followed behind while I showed him the cat room, where we had about six kennels filled with cats needing new homes.

"Not very many in here."

The sound of his voice after so much silence was jarring, and I blinked up at him in surprise.

"We're mainly a dog rescue," I explained. "Older ones, actually. We have a handful of foster homes that take in mamas and puppies when we do get them. Right now I think we have eight others split between three foster homes. It's not that we don't get cats or puppies or younger dogs—sometimes the need is so great that we have to take on what we can. But it's so much harder for older dogs to find families. Muriel, the woman who founded the shelter, adopted an eight-year-old Lab when she and her husband first got married, and he'd been sitting in a shelter for two years when they took him home." I gestured to the logo on the wall. "That's his paw print."

Next were the adoption rooms, where prospective families met with dogs.

"We also do temperament-testing in here—check for resource guarding and see how they might handle kids, other dogs, that sort of thing. And when our local vet partners come in for routine exams, they can handle all of that on-site."

I gestured to the door that led to the side yard. "You know what's out there—or used to be," I added icily. "It was an outdoor space we'd just added for families to play with dogs they're considering adopting. It was less than a week old. My grandfather gave me two benches that he bought for my grandma thirty years ago. Took him months to refinish them." I cleared my throat. "They're destroyed too."

Archer's profile was stony as he stared at that door. A muscle in his jaw flexed. He took another deep breath, and without turning to face me, he spoke again.

"It was raining."

"What?"

"It was raining," he repeated. "The roads were wet, and I thought I saw an animal. Maybe it was that dog—"

I let out a shocked huff. "Are you trying to make excuses for getting behind the wheel and driving when you were drunk?"

"I'm just saying you don't need to try and make me feel like shit. I already do."

I thought about what Muriel had said. Professional. Kind. Don't step a toe out of line with Mr. Football.

So instead of telling him that he needed his head dislodged from his ass, I was glad my son tossed his jersey, *and* I wanted to slap the perfect teeth out of his face, I took a deep breath and let the bad juju out on the exhale.

"You want an easy job while you're here?" I asked.

"Preferably."

"Good. Then let me introduce you to the poop shovel. Easy enough to shovel dog shit for fifty hours, isn't it?"

Chapter Four

Remi

Vanessa—also known as Ness, Auntie Ness to Gavin, or the pink-haired monster of chaos to Muriel—showed up for her afternoon shift in an absolute tizzy.

"Holy shit, you'll never believe what happened last night with Christian."

I looked up from my computer and blinked. "Hi. What?"

"God, it was amazing. I kinda thought the party was it, because he was playing it cool and he didn't call me for three weeks while he was on tour, right? But then he called me four times last week. I could've strung it out longer, but he's *so* gorgeous, I figured that it was a pity to torture myself when I wanted the same thing he did, you know?"

I could take you right here, couldn't I?

Shit. No. Bad Remi.

"Uh-huh. I hate that feeling. So we're not talking to the guy with the piercings anymore, right?"

"The guy with the piercings was psycho. He wanted to name our future children after one night together." She widened her eyes. "One night."

"Maybe if you weren't so sensational at everything, he would've been like every other guy and moved on after."

"I know," she sighed. Then she tilted her head. "You look pretty today."

"I—what? I look the same as I do every day."

"No. You put on blush or something."

I gave her a crazy look. "No, I didn't."

"Did you have sex?" she whispered.

"*No.* And why are you whispering? There's no one in here. Muriel is already gone for the day."

"There was another truck in the parking lot." She set her feet up on the edge of my desk. "New volunteer?"

A frown pulled at my lips before I could stop it. "Sort of. I'll explain after you tell your story."

Her feet dropped off the desk, and her head briefly disappeared as she rooted around in her giant bag, resurfacing with a piece of licorice in her mouth—a sure sign that she was spiraling.

"Oh boy," I muttered.

She yanked off a piece with a violent snap of her teeth. "'Oh boy' is right. I am *shook*, Remi. We go back to my place after dinner, because I'm not stupid enough to go to his place, right? Like, what if he's a serial killer?"

"I'm guessing the choice of venue wouldn't matter too much if that was the case."

Ness blinked. "Right."

"Continue," I prodded, flipping through some adoption applications that had come in over the weekend. "Clearly, you didn't die."

"Almost," she said glumly.

My hands paused and I glanced up. "Explain."

Ness leaned in. "He wouldn't sleep with me."

"Why not?"

"I don't know!" she wailed. "We had this amazing dinner, and the sexual tension was off the fucking charts. He had his hand over my thigh—you know what I mean. All *I'm staking my claim* and shit. Just parked there. Little movements of his fingers . . . But he never strayed too far, and I was ready to climb into his lap in the middle of the entrée."

"Goodness," I mused. "That's a powerful hand he must have."

"I wouldn't know, because he wouldn't *use it on me*." She pouted. "We kissed and it was so hot, and he had his hands up the back of my shirt, and I thought we'd mosey on back to the bedroom and make a night of it, but . . ." Her voice trailed off. "Then he pulled back and said he couldn't wait to go out with me again."

"And we're mad about this?"

"Yes!" she cried. "I damn near begged him to stay. It was pathetic."

I smiled. "What did he say?"

Her head flopped back and she laid her forearm over her eyes. "That he changed his mind and didn't want this to just be one night or some casual fling, and he wanted to take his time because it felt . . . big. Felt important."

She whispered this last part, and my smile grew.

"Aww, he's got a crush on you, Ness."

"Fuck off," she said without any heat behind it. "I've got a crush on him, too, but can't we have mutual crushing and also bang the bejeezus out of each other?"

"In theory, yes."

She sat up, her cotton-candy pink waves falling forward over her shoulder as she pinned me with a look. "Not *your* theory, Miss Eight-Date Rule."

"The eight-date rule was born from abject misery and lessons about modern dating that I did not feel particularly keen on learning."

"That it sucks," she said knowingly.

"Big-time."

"Good thing I can come here and distract myself from this shit." She tapped her temple.

"And what's in there?"

She gave me a miserable look. "I thought about baby names this morning while I was drinking my coffee. Now *I'm* the psycho."

I burst out laughing. She did too.

When we'd calmed down, I handed her two applications. "Got these in for Coco. Why don't you call and set up meetings for both families. You can get a feel for who might be the best fit. And I've got one for Charlie, one for Belle. If the meetings are good, we should be able to get all three kennels turned over this week."

"Sweet. I'm on it." She hopped up from the chair and adjusted her short denim shorts. "Does the yard need cleaned up?"

I sighed. "No."

Her eyebrows rose slowly. "You were on shit duty?"

"Not exactly," I hedged.

A deep voice came from the doorway: "That would be me."

Ness froze, then turned slowly, her eyes widening comically as she took in the sight of Archer at the entrance to my office. "Oh, holy fuck me in the eardrum."

Archer's eyes narrowed. I pinched the bridge of my nose.

"You're Archer Evans," she breathed.

His entire body seemed to brace for impact. Couldn't even blame the guy. I'd hardly given him a warm welcome. "I am."

"You're Archer-fucking-Evans." She pointed at him. Then pointed at me. "Did you know about this?"

"When he showed up in the parking lot this morning, yes, I was officially made aware."

"Archer Evans is volunteering here?" she squeaked.

"Can you stop saying his name?" I snapped.

Ness whistled. "You feeling feisty today, friend?"

"She hates me," he said.

My eyebrows shot up. "I never said that."

He arched a brow right back, and I tore my gaze away. Direct eye contact with this man made me feel all squirmy inside, and I did *not* like it.

"Her son was obsessed with you," Ness said. "Like, *obsessed*."

However Archer reacted to that news was none of my damn business, so I kept my focus locked on my best friend. "Vanessa Marie, you have things to do."

"Don't use my full name on me, Remi Elizabeth."

"'Was'?" Archer asked, and I cursed quietly under my breath.

Ness tilted her head. "Yeah. Past tense. The whole drunk-driving thing is a real turn-off when picking your heroes. He requested to toss the jersey he got for his birthday a few months ago. Right in the trash."

This time, I couldn't help myself. My gaze flicked back up, catching the brief flash of emotion in Archer's eyes. He masked it immediately.

The phone on my desk started ringing. "Ness, please go schedule those visits. You," I said to Archer, "sit."

Ness grinned. "I love it when you get bossy."

Archer's unreadable gaze stayed on me while I rolled my eyes and hit the button to answer the call on speaker. "Second Leash Sanctuary, this is Remi."

"That nurse won't leave me the hell alone."

I sighed. "Pops, we've been over this. You have to take your meds."

"I did. She says I'm lying."

"Did you hide them under your pillow again?"

He paused. "How'd you know about that?"

"Because I know *you*. You'll get no sympathy from me. She's just trying to do her job, okay? Don't make it harder than it has to be. She's there to help."

"I thought *you* were going to help."

Guilt shredded my insides. "Hiring her *is* my way of helping right now. Until we can get you moved in, I still have to work. Someone has to fund our lavish lifestyle."

He snorted. "Lavish, my ass. Tell me the last time you bought yourself anything."

"I bought groceries yesterday. That's as big of a splurge as you can get right now." I shuffled the stack of papers to the side and tried to ignore Archer as he sat silently in the chair pressed against the wall of my tiny office. God, he made that thing look half its size, with his legs spread out and his arms crossed over his wide chest.

"Can I still watch my show when she leaves?"

"Yes. I'll be over later to get you some dinner and do the laundry she can't get finished, all right? Gavin has soccer practice, so I'll have about an hour at your place while he's there."

"Okay. Love you, bug."

Allowing Archer this glimpse into my life made me want to crawl under my desk. It seemed like he knew it, too, because he kept that knowing gaze leveled at my face.

"Love you, too, Pops. Go take your meds," I added, just before he hung up.

"He gets to call you a nickname?"

My glare was unavoidable. "He's my grandfather, and I like *him*. Did you get the yard cleaned up?"

"How much do you feed these dogs? Or did you plant some extra shit just before I got here?"

"Oh, Archer. I'm thrilled you think I have that kind of foresight. Alas, they just poop a lot." I smiled. "Lucky for you. You'll be a pro by the end of your time here."

He shifted in his seat, widening the spread of his legs. "Can I do a few long days here and get this over with?"

I shuffled some papers into a neat pile. "No."

"Excuse me?"

"I want you disrupting as little as possible while you're here. This isn't a circus, where people can come gawk at the sideshow. We're trying to run a rescue, and I don't need your dwindling fan club lining up for autographs."

Archer expelled a sharp punch of air. "'Dwindling fan club,'" he said quietly. "I've still got a few."

"Less than you did last week, I promise."

His jaw tightened, but when he looked away, I felt a sharp twist of victory. It was short-lived, though, thinking about Gavin's face when he'd brought the jersey into my bedroom.

"Fine. I work out early right now. I'm done working with my QB coach by nine."

"No practices or anything?"

"Not yet. We start OTAs at the end of the month, so I'd like to be done by then. Everything until then is voluntary."

I sighed. "I don't know what OTAs are, but fine."

"Organized team activities."

I nodded briskly. "I can work with that. If opportunities for additional hours come up, I'm willing to work with you on more. But we have open hours for people to show up to check out the dogs on Mondays, Wednesdays, and Saturdays, so I don't want you here then."

Before he could say anything, the phone rang again, and I answered that too.

"Remi, it's Cass. I'm almost out of food and pads."

"Already?"

"Hungry litter. They're sweet, though. I'll have updated pictures to you by tomorrow."

"Great. You thought of some names?"

"Yeah, my kids went for cartoon characters on this group. We've got Minnie, Mickey, Donald, and Goofy. They're already campaigning to keep Goofy."

I smiled. "You going to become a foster fail on me already?"

"No," she said on a laugh. "They'll be just as excited about the next batch of puppies."

My relieved exhale was loud. "Good. It would be hard to replace you."

"No need for that. Just another bag of food and a box of pads, and I'm a happy girl."

I snatched a Post-it from the stack next to my computer and scrawled out what she needed. "I'll drop some off on my way home from work. Thanks for letting me know."

The call that came in right after that was a quote to repaint the outside of the building, and the number he gave me made me sick to my stomach. "Okay, thank you. I'm going to have to talk to our owner before I make that decision."

When I hung up, I braced my elbows on the surface of my desk and speared my hands in my hair. Ness wanted to know what I was doing differently today? Having a complete and utter fucking meltdown, that's what.

"I noticed the paint peeling when I was outside. The whole exterior needs to be redone or you'll start having issues with the siding."

I kept staring down at the desk. "Observant of you. I'm fresh out of gold stars, unfortunately."

I was on a roll today, sailing past my own personal record of bitchy retorts. Archer was quiet for a second, probably wondering just how hellish I'd make his life for the remaining forty-seven hours.

"That's not a bad estimate," he said. Something about his voice left my lungs feeling tight, like someone was squeezing them with a fist. "Maybe some of the money I have to pay can go towards that."

It took me a moment to gather my words. A long moment, with many internal pep talks about why it was bad to say swear words to men who were mandated by a judge to be here.

I looked up, and based on the way his eyes darted around my head, my hair probably looked insane, but I really didn't give a shit.

"The money you're paying will cover the repairs in the outdoor area. The fence. The seating. The equipment. Every penny will go towards what was destroyed by the *accident*. And once that's done, we have a list of a dozen other things that need updated." I held his gaze, no matter how squirmy it made me. "We have to work our asses off for every penny that comes in from donations. We are constantly asking and asking and asking for more because we *always* need more. But first we need food. We need to pay for medical care. We need to pay the few employees we have. We need puppy pads and flea shampoo and crates for our fosters. I have an online wish list that will never come close to being filled.

"I wish the money you were giving could cover all that, Archer, I really do. But it doesn't matter what I wish." My throat felt tight and achy, that familiar wave of anxiety crashing over my frame, just like it did every single day. "I know that you don't want to be here, and I really don't want you here either. I would have much rather taken a bigger check to pay for paint and a new roof and updated floors, and picked up the dog shit myself."

He studied my face so intently that I almost flinched, but instead held myself perfectly still.

"You're not going to make this easy on me, are you?"

"Should I? You're the one who had some beers and accidentally destroyed private property. Tell me why I should cut you any slack at all."

The chiseled features on his face were so hard to read, and I couldn't help but wonder what was going on in that brain of his.

"Okay."

I blinked. "Okay, what?"

He stood up, and I fought the urge to fidget under his perusal. "Don't go easy on me, Red."

I breathed out an incredulous laugh. "You think I'll back down?"

His eyes were center-of-the-flame blue, and I hated them. I hated *him*. "I guess we'll see. See you tomorrow, boss."

My mouth hung open as he strode out of the building.

Ness sprinted back into my office the moment the door slammed closed. She skidded to a halt in the doorway. "What happened to your hair? Did you make out with him?"

"Ness," I sighed. "No, of course not."

"Looks like you did." She came around my desk, wincing as she tried to smooth down the wild strands around my face. "This is how my hair looked after my no-sex make-out session with Christian last night."

I swatted her hands away. "Muriel already told me how I handle this entire . . . situation will basically be the deciding factor if she lets me take over officially."

"No making out, then," Ness stated on a disappointed sigh. Her lips curved in a sly smile. "Can we still look, though? His ass is perfection."

I smacked her arm as she laughed. "No. No looking at his ass."

"You are no fun when you're in boss mode. If we can't even look, what are you going to do with him?"

Through the window in my office, I had the perfect vantage point as Archer crossed the parking lot with long strides of his legs. Just before entering the truck—not some gleaming monster straight from the showroom, but something a few years old, dirt covering the bottom half—he paused, staring out into the tree line of the wooded area surrounding the shelter.

Did I believe him about the dog? I wasn't sure.

The timeline matched up. We'd had sightings of Bandit, as I'd started calling him when he evaded every single live trap we'd set, for the last two weeks. Based on the state of his coat, he'd been on his own for longer than that.

If it were that simple—wet roads and an animal's shadow—why wouldn't he tell the press that? The shelter didn't have the budget for exterior cameras. It was enough of a stretch to install them inside, but it was the easiest way to monitor the kennels after hours. Our neighbors in the mini-mart across the street had them, but they'd been down for maintenance the night of the accident, so there was no way to prove or disprove his story.

The truth of it was, I didn't want to believe him. My anger hadn't quite dissipated. It still boiled dangerously close to the surface, seeing something I loved and had worked so hard for come within four feet of being damaged far, far worse.

Four feet. That was how close the car had been from the front edge of the kennel. To breaking down walls, to driving straight into the room with all the dogs.

Into Scout and Daisy and Edgar and Sherlock and Pip. Into the others too. It would have been devastating. If he'd hurt a person by veering in the other direction, it would have been even worse.

That was why it didn't matter if I believed his story or not.

Because the consequences weren't simple either. Not for us, and not for all the kids like Gavin who looked up to this guy because he was big and strong and could throw a ball down a field. They idolized him, and now they had a mug shot to add to the pictures on their walls.

Just because he hadn't killed someone didn't mean he should get off the hook easily. And yes, he had money to throw at the problem, but it wasn't what the judge wanted.

The entire point was that this guy learned his lesson. And apparently, I was the one in charge of what lesson he learned. I thought about what I'd told Gavin when he was so upset about this. About not judging too quickly and not hating people we didn't know.

The best part of adulting is the ability to ignore your own advice sometimes. Parents' prerogative and all that.

I was judging. He was arrogant and rude and thought I'd roll over and make this easy on him because we'd had one stupid night where he managed to get his hand down my pants. His judgment of me gave that embarrassment and shame an angry edge, and it was hard to recognize as it pumped through my body.

"Remi?"

I didn't turn to face Ness. Instead, I kept my eyes on Archer as he slid into the driver's seat of the big vehicle.

Damn it, he really did have a great ass.

"What am I going to do with him?" I asked.

"That is the question of the day."

"I'm going to make him miserable."

Chapter Five

Archer

The weight room was quiet. I'd expected that, of course, after showing up at four thirty in the morning to get my reps in. PT for my ACL for all those months last year meant I'd hardly ever been alone in the training rooms. There was always someone analyzing my movements, watching my reps, making me run in a pool, recording the way I walked and ran and jumped and squatted.

So many eyes on me, so many boxes that needed to be checked before I could return to the field. And now, with a knee that was fine, I had a team that gave me sidelong looks when I walked through the building with earbuds in at all times.

Angry music screamed into my ears when I did my work, while I lay on the table and let the team's PT work on my body, and while I took reps with my quarterback coach alongside Carson.

Morning, I saw him mouth through the blaring music.

I nodded, leaning over to pick up a ball and toss it toward Mitch, our coach. They shared a look as Mitch caught my throws. We'd do this for a while, and as I threw, the repetitive motions soothing despite the constant knotting of my stomach, I felt my teammates' eyes on me as they filtered in and out of the practice fields.

No one knew how to approach me. Some of the veteran players, the other captains, wore their disappointment more plainly, but the rookies tended to edge around me with distinctly nervous energy.

Mitch held up his hand, and I stopped, holding the ball on my hip while he jogged over. He motioned to my earbuds, and I let out a slow breath as I pulled them out.

"You want to work with your receivers?" he asked, tilting his head in their direction. Three of them were here, doing sprints with their trainers. One, the rookie, stopped at the end of his run and looked over, lifting his hand in an awkward wave.

"No."

I put my earbuds back in, the screaming guitars drowning out all the thoughts in my head that I didn't particularly want to dwell on.

Over and over, I threw the ball, and I'd do it as long as Mitch would stand there. The muscles in my arms knew how to do this better than anything else in my life. Anchor my fingers along the laces, feel the pebbled leather under my palm. I'd known this for the majority of my life, the one place I felt the most sure, where all the noise faded away and the feel of the ball in my hand kept me grounded.

Find a target. Pull my arm back.

Release.

Watch it sail through the air and go exactly where I wanted it to go. In the moments where it did, nothing felt better. Even if it wasn't perfect, it didn't matter as long as the catch was made and the game stayed in our control.

Since I was nine years old and threw my first touchdown pass in flag football, I'd always known what I was supposed to do. It was only as the years passed that everything else in my life complicated the one thing that was the simplest: holding a ball in my hands and throwing it where it was supposed to go.

Mitch tossed me another ball, even though his face was pinched with disapproval. I danced back, snapping my arm forward, and he caught it, then tossed it into a bin next to him instead of back toward me. His eyes were focused on someone past my shoulder, and he gave a slight shake of his head.

A warning.

I tipped my chin up and stared at the metal roof of the practice fields. Only one person would interrupt without fear, and I swiped a hand over my mouth before turning.

Coach King was standing a few feet behind me, arms crossed over his chest, watching with a steady expression. He was the youngest coach in the league, and following orders from someone only a few years older than me had taken some getting used to.

The guy had fucking ice in his veins, or that was what it seemed like. After a rough first season together—me pushing him, him pushing me—we'd reached a tentative peace.

Until this.

It wasn't that he looked at me with distrust, more like I was a puzzle he was still trying to piece together, if I'd only stay still long enough for him to do so.

When he kept watching, I knew this was a battle I'd lose. With slow movements, I pulled the earbuds out and then stopped the music.

"Coach."

He didn't say a word. Just watched. The knot in my stomach grew, twisting around itself until I felt like I might choke on it, and I literally bit down on the tip of my tongue to keep from saying anything else.

I could only imagine what he was thinking.

That I was a fuckup.

A disappointment.

Benched for another season if I didn't get my ass in line and live up to his standards. He didn't expect perfection like my father, but he wanted the men on his team to show respect to each other. To work harder than we've ever worked as a team. To be good people in our lives off the football field as much as on.

You make me sick.

I heard my father's voice as I waited for similar words to come out of Coach's mouth, and before I could stop it, I felt a brick wall climb higher and higher in my mind, crowding out any weakness.

I was impenetrable before he ever opened his mouth.

"Do I need to be worried about you?"

The unexpected question landed like a shot to my chest, and I clenched my teeth, fighting to keep my expression even.

Remi's face was the first thing that popped into my mind, the shock and disgust and anger as she cradled her hand to her chest after landing that well-deserved blow.

Yes.

That was what I wanted to say. *Yes, you should be worried about me.* I was worried about myself. But I didn't know how to admit that. To stop the ugly cycle I'd found myself in.

So I took a deep breath and gave him an arrogant smirk.

"No, Coach. I'm right as fucking rain."

I clipped his shoulder as I walked away, marveling at how much you could hate yourself and still stay standing.

Chapter Six

Archer

For a long time, I'd wondered whether there was something wrong with me. There was enough questionable shit I'd done in my life—stemming from the way my father raised me—that I'd always struggled to understand why I did some of the things I did. But the thrill I got from antagonizing Remi Sinclair had me asking myself that question all over again.

I swear, she was giving the dogs something to make them poop more than usual.

The second day I showed up, she took one look at me and pushed the shovel into my hands. Not a single word. There was no one else at the shelter besides the two of us, and while I cleaned up the yard, I watched her work her ass off—feeding each dog, filling their water bowls, answering the phones, and generally being very skilled at not asking me for a single thing.

If I was doing just about anything else, it would have been a beautiful day. It was hot and sunny, and the smell was . . . well . . . suffice it to say, I'd have given anything for my community service hours to take place during the winter, when everything was frozen over.

Three hours of picking up dog shit—while being ignored—was starting to feel like *hell* would freeze over before the leggy redhead with pretty eyes would be civil to me. Never, in all my years of playing football, had someone disliked me this much from the moment they met me.

Not only did she not expect me to be perfect, but she also glared at me like I'd personally done her harm. It was fucking exhilarating. Maybe because I'd finally met someone who let their worst impulses out to play, just like me.

Remi said nothing to me, simply signed the paperwork when I was done and tightened her jaw when I said, "See you tomorrow, boss."

On the third day, she was waiting for me with a mop bucket. Her fiery hair was slicked back from her face, knotted in a bun low on the nape of her neck. Lazily, I perused this neater version of the woman I'd seen before.

"I like it the other way."

Her eyes flashed. They looked blue today. How did they look blue? "Good thing I didn't ask your opinion."

"Your eyes are a different color."

Remi's mouth fell open for a moment, then snapped shut. She straightened her spine and squared her shoulders. "Let me guess—you like the green better. I really don't care."

"I—"

"You ever used a mop?" she asked.

Five words, and a sick urge to keep stoking whatever pissy energy she was aiming at me gripped me by the fucking throat.

I pursed my lips and studied the bucket, the long wooden handle she held in her hand. "Looks pretty complicated. You might want to show me."

Her eyes narrowed slightly, then a soft smile curled her lips up at the edges. "If you've got enough IQ to hurl a ball down a field, I think you can manage just fine. But if that floor isn't clean enough to eat off of? Don't worry, you'll get plenty of practice, because I'll make you do it again until it is."

I took a step closer, wondering how far I might have to push her before she slapped the shit out of me. "How you gonna test that out, boss? You gonna let me take you out to dinner in Pip's old kennel?"

The bright flash of shock on her face was worth it, because she took a step closer too. My stomach tightened at the way she had to tilt her chin to look at me, even though she was taller than average. "Mop the floors and quit trying to piss me off, Evans. It won't work."

"Won't it?"

Remi stepped back, her face smoothing out. "No. Make sure to swap out the dirty water with clean after every kennel. The sink is back and to the right. Cleaner is in the cupboard above."

I gave her a crisp salute. "Whatever you say, boss."

She hated that nickname, her eyes gleaming every time I said it.

"And when you're done with this—"

"Let me guess—I can clean up the yard."

She smiled sweetly. "No. Today you get to clean litter boxes. Clio had diarrhea last night, so you're in for a real treat."

"That sounds delightful," I said smoothly. "I can't wait."

The glare I got in return was fierce, color slipping into her cheeks—a delicious pink that covered her chest too—and I was damn near ready to knock the mop out of her hands and see what would happen if I tried to kiss her.

She'd probably knee me in the balls, and I'd be half in love with her.

When she whirled around and left me alone with the mop, I smirked, wondering what it said about me that I was almost hard from her trying to make my life a living hell.

By day four, I was certain that I needed some emergency sessions with a shrink, because I'd developed an unhealthy obsession with pissing off Remi Sinclair. Maybe this was something a professional would pinpoint back to my childhood. I didn't get enough affection as a baby. Having had no real mother figure caused me to seek out attention—positive or negative—from wherever I could get it.

And Remi seemed to know that.

As I mopped the aisle again, Scout leaned up against the cinder block wall, watching me work with his big dark eyes.

"She's probably really nice to you, isn't she?"

He yawned, slowly sliding down into a lying position on the floor.

The back wall of the kennel room was one long window that stretched the entire length of the space. Like one of those observation windows where people used to go see their babies in the nursery after they were born. With that clear glass separating me from the offices and meeting rooms, it was easy to watch how often Remi was back and forth throughout the morning.

She'd asked that I come in Tuesdays, Thursdays, and Fridays.

All my shifts fell in the late morning, averaging three hours every time I was there. Mainly because the crappy jobs only took about that long, and God forbid she let me cuddle a puppy or something, because that might make my time pleasant.

Once the mopping was done, I walked to her office and paused outside the door when I heard her talking on the phone.

"Baby, I already told you, you cannot skip practice because you're tired."

I tucked my hands in my pockets, thinking about what her friend had said about Remi's son. Throwing my jersey away, as a young fan, was a big fucking deal. One I hadn't anticipated in the split-second decision that seemed to be bleeding into every aspect of my life.

"Mom," he groaned. "*Please*. We only have one game left, and I'm on the bench most of the time."

I tucked my chin into my chest and peered just around the edge of the doorframe. Her eyes were closed, exhaustion stamped all over her face. Her head was in her hands—and you're fucking right, I'd already checked for a wedding ring, and the fourth finger on her left hand was bare. No tan lines, no indents, nothing.

"Gavin," she sighed. "We talked about the responsibility of signing up for a team, right? You can't just pick and choose when you show up for the things that matter. We always have to show up for the people who depend on us. That's your teammates and your coaches."

"I know. But what if I don't even play?"

Remi adjusted the edge of a picture frame on her desk. The kid in the picture—ten or maybe eleven—had a mop of strawberry-blond hair and dimples. "Then I will be the proudest mom in the world knowing you're ready to go whenever they need you. The people on the bench are important too. You can cheer on your teammates, encourage them when things are hard."

He groaned, and the sound of it lifted the edges of her lips in a smile. It didn't lift mine, though.

At Gavin's age, I never would have received such a logical pep talk. There would've been guilt. Would've been shame. And the dangling of my father's affection over my head like a fucking carrot on a stick.

"Do you think if I had someone to help me play soccer in the backyard, I'd be good enough to start?" the kid asked quietly.

Remi pinched her eyes shut. "Maybe. I could . . . I could try to find some lessons or something if that's what you want."

"Lessons are expensive, right?"

She tipped her head back and let out a slow, soundless breath. "Sometimes, yeah. But you let me worry about that."

"Cory's dad helps him," he added quietly. "He played soccer in college, so they work on dribbling and shooting and stuff. Do you . . . do you think my dad played soccer?"

Heartbreak. It was the only way to describe Remi's face. The pit of my stomach pitched and rolled, the discomfort so thick that I fought the urge to back away, to not look anymore.

"I don't know, buddy. Maybe." Remi rubbed a hand over her forehead. "I'll look into getting some lessons this summer, okay? Maybe they've got someone at the rec center who can help."

"Okay. Thanks, Mom."

"I love you," she said softly.

"Love you more."

Remi smiled. "Impossible."

Don't you want me to be proud of you, Archer? I'd be proud of a son who's the best.

Slowly, I stepped back from her office, wondering what the fuck I was doing trying to get under her skin the way I had been. The lobby was empty and quiet, and I gripped the edge of the front desk, hanging my head down toward my chest as I tried to make sense of why I was like this.

Always seeking the wrong kind of reaction. Looking for attention in a way that made everything difficult. From my coach, from my father, and now from Remi.

Attention from women was easy. If I wanted, I could've had a different woman in my bed every night, but not long after I got drafted, that felt stale. Ugly. Fake. And I'd had enough of that around the dinner table growing up. Putting on a mask and pretending like everything was okay.

Now a beautiful woman had caught my eye, turned my fucking head, and I was poking and poking and poking at her, tugging on her braids and hoping she'd look my way.

But all I was doing was adding to the weight she already carried.

I felt sick to my stomach, shame turning my skin cold and clammy.

Coach. I could call Coach. He'd listen to me, right? I couldn't call my father. Didn't have a mom to ask, because she left him so long ago, not caring enough to take me and Analise with her.

There'd been no one in my life to teach me how to do this shit, but I'd seen Coach with his wife, knew what kind of man he was. What kind of husband and father. He loved them, unreservedly, and didn't care who saw it. There were no strings to his affection, and that was probably the kind of person I needed to talk to right now.

I stood up and pulled out my phone, ready to search for his contact info, when movement caught my eye in the parking lot.

The dog was sniffing around my truck.

In the light of day, I could finally see him clearly. He had a medium build, mostly black with some brown markings, a hint of white on two of his paws. A Lab mix, or maybe a hound.

I thought about interrupting Remi, but I could hear her on another call. Sitting by the front door was a small bag of hot dog pieces and a simple leash that could be looped around a dog's neck. She'd set them there just in case anyone saw him.

I took a deep breath and tucked the hot dogs in my pocket, then looped the leash around my hand, cracking the front door just enough that I could slip out without triggering the bell attached to the frame. I kept my steps quiet, steady, but he lifted his head when he saw me.

His eyes were blue.

I slowed, setting the looped end of the leash on the pavement as I kept the other end tight in my grasp. I'd seen Remi do something similar the last time she'd tried to get him to come close, but that time, the blare of a car horn on the street scared him off.

Even though his body language was tense, he didn't run.

I held eye contact while I eased myself onto the ground. "Nice to finally meet you," I told him. "You caused one hell of a domino effect in my life."

His head tilted, his frame relaxing a little at the sound of my voice.

"I know you didn't mean it. I'm like that, too, you know. I do stuff and I don't always know why. Can't see what might happen as a result." I carefully opened the bag of hot dogs and tossed a few in his direction. One bounced close enough that he lowered his nose to smell it, then took a step closer to eat it off the ground.

I stayed still. He took another step and ate another one. Then another.

When the pieces I'd thrown were gone, he lifted his head and watched.

"Still hungry?" I tossed a few more, making sure the majority of them landed inside the loop of the leash. "I tell you what, dude, if I could bring you in there safely, I'd get some pretty major brownie points with her."

Remi had been calling him Bandit, and he paused again, not moving closer to get more food.

"Not that that's your responsibility," I told him. "It's my problem to fix. Sometimes things that come easily to other people don't always come easily to me. Usually relationship stuff, you know. I didn't have a good example growing up. And I shouldn't find it this hard to be around a beautiful woman who interests me without acting like a jackass, but I've spent the entire week doing that."

He ate another piece but kept his gaze flicking back to me, just to make sure I wasn't moving.

"In college, and even the first couple years in the pros, no one cared much if I was a nice guy. I didn't have to be the best version of myself. I just had to win."

I tossed a couple more pieces closer to him, and he ate them quickly. When he stepped forward to eat the pieces inside the loop, I held my breath, making sure my body stayed perfectly still.

"When Coach benched me, then I got injured, that all seemed to change." My stomach sank as I actually said the words out loud. "People looked at me differently, and I didn't know how to change it. I still don't. Definitely not now."

All the pieces were gone, and Bandit stared at me expectantly.

I tossed him a few more, keeping them inside the loop. He ate them.

I threw a couple more.

"Maybe it's just about being patient," I said as I watched him. "Doing little things that add up to something big."

Bandit lowered his head to eat, and I moved quickly, shifting onto the balls of my feet and tugging backward with the leash so that the loop pulled over his head. He jerked back with a yelp, but jerked in exactly the right direction—darting to the side instead of back—so that the leash was firmly around his neck.

I stayed down at his level. "Easy, buddy, I'm not going to hurt you."

He wrenched his body as far away from me as possible but wasn't fighting the restraint like I thought he might. I gave him the last pieces of hot dog, and he only hesitated for a moment before inhaling them like he had all the others.

"You've probably been struggling out here a long time, huh? Nowhere soft and warm to sleep. That's gotta get old. You come inside and you'll have the cleanest floors in the world, I promise."

I let out a slow breath when he raised his head—there was slack in the leash.

"Good job. Should we go inside and say hi?"

The door flew open behind me.

"How did you—"

Remi was wide-eyed, glancing incredulously between me and the dog. I held out the leash in her direction. Bandit stared between us, much in the same way she'd just been doing.

"I guess he was ready today."

Her mouth fell open, and the way she looked up at me made me feel ten fucking feet tall.

"Archer," she exhaled softly, then shook her head. "Thank you."

This. This was so much better than her anger.

It was a heady thing, and my mouth went dry at the way her eyes held mine. It wasn't how she'd looked at me when we sat in that darkened corner in the bar. It wasn't how she'd looked at me on the dance floor.

She didn't know me then. I didn't know her either.

Those were looks based on only the superficial, only the things our eyes could see.

This was something different.

Something better. Something powerful and slick as it swelled in the space between us.

Oh, how I wanted more.

As I took a step back, I refused to drop her gaze. The color climbed slowly up her cheeks.

I wanted more of that too.

"See you tomorrow, boss."

Chapter Seven

Remi

I was thinking about blue-eyed dogs and blue-eyed men and how much trouble they'd caused in my life recently, and that was the only reason why I burned dinner.

"Holy shit, bug, what is that smell?"

I'd been staring at the tile backsplash, stirring absently, not paying the slightest bit of attention to the black edge accumulating on the pan of meat sauce. When Pops asked the question, I blinked down at the stovetop and grimaced. "Oh, um, it's dinner. It'll be fine. I can add more seasoning."

I picked up the garlic salt and the Italian seasoning, and Pops quickly snatched them out of my hand. "I'll do that," he said, nudging me out of the way.

I sighed, handing over the wooden spoon with a lift of my eyebrows. "Fine. But you weren't supposed to come over and do the work. I'm supposed to be taking care of you."

"Oh, come on, I'll get dementia faster if I sit here and do nothing. You don't want that, do you?"

"I'm not sure that's how it works, but fine, you can finish dinner."

As I sat in one of the chairs at the kitchen table, Pops brought the sauce to his lips, wincing slightly when he tasted it.

"What's wrong? I didn't burn it that much."

"Just needs a little garlic, is all." On his way to the pantry cabinet, he patted my shoulder. "How was work today?"

"Weird."

"What did Ness do now?"

I laughed. "Nothing, actually. It was just . . . weird."

He must have caught something in my tone, because Pops gave me a long look over the rim of his glasses. "Something you want to talk about, bug?"

I shook my head. "I'll get it figured out."

Maybe.

Probably.

It was so much better when Archer stayed in his damn lane. We had roles now—I was professional and didn't hit anyone. He was smug and annoying and tried everything he could to get under my skin.

If he was thoughtful and did nice things, where the hell did that leave us?

Nowhere I wanted to be, thank you very much.

Except he *was* doing nice things. In another life, Archer must have been a professional dog wrangler. I didn't know how to process what had happened. Couldn't even think about trying, because my entire life was a wobbly house of cards. One stiff blow—or dog rescue, as it were—would knock the entire damn thing over, and I'd be left to pick up the pieces for everyone involved.

Processing could happen later, when he was back in his life and no longer the number one threat to my sanity.

Pops crushed some garlic with the flat side of a knife, a move I'd never quite mastered, but his worried gaze kept flicking to my face.

"I'm fine," I told him. "I promise."

Gavin ran into the kitchen, his eyes bright and smile wide. "Pops, I just saw the first oriole in the backyard!"

"Oh baby, did you get a picture on my phone?"

Gavin nodded and turned the screen around so Pops could check it out.

He held the phone away from him. "Nice one, buddy. Add it to the folder."

"Okay."

He took off toward the backyard, and Pops chuckled under his breath. "What I'd give for a tenth of that energy."

"No kidding."

"Honey, you're not even thirty. Don't talk to me about feeling old and tired until you're past fifty."

I scrunched my nose. "I feel like I'm going to be an old lady by the time I turn forty. I'll have a kid in college." My mouth fell open as that realization hit. "Oh God, I'll have a kid *out* of college when I turn forty. What the hell will I do with myself when he's gone?"

Pops interrupted the maternal spiral with a deep laugh. "Maybe you'll be married and have more kids by then."

"Doubtful. Unless the perfect man literally drops out of the sky and into my lap, I'm not looking for any kind of relationship." I eyed the way he kept adding spices to the sauce. "I've got enough men stressing me out, thank you."

Pops took another taste and nodded approvingly. "I know you don't mean me."

Gavin yelled from the other room, "Mom, does Sharpie come off if someone accidentally colored on the walls?"

Pops chuckled. I dropped my head into my hands and groaned.

"It's just a little touch-up paint," he said. "Now, come on. You set the table and let's eat."

Chapter Eight

Archer

"This steak is overcooked." My father set down his fork and knife with slow, purposeful movements. Without trying it, he'd sliced into the middle, the vivid red of the expensive meat clearly visible even across the table. Medium rare, the way his was always prepared. "Hundreds of dollars a pound and our chef doesn't even know how to properly prepare Kobe beef. It's embarrassing."

My knife hovered in the air, just above my own cut of meat, which was cooked to a textbook medium—seared on the outside and pink on the inside—exactly how I liked it.

Analise glanced in my direction, but we didn't hold eye contact for long. She managed a tiny eye roll and shoved a spear of broccolini in her mouth. There was no steak on her plate. She'd been a vegetarian for about two years.

She'd never admitted it out loud, but I was increasingly certain she'd forgone eating meat in equal measure about not wanting to eat animals, and because it pissed him off.

Both Evans children, all in all, were a great disappointment to my father.

The entire life he'd built was a disappointment to our mother, too, which was why she'd packed her shit and left when Analise was two. Turned out, he didn't earn quite enough to keep her happy, and raising children—even by proxy, with the help of two nannies—was just a bit too messy for her.

No doubt if she'd been here, she'd have been bitching about the $200-a-pound steak too.

Instead of reacting immediately, I adjusted my grip on the fork and watched with satisfaction as the knife cut through with hardly any effort. When the steak was in my mouth, practically melting as I chewed, I sat back in my seat and let out a contented groan. The sound was obscenely loud in the uncomfortably quiet formal dining room.

Father sighed quietly but didn't comment.

I hated this room. The ostentatious crystal chandelier. The giant table for twelve, even though it was hardly ever more than just us three. The walls of this place only ever saw polite veneer and better faking than a porn star's bedroom.

Father gave me a narrow-eyed look as I patted my stomach.

"Mine's fucking delicious."

His eyebrow arched. "Do we curse at the dinner table now?"

I set my fork down, crossed my arms over my chest, and pinned him with a look. "I guess I do, yeah. Gonna kick me out, Dad?"

He hated when I called him that. *Uncouth,* he'd said.

His lip curled in disgust, but when Rebecca pushed through the serving kitchen door with another batch of crusty yeast rolls fresh out of the oven, his features smoothed out. She'd been with our family for over a decade, so I wasn't as close to her as my sister was, given that I was a junior in high school when Rebecca started. But even those couple years at home, I gravitated to the kitchen as much as Analise, simply because we both sought out her warm, soothing presence.

Her hair was more silver than blond now and her steps a little bit slower, but the woman was an absolute dream in the kitchen. On death row, I'd ask for her lasagna and garlic bread as my last meal.

"More bread," she said, setting the plate right by Analise with a tiny wink that my father couldn't see.

My sister beamed. "Thank you, Rebecca. It smells delicious."

"You're welcome, honey."

Father cleared his throat—a sharp, piercing sound. "She has a name, Rebecca," he drawled. "Do try using it."

I caught Rebecca's eye and gave her an encouraging nod, just before her face slipped into a mask of deference when she turned to my father. "Is there anything else you need, sir?"

"Yes." My father tugged at the sleeves of his starched white oxford. Even at dinner with his family, he couldn't fucking relax. He set his hand on the silver-rimmed bone china plate in front of him and pushed it away. "When I ask for medium rare, I expect medium rare. Try again. I pay you an ungodly amount to get this right, Rebecca."

Her eyes were downcast immediately as she picked up the discarded plate, the flush of her cheeks giving away her embarrassment. "Yes, sir."

There might have been a time, even recently, when I kept my mouth shut and let him treat the staff like shit because it was easier to just let the tempest pass.

Maybe those rocks in my gut were finally thawing, because it wasn't very difficult to push away from the table with an angry screech of the chair legs against the hardwood floor.

"For God's sake, Archer," my father muttered.

Analise gave me a confused look. "Where are you going?"

"Home." I picked up my plate and handed it to Rebecca. "Can I please get this to go? It's far too delicious to waste."

She smiled gratefully. "Of course."

Analise's face drooped in disappointment. "You're leaving already? We hardly had time to talk."

Sometimes I thought the only reason I could carry on a decent conversation at all was because of my little sister. Born when I was ten, Analise had been my shadow until I moved out. She wanted to know everything—insatiable curiosity paired with a healthy dose of loneliness from being the only one left at the house with Dad. I called her every day on my way home from the facilities.

What she didn't know about yet, and I suspected she'd grill me about at the first chance, was my community service. I thought about trying to explain Remi to her without giving myself away, and winced internally.

Gently, I nudged her shoulder. "Want to come with?" I asked. "You don't have school tomorrow. You can stay over if you want—"

She was halfway out of her seat before I'd even finished speaking. *"Yes."*

"No," my father snapped. "She has tutoring tomorrow morning at eight. Which you wouldn't need if you'd figure out how to focus on your schoolwork and get the grades I expect from the Evans name."

"Shit," Analise muttered under her breath.

"I see the language in this family is an epidemic." He pulled the linen napkin away from his lap, plucking at an invisible piece of lint after it was folded in front of him. "I think maybe less time with your brother is in order, until he can remember his manners."

I had fantasies—deep fantasies—about what it would feel like to knock his veneers out with my fist.

Dipping so I could see her face, I waited until Analise finally looked up. "Text me when you're done tomorrow. I'll pick you up and we can go do something."

She smiled. "Okay."

She stood and wrapped her arms tight around my middle, Father watching us with an inscrutable look on his face. I did a lot of things to piss him off, but showing my little sister affection was not one of them. Because if I didn't, she'd have nothing. Just like I'd have had nothing without her. I hugged her back with a deep sigh, then pressed a kiss to the top of her head. "Love you, little A."

"Love you, big A."

Father's eyes gave nothing away at our shared nicknames, something that had started when she was a toddler, running around the house after me. *Archer* had been too hard for her, so she called me A.

I didn't let go right away. Neither did she.

Analise didn't want to stay in that house any more than I wanted to leave her, but until she turned eighteen, there wasn't much either of us could do.

My father didn't say a word as I strode out of the dining room. Rebecca was waiting with a glass container holding my steak, potatoes, and broccoli.

"Eat all your vegetables," she instructed.

"Yes, ma'am." I tilted my head toward the front door. "You sure you don't want to come work for me? I'll double whatever he's paying you."

Her eyes glittered. "If I leave, who's watching out for her all the time?"

I don't know what possessed me—maybe this entire experience was softening me more than I'd expected—but I leaned in and kissed her on the top of the head too. "You're a good one, Rebecca. I don't think either of us would've survived him without you."

Her cheeks were a brilliant red when I pulled back. "Oh, go on with you. Your flirting's wasted on an old lady. You should save that for a pretty girl in your life."

"Don't have one of those right now." Green eyes flashed through my mind. "None that want me to give any kisses, at least."

She studied me speculatively. "But you have someone you like?"

"Good night, Rebecca."

Rebecca laughed. "Drive safe. No beers tonight?"

The gleam in her eye told me she knew more than she was letting on.

Instead of asking, I said, "Just water."

"Good boy."

Fifteen minutes later, I let myself into the garage door of my house in the woods. Construction had been completed a few months earlier, but furnishing the home was still a work in progress. I didn't want to hire someone to pick stuff, because it was always too small or too fussy. Trends didn't interest me, because I was the only person who saw it, and the only person who mattered.

But I didn't care enough to get it done quickly. I had a place to sleep, a place to watch TV or read, and a place to eat my meals, and for now that was enough. As I walked through the kitchen, I kept it dark, only turning on the light above the stove. I stood in front of the sink and ate my dinner straight from the container, ignoring the empty, quiet house around me until it was time to shower before bed.

My bathroom suite was the size of my college apartment, one of the only places where I truly went overboard. The vanity was imported marble, eight feet long with a sink on either side. In the corner of the bathroom was a custom soaking tub I'd had made just for me. Not being able to stretch my legs out in a bath was the curse of being tall. Being rich meant I could sidestep that pretty easily. It was square, six and a half feet long from end to end, with just enough slope on two of the sides that I could lie in it with only my shoulders and chest above the water.

For a moment, I eyed the tub, trying to decide if I was patient enough to wait for it to fill up, but in the end I decided the shower would suffice.

The tiled shower was even bigger than the tub, with multiple showerheads and a bench stretched along the side. Every night, I cleaned off the day before climbing between the sheets. It was the only way I could sleep.

The water heated quickly, and I stripped off my clothes, tossing them in the laundry basket off to the side. When I stepped under the spray, I closed my eyes and tipped my head back, letting the scalding-hot water course over my body.

It was the first time all day that my mind quieted. And as had been the case for the last few weeks, it was in those quiet moments that she crept in.

Red hair.

Blue-green eyes.

A big laugh.

A vicious streak that was hotter than it should be.

I braced my hands on the tile and hung my head under the ruthless water. My chest heaved, because all it took was a few scattered thoughts of Remi and all the blood rushed straight between my legs.

Prying my eyes open, I stared down at my hard-on.

The last time I'd thought with that stupid prick was in the bar. How was I supposed to resist her? She was nothing like I'd been expecting, and it was in the genuine rambling nerves, the big eyes, and the delicious curves of her body that desire had knocked me breathless before I knew what was happening.

I clenched my teeth and took myself in hand, rolling my forehead on the cool tile while I let my thoughts drift.

Her breast in my hand—skin warm and soft and big enough that I wouldn't be able to take the whole thing in my mouth.

A groan tore from my chest, my hand working in slow, steady strokes. I imagined her writhing under me while my brain conjured the taste of her, the feel of her flesh against my tongue and teeth and lips.

Remi naked, lush curves and greedy hands.

Remi's red hair wound between my fingers as I gripped it in a fist and took her from behind.

Remi on top of me, rolling her hips like she had on the dance floor.

Remi underneath me, crying out into my ear while I worked my hips between hers.

"Fuck," I bit out, hand working faster.

Remi's face, her big eyes staring up at me, brow pinched as she chased her release.

Tight. She'd be tight. She'd fucking suffocate me, wouldn't she?

I wanted it. I wanted to see the play of it across her face. She showed everything on her face.

Her happiness. Her stress. Her anger.

Her shame.

My hand slowed.

Remi's big eyes as she stared up at me on the dance floor. Horrified. Embarrassed. Cheeks flushed with shame.

"Fuck," I said again, tearing my hand away and slamming my fist down on the tile.

With my heart racing, my balls screaming because I was on the edge of release, I cranked the shower handle to cold and stood there until my skin pebbled with goose bumps.

The ghost of my unfulfilled orgasm left an ache behind, and I strode out of the shower, letting the pain remind me how thoroughly I'd fucked up my chance to see any of those sides of her.

I didn't deserve it.

Didn't deserve her.

Chapter Nine

Remi

The list of reasons why I didn't sleep well at night was long, a constantly rotating battle for what was currently stressing me out the most: raising a preteen on my own, my aging grandfather who needed to move in with me because he was stubborn and ornery and we couldn't afford for him to go anywhere else, the shelter. But the most frequent visitor at the top of *that* list was—wait for it—my to-do list.

Sometimes I lay in bed and thought about the bullet points that I hadn't checked off.

Had I showered? Maybe.

Shaved my legs? Don't be ridiculous.

Gavin's laundry was done but definitely not put away. Which was fine, because laundry was a morally neutral task. Getting it done didn't magically make me a better person. But God, the way it piled up made me crazy.

Had I picked up Pops's prescription?

Did the foster home for the new litter of puppies have enough formula to feed them through the first week? Maybe I should have sent more.

Truly, it was a miracle I slept at all. I'd often fade somewhere around two a.m., only to be woken, bleary-eyed, by the obnoxious scream of my alarm clock, reminding me that there was another day of *this* ahead of me. Always going, always needing more than I had, and always feeling like I wasn't quite enough to take care of it all.

My day off, for whatever it actually was, was even busier than my days at the shelter, because then I had to cram roughly two hundred things into my waking hours instead of one hundred. And on this particular day off, I didn't even get a full day. Stuart was sick, and I had told Ness I'd take his evening shift and do the last feeding and let the dogs run before closing up the shelter for the night. I remember feeling tired in high school. What a fucking joke. Sixteen-year-old me didn't *know* what tired was, that little shit.

The exhaustion that hung off my frame was deeper than anything I'd ever experienced. No amount of sleep could erase it, and even though I joked with Ness that I didn't want a sugar daddy, if there was some kind old gentleman who'd pay all my bills just for some pictures of my feet or something, I'd be tempted.

Maybe then I could take a day off on my day off, instead of whatever it was I was doing now. Surviving. Hardly.

That was the only reason why I fell asleep on the floor of my guest room when I was supposed to be scrubbing baseboards, readying the space for when Pops moved in.

The floor wasn't even particularly comfortable, but the midday sun was streaming in through the window, an inviting warm spot, and there was a blanket in the basket next to the end of the bed, so I tugged it down next to me and thought, *I'll just enjoy the sun for five minutes. I can take five minutes for myself without the world falling apart.*

Brrrrrring. Brrrrring.

I jolted up from the floor. "Wha—" I scrubbed my hands over my face as my phone kept on with its incessant blaring ring. There was dried drool on my chin, and I groaned when I realized I'd been asleep for an hour. An hour!

"This is Remi," I said around a yawn, not even stopping to look at the screen.

"Ms. Sinclair, this is Katie at your grandfather's doctor's office. He's supposed to be here for an appointment, and we were just checking to see if he's all right, because he was a no-show."

I ran a hand over my forehead and sighed. "Yeah, I talked to him a couple hours ago. He was fine. I, uh, I probably should have driven him myself, but he said he was going to go with a neighbor who was running some errands."

She made an understanding noise. "He's been a little reluctant to see us lately."

"I know. I'm so sorry for the wasted time. I'll talk to him and reschedule when I can bring him myself. He's moving in with us shortly, and that will make it easier."

"He's been receiving private-duty nursing support, correct?"

I stood up from the floor and winced at the ache in my lower back. "Yes. For the last month. It's helped, but he's so stubborn about people taking care of him."

"Please make sure you're getting adequate support when he moves in with you," she said gently. "Caregivers often neglect their own physical and mental well-being when they're stretched too thin."

I couldn't help it. I started laughing. "I'm sorry," I wheezed. "It's just . . . that's my entire life in a nutshell, and I think I'm falling into a sleep-deprived state of hysteria at this point."

There was a smile in her voice when she answered. "Well, I hope you can carve out some time to rest and relax."

I scrubbed at the drool mark on my chin. "Yeah, me too."

When the call disconnected, I sank onto the edge of the bed and sighed. Something had to give. Pops moving in would help. A little. There'd be another adult at the house with Gavin, and I could stop having to rely on my neighbor to watch him. He'd save money by not having to rent his apartment anymore, and he'd already insisted on using some of his social security payments toward my rent.

The weight of my entire existence kept getting heavier and heavier, and I wondered when it had started to feel like too much for me to handle. I loved them both so much, so fiercely, that it was hard to breathe through most days. I'd do anything for them, and I wondered when I'd have to admit there were some things I couldn't do, couldn't fix, in my endless pursuit to make their lives better.

My phone rang again, and I sighed before flipping the screen over. It was the school.

"This is Remi," I said.

"Hey, Remi, it's Marie from the school office."

"Is Gavin okay?"

"Oh yeah, he's fine. I was actually calling because we were going through our list of people who volunteered at the beginning of the school year to help out where the PTO might need it, and we've been covered for the last couple events, but we're really short of bodies for Field Day."

Field Day, I thought, barely keeping my groan contained. Organized chaos and sweaty kids and teachers and parents who were just trying to make it to the last day of the school year. I'd helped every year, because just like with the class parties and the field trips and the reading groups in the classroom, I knew there'd be a day when Gavin didn't need me around as much. And the teachers . . . they were so appreciative. Dogs couldn't really say thank you, so it was nice to help out the human variety too.

"Yeah, of course," I said, injecting some enthusiasm into my voice. "You know I'm always there."

She chuckled. "Everyone regrets it when they get these phone calls, if it makes you feel better."

"Past me thought I'd have more energy at this point of the year."

"May really is the worst. No one warns you about May before you have kids in school."

"They don't. I wonder why," I mused.

She laughed quietly. "Is that a yes for Field Day?"

"Of course."

"You are the best, thank you. I told our PE teacher we can always count on you to help."

See, that was why I did it. Being needed, being someone people could count on, was such a good feeling. No doubt about it, I had a praise kink left untapped somewhere.

"I try."

"Besides, even if you'd said no, I know how to wear you down." It was said with a teasing lilt, but we both laughed because we knew the underlying threat was so frickin' real.

For about thirty minutes, my phone was blissfully silent, and I finished cleaning in the guest room, then moved on to getting dinner into the Crock-Pot. There was no soccer practice that night, so Gavin would be home with the neighbor while I went to the shelter.

Paying a babysitter usually made any post-school hours I worked a fairly moot point.

After securing the lid so the roast and vegetables could cook—it would be done by the time I got home for a late dinner, and heat up well for the rest of the week—I pulled out my phone and sent Pops a text.

Me: You are in so much trouble.

Pops: I don't know what you're talking about.

Me: Did you think the doctor's office wouldn't call me?

Pops: That's a breach of confidentiality.

Me: If I wasn't your medical power of attorney, yes, it would be. Don't deflect.

Pops: Those doctors never tell me anything important. I saved myself some money.

Me: You are a stubborn old goat and I love you. Want to come over tomorrow for dinner?

Pops: Not tonight?

Me: I'm covering for Stuart tonight. G will be home with Mrs. Patterson.

Pops: Okay. See you tomorrow, bug.

I set my phone down and glanced at the clock. I had about two hours before I needed to head to the shelter.

The top of my to-do list was in Ness's handwriting.

For the love of God, take a shower, dry shampoo can only do so much.

I smiled and decided to listen to my best friend.

An everything shower was a luxury I often skipped. Two rounds of shampoo. Hair mask. Face wash. Armpits and legs shaved. After thirty minutes, I hopped out of the shower feeling like a new woman, my skin pink and pruny from the hot water.

The mirror was steamed over, and I ran a hand through the condensation so I could see my reflection. I dropped the towel and turned to the side to study my profile.

My legs were still toned from all the physical work I did at the shelter, my stomach softer than it had been in my early twenties. Faint stretch marks left white streaks on my lower belly from my pregnancy with Gavin, and I dragged my hand over the white lines, trailing up my stomach and between my breasts.

Now *those* I was proud of. Yes, they often hid behind a baggy T-shirt, encased in a sports bra, but I had a great rack. My chest held light freckles, just like the bridge of my nose. I sighed as I pulled on my cotton underwear and some lightweight shorts. The tank I'd picked had a bra built in, and it gave me the kind of cleavage I used to show off ten years ago.

Like I showed off the night at the bar.

Oh, but we were ignoring that night because it never happened. It didn't *exist.*

The entire thing was a fever dream, best banished to the dark, scary part of my brain where I kept algebra and laundry best practices and how to iron clothes and all manner of things that were pointless.

No, today, we were focusing on the fact that I was proud of my body.

"Not bad, Sinclair," I muttered, brushing through my wet hair and then twisting it up onto the top of my head.

While I slathered lotion over my legs and arms, Archer kept trying to elbow his way into my thoughts. Talking to him. The sound of his voice. The way he'd watched me. The way he'd touched me. My hands slowed, goose bumps lifting along my arms. Ness joked about my impossible standards and the eight-date rule attached to them, but that list came in handy.

Hadn't I learned that in excruciating detail with my didn't-really-happen run-in with Archer?

He was the *antithesis* of my list.

Too good-looking.

Too rich.

Too successful.

Arrogant.

Sex on legs.

Eyes on him all the time.

Nothing about him was quietly average, and that was why he was a big ol' no for me.

Only one person in the last five years had gotten past dates five and six. He'd met every criterion on the list, and still I was reminded why it was best to proceed with caution.

I wanted a partner. A best friend. I didn't want someone else to take care of, an overgrown man-child who needed another mom. I also didn't want an easy lay, because holy hell, was a vibrator a lot less hassle. That was collecting dust in my drawer too. By the time I hit my mattress at the end of the day, just reaching for it felt like more effort than I could spare.

I wasn't even sure who I'd think of if I did.

Liar, liar, sensible panties on fire, a voice whispered in the back of my mind. It sounded an awful lot like Ness. If she was the voice of my conscience, I was in *so* much trouble.

Unbidden, a face slipped into my mind while I ran my hands over my shoulders and chest to rub in the last of the lotion. A strong jaw and blue eyes. Firm lips. Unsmiling mouth.

He sure didn't look at me like I was a messy, tired single mom, but I didn't know what his looks meant either. Eighty percent of the time, I wished I'd never met him.

Another ten percent didn't necessarily regret what had happened. I just wanted him to go away.

Unfortunately, the last ten percent never should have seen the light of day. Blame it on hormones, blame it on a dry spell—whatever. It was there, and only when my life quieted down enough that my mind could wander away from to-do lists did it land on questions that I never should have been asking.

As you got older, it was easy to let certain parts of your personality fade, caught in the cycle of routine and just trying to get through each day. What faded in me over the last ten years was that slightly rebellious girl, the one who'd snuck out when she was supposed to be asleep, and allowed the curious part of her nature to crank the engine and stomp on the gas.

The inquisitive, rebellious girl wasn't gone, but it was only with Archer that she'd come out to play. *She* asked questions. *She* wanted to know things. *She'd* take a list meant to restrict potential partners and burn it to the fucking ground.

Even though I'd allowed her to fade, the questions remained.

What if I'd let him take me home that night? What would he be like in bed?

My hands trembled slightly as I rubbed lotion underneath the strap of my tank, because I *knew.* He'd be bossy. Demanding. Relentless.

Unwelcome desire curled through my veins, spinning heat through my stomach before I could stop it, and I squashed it like a bug.

Archer was the kind of man who'd have a veritable buffet of sex at his disposal, whenever he wanted it. Maybe he didn't look at me like I was a tired single mom, but that didn't mean he was having naughty thoughts either. His looks probably fell in the category of *What's wrong with her hair?* and *Why isn't she throwing herself at me like the rest of the Straight Female Under Fifty demographic?*

Because I had standards. Because I had no time for playboys or Neanderthals or idiots who decided to drink and drive. No matter how big their muscles were. Or their hands. Or feet.

He had really big hands. And really big feet.

My eyes slammed shut.

Professional thoughts only, I scolded myself, my hands moving more briskly than they had been before. No thinking about Archer while hands were moving anywhere near my nipples.

I glared at the mirror because they had perked right up at the shift in my thoughts.

"Traitors," I murmured, then flipped the light off and left the bathroom.

Halfway through putting away Gavin's laundry, my phone rang again, and I wondered what would happen if there was a blood pressure monitor connected to my body.

That shit would probably jump so high every time I heard the ring.

The shelter's number flashed across the screen.

"Ness, I have ninety minutes of freedom left. This better be good."

"It is. You need to get over here."

"Now?" I whined.

"Remi."

"Ness."

"Get your fine ass to the shelter."

"Is it one of the dogs? Is Bandit all right?"

"That dog is so obsessed with me already. He's not ready to show it, but I can tell in his eyes."

"So what is it?"

"I'm not telling you shit, I want to see your face. Now, get over here."

Chapter Ten

Remi

Ness stared at my boobs the entire time as I walked toward her. "Wow, I must've really gotten through to you with that club shirt. We'll get so many more adoptions this way."

I glanced down and cursed. "No, I just ran out of the house because someone was being very dramatic." Then I pointed at the giant delivery truck sitting in the parking lot. "What is this?"

A bored-looking driver with greasy, limp dark hair stood next to the cab of the truck and wandered over with a clipboard. "You Remi Sinclair?"

"That's me."

"I, uh, I've got a . . . a thing for you." He licked his lips. "A thing for you to sign, I mean."

While he fumbled with the clipboard, his eyes were locked on my tits, and Ness coughed out a laugh. I glared at my best friend. "Please go get the denim shirt in the back seat of my car."

"Why? Those babies are a weapon if you know how to use them right."

The delivery driver looked like he was going to pass out.

"Vanessa. The shirt."

She rolled her eyes, sauntering off to my car like she didn't have a care in the world. Why would she? It wasn't her nips showing to the entire world.

I scrawled my signature on the paper and crossed my arms over my chest. Disappointment flashed in his eyes.

He'd already turned to go back to the truck when Ness returned with my shirt. I slipped my arms in and hastily buttoned the middle button, just enough that I didn't feel like I was flashing everyone around me.

"May I?" Ness asked.

The driver waved. "Go ahead."

She hopped up onto the back bumper of the truck, gave me an anticipatory grin, and yanked on the handle holding the door of the truck shut. It rolled open with a groan of metal on metal, but when the contents came into view, my jaw dropped.

"What the hell?" I breathed.

Boxes upon boxes of dog food—the good kind too. Some for puppies, but mostly for adults. I took Ness's outstretched hand and hopped up into the back of the truck with her, exhaling an incredulous laugh as I cataloged the contents, my hand skimming along the top of each stack. Puppy pads. Blankets, new dog beds. Dog shampoo, leashes, and toys.

My eyesight went blurry when I did the mental math on just the dog food alone.

"Ness, this is enough dog food for the next . . . eight months? Maybe more."

"I know." She tore open the top of one of the boxes. The first thing she fished out was a sleeve of extra-strength tennis balls. "Oh man, Scout is gonna love these, isn't he?"

I smiled. "Who did this?"

She shrugged. "I was hoping you'd know."

The driver came around the side of the truck and peered up at us. "Where do you want me to unload it?"

Ness and I shared a look. "The big conference room for now?" I suggested. "We'll have to disperse this to some of the foster homes, but we may need to take over one of the smaller rooms that doesn't get used as much."

She nodded. "I'll go push those tables off to the side of the room. Should I email all the fosters and tell them to come in today to load up?"

I shook my head. "Let's wait until we get an inventory of what we have."

"Oh," the delivery driver interjected, "I've got that right here."

He ripped a piece of paper off the stack wedged underneath the clip of the clipboard and handed it to me. I scanned the list, mentally tallying how we'd need to divvy up this food.

Ness hopped out of the truck first and went to unlock the side door while he lowered a metal ramp off the back. As I was not in the mood to break an ankle by hopping out of anything, I waited until the ramp was connected and walked down that way. The sun was warm on my back, and I plucked at the denim shirt, wishing I could ditch it.

Based on the occasional looks the driver gave my chest as he descended the ramp, I decided that sweating was the preferable course of action.

It was odd to just stand and watch him load up his dolly, bringing stack after stack of boxes around to the side of the building. Normally, I was the one doing the heavy lifting—literally and metaphorically—but as I watched someone else do it, I felt the strangest sensation take root in my chest.

Relief.

I could breathe, just a little bit easier than I'd been able to breathe that morning. It was an embarrassment of riches, and I wasn't even sure who to thank.

Ness sidled up next to me, fixing the pink ponytail on the top of her head while we watched the room slowly fill with much-needed supplies. "I sent Christian a text asking if it was him."

My eyebrows shot up. "Seriously?"

She shrugged. "We had great phone sex yesterday. It's one hell of a way to show his gratitude."

I snorted. "Indeed. And was it him?"

"No."

"Is he still waiting?"

Her lip pushed out in a mighty pout. "Yes."

"So rude," I teased.

"If he's trying to make me feral, it's working."

"I'm not sure that's what he's trying to do, babe. I have a feeling he really means it." I nudged her shoulder with mine when she let out a beleaguered sigh. "Brutal, huh?"

"The brutal-est."

"Not a word, but I'll accept it." The stacks in the truck dwindled with each trip back and forth, and by the time the driver left, Ness and I had already started unpacking the smaller items we knew had a home in our usual storage closet. As soon as we were alone, I ripped off the denim shirt, ignoring Ness's approving whistle.

"What about Muriel? You don't think she ordered all this, do you?"

"And not tell us?" Ness asked, smiling as she unpacked a box of stuffed animals. She held up a fluffy yellow duck with sunglasses sitting on his orange bill. "I'm saving this one for Bandit."

"Why?"

She gave an airy sniff. "Because it's the biggest one, and my good boy needs some spoiling."

"We're not supposed to have favorites, Ness."

"Oh bullshit, like you don't give Scout extra treats. And didn't I walk in the office last week and he was taking a nap next to your desk?"

I refused to make eye contact, instead focusing on cutting through the packing tape holding a box of puppy formula closed. "He was stressed out. He needed some quiet."

"Mm-hmm."

"So he's in love with you, huh? How did that happen? We've only had him for, like, forty-eight hours."

Ness pulled a cat toy out of the box and set it in the pile that needed to go to the feline room. "We bonded on a soul-deep level, that's how. I got some great footage for social media. Combined with what you filmed while you were trying to catch him, I think we could get something viral out of it." She set an extra-strength chew toy aside. "Too bad Archer wasn't filming when he caught him. God, can you imagine? We'd break the internet with that one." Her eyes took on a faraway quality. "Especially if he was shirtless. Was he shirtless?"

I was juggling three boxes in my hands when his voice came from behind us.

"I try to keep my shirt on when I'm rescuing dogs."

I squeaked, and the boxes went flying.

Ness laughed, and I gave her a dirty look, even though the flaming red of my cheeks probably made it a little less intimidating.

Archer leaned against the doorframe, his eyes dragging over all the boxes. My breath snagged in my chest at the flex of his shoulders. "Looks like Christmas came early."

"A few Christmases, actually." I swallowed. "What are you doing here?"

After a few more seconds of studying the deliveries, Archer lifted his eyes to me. They never dropped below my face, and my stomach executed a dangerous flip when I realized it.

"I was in the neighborhood."

Ness was boring holes into the side of my head, and I kicked at her behind the stack of boxes.

"Do you happen to know where this came from?" I asked.

For a moment, Archer stayed quiet, his chest rising and falling on a deep breath. "A store, I'd reckon."

Ness laughed.

"Oh, for fuck's sake," I muttered. I gave her a look. "Do not encourage him."

She rolled her lips together and mimed dragging a key over her mouth.

He tucked his hands into his front pockets, and the swell of his biceps rippled under the seams of his shirt. "Need help moving anything?" he asked.

"No. You can go."

"Yes. Ignore her," Ness answered for me. "That stack of senior dog food closer to the door can be taken out of the boxes, and the bags can go in the storage closet in the kennel room. Just start with four bags, maybe. The rest can be stacked along the back of the wall in here."

Archer gave me one last look, his gaze lingering on mine before he ripped open a box and hefted out two bags. He hoisted them over his shoulder easily, walking out of the room as Ness and I stared silently at the shift of muscles in his arms and shoulders.

"God bless," she whispered. "Whoever is training that man should get a raise."

I shook my head, brow furrowing as I directed my attention back to the box I was unpacking. "They're just muscles, Ness."

"Oh please. Your mouth was hanging open. You could be using that pretty man in so many ways, young lady. What a shame that his time here is going to waste."

"I am not going to use him," I hissed. "Even if he *wanted* to sleep with me, do you think I have any desire to be a notch in some playboy's bedpost?" I slammed a box of puppy formula down on the table next to me. "I mean, fine, it would be good, I'm sure. Maybe even better than good, if he understands basic female anatomy. Except he probably doesn't because he's never *had* to. I'm sure he's horribly selfish in bed. No kissing and a few grunts, and then he'd smack my ass and leave me unsatisfied."

Ness chose to keep her mouth shut, watching my increasingly unhinged rant with a purse of her lips.

I yanked out another box. "That's where my list makes *sense*, Vanessa. Because then you *know* if someone's going to be horrible. You have time to figure it out. I don't have or want that time with Archer because he's a dick." I pinched my eyes shut and pressed my hands to my face before letting them drop on the table. "Except it would be great if he wasn't actually an asshole, because I don't *want* him to be an asshole. But that doesn't mean I'm going to sleep with him."

All the blood in my poor little body flooded my cheeks, and there was no stopping it, especially when I clocked the pitying expression on Ness's face.

"What?" I snapped.

With her mouth set in a firm line, she reached and gave me a condescending pat on the head. "I wasn't talking about sex, babe. I meant for the shelter. You could be using him for social media reach and it would be amazing publicity."

"Oh."

She wheezed. Absolutely wheezed. As my best friend tried to get her cackling under control, I calmly unpacked the rest of the formula and moved it over to the cabinets in the back corner of the conference room.

"Are you quite finished?"

Ness wiped her hand under her eyes. "Yes, I think I am. Holy shit, I wish I was filming. I'd replay that every night before I went to bed."

"I hate you."

"No, sweet pea, you really don't."

I scoffed, lifting one of the bags of senior dog food under my arm and marching it toward the kennel room. The dogs barked happily at my entrance, and I smiled to see Bandit wagging his tail a little when I came through.

As I turned the corner, I was greeted by the sight of Archer Evans's exceptional ass just as he straightened.

I tripped over a ledge in the concrete, but with no hands free, I resigned myself to a face-plant on the kennel floor at his feet, and then I'd never be able to look him in the eye again.

Except I didn't fall.

Because he caught me.

His hands, big and strong, caught me right around the upper arms just as I pitched forward. "Whoa, steady." Archer helped me up as I got my feet under me, then took the thirty-pound bag of food once they were. "You okay?"

I rubbed my arms where he'd grabbed me. "Yeah, great."

He set the bag of food on top of the stack he'd already started, his face unreadable as he turned back in my direction. My chest was heaving from the almost-catastrophe, and with the flimsy barrier of my trusted denim shirt gone, I braced myself for his eyes to drop. But they never did.

They stayed right on my face.

"Was it you?" I blurted out. "All of this. Did you order it?"

I didn't mean to ask. The words just tumbled right out. Something in my locked-up subconscious had unlocked with my little ramble to Ness. Even though I hated what he'd done, even though he'd been an absolute dick when he showed up, there was still some ridiculous part of me that wanted him to be a good person. So I could look my son in the face and say, *Yeah, he was worthy of the jersey and all the stats you memorized and the game clips you watched.*

So I could tell him that I understood why he idolized this man so much.

So I could admit to myself that my harsh treatment toward him had as much to do with *me*, and how I felt seeing him again, as it did with him. It would be like swallowing sandpaper to give that admission ground, but I wanted to feel the burn.

I wanted to be wrong about him.

"No," he said, voice slow and deep. "I didn't order it."

I *felt* the color drain from my face. "Oh. Okay."

Archer's brow wrinkled. "There was no note or anything?"

Slowly, I shook my head. "No. The delivery driver didn't have any information on where it came from either."

"A mystery."

Even though it was hard—what with the almost-falling and the nipples visible through my tank top—I held his gaze. "There seems to be a lot of that going around. It would be nice to know what to expect once in a while."

Archer's eyes flickered, but before he could say anything, my phone rang.

I sighed, pulling it out of my back pocket. "This is Remi."

"Remi, it's Nora. I am so, so sorry to do this, but I can't watch Gavin today when he gets off the bus. Michael just came home sick from school. He's throwing up, and if I'm being honest, I don't feel great, either, and I'd hate to get him sick if he's around Pops at all this week."

I rubbed my forehead. "Of course. No, I understand. I don't want him to get sick either." The clock on the wall told me I had about forty-five minutes before G got home, and my mind started racing through options. "I'll find someone else to watch him, don't worry about it. Just feel better."

"Thanks, I'll try."

"Do you want me to bring you some chicken noodle soup?" I asked.

"No."

I blinked at the rushed tone. "Oh. Okay."

She cleared her throat. "I mean, no thank you. You're so sweet to offer, though."

"Sure. Thanks for letting me know."

With a whispered curse, I disconnected the call, my eyes falling shut as I realized I was either going to leave the shelter shorthanded, or Gavin would have to spend another evening here, which I tried not to do too often, especially on a later night like this one, when I'd hardly get home before he needed to be in bed. "Shit," I said one more time.

"Everything okay?" Archer asked.

"No. My neighbor was supposed to watch my son, and she can't." I gave him a quick look. "He doesn't mind having to hang out here every once in a while, but I like him to stay on a routine at home if I can help it."

"How old is he?"

"Ten."

Archer took a deep breath. "I have someone who can watch him."

My brows lowered. "What do you mean?"

"Babysitter. She's first-aid certified. Knows CPR and all that shit."

I blinked. "How old is she?"

"Seventeen."

"Who is it?"

The heavy skepticism in my voice made his lips curl up in an amused grin. "You don't trust me?"

I snorted. "Hardly."

"What's your address?"

"I didn't say yes."

He cocked a brow. "You didn't say no, either, did you, boss?"

"Do not call me that."

Archer smirked. "I can't call you *Red.* Can't call you *boss.* What nicknames *can* I use?"

"None."

His eyes traced over my face. "We'll find one. What's your address? I'll go get her."

"Go get her?"

He nodded. "She doesn't love driving."

I crossed my arms. "I thought your license was provisional. Only your hours and work."

Archer adopted an innocent expression. "It's for you. Doesn't that count as my hours?"

When I mumbled under my breath, he let out a brief chuckle.

"Fine. Only because I'm desperate." I rattled off my address, watching his expression as he typed it into his Maps app. It was a humble home in a humble neighborhood, but I would not apologize for where we lived. "It better not be some underage football groupie who answers to your beck and call because she's not allowed to sleep with you."

Archer gave me an unamused look.

"What? How am I supposed to know?"

"Trust me," he said.

I crossed my arms over my chest and breathed through a wave of anxiety because I just *knew* I was about to do something really stupid.

"Fine. But don't make me regret it."

Chapter Eleven

Remi

"Mom, you're freaking out."

"No, I'm not."

Total bullshit answer. Sometimes it wasn't just okay to lie to your kids—it was a matter of public health and safety. Gavin had gotten off the bus and found me tearing through the house, shoving piles of laundry into closets. My face was flushed, sweat beading at my hairline.

Would it have killed the man to give me a clear arrival time?

It's not like it was hard.

Thirty minutes since we'd both left the shelter and only a vague "I'll be there in less than an hour." It could be fifteen minutes, could be two. Could be another thirty.

I'd lose my mind if I had to prepare for Archer Evans to walk through my front door for another thirty minutes.

So what if my house wasn't cute and perfectly decorated or brand new? The trim I'd painted white a couple years ago was chipped and dusty because who the hell had time to scrub baseboards on a regular basis?

There were marks on the wall next to the kitchen table where Gavin tapped his pencil when he was doing his homework. Last week, I'd told him he needed to wash them off, but as soon as we had one conversation about it, it was forgotten.

The couch—a hand-me-down leather sectional from the neighbors across the street—was new to us but still worn on the arms, and the recliner end that faced the TV had a few small cracks from sitting in the sun underneath their front window for ten years.

My hands were trembling as I tried to wrench my hair into submission. How stupid this was. He was just a man. It didn't matter that he made more money than I could ever comprehend in my entire lifetime or had the body of a god—he was still just a man.

I blew out a short breath. A man who'd made mistakes. He had flaws. And if he walked into our house and said *anything* about the size or the decor, I'd have no choice but to punch him in the balls.

I rolled my hand into a fist and tried to imagine it. No, no punching. The angle was wrong.

Leaning in the corner next to the couch was Gavin's bat.

That would work.

I groaned, wiping a hand over my mouth.

God, did I have time to scrub the baseboards before he got there?

"You've got those crazy eyes," Gavin said, gesturing at my face with a dubious expression. "Who is this new babysitter again?"

My legs went a little rubbery, and I managed to sink onto the corner of the couch. "About that . . ."

The slow, intentional words caught his attention. "Mom?"

"Why don't you take a seat, bud."

"Am I in trouble?"

"*No*. I promise." His little face was still pinched with worry, and I forced a smile. "So, I'm not exactly sure who your babysitter is, but I know who's bringing her over."

His eyes widened. "You're leaving me with a stranger? What if they're mean? Or . . . even worse, irresponsible!"

My smile spread. "Is that worse than being mean?"

"You tell me—you're the one leaving your kid with someone you don't know."

I ruffled his hair. "You're right, irresponsible would be bad. But that's not what this is about."

"Okay. Who's dropping her off?"

When had I swallowed a cup of sand? I tried to clear my throat, but my voice came out all raspy. "Remember when you saw a picture of the shelter in that article about Archer Evans's car accident?"

"Yeah."

"Well, he's been volunteering at the shelter because the judge told him he has to do that in order to make amends for what happened."

Gavin's mouth fell open. "You *met* him?"

I nodded.

Color crept up his freckled cheeks, his eyes flickering while he waffled between excitement and awe and confusion. "What's . . . what's he like?"

There it was. The reason why I hadn't told him.

Shining in his eyes was hope.

At the end of the day, he still wanted to know that this person he'd idolized was good and nice and kind and cool. I wasn't the only one who wanted to be wrong about Archer.

Which meant I had to tread carefully. It took constant vigilance not to let your kids carry your own baggage, and I did not need to give Gavin mine when it came to his idol.

"We haven't talked a lot since he started, but Archer has done everything I've asked him to, and I've given him some pretty crappy jobs. He's never complained."

Gavin, as usual, saw absolutely everything I didn't want him to see. "You don't like him, do you?"

"I don't know him very well." Yanking at the hair tie holding my hair back allowed me to drop my gaze, and while I wrestled it into something a little bit neater, a little less *crazy lady who's rage-cleaning her house*, I tried to think of how I'd want to prepare him to meet someone who'd always been larger than life. "But you'll be able to form your own opinion of him."

Gavin's eyebrows shot up. "He's coming here? To our house?"

I nodded slowly, dropping my hands back in my lap. "He knows someone who loves babysitting. She's seventeen, and he told me she's first-aid certified and took CPR classes, all the really important stuff."

"Great, so if I choke, she'll know what to do."

I laughed. "Yes. Let's try to avoid that, though."

He blinked rapidly, eyes locked on the floor. "He's really going to be here?"

"Yeah, buddy. Any minute." I glanced at the clock on the family room wall. "I need to get back to the shelter, so we won't be able to hang out long. And Archer may not even come out of the car, so it's possible he'll just wave and be on his way."

Gavin's face fell. "Yeah, maybe he doesn't like talking to little kids."

Oh, my. Parenting was not for the faint of heart, that was for sure.

The sound of a truck came from the driveway, and I stood up quickly. Gavin did too. His breath came in short, excited pants when the driver's-side door opened and Archer got out.

"Holy shit," he whispered.

"Gavin Michael."

"You can ground me. It's totally worth it."

His eyes hadn't left the man walking around the front of the truck. Even from an adult's perspective—a single-mom-variety adult—Archer was impressive enough. More than impressive, unfortunately. He was always wearing a solid-color T-shirt, and today's option, white and simple, clung to his chest, highlighting the shift of his carved muscles in a way that made my mouth go dry. Everything about him was strong and solid and big.

Trying to imagine what he looked like to a ten-year-old boy who wanted nothing more than to be a professional athlete someday . . .

I decided to let the swearing slide.

"I won't ground you," I told him. "But why don't you wait here a second while I go meet your new babysitter."

The teenager who hopped out of the truck had lighter hair than Archer, more of a true blonde. It was shiny and straight, hanging past her shoulders, and she wore pink-hued sunglasses and denim cutoffs over long, tanned legs.

She smiled at Archer, and the breath hitched in my throat when he smiled back.

Damn him. Damn him all the way back to the place he came from.

Who did he think he was? Showing up here and *smiling*.

I'd swapped the cleavage-happy tank top for something with a bit more coverage, opting for a worn Buffalo Storm T-shirt that Pops got me for my birthday a few years ago. Archer's eyes locked on the logo as soon as I walked out the front door, and I mentally cursed my choice.

"Hey."

"Boss."

I rolled my eyes.

The punch of his blue eyes out in the direct sunlight was awful. The girl next to him had the exact same eyes, and they were currently bouncing between Archer and me, a slow smile covering her pretty face.

"Everything makes sense now."

"Analise," he growled.

She beamed in my direction, all straight white teeth and deep dimples. "I'm his annoying little sister, and he'll regret bringing me in about five minutes if he doesn't already."

Archer said nothing, but his jaw was tight with tension as he crossed his arms over his chest, his biceps testing the seams of his very nice white T-shirt.

I couldn't help but smile. "Nice to meet you, Analise. I'm Remi. I can't thank you enough for being willing to watch Gavin."

"Remi," she said thoughtfully, cutting a sly gaze to her brother. "Someone wouldn't give me any details in the car, and I'm starting to realize why."

His chest expanded on a deep breath, his eyes briefly closing as he muttered her name again.

Analise ignored him. "He's always pretty quiet, right? But this was *extra* quiet. *Extra* grumpy. Which is saying something for him, because he's not usually grumpy with me. And no matter what I asked him—Who am I babysitting? Why is this so secretive? When have you ever volunteered me for jobs before?—he kept his mouth totally shut. Not a single word about a hot redhead."

"Analise," he barked.

Behind my sternum, my heart thrashed wildly. "Oh," I said in a weak voice.

"Don't sweat it. I'm sure your general attractiveness has nothing to do with the fact that he won't tell me anything about his community service hours other than you hate him."

Archer scrubbed a hand over his face as I breathed out a shocked laugh.

She pointed at him. "Do you think I can get him to say anything besides my name? It could be a fun challenge."

"That is enough," he said tightly. "I told you to be on your best behavior."

"That's what I'm doing." She patted his shoulder but kept her smile aimed at me. "Now, I'd love to meet your kiddo. I haven't had much time to babysit lately because my dad thinks if he crams all my free time in with tutors, I'll magically love school and get A's and desperately want to spend the next four to six years in college." She rolled her eyes.

I smiled. "I didn't love school either. I got a job straight out of high school because I was sick of doing homework and going to class."

"That's what I want to do," she said, her eyes wide and pretty.

"Granted, I also had a baby on the way at my high school graduation." I shrugged. "College didn't seem more important than my ability to pay the bills."

"Well, you're clearly doing something right. Your house is adorable," she gushed. "I love the color you painted it. And the . . . flower boxes are nice."

The empty flower boxes. I laughed. "Someday they'll have flowers in them."

"I have no green thumb," she said. "But honestly, the house doesn't even need it. It's so friendly."

Archer had relaxed slightly, and at Analise's genuine nature, I did as well. "Thank you. It's not big, but it's home."

The front door to the house opened, and when the three of us turned around, Gavin's face poked through the opening. "Am I allowed to come outside now?"

"One second, bud." I locked eyes with Archer, ignoring the fact that his sister was watching the exchange with a rapt expression on her face. "My son has never met one of his idols before," I said in a hushed tone. "If you do anything to upset him, I will take a baseball bat to your testicles."

Archer's gaze flickered. "That so?"

"With a smile on my face, Evans."

A muscle in his jaw flexed. "You should've warned me I might need to wear my cup."

"Only if you're a dick." I smiled sweetly. "Let's hope it doesn't come to that."

The air between us was heavy, thick with tension that made it hard to breathe.

"You got it, boss."

Analise sighed happily. "This is the best thing I've ever seen."

The thread of tension snapped, a clean break when Archer dropped his gaze from mine, and in the vacuum of silence when he did, my heart clanged around behind my ribs.

"Come on out, Gavin."

His steps were tentative, but the excitement and nerves were stamped all over his precious little face. More than anything, I wanted to make this perfect for him. It was the curse of being a parent. There was nothing we could do to shield our kids from the things that worried them, and I just prayed there wouldn't be much fallout to deal with.

The tears in his eyes the day he'd brought me the jersey were all I could think about as I watched him approach the man at my side. The man who was tall and big and strong and looked like one of the superheroes on the movies he loved to watch—the ones who could save cities and bring down a bad guy with a single punch.

Analise must have read the tension in my pose, because she stepped forward first. "You must be Gavin. I'm Analise Evans."

At the sound of her last name, his eyes widened. "E-Evans?"

She nodded, giving him a conspiratorial nod. "He's my brother."

"Whoa," Gavin breathed. "I didn't know he"—his gaze darted behind her, at the man in question, like he wasn't sure who to address—"had a sister."

"I asked him to keep it on the DL," Analise admitted. "I prefer to keep a low profile. Otherwise it's hard to know if people like me for me or for my brother. His job is the best, but every once in a while it can be hard when you're related to someone famous."

Gavin nodded like he knew exactly what she was talking about. "Yeah, totally."

"Is it okay if we hang out for a while tonight?"

His eyes darted between Analise and me, and he finally gave her a nod. "Sure."

"Sweet. What do you normally do on a school night?"

Gavin shrugged. "Homework, if I have any. Or soccer practice. If I finish my stuff on time, Mom lets me play video games."

"I love video games. What's your favorite?"

His eyes lit up. "I'm kinda playing a lot of *Mario Kart* right now. I got bored with *Fortnite*."

She whistled. "I see a race in our future. I won't let you win, though. I'm really good."

"Do you know all the tricks?"

Her eyes narrowed. "I don't know. What kind of tricks?"

"Nothing," he said innocently. "I'm sure you don't need them."

Analise laughed. "I guess we'll see."

Gavin finally got the courage to look over at Archer, and his chest puffed out on a deep inhale. "I'm . . . I'm Gavin. Gavin Sinclair."

Archer crouched, holding his hand out to Gavin.

"Nice to meet you, Gavin. I'm Archer."

Gavin hesitated, and my lungs squeezed at the expression on his face. It was so serious. So direct.

"You ran into my mom's shelter, didn't you?"

His chin was notched high, his nerves completely gone. Tears coiled tight around the back of my throat at the sight of my protective boy.

Analise rolled her lips together and stared down at the ground, her cheeks reddening.

Finally, Archer nodded, his hand dropping back down when it became clear Gavin wasn't going to reciprocate. "I won't make excuses for what happened. But I promise, I regret a lot of things about that night, especially when I think about kids like you who lost respect for me." He let out a slow breath. "I'm really sorry." Then he looked up at me, the intensity making his eyes glow brighter than usual. "I'm trying to make amends."

I sucked in a sharp breath and licked my lips as I tore my gaze from his. Gavin glanced up at me, and I gave him a tiny encouraging nod.

He shoved his hand out. "Pops says that our actions are what matter the most in this world. So if you're trying to make things better, then I can forgive you."

A tear slid down my cheek, and I wiped my palm over it before anyone noticed.

Archer's throat moved in a slow swallow, and his big fingers completely dwarfed my son's as they shook hands. "He sounds like a smart man."

Gavin smiled. "The smartest."

Archer's shoulder brushed my arm as he straightened to his full height.

I cleared my throat. "I have to get back to the shelter. Analise, there's plenty of food in there, and Gavin can show you where everything is." I snapped my fingers. "Oh, and the dishwasher isn't functioning right now, so any dishes have to be hand-washed. Don't load anything in there."

Her cheeks were still red as she nodded, her eyes darting over to her brother briefly. "Great. Any food allergies I need to worry about?"

"He's good, but thank you for asking." I squeezed Gavin's shoulder. "Finish your homework before video games, okay? And you need to shower tonight."

"Mom," he groaned. "Do I have to?"

"Yes. I'm not gonna send a stinky boy to school tomorrow. Shower by eight, please. I want you in pajamas when I get home around eight thirty."

"We can manage that." Analise smiled at him, then me. "We'll have a great time."

Gavin chewed on his bottom lip before looking back up at Archer. "Are you coming back too?"

He nodded. "I'll pick her up after your mom gets home." Our eyes met briefly, and my stomach twisted as I thought about Archer walking back up to my house as the sun faded. "You said eight thirty?"

I managed a quick nod. "Maybe nine, if the dogs aren't cooperating."

Gavin inhaled through his nose, visibly shoring up all his courage. "Maybe I . . . maybe I could show you my room later when you pick her up. I've got lots of Buffalo stuff."

Archer gave him a small smile, just the slightest curl to the edges of his lips. "I'd like that."

"Okay," Gavin breathed. His cheekbones were washed in pink, and the excitement in his eyes was almost my undoing.

Standing in the driveway bawling over my kid was not on the to-do list, though, so I cleared my throat and tilted my head toward the car. "I need to go."

Gavin wrapped his arms around me in a tight squeeze, and I kissed the top of his head.

"Be good. Love you, buddy."

"Love you more," he said, voice muffled against my stomach.

"Impossible."

He grinned as he pulled away, then ran into the house with Analise trailing behind.

She paused with her hand on the door. "I approve of whatever's happening here, brother."

"Fucking hell," Archer muttered under his breath.

I slid my hands over my cheeks and laughed. "She's sweet."

He wouldn't look at me. "She's a menace."

"But you love her."

That made him pause, his eyes finally coming to rest on mine. "More than anything. Don't tell her that, though. It'll go to her head."

There were hidden sides to everyone. Sometimes we were lucky enough to discover what they were. But mostly, we never saw what was under the surface. They stayed hidden behind ego and short tempers and shitty moods that soured our disposition for really good reasons. Wasn't that a shame? If we had moments like this with all the people who did us wrong, or who we caught on a bad day, maybe we could extend more grace in a world that seemed to do nothing but sow anger.

This wasn't the same man from the shelter—hard and arrogant and proud. The same man who got behind the wheel of his car and did something stupid. It wasn't the same man from the bar, either, unashamed of taking what he wanted because he saw that I wanted it too.

Except it was, and I didn't really know how to reconcile all the sides to him.

"Are you sure it wasn't you?" I asked quietly. "Who ordered the stuff?"

Archer didn't answer right away. His eyes traced over my face, then moved to my house. What did he see when he looked at it?

The yard was neat, the grass green and lush, even though it was in need of being mowed. The deep-blue paint color was cheery, something I'd splurged on a couple years earlier, as was the pale-aqua front door. The empty flower boxes and cleared beds simply said *I'm too busy to do this*, but to him, it might look like something else entirely.

"Wouldn't I tell you if I did?" he said after a while. The sound of his voice felt like someone had struck a bell affixed to my spine. His eyes moved back to mine. "Wouldn't I want credit for that?"

"That's not an answer," I said, banishing any hint of a tremor from my voice, even though there was a dangerous quaking in my ribs.

Archer's mouth softened in a hint of a smile. He twirled his keys around his pointer finger and started walking backward. "See you at eight thirty, boss."

Chapter Twelve

Archer

At this time of the evening, the buildings were almost empty. Mostly maintenance staff, but there were still lights when I walked past the lobby of the executive-staff offices—the team owner, GM, head and assistant coaches.

The weight room had been empty, too, and I worked myself harder than I should have, considering I'd already done a workout that morning.

But my muscles felt better, holding none of the tension from earlier.

Every time I was around Remi, the energy around us was like an idling engine, and the longer it went on, my body braced for the moment we'd take off. If I didn't work through that, I couldn't get the kind of release I wanted, so abusing my body with weights felt like the next best step. It didn't make sense to drive home, because I didn't really have anything to do there, and if I showed up at the shelter unannounced, I had a feeling Remi would tell me to get my ass back in the car.

"Evans."

At the sound of Coach King's voice, I slowed, wishing I'd been just a little bit less of an asshole the last time we talked, but when I turned and saw his wife, Lily, at his side, my stomach crashed to the bottom of my feet.

They were hand in hand as they came down the hall from the area of his office. Coach was a big dude, only an inch or so shorter than me, and still in the same shape as when he'd played. His wife, Lily, was striking—tall and slim, jet-black hair, and piercing eyes that were locked right on me with an unreadable expression.

I knew why too.

She wasn't the bubbly, outgoing wife you'd expect a head coach to have, but she'd earned the admiration of every single guy in the locker room over the last year. They'd recently welcomed twins, but if she was tired from taking care of the two babies, plus Coach's two preteen kids, it didn't show.

It was easy enough to recognize someone who kept their guard up like me, and when they approached, I sucked in a quick breath, lifting my chin like it might protect me if this went south.

"What are you doing here so late?" Coach asked.

"Decided to get another workout in." I kept my hands loose by my sides. I gave Lily a quick nod. "Ma'am."

She arched a dark eyebrow, clearly unimpressed with my attempt at manners. "I'm only two years older than you, dude."

"Right." My jaw clenched. "Mrs. King."

"You can call me *Lily*," she answered with a wry smile.

Coach glanced sideways at his wife, a soft smile playing around his lips. Lovesick.

Not that long ago, I might have scoffed, thought him weak for it. But now, all I felt was a curl of envy so deep that I knew it would never go away.

What was it like to be so at peace with yourself in a relationship with another person? Someone not related to you, someone who chose you?

"Not sure you need extra workouts," Coach said. "You're already bigger than you were the last time you played."

"Just trying to be perfect when I come back, sir."

"Sometimes when we chase perfection, we don't see the damage we do as a result. Trust me."

His eyes saw way too fucking much.

Lily gave him a quiet smile, wrapping her hand around his arm. But when she turned her sharp-eyed attention back to me, a chill coiled around my spine.

"You know my stepdaughter, Maggie."

Everyone on the team did. Coach's kids were always running around the facilities, but Maggie had ingrained herself in part of the Storm's team culture—she regularly made cookies for practices and hosted a popular social media show where she interviewed players.

"Of course," I answered. "I haven't seen her much lately."

Lily hummed. "The other night at dinner, she asked about interviewing you for *Midfield with Maggie*."

Apprehension twisted my gut. Knowing that kid—smarter than she had any right to be—she'd sit me down in her infamous yellow chair and grill me like a cross-examiner. "She's a good kid. But I don't know if I'd be the best guest right now."

Coach regarded me steadily from under the brim of his hat while his wife tilted her head in consideration. She was fucking terrifying.

"How's your community service been?" she asked.

I swallowed. "Fine, ma'am. Lily," I corrected. "It's fine."

"Hopefully, it's successful in teaching you something."

Coach glanced down at the ground but didn't interrupt.

"I think it will."

She arched an eyebrow again. "Did you know that over twelve thousand people died from alcohol-related car crashes last year?"

I kept my face even. "No, ma'am. I didn't."

"I lost people I love very much to someone who drank too much and got behind the wheel, which is why my husband and I support charities related to education and awareness of this issue. It's avoidable. Entirely, completely avoidable."

Shame tried to claw up my throat, a thick wedge of icy emotion that wouldn't budge when I tried to swallow. "Yes, ma'am."

"I hope you're willing to learn and make different choices when this is over. My husband said you have amazing potential to lead this team."

My eyes darted over to Coach. He'd lifted his head to stare at his wife but turned to me when she said it. He held my gaze and didn't say anything.

How was he still giving me chances? It didn't make sense, no matter how many times I turned it over and over in my head.

I exhaled slowly, shifting my attention back to her. "Yes, ma'am. I'm going to try."

Her features thawed slightly. "That's all any of us can do. We're rooting for you, Archer."

Coach leaned in and kissed her temple, and I stayed frozen in place as they said their goodbyes and walked away, still hand in hand.

When they turned a corner, I leaned my back against the wall and sank down to the floor, my head in my hands while I tried to breathe through the wave of prickling anxiety that crashed through my body.

I wasn't sure how long I sat there waiting for my hands and feet to stop tingling, for my heart rate to even out, but an alarm went off on my phone, and I was stunned to see that it was already time to head back to Remi's.

As I stood, I scrubbed my hands over my face. Eventually, this would all be over.

Eventually.

Chapter Thirteen

Remi

For once, the dogs behaved. Scout might have lingered a bit too long at the spot where Edgar had peed right before him, and had to squat in the exact same spot three times, but he finally came when I called his name.

I took one last loop through the building, double-checking water bowls and bed setups. I stopped by the supply closet in the kennel room and snagged one of the new fleece blankets from the top of the stack, then slipped into Bandit's kennel.

He was sitting in the corner, his blue eyes watchful and his body language relaxed as I added a second blanket to his bed.

"Don't tell the others, because they'll think I'm playing favorites." I'd watched him on the camera earlier and noticed that he liked to burrow into the blanket. I bunched the new one up alongside the other to create a little blanket barrier.

His head tilted slightly when I was finished.

"What do you think?" I asked.

Bandit blinked.

"I'll take that as approval."

Because we'd gotten through the evening routine fairly quickly and I had a little extra time, I slid down against the wall of his kennel and left my hand resting on my leg, palm up, fingers relaxed. Slowly, I inched my hand out, and he extended his snout a few inches like he wanted to sniff me, but stayed right where he was.

"It's okay. We'll get there eventually."

The pocket of my hoodie held the last pieces of hot dog, so I pulled the bag out and tossed him the few left over. His eyes stayed on me as he lowered his head, but as he ate, his tail gave a few uneven thumps, and a smile overtook my face.

For a few moments longer, I stayed and enjoyed the relative quiet.

Relative, of course, because Daisy was barking at a fly in her kennel, Scout's collar jangled as he scratched at his neck, and Eddie howled at something I couldn't see.

But still . . . it wasn't bad. Finally sitting felt like a small kind of win.

My muscles were screaming for a hot shower after unloading all the boxes. More than once, I wished I hadn't said no to the extra help unpacking. Throughout my evening shift, between answering the phones and doing some admin work to lighten my load the next morning, most of our fosters came through and picked up more food, toys, and puppy pads, all of them curious to know who our mystery donor was.

Join the freaking club.

In the past, Muriel had friends who'd spontaneously show up with items off our wish list, but no one in Second Leash's ten years had ever come in and cleared that list completely.

It had to be him, didn't it?

Or did I just want it to be?

Archer Evans was a mystery, and I didn't much like those. Figuring him out was priority number one.

Or ten, or twenty, depending on the day. But on the to-do list surrounding hot, pompous football players currently infiltrating my life, he was definitely in the top spot. How else was I supposed to compartmentalize his overwhelming presence?

As it was, he invaded far too much brain space, slipping unnoticed into areas he had no business being in.

"What do you think about him, Bandit?"

The dog slowly lowered his body to the floor, keeping his eyes trained on me as he settled his muzzle between his paws. His ability to relax in my presence was a good step, and another one of my wins for the night.

Not wanting to disturb his well-earned quiet, I stood slowly and left his kennel. After securing the latch, I turned off all the lights and let myself out through the front doors.

The sun was going down as I drove home, and I yawned about seven times, praying that Analise would have Gavin ready for bed, because there was no way I'd make it past nine thirty. As I neared home, I glanced in the rearview mirror and swore to try some new mascara. It should not be so hard to find something that didn't give me raccoon eyes the size of a softball after a shift of mild physical labor.

It was pure vanity that had me licking the edge of my thumb to clean off the dark smudges. The car behind me honked when the light turned green, and I waved my hand in acknowledgment.

"Sorry, sorry," I muttered. "If you had to face Archer Evans when you got home, you'd clean up a little bit too."

When I turned onto our street, there was no sign of his truck, and I let out a sigh of relief. The thought of him waiting for me there was a bit too much. Then I started picturing him in my home, manspreading on my couch, taking up way more space than anyone else usually did.

Other than Pops and Vanessa, I'd never had a true guest sit on that couch. Or look at the inside of my house. Being allowed into my sanctuary was a privilege. I wasn't showing off that family room all willy-nilly—they had to *earn* it.

Home visits usually came after date six. By that point, I knew I'd sleep with them, but the extra two dates, and their meeting Gavin, were what kept my head on straight.

Date six was where the last one had gone off the rails—a disastrous meeting of his friends, where I found out that not only did he not view our arrangement as exclusive, but I was also the butt of jokes for holding out on going to bed.

Thank you. Next.

Exhausting wasn't even the right word. It was something much deeper than that. To want something that feels so wildly out of reach sapped me of something vital. It would be one thing if I didn't care. Or didn't lie in bed at night and think maybe it would be nice to have someone there with me. To talk about our days and figure out what dinners we might make that week. To share the emotional load of life.

I did want that. And I wanted it enough that I kept trying.

But as I pulled my car into the garage and leaned my head against the headrest, I couldn't deny that my entire existence seemed hell-bent against making romance a priority.

As the words floated through my mind, the garage door opened and Gavin poked his head through.

"You're home!" he yelled.

His hair was wet, sticking up straight in the front, cheeks still rosy from the hot shower.

With a groan, I hauled myself out of the car and braced for the impact of his hug.

"Hey." I kissed the top of his head. "You smell nice and clean. Did you soap up everywhere?" I asked meaningfully.

Gavin nodded. "Pits and privates got extra."

"Excellent work."

Analise was curled up on the couch when we came through the garage door, and her smile was bright and happy. "Hey, how was work?"

"Great. I'm exhausted." Gavin leaned against me, and I curled an arm around him, soaking up the easy affection. "Did you two have fun? Were you a good, respectful child?"

"Yes and yes. We made chips and cheese for dinner, and then we played *Mario Kart* for an *hour*."

Analise grinned.

"Lucky boy," I said.

"She helped me with my homework, even though she hates math too."

I laughed. "Oh man, she'd fit in great at this house, wouldn't she?"

Analise tucked her phone into her pocket and gave a self-deprecating shrug. "I'm not great at school, if I'm being honest. Reading makes my brain hurt and it's so hard for me to focus, but I have enough tutors dragging me through my classes that I'll graduate with a three-point-five."

"That's great," I told her. "I was a solid B-minus student, and I did not lose sleep over that. My grandfather raised me, and it was a struggle to get him to help me with math because we 'didn't do it the old way.' I'm just glad he didn't expect A's out of me."

Gavin tugged on my arm. "Can I go have a bedtime snack?"

I glanced at the clock on the wall. "A quick one. A glass of milk and a graham cracker, okay?"

He groaned. "Can't I have cereal?"

"Too much sugar. Take it or leave it, dude."

Gavin heaved a dramatic sigh. "Fine."

Analise smiled as he took off for the kitchen. "He's a great kid."

"Thank you. I kinda like him."

She chewed on her bottom lip as she studied me. "Can I ask you a question?"

"Sure."

"How has my brother been during his volunteer hours?" she asked carefully. "He won't tell me anything, and I'm usually the only person he talks to. Made me curious if he's been absolutely impossible, because I know he can be."

"Oh boy." I laughed. "You're diving right in, aren't you?"

She scrunched her nose. "Sorry. I have zero filter on a good day. It drives my father crazy." Her eyes dropped to the floor. "Most things about me drive him crazy, though," she murmured. "Starting with the not-impressive-enough GPA."

My chest ached at the expression on her face. "That can't be true."

Her face brightened, but something about it seemed forced. "Believe me, it is. I'm used to it. We've always been like oil and water."

"That's what Pops said about him and my mother." I crossed my arms and leaned against the wall. "They never got along either."

"Do they now?"

I gave her a sad smile. "She passed away when I was little. She wasn't very healthy, and she had a heart attack when I was five. I don't even really remember her."

Her face was stricken. "Oh, I'm so sorry, Remi. I didn't mean to pry."

"You're fine. It is what is. I had a wonderful childhood with my grandfather. He's the most important man in my life."

She smiled. "That's Archer for me. He's the best brother in the entire world."

"Archer?" I asked disbelievingly.

Analise laughed. "Yeah. No one believes me when I say that. He's . . . he's pretty guarded."

I snorted. "That's one word for it."

"Has it been bad?" There was something so sweet about this girl—perceptive, too, because she clocked my hesitance to answer and gave me an encouraging smile. "You can be honest."

"Okay. Then, honestly, I wanted to slap the shit out of him the first three or four days he came in. I thought he was arrogant and cold. Too good to do menial labor." I shook my head, inhaling slowly. "And he is so talented at pissing me off. He could walk in and say one thing, and my blood pressure goes sky-high. Also, I cannot tell if he hates dogs, and that really bugs me for some reason."

Analise smiled. "Yeah, that's how he acts when he's unsure."

"Oh, come on."

"I'm serious. Archer doesn't let himself relax very easily." Her eyes were earnest, like she was begging me to understand something. "But when he does, he's . . . he's thoughtful and he's supportive. He'd literally do anything to protect me. And I think I'm the only person he's had the chance to love, you know?"

"Analise . . ."

She kept going. "I know this seems crazy to tell you all this, but if he brought me here, if he's trying with you, it's because there's something there. He probably doesn't know how to show you that he's interested, but he's such a good person underneath his shell, Remi, I promise—"

"Analise," I said more firmly. "I hardly know your brother. He just happened to be there when I found out I didn't have a babysitter." She opened her mouth to argue, but I held up my hand. "I appreciate what you're trying to do, but you don't need to try and sell me on him. He's not the kind of guy who would fit in my life. He's a professional athlete, and I can't deal with all the things that come with that—even if he was interested, which he's not."

"But if he was—"

"He's not. We don't . . . we don't mesh. I can't invite someone into my life who's done some of the things he's done," I answered carefully. "I have a son to think about."

Her expression never wavered. "No, you don't understand. He's . . . he's not the way he portrays himself to be. I know what the media says and how all this looks, but he doesn't care what other people think of him."

"I'm glad he's such a good brother—"

"He's the *best* brother. He'd do anything to protect me, even if it ruined him," she said fiercely. It was the light in her eyes—not angry, not stubborn, but so genuine, so steadfast—that made my head rear back. She closed her eyes and took a deep breath. "I'm sorry. Maybe I got too excited when he brought me to meet you," she said, opening her eyes again and giving me a meek smile. "He's never done that before."

"It's okay," I answered gently. "I'm glad you two are so close."

"Hey, Analise, come here!" Gavin called from the kitchen. "I want to show you something on my iPad."

I tilted my head. "Go ahead. I'm gonna go get the mail."

She left the room with a smile, but I saw the hint of regret in her eyes—probably worried that she'd shared too much. As I let myself out the front door, my head was spinning.

"What the fuck was that?" I breathed.

Just as I said it, Archer's truck parked in the driveway, his gaze on me as I pulled the mail from the mailbox.

As he hopped out of the truck, I kept circling and circling around what she'd said, the urgency with which she'd said it. My steps slowed until I stopped halfway up the driveway.

Archer adjusted the hat on his head, concern etched on his face.

I stared up at him, my heart racing. It would be so much easier to keep my mouth shut. So much easier to let him take his sister and leave my house and keep a safe, healthy, professional distance between us when I saw him again at the shelter.

"Are you okay?" he asked.

It was the sound of his voice that did it. Low enough to send a pleasant shiver down my spine. Sure enough to unlock the self-preservation that I usually held so tightly in check.

"It was her, wasn't it?" I asked.

His brow furrowed. "What do you mean?"

"Your sister was the one driving that night, wasn't she?"

Chapter Fourteen

Archer

Fuck.

Fuck.

My brain could do a lot of things—read a defense in seconds, adjust a route when a lineman was barreling down on me, memorize a playbook week after week—but in moments like this, when an emotional tsunami held me by the scruff of my neck, my cognitive function sputtered to an ungodly slow crawl.

Maybe if my heart wouldn't clench painfully every time she looked at me, I'd have the ability to speak. But standing in her driveway, the setting sun catching on those wild red strands of hair that always seemed to fall around her face, it was very much like she'd reached her fist inside me and was squeezing my throat until it closed.

"I—" My voice was dry and rusty when I tried to say something, anything, and her eyes flickered with a look I couldn't define. I cleared my throat, staring at a point just over her shoulder to see if that helped. "I—"

Then she took a step closer, and when a breeze picked up behind her, hitting me straight in the face, God, I could smell her.

Remi didn't smell like perfume or a bed of wildflowers. It was a light, clean scent that made my mouth water. *She* made my mouth water.

Even as I tried to avoid eye contact, she refused to let me, adjusting her stance so that she was in front of me again. Her eyes looked bluer tonight. Less green. How?

"Was she driving the car?" she asked again.

My jaw clenched tight, and I gave her a pleading look. "Remi," I warned. "Please . . ."

"Oh my God," she whispered, her hands covering her mouth for a moment. "She was."

"Please," I begged. Maybe Evanses didn't humble themselves, but I'd beg this woman without a second thought. For many things, probably. But right now, I'd beg for her silence. And hopefully, I'd get her understanding. "You cannot tell anyone."

"Archer, you could've gone to jail!" It seemed that her processing skills had slowed as well, because she blinked rapidly as she stared up into my face, seemingly unaware that the space between us had shrunk to almost nothing. "Everyone thinks you . . . you were drunk and behind the wheel. Why would you let them think that? Was she drinking?"

"No."

The gruff answer landed like a slap, and she straightened, swallowing quickly. "Okay. So why . . . *why*?"

I slicked my tongue over my teeth as I finally dragged my gaze back to hers. With the way she was staring up at me, something inside me softened. Unwillingly, too, which made it even worse.

I didn't want to soften for her. For anyone.

"It's a long story."

"Tough shit. Try shortening it."

I couldn't help it. I laughed.

I didn't laugh very often, but this particular one cracked something open inside me that had been pressed closed for a long time.

Remi's brows furrowed briefly, then she seemed to soften too. Her arms dropped from where they'd been tightly crossed over her stomach, and the hard line of her mouth curled in a smile.

"Why is that funny?" she asked.

"Because I get the feeling you always get your way in the end, don't you?" I asked, fondness creeping into my tone before I could stop it.

"Oh, buddy, if that were true, I'd have a functioning dishwasher and someone to put away the laundry for me."

"Maybe you just always get your way with me, then," I added. Her gaze snapped to mine, and for a breathless moment, nothing else happened. Pretty pink flushed the tops of her cheekbones before she broke the eye contact and stared down at the ground. I blew out a hard breath. "Okay. It's not a very exciting story."

"I don't mind."

As I scrubbed a hand over the line of my jaw, I checked the house, but neither Gavin nor my sister seemed to be paying us any attention. "We went out for dinner. I try to take her out at least twice a week during the offseason. She wasn't supposed to be out that night—he was upset about a test. Her tutors report to him, and he felt like she needed to study more than she already had. But he was gone at an event. She took her car out because she needed a breather, even though she hates driving."

I yanked my hat off, just for something to do, and she watched quietly, waiting for me to continue at my own pace. "We met at the restaurant. It should've been easy for her to get back home before him."

"It's that bad with your dad?"

I nodded. "She stays at my house sometimes too. I try to give her a break when I can. They don't . . . they don't get along."

"Analise told me that," Remi said. Our eyes met and held. "Before you got here."

"What'd she say?"

"That they're like oil and water."

I let out a dry laugh. "Something like that."

"But *you* get along with him?"

A simple question with a complicated answer, and again, I struggled to find the words. "I know how to handle him," I answered carefully.

"I've had ten more years of experience than she does. And when I was her age, I was far more pliable."

Far easier to manipulate. And I'd developed a protective shell that my sister hadn't managed yet. God, I hoped she never needed to. Thinking about Analise being anything like me . . . it fucking hurt. My biggest problem was that I didn't know when it was time to put that shell off to the side, and that armor bled into everything.

"Why did you cover for her? I still don't understand that part, especially if she wasn't drinking."

It took a moment to release the tension in my jaw. "My father expects perfection, excellence, in everything. Less than perfection is failure. There's no shades of gray in his house." Her eyes were sad, her sweet mouth turning into a tiny frown. "I don't want Analise to lose the parts of herself that he'll crush, given the chance. The shit he crushed in me when I was too young to know what was happening. Anything sweet and kind in that girl is in spite of him, and I don't give a *fuck* what happens to me if I can help her keep that side of herself intact."

Remi's eyes were glossy, like she was trying not to cry. "And the accident . . . ?"

I smiled wryly. "I already told you."

Her brow furrowed. "You did not tell me this."

"The animal we saw—Bandit," I said pointedly, and her eyes fell shut for a moment. "The wet streets from the rain. I'd had a few beers at dinner, so she said she'd drive me home." I laughed under my breath. "That's the fucking irony, Remi. She offered to drive me home because neither one of us wanted the risk of me getting behind the wheel. I was going to get my truck the next morning. She'd be home before my dad. No harm done."

Remi covered her cheeks with her hands, shaking her head slightly. "Archer, you have to tell someone."

"No, I don't. And neither do you." Her mouth fell open, but I took another step closer, enough that she had to tilt her chin to look up at me. The proximity made my stomach muscles clench, because I could have touched her so easily if she'd let me. God, I wanted to touch her again. "She wasn't supposed to be out with me that night. He thought she was studying for a test in her room. Instead, she wrecked the car he bought her, even though she didn't want one."

"What would have happened if he knew it was her?"

"He's always threatening to send her away." I held her gaze. "I'm completely convinced she's got ADHD, if he'd care enough to get some testing done, get her support and tools and medicine if she needs it. But he won't because he thinks it's bullshit. An excuse. Instead, he thinks he can discipline her enough that she'll change. He'll send her off *if*. . . if she doesn't get her grades up. If she doesn't start paying attention in school. If she's not better, if she isn't *perfect*, if she doesn't pretend to be exactly what he wants, he hangs it over her head like a weapon. A school for girls on the West Coast that can 'handle problems like her,'" I repeated dully. "I will not let him do that. It's a hidey-hole for rich assholes to send the kids who can't get in line, and it would destroy her to be treated the way they treat those girls."

Her chest rose and fell as she listened to me talk. "How long until she turns eighteen?"

"She just turned seventeen." Analise's face appeared in the front window, her happy smile turning a crank underneath my ribs. I raised my hand in a short wave. "When she turns eighteen, she's coming to live with me."

"Does your father know that?"

"No, and I can't wait to see the look on his face when he realizes he can't use her as a weapon against me anymore. I'll be the source of his anger every fucking day of the week if it means he ignores her. It's when he notices her too much that things get bad for Analise."

My fists clenched at my sides, and Remi noticed. I wanted to tell her that I hated him. That my hatred made me more like him than I wanted to admit. Now that I'd unlocked my words, I wanted to give all of them to her.

Slowly, she reached forward and slid her palm down my forearm, holding my clenched fist with her cool, slim fingers. My pulse raced at the simple touch, and she seemed oblivious, staring down at our hands until my fingers relaxed. She didn't wind them together, instead wrapping her fingers around my palm and setting her other hand on top of mine.

"You're a good man, Archer Evans." Her gaze was so direct, so forthright, that it almost took me to my knees. *She* almost took me to my knees, and I wondered if she had any idea. "You're determined to hide that, though, aren't you?"

I pulled my hand from hers, wishing I could slow the frantic pounding of my heart. "I don't need anyone to know what happened that night."

Remi tilted her head. "I won't tell anyone about the accident," she promised. "But I wish you would. Someday, at least."

There was no point, but it didn't feel like the right moment to tell her that. Athletes had overcome far worse scandals than this one, and I'd do the same.

Even kids like Gavin, sweet and impressionable and kindhearted, would forgive me eventually, as long as my performance on the field was impressive enough. It was a double-edged sword, being a celebrity in the world of sports. We were forgiven probably far more easily than we should have been.

The sky had gotten darker as we stood and talked, and a slight chill in the air made her shiver.

"You're cold. We can go inside."

She breathed out a laugh. "Family room before date six," she said under her breath. "Unbelievable."

"What?"

"Nothing." Remi smiled. Not a forced one, not tight or uncomfortable, but an amused, secretive smile that made me want to kiss her soundly on the lips. "Yeah, we can go inside."

The sound of the front door opening made us both turn toward the house. Analise was pulling her bag over her shoulder. "We need to go, Archer." She gave me a meaningful look, and the worry in her eyes was enough to make me stand up straighter. "Dad's on his way home."

"Ah."

Gavin was behind Analise, wearing plaid pajama bottoms and a shirt with a sleeping moose on it.

"So you can't see my room?" he asked. I swear, the way that kid looked at me gutted me in an entirely different way than his mother. Scooped hollow. Scraped raw by both members of the Sinclair family.

Remi and I traded a look, and she slid her hand over Gavin's back. "They have to go home, bud. And you need to get to bed anyway. It's a school night."

The disappointment in his face broke my fucking heart. I found myself crouching in front of him again, like I had when I'd arrived. "Will you show it to me the next time I come over?"

His eyes lit up. "Really?"

"Yeah."

"You're coming back?"

Even though my sister was watching and Remi's eyes were wide with shock, I looked at Gavin, then up at his mother and held her gaze. Her breath caught audibly in her throat. If she could hear my heart, it was the unsteady thrumming that would've given me away.

"Yeah, I'll be coming back."

Chapter Fifteen

Archer

There was pink hair at the front desk. Not red.

I stopped short when I walked through the doorway of the shelter lobby.

Vanessa smiled. "Hey." Then she tilted her head. "Why are you all dressed up?"

Fuck.

"I'm not," I lied, tugging at the collar of my favorite blue polo shirt. Analise told me my eyes looked the best when I wore this shirt, and against my better fucking judgment, I pulled it out of the closet when I showered after my workouts.

She hummed disbelievingly, one dark eyebrow arched. "Okay."

I cleared my throat. "Is Remi here?"

Vanessa shook her head. "Her grandpa wasn't feeling well, so she took the day off to make him some soup or something. Honest to God, it'll probably make him worse, but I don't have the heart to tell her that."

Disappointment was so much heavier when it came hard on the heels of anticipation. I'd never felt like this. Walking around like a fucking zombie, holding on to an aching need to see her. Be around her. Do whatever would make her smile. Well, maybe not *whatever* would make her smile.

You have to tell someone.

I couldn't do that for her, and I just prayed she understood why.

I had heard her voice over and over and over in the three days since she'd said it. No hours scheduled at the shelter meant I hadn't seen her. Hadn't talked to her. Heard her voice.

I'd picked up my phone a dozen times to send her a text, but I couldn't find a reason that was good enough.

Analise, in her extremely unhelpful way, gave me a few ideas.

Option 1: *Please help settle a debate: Is cereal a soup?* (Absolutely fucking not, and anyone who thought so was psychotic. If Remi said yes, I'd never be able to get over it.)

Option 2: *I saw someone who looked like you today. Almost broke my neck turning to look at her.* (Had a sneaking suspicion that this would backfire.)

Option 3: *If I had a dollar for every time I thought about you, I'd still text you for free.* (With option three, I was fully convinced my sister was plotting my demise.)

Despite a screaming gut instinct that I shouldn't take advice from a hopelessly romantic seventeen-year-old who'd never gone on a date, I gave my sister the benefit of the doubt and typed them out one by one. Seeing them like that, only one tap on the screen away from either endless humiliation or being pleasantly surprised if it worked, I made myself wait fifteen seconds to see how they looked.

Each one got deleted more violently than the last. By the time I got to option three, I was surprised I hadn't cracked my phone screen.

In the end, I had to wait. Wait to see her and hope we'd get some time to talk. It would be different today, I told myself. We'd had a moment at her house, hadn't we?

I saw her home. Met her child. I was *honest*. Vulnerable, even. Didn't royally fuck up anything in the process.

Which was why I'd dressed nicely. Put on a little cologne. Shaved off the ever-present stubble.

I'd ask her out today. For coffee or dessert, if that was all I'd get. I was more than halfway through my hours, and the desperate desire for more time with her had me thinking things I'd never thought before.

Except all those things were for naught because she wasn't even fucking here.

Vanessa was watching me with a knowing look on her face. "Don't worry, troublemaker. She'll be back tomorrow and you can fawn over her then."

I glowered. "I'm not fawning."

What a fucking liar.

"If you say so." Her voice was dripping with condescension. "Don't get me wrong, I love this journey for her. She needs to be chased."

"I'm not—"

"Oh, zip it, quarterback. Yes, you are. You put on your pretty shirt and you smell much nicer than you should, considering you're going to clean cat shit for the next hour."

"Maybe the animals will appreciate that."

"I'm sure they will." She smiled. "Especially Pumpkin. She'd scratch your face off for smelling so good. But I'm gonna tell you right now, that woman is looking for the kind of perfection that doesn't really exist anymore."

My brow furrowed. "What do you mean?"

"Her standards are almost impossibly high, in that she is looking for complete and utter mediocrity. She wants the most vanilla man in the world, to avoid getting hurt again." Her face gentled. "It doesn't mean you shouldn't try, but if you want to overcome her reservations about you, you're about to scale Mount Everest, baby. I hope you're ready."

I took a deep breath and managed to nod.

"Excellent," she said. "I assume you recall where the bags of kitty litter are."

"Yeah, I remember," I answered dryly.

"Good boy. I'll be up here if you need anything."

◆ ◆ ◆

I couldn't turn my brain off.

At workouts and drills, Remi was always hovering at the back of my mind.

You're about to scale Mount Everest, baby.

What the fuck was I supposed to do with that?

I could buy her a million trucks of dog food, and I still wasn't convinced that was the right way to go about any of this.

With the level of distractions on my mind, it was a fucking miracle I was still able to do my job.

I caught the ball as Mitch snapped it to me, the hundredth rep of the morning. There were ten routes on the route tree, and as the receivers rotated in and out, we ran the route tree twelve times so they each had four cycles through.

Quick out.

Slant.

Comeback.

Curl.

Square out.

Square in.

Corner.

Post.

Go.

I had music blaring in my ears, my body humming as I made each throw to the receivers doing drills today. We had six receivers on the roster this year and two more on the practice squad. Today, we were working on the guys in the one through three spots.

Williams was a rookie, and we'd only talked a few times. He was quick and eager, his eyes lighting up every time he caught the ball to his chest. He'd do well. Better than I had my first year, probably because he wanted to listen and took down everything anyone was willing to teach him. Smith and Brooks waited on the sideline, watching with sharp eyes, even though they had their own music in their ears.

This wasn't a time for conversation.

This was the kind of repetition that was the foundation for every guy who wanted to play this game. It was the repetition I'd missed when I was injured. And what I'd taken for granted when I wasn't.

Football was easy to figure out. I'd known how to do that since I was in high school.

It was the relationships in my life where I always struggled most.

My father.

My nonexistent mother.

My teammates and coaches.

Remi.

I didn't know how to do any of it, not when it mattered.

I snapped the ball a little too hard on the last go route. Williams had done his job, sprinting straight down the middle of the field about twenty-five yards, but the ball sailed over his head, easily ten yards past him.

"Fuck," I muttered, then tapped my chest. "That's on me."

Williams jogged back with an easy smile on his face. "No worries, QB. I shoulda run faster."

I pulled out an earbud and tucked it into my wristband so he knew I was paying attention. "You ran fast enough. I was distracted with my own shit."

My QB coach glanced in my direction, his eyebrows lifting slightly at the admission. Brooks and Smith shared a look on the sideline.

Williams set his hands on his hips. "Anything you want to talk about?"

I froze.

So did Brooks and Smith.

Mitch sucked in a quick breath and held it.

"You want to talk about my problems," I said slowly.

He shrugged. "We're teammates, right? If you're struggling with something, we should feel secure enough to ask if you need help."

Brooks swiped a hand over his mouth, and Smith stared down at the ground.

I stared at Williams with narrowed eyes, my chest tightening uncomfortably.

He was trying to help.

Tell someone.

I banished the sound of Remi's voice out of my head. Other than Coach, I couldn't remember the last time anyone around me had offered something so simple. Not that I blamed my teammates—they were all living their own lives. It wasn't their responsibility to fix me.

"I don't know if you can," I told him, crossing my arms over my chest.

He nodded. "Is it about the DUI?"

"Fucking rookies," Smith muttered. Brooks choked on a laugh.

"What?" Williams asked. "Are we not supposed to talk about that?"

"It's not about the DUI." I rolled my neck until I heard a crack. "I, uh, I like someone."

My QB coach dropped his phone. Brooks's head snapped up and Smith's mouth fell open.

Williams nodded eagerly. "That's . . . that's good. What's the problem?"

"Well, she hates me. Sort of." I grimaced. "Maybe."

Remi might not have hated me anymore, but I wasn't sure she really trusted me either.

"So she knows you?" he asked carefully.

Brooks lost his battle, leaning in to Smith as he burst out laughing. I glared, which made them both laugh harder. Mitch coughed, but he couldn't hide his smile either.

The rookie's face turned red. "Fuck, that's not what I meant. I just . . . I meant, you two have met and everything."

"Yes," I answered dryly. "And everything." I pulled the hat off my head and ran a hand through my hair. "Her life is complicated. She's a single mom. Always working, taking care of people. Her friend, uh, she said that meeting her standards would be like climbing Mount Everest."

All of them made an "oh" sound.

Brooks straightened. "Look, Archer, you gotta be straight with women like that. Single moms don't fuck around with liars or playboys."

"I know, I'm trying. I'm not either one of those things."

"Yeah, but you're not a saint either," Smith said.

Tell someone.

I pushed my tongue into the side of my cheek. "Yeah, I know. I met her doing my community service. Well. Met her a second time. The first time was . . . complicated."

Williams's eyes widened. "What does she do?"

I gave him a dry look. "She runs the animal shelter."

"Oh."

Brooks smiled. "Oh shit, for real? I've been thinking about getting a dog. They got any cute ones?"

"Lots of them. I'm not there when people come in for adoptions. She doesn't want it to become a circus with me there the whole time."

They all nodded.

"So this is, like, important to her."

I looked over at Williams. "Yeah."

"Have you asked her out yet?"

"No," I said with a roll of my shoulders. "Like I said, it's complicated."

"Dude." Smith smacked my chest. "You're a quarterback for a professional football team. That uncomplicates a lot."

"I think my résumé is a strike against me, unfortunately."

"You gotta play it smooth," Brooks said. "Under the radar. You don't want to scare her off."

"Right."

Brooks nodded. "But let her know you're interested. Not, like, too much. Just enough."

"Okay. Fuck. How do you know if it's too much?"

"You know," they replied in unison.

Williams shrugged. "I think you should ignore her about coming in during adoption hours."

Brooks and Smith immediately started shaking their heads.

"No, man."

"Bad, bad idea."

The rookie held up his hands. "I'm just saying. I think you should go. More people usually means more dogs adopted."

I stared at the kid. "You're single, right?"

"Yeah," he sighed. "My girlfriend dumped me right before the draft because she said I wouldn't do shit."

Brooks whistled. "She know you got drafted?"

Williams nodded. "Tried to call me the next day."

Smith narrowed his eyes. "What'd you do?"

"Told her I was too busy spending my signing bonus to talk to her."

The guys burst out laughing, shoving the rookie as he grinned.

I smiled, shaking my head.

"I can't just show up if she told me no," I said once they'd calmed down. "I know her well enough. It would piss her off."

"Shit, I'd go down there and look at dogs, but I don't want to make it crazy either," Brooks said.

My gaze snapped to his, brain stumbling over a thought.

That was it.

"What are you guys doing tomorrow?" I asked.

"Nothing, why?"

When you've gone your entire life believing that asking for help made you weak, it was so fucking hard to force the words out.

Despite my upbringing, I was so far from perfect, we weren't even circling the same orbit. But neither was I weak, no matter what my father might have said to the contrary.

I was trying.

"You know anyone else on the team who wants a dog?"

We all turned to my QB coach. He held his hands up. "I already have three, and my wife would murder me if I brought home another one."

Williams laughed.

Smith held up a hand. "I heard Justice say something about it a couple weeks ago. He might be looking."

"Good." I sucked in a deep breath and fought through the instinct to shut down, pretend like I was fine. "I need your help. Will you guys come with me tomorrow?"

Chapter Sixteen

Remi

Ness pounced on me the moment I left my office.

"I'm going to find a new best friend," I told her.

"No, you're not."

"I was in a meeting, Vanessa. You can't come to my office door and do your little excited dance and wave your arms around when I'm trying to secure a grant for the shelter."

She kept tugging on my arm. "They couldn't see me."

"I could." I snatched my arm back. "What are you doing? Quit manhandling me."

"You have got to see this."

We came around the corner to the meeting room, and I skidded to a halt.

Four giant, beautiful men were sitting on the floor, playing with Scout and Daisy.

"What is happening right now?" I whispered.

She leaned in. "Archer brought friends. Aren't they pretty?"

"I'm not sure *pretty* is the right word," I answered absently, tilting my head as Archer rolled to the side of one hip to snatch a toy and toss it across the room for Scout. Those jeans, and what they did to his ass, should have been illegal. "When did they come in?"

"About an hour ago, hence the dancing in front of your window during a donor meeting."

"Ah."

"One guy was here and adopted Razor. He's already gone. But these guys have taken their sweet time. They played with a few others, took some videos and stuff on their phones, but Scout and Daisy seem to be the winners of the dog lottery today." She lifted her chin. "Look at them."

Daisy was in her element, prancing around with her fluffy tail in the air. They were tossing a ball across the room and playing tug with a frayed rope toy she always kept in her kennel. Scout, sweetheart though he was, was a bit more reserved with strangers. He was often overlooked because he was missing a leg and didn't give out affection quite as easily. I was completely convinced he had a doggy eight-date rule, too, which was probably why we got along so well.

"This is amazing."

"I know," Ness replied. "I guess Archer was talking to them at practice, and a couple of them said they were interested in adopting a dog, and he convinced them to come here today so they didn't turn an adoption day into a circus." She gave me a sidelong look. "I still think it's a circus we could handle, but you cannot fault that man's listening skills."

There was a knot buried under my sternum, and my hand rubbed uselessly at my chest to see if it would disappear. The other guys were just as big as Archer, and even if they all looked different—different eyes and smiles and skin color and hair, some with ink, some without, some laughing and smiling, one a little bit quieter, like Archer—it was overwhelming to see them as a group.

To be perfectly clear, I was not the kind of woman who got weak-kneed by a group of celebrities, but it was entirely possible that seeing him play gently with Scout for the first time, then scratch behind Daisy's ears and smile at the play bow she gave in return, made my knees a teeny bit wobbly.

Worse, it wasn't just my knees. My entire body—head, heart, and all my instincts—was freaking Jell-O at seeing him finally let his guard down with the dogs.

"I don't understand," I admitted quietly. "I don't even know him all that well, Ness. And I feel . . ."

"Seen? Pursued?"

My eyes fell closed. "Maybe."

Her shoulder nudged mine. "Good. You should be seen and pursued."

"I don't have time. It's a horrible idea."

"Bullshit," she said lightly. "I call complete and utter bullshit."

I rolled my eyes. "Easy for you to say. Muriel didn't leave you in charge."

She ignored that. Ness didn't like for things like logic to get in her way.

"Would you allow me to prove a point? Even if nothing comes from it."

"What's that?"

"Try—just for one day—to give the man the benefit of the doubt." She said it so gently, which was a word I'd never used to describe her, and it was enough to pull my attention from the scene in front of us. Ness smiled. "You give everyone the benefit of the doubt, Remi, but not him. It's not like my friend to do that."

Even if a harsh truth is wrapped up in the softest package, it still stings when it lands.

"I'm trying," I told her. "It's hard to let myself look at him and think . . . *what if*."

"I know, babe."

"I don't want to get hurt," I whispered. "And I don't want Gavin to get hurt either."

Ness set her head on my shoulder.

One of Archer's teammates was sprawled out on the floor, and Scout stood above him, wagging his tail. Ness and I paused our conversation, watching to see what would happen. The dog dropped his big head and nestled it into the guy's neck, flopping onto his side for a full-body cuddle. The burly football player smiled, turning over to wrap his arm around Scout's middle.

"I think this is my boy," he said loudly. "You wanna go home with me, Scout?"

Scout's tail smacked wildly on the floor, and he angled his head to lick him along his chin.

My eyes watered instantly. Ness sniffled.

I reached over to rub her back. "It never gets less cool, does it?"

"Nope." She sighed, swiping at her cheeks. "Now you just need to convince Archer to adopt."

I snorted. "This is the first time I've ever seen him touch one of the dogs. I'm not sure he wants a pet."

Archer lifted his head as if he sensed me watching him, and through the glass window separating us, our gazes locked for a few breathless seconds.

"No, I'm not sure that's what he wants either," Ness added airily.

The tension in my body knotted around itself, over and over until an unbearable weight filled my stomach, but when Archer broke our eye contact to answer something one of his friends said, I could actually breathe again.

"Want to come in?" she asked.

I shook my head, glancing at the clock on the wall. "I have one more meeting. You can handle it."

Ness nodded, reaching down to squeeze my hand before she pushed open the door into the larger room.

"Okay, boys, how many adoption applications should I bring in?"

Two hands shot into the air. Archer laughed, a dimple appearing in his cheek, and when that squirmy sensation shot from head to toe, a restless bolt of energy coursing through my body that could've powered the entire greater Buffalo area, I tucked my chin down to my chest and walked back into my office and tried to will it away.

An hour later, I was able to escape for a quick pee break. The meet and greet room was quiet, and disappointment swelled before I could stop it. I thought about doing my morning rounds through the kennel without Scout's patient gaze and Daisy's happy dance, and my throat felt tight at the fact that I didn't get to say goodbye.

Rescue work was like this—a yo-yo of emotions you never quite got used to. Watching them go to their new homes was good, the outcome we'd been working toward for so long. But there was always, always a pinch when thinking about never seeing them again, and I didn't want to lose that.

My entire body sagged, my forehead resting against the cool glass while I waited for the thick squeeze of tears to disappear. Before any could fall, the front door opened. I straightened, blowing out a quick breath.

I turned with a polite smile. "Can I help—"

It was Archer.

"Oh." Mentally, I cursed the breathy sound of my voice. *Get a grip, Remi.* "I thought you'd have left by now."

His chest expanded on a deep inhale. "I asked the guys to wait around until your meetings were done so you could say goodbye."

My heart stopped, then kicked violently against my sternum when it jolted back into rhythm.

"Really?"

In an endearingly bashful display, he ducked his head down and pushed his hands into the front pockets of his jeans. "I know Scout's your favorite, even if you wouldn't admit it. You always give him extra treats when you walk through the kennels."

I breathed out a shocked gust of air but recovered quickly, fixing my expression into a mock glare. "Don't you dare tell the others."

He mimed pulling a zipper across his mouth, then tilted his head toward the parking lot. "Brooks is already planning to add a doggy suite so that Daisy can have her own bedroom."

My laugh was watery, and I didn't even try to stop it. "Thank you. For bringing them in."

"You're welcome."

The harsh fluorescent lighting of the lobby did nothing to dim the wild blue of his eyes. It made *me* look like I'd walked out of a crypt, but he stood there, tall and impossibly strong, one of the most handsome men I'd ever seen. That was bad enough, wreaking havoc on my slowly weakening defenses.

But this . . . this thoughtfulness was more than I could handle.

Archer stepped to the side, letting me through the lobby door first, and the feel of him walking closely behind almost caused me to stumble. He settled a big hand on the small of my back.

"Okay?" he asked in a low voice.

I nodded, unable to speak.

This was bad. *Bad* bad.

Was I so hard up for affection that a little lower-back action felt better than my last round with a vibrator? God bless it, who came up with this stupid eight-date rule and unwavering sense of professionalism? I wanted to slap my past self.

The shelter's parking lot had been turned into a car show for the rich and famous. They'd all driven separately, and while Archer's truck was clean today, it looked damn-near shabby compared to his three teammates'.

Two huge, tricked-out SUVs with gleaming rims and custom paint jobs—one a deep hunter green and the other a charcoal gray so dark that it was almost black, but when the sun hit it, it gleamed iridescent. I'd never seen anything like them.

And a low-slung sports car in a pearlescent white with black rims. The happy dogs were leashed and sniffing around the vehicles while the three men talked about each other's cars and pointed out things they'd done to them.

I thought about my paid-off Toyota with a few rust spots and a back door that opened with a loud creak, and couldn't help but smile.

Maybe I'd pull her around from the back and show off the new brake pads that had about sent me over my budget two months ago.

When the youngest of them pressed a button and the doors of his white sports car lifted straight up, the other two hooted and hollered, shoving him in the back as he grinned. The tallest one noticed my approach, elbowing the guy next to him. His eyes widened, and he smacked the youngest one in the stomach. He turned, eyeing me with undisguised interest.

"Hey," I said. "Thank you for waiting so I could say goodbye. I'm Remi Sinclair, the interim director of the shelter. I'm so grateful to both of you for giving them such good homes."

"Remi," one of them said knowingly, trading a quick look with the others. "Yeah, we figured."

My brow furrowed. "Okay."

Behind me, Archer cleared his throat. All three of their faces smoothed out.

"What's your sign, Remi?" the youngest one asked.

I blinked. "Um, Virgo. Why?"

He nodded. "That makes sense."

Archer cleared his throat again, more pointedly this time.

Still very confused, I crouched down and called for the dogs.

Daisy got to me first, almost knocking me over with an enthusiastic kiss to the face. I laughed, bracing my hand back on the asphalt. "Hey, sweetheart. You're going to have a lot of new people to meet." I scratched behind her ears and pressed a kiss to the top of her head. I glanced up at her new dad. "She loves chew toys, but she needs the extra-strength kind," I said, my voice already thick with tears. "And during thunderstorms, she'll want to hide in the bathroom. She doesn't like the lightning."

He smiled kindly. "You got it. I'll give her her own bathroom without windows, then."

A tear slid down my cheek, and I brushed it away quickly. "Perfect."

I clicked my tongue and Scout lumbered over, pressing his face into my chest.

"I'm gonna miss him," I said in a shaky voice. "He's been here for a year."

"I'll give him the best life, I promise. Spoiled rotten, all day, every day," the other guy said, and the genuine look in his eyes was my absolute undoing.

As if he could sense my impending emotional breakdown, Scout pressed harder, and I gave up, my ass hitting the asphalt under the big dog's attention.

I wrapped my arms around Scout with a soft laugh, hiding the tears that flowed harder now. "You're the best boy, aren't you?" I whispered, nuzzling into his neck. "You're going to have such a good life, I know it."

I tried wiping my cheeks when I pulled back, because good Lord, I'd gone past humbling and into embarrassing as I sat in the parking lot, with four professional athletes watching me weep over these dogs. To be sure, this was not on my to-do list today.

Before I could try to stand with some semblance of grace, a large hand moved into my peripheral vision. Archer's hand.

It would've been easy to wave him off. Say that I was fine.

Could I stand up on my own? Of course.

For this moment, though, I wanted to let him help me. It didn't mean anything, even though finding my balance around him seemed to be a continual work in progress.

Give him the benefit of the doubt.

I let out a shaky sigh and slipped my fingers along the rough skin of his palm as his closed around mine, my stomach swooping when he tugged me to standing like I weighed nothing.

News flash: I didn't weigh nothing.

Even worse, he didn't let go of my hand right away. His thumb dragged along my knuckles while his gaze bored into mine. "Are you okay?"

I nodded, giving the other three a tiny smile. "This is the bittersweet part of rescue work."

While no one spoke, they all glanced at Archer, and I rolled my lips between my teeth when he seemed unsure of what to say.

Brooks, I'd heard them call him, elbowed the younger guy, who gave him a helpless look.

"So, um, Remi, what are you looking for in a partner?"

"What?"

His cheeks were flame red, and the other two guys stared down at the ground, mouths covered by their hands. Archer sighed.

"I mean, in a boyfriend. Or husband or whatever."

"Shut up, rookie," Archer growled.

He shrugged. "I'm just trying to help."

"You're not."

"Don't you want to know this stuff?" he asked.

"Who does?" I asked.

"Fuck's sake," Archer muttered.

Brooks lost his battle, wheezing immediately. The third guy covered his face with both hands. "This is so fucking bad. No wonder your ass is single."

"Do *you* want to know?" I asked. *What* was going on? I'd exchanged less than five words with this guy.

It seemed unlikely—highly, highly unlikely—that I'd gone from zero male attention to having multiple athletes flirt with me in strange, unorthodox ways.

His eyes widened. "No. No, I don't care."

Smith groaned.

I folded my arms over my stomach.

"Listen, you're . . . really hot, it's not that I don't find you attractive. I do, actually. The red hair is really working for you."

"If you do not shut the fuck up, Williams . . ." Archer warned in a gruff voice. "Not a single pass. All year."

Williams swallowed audibly. "Right. I think I'm just gonna go."

"Is someone going to explain what the hell is going on?" I asked.

"No," they said in unison.

I glanced at Archer, who couldn't meet my eyes. All our interactions flipped through my head like a Rolodex.

Not like I had much experience with guys like him—a celebrity in his own right. Maybe all the little things he'd done weren't real, or they weren't indicative of some unspoken attraction. Maybe it was a giant fucking joke.

It was too easy to imagine them huddled around in some fancy locker room, or on the practice field, joking about the desperate single mom who'd practically screwed him on the dance floor.

The knots in my stomach iced over, dropping like blocks of concrete, and I kept staring until he finally looked over.

"Did you . . . did you tell them?"

His face bent in anguish. "No. *No*, I swear."

The other guys all stepped forward, talking over each other.

"That's not it, we promise."

"Not at all!"

"We'd never do you like that."

I let out a slow breath. "Fine, whatever. I, um, I have to get back to work." I gave the other guys a smile that felt tight at the edges. "Take good care of them, okay?"

"Yes, ma'am."

"We will."

Now it was my turn to avoid eye contact with Archer as I turned to walk back to the shelter as fast as humanly possible.

"I wanted to ask you out and didn't know how!" he shouted.

I froze.

"Oh shit," one of the guys whispered. "That was stupid, bro."

It took an entire *year* to turn around and gape at Archer. "Excuse me?" My voice was hardly a whisper, but my heart . . . it was thrashing somewhere in the vicinity of my throat.

His eyes fell closed. "Fuck. That's not what I meant to say."

"I don't have time for your games," I said firmly. "Go home, Archer."

Chapter Seventeen

Remi

The kennel room was quieter without Daisy and Scout, and as I sat down in Bandit's space, I closed my eyes and prayed for the cinder blocks to, I don't know, come to life and bash me to death instead of having to face whatever had just happened out in the parking lot.

Yes, death by kennel block sounded fabulous.

Bandit was sitting in the corner, watching as the embarrassment threatened to swallow me whole.

It was truly amazing that until Archer Evans had walked through these doors, I hadn't realized just how badly my trust in my own instincts were broken. That twisty knot of embarrassment was impossible to untangle when you were unsure of where you stood with someone.

I wanted him—that much was undeniable. Wanted him enough that the idea I'd been any sort of joke to him and his friends was a frigid slap of reality that stung to my bones. Those were trust issues tied to far more than him, not that he could've known it.

I shouldn't want him, because despite what I knew now, I still wasn't sure I could trust him.

I'd lied to myself so thoroughly since the night we met. That was the scariest part of the lies you told yourself: If you said them long enough, even knowing they weren't true, eventually you'd believe them.

I don't want Archer Evans. I'd repeat it over and over and over until my belief was unshakable. The words needed to be inked not just on my brain, but on my heart. The kind of ink that would never wash away and couldn't fade with time and circumstance. Wanting him would gain me nothing but heartbreak.

I lightly tapped the back of my head against the hard, cold blocks behind me.

A concussion might help all this sink in, come to think of it.

Bandit tilted his head.

I stopped the possible head injury and breathed out a small laugh. "Sorry, bud. Not trying to freak you out. But if you'd seen me out there, you'd try to erase the memories too."

The door into the kennel room opened and closed.

Ness was around somewhere, as were a few volunteers, so I stayed where I was and tossed Bandit a few more of the treats I'd snagged from the supply closet.

He inched forward, snuffling them off the ground. With a lick of his chops, he looked at me expectantly. When I slowly reached my hand forward, he backed up again.

"All right," I said gently. "It's okay if you're not ready."

The dog's attention wasn't on me anymore, though. It was on the entrance to his kennel, where a giant lurking presence made my stomach flip inside out.

I slammed my eyes shut.

"Remi, can I talk to you?"

"No."

"Remi."

What made it worse was the tone of his voice. It wasn't gruff or demanding. As deep as normal, but there was something steady in it that made me want to plug my ears. I didn't want steady, deep voices that would make me feel better about . . . anything. Even worse if they made me feel better about everything.

The moment I had the thought, my eyes caught on the tip of Bandit's tail.

The tiny wagging motion at the mere sight of Archer. My mouth fell open.

"Archer, slowly open the door and come in here," I told him, keeping my focus on the dog. "Please," I added as an afterthought.

As instructed, Archer lifted the latch and soundlessly walked into the kennel. When he caught sight of Bandit's hidden tail wag, his movements slowed.

"That's for me?" he asked, clearly incredulous.

"It is. Usually it's just the presence of processed meat that gets him going."

"Thanks," Archer answered dryly.

"Anytime."

See . . . this was better. An even playing field, where I had solid footing in our interactions. The moment we stepped outside the walls of the shelter, everything went topsy-turvy, which was the surest sign of all that whatever this was, it needed to stop.

When Archer mimicked my seated position—back against the wall and legs stretched out—the free space in the kennel shrank. In an effort to avoid accidental leg brushing (I'd just shaved and all, but still . . . no one needed calf-on-calf action if it could be helped), I tucked my legs up against my chest.

Finally, I allowed myself to look at him.

I thought maybe he'd be staring at the dog, or avoiding my gaze after what had happened in front of his friends, but no, the man was looking directly at me. The broad stretch of his chest rose and fell beneath his plain T-shirt, and under the harsh light of the kennel room, the veins mapping his forearms stood out against his tanned, golden skin.

Everything about him screamed strength. In all his features and limbs. In the graceful way he moved and the ease in which he interacted with the world around him, like it bent to his will simply because it was easier that way.

I don't want Archer Evans.

The thought didn't come quite as easily now that I was faced with him. If I didn't want Archer, I never would've reacted that way outside. It was the wanting that turned me into a basket case. Emotion, a big wall of it, twisted my ability to speak clearly, so I kept my attention on the dog while Archer carefully extended his hand in my direction.

"Can I have a few of those?"

Absently, I nodded, digging into the bag to give him a few pieces. My fingertips brushed the rough skin of his palm as I released the treats into his hand. The weight of his gaze was heavy on my face, but like an absolute chickenshit, I stared at Bandit.

The dog was watching the exchange with subdued interest. Archer tossed him a couple pieces, waiting patiently while Bandit eased forward to eat those too.

"Try from your hand," I suggested.

"It's not too soon?"

Briefly, I allowed my eyes to meet his. "I guess we'll see."

Archer's chest expanded on a deep inhale, and he refused to drop my gaze. Almost like the steady eye contact fortified him. The thought caused a trembling deep, deep inside, tugging on a chord attached to my heart that hadn't been tugged . . . ever.

I broke first, but only when it became hard to breathe.

Archer kept his movements slow, holding two pieces on the tips of his fingers as he rested his hand on the floor just out of reach. Bandit glanced up at him, then back down at the treats.

For a moment, no one moved. Not me, not Archer, and definitely not the dog. Even the other animals in the kennel room seemed to quiet.

Then Bandit, staying on his belly, inched forward. He sniffed the treats, lifting his gaze to Archer, who was staying unnaturally still. I wasn't even sure he was breathing.

Another inch. Another look.

Then another.

With each shift forward, my heart picked up speed, until Bandit finally sniffed Archer's fingertips.

Instead of inching forward on his belly, Bandit got up off the floor and stood, lowering his face to Archer's prone hand, delicately eating the treats from his fingers.

I breathed out a small laugh. "You did it."

Then I made the absolute, utter mistake of lifting my gaze to Archer's.

He was smiling.

Wide and happy, deep grooves on either side of his mouth, straight white teeth, and the gleam in his eyes made my pulse skip erratically.

I don't want Archer Evans, I thought with frantic urgency. *I don't want Archer Evans.*

I *couldn't* want Archer Evans.

He added more treats to his hand, and Bandit ate them more easily this time. When they were gone, he slowly raised his hand to scratch the side of Bandit's neck.

My chest cracked wide open, watching the care he was taking. The slow movements, the incredible patience he'd shown.

"You're a good boy, aren't you?" he whispered. "I bet you haven't heard that enough before you got here."

Oh no. This would not do.

My grip on my emotions had been tentative at best before he'd walked into the kennel, but this, I simply could not abide. Before I did something insane, like climb into his lap for a hug or burst into tears, I stood as slowly as I could manage.

Bandit backed away from Archer when I did, but not for very long.

Archer's concern was evident, but I ignored it. Ignored the furrow in his brow and the wave of emotions that threatened to hit all at once.

"Remi?"

"I—I need to go."

My muscles screamed to run, sprint, high-jump, whatever the hell I needed to do in order to get the fuck out of the enclosed space with the man I did not want, but I managed to cinch the untapped energy coursing through my veins.

This, folks, is what we call fight or flight.

Unfortunately for me, my nervous system couldn't tell the difference between fleeing from a serial killer and facing my feelings for the hot, emotionally stunted football player who may or may not want to ask me out on a date.

The sanctuary of my office was short-lived, because about only thirty seconds after I sank against the closed door, there was a knock on the outside.

I groaned. Couldn't a girl wallow properly?

"Remi?"

I do not want Archer Evans.

"Act like a grown-up, you coward," I whispered harshly. Straightening my shoulders, I tossed my hair back and opened the door like I was totally and completely fine to be facing him again.

Archer studied my expression, then glanced down the hallway. "Can I talk to you?"

"I don't know if that's—"

His eyes burned. "You are not a joke to me. I didn't tell anyone."

A burst of laughter came from the vicinity of the meet and greet room, so I opened the door wider and motioned him inside, despite the uneven thudding of my heart when I closed us into my office together. "I don't want anyone hearing this."

I pushed my hair behind my ears with shaking hands, then leaned against my desk. I should've been on the other side, but my feet seemed bolted to the floor.

A barrier was good. A ten-foot wall would have been better, but I couldn't afford to be so picky. And yet my ass stayed right there, with nothing but a small stretch of air and tenuous control separating us.

Archer stayed focused on me as he leaned against the wall just a few feet away, checking my reaction to see if that was what I wanted.

Good luck with that, because even I wasn't sure what that was.

"I didn't handle it well," he continued. "I haven't handled anything well since I got out of that car."

This wasn't a time for me to speak, because it was important to hear what he had to say. Words would come. Plenty of them.

"But I swear to you, I told no one about how we met, and I'd never let my teammates or anyone disrespect you, even if they knew."

"*You* disrespected me, Archer. The very first day," I said. "You all but called me a whore."

The anguish on his face was contagious, because I felt it twist my chest like it was attached to an invisible crank. "I have no excuses for why I spoke to you that way. There are none."

"Try," I said on a shaky whisper. "Try to explain it to me."

He blew out a harsh breath. "I was embarrassed. You were on my mind constantly after we met, and to see you again . . . like this"—he spread his arms out—"it was my nightmare. I was showing up as the worst version of me."

That was contagious, too, it seemed. "I've been doing that too," I admitted quietly. "I'm sorry."

"No, you don't need to apologize." He shook his head. "It was inexcusable. I know that. I felt sick saying it, and when you slapped me . . ."

"About that—"

His gaze flared. "Do not apologize for that. I deserved it."

Somehow I managed a nod. I'd been about to do exactly that, even though I didn't really regret it. Not then and not now. He *had* deserved it, and it felt really fucking good to stand up for myself.

It just felt like slapping someone in adulthood should come with at least a cursory apology, but what did I know? He'd been the one to pop that particular cherry.

Archer pushed off the wall, stepping closer. The space between us shrank by a foot, lifting the hairs on the back of my neck. His voice was rough when he asked, "If I apologized for that, would you believe me?"

Even a week earlier, I might have answered differently. At any other point on this strange roller coaster since he'd appeared in my life, we would have ended in a different place, but right now, I was able to meet his eyes unflinchingly and answer with naked honesty.

"Yes."

His entire frame sank in relief, his eyes falling shut momentarily. When he opened them again, they were blazing. "I wasn't taught how to apologize, because my entire existence was built to be above reproach. But I am more sorry for what I said to you than anything I've done in my entire life." He settled his hand on his chest, fingers spread. My hand itched to touch his, but that would be kindling in the middle of a wildfire. There'd be no hope of ever putting out the flames. "I haven't felt right inside since I said it. I don't deserve your forgiveness, but I hope someday you feel like I've earned it."

Twin tears tracked silently down my face. "Damn you, Archer," I whispered shakily.

His brow wrinkled as if he were in pain. "Please don't cry."

"I cry over everything," I told him with a wobbling smile. "Commercials. The movies Gavin makes me watch. A pretty sunset. It doesn't take much. I swear, I gave birth and my hormones quadrupled, and now there's no hope of keeping them contained."

He wanted to reach for me, I could tell in the way he held himself perfectly still. Now I was the cagey one he was trying to coax closer, holding himself carefully so that I wouldn't run.

The irony was not lost on me.

I brushed my cheeks and let out a deep breath. "You're forgiven."

There was no relief on his face. "Why do you still look so sad?"

Because I *was* sad. Because it made no sense if I tried to reason through it, and somehow that made me even sadder. I'd followed a pattern to keep my life making sense, and he was the biggest deviation on that path, and I didn't know what to do about it.

"I have a list," I blurted out.

"Okay." He blinked. "What's on it?"

"The kind of man I can handle having in my life."

Archer sucked in a quick, sharp breath. "Tell me."

I licked my dry lips, wiping at my chin. "You have to understand something first. When I met Gavin's father, he was . . . he was *everything*. Charming and so handsome that it hurt. He wooed me and said all the right things. His family was wealthy, and so he spoiled me with gifts and extravagant dates. For a few weeks, at least." I let out a dry laugh. "Pops warned me to be careful. But there was only so much he could do, you know? He was in his late sixties raising a teenager. He did his best, but I thought I was so smart. That I knew exactly who this guy was."

His jaw was tight, but he listened patiently.

I closed my eyes and let out a heavy sigh. "We dated for two whole months," I said lightly. "And a couple weeks after I slept with him for the first time, he stopped calling me. Stopped answering my texts. I was the worst sort of cliché, and it's embarrassing."

"You were a kid."

"I was. And I got pregnant after having sex four times."

He glanced up at the ceiling, then back down at me. "What did he do?"

"Once I tracked him down at baseball practice, he handed me three hundred bucks and told me to take care of it because he didn't want some bastard kid coming after him in eighteen years."

His eyes fell shut. "Fucking hell."

"Pretty much. Pops and I had some hard conversations, but in the end, he left it up to me. He'd support me no matter what. I decided to keep him and used the three hundred bucks to buy a car seat and some diapers." I glanced at the picture on my desk. "And he's the best thing I've ever done."

"You never reached out to his father."

"Never." I held his gaze, daring him to tell me I should have done otherwise.

Archer's face was implacable. Terrifying. "What's his name?"

"Why, you gonna take him out for me?" I asked with a smile.

He didn't smile back.

I rolled my eyes, but there was no heat behind it. "Archer, it's fine. It was a decade ago, and I'm thankful I don't have to share Gavin. I don't have to undo someone else's influence in trying to raise a good human. He's *mine*. No one else's."

There was a thoughtful expression on his face. "So your list . . ."

"It's protection. For me and for Gavin." I shrugged weakly. "Sometimes it works, and sometimes it doesn't."

Understanding lit up his eyes. "The guy you told me about at the bar."

I smiled. "Yeah. I was the butt of a joke to him—or his friends, at least. But I shouldn't have taken that out on you. It just . . . triggered me, I guess." Now it was Archer's turn to look sad. "I want . . . I want safe. Normal. A quiet love with someone perfectly average. Someone nice. Kind. Humble."

The last word made his eyes flicker, the muscle in his jaw flex. "Normal."

Slowly, I nodded. "You've seen my life, Archer."

"It's a good one. You're a great mother. Great friend. Granddaughter. Boss." He hooked a thumb over his shoulder at the hallway outside my office. "And this? You're actually making the world better. You're not average, Remi. You are so far above it."

The sweet, perfect words drenched some long-dried-out part of me that still wanted poetry and grand gestures. I wasn't just the rebel or the Siren. Once—even if it was a long time ago—I had been a romantic. I'd forced myself to forget that too. "I'm no angel, Archer. I gave as good as I got when you showed up."

His heated study of my face made my stomach clench. "I'm aware. It made me fucking crazy."

Another step, and Archer was closer again.

"Archer," I warned.

"What?"

My hands gripped the edge of my desk so hard, I thought it might snap off in my hands. "Don't put me up on a pedestal."

"I'm not. Tell me all your flaws, and I'll decide if they're a deal-breaker. Maybe I have a list of my own."

"No, you don't," I chided.

He was unrepentant, inching closer with another step. "No, I don't. But if I did, I can tell you what would be on it."

"Don't."

"She'd have red hair." The way he looked me over—thorough and intense—heated me to my throbbing core. "Green eyes that look blue sometimes. Hell of a swing."

"Archer." My eyes fell closed. "I was horrible to you. Do you know what I told Ness your first day?"

"Tell me." His nose traced my temple, his exhales against my skin sending a shiver down my spine. "Tell me something bad. Please."

My hands shook where I kept them anchored on the desk. "I wanted you to suffer while you were here. I told her I'd make you miserable."

"You do. God, do you make me miserable." Archer's fingertips traced the edge of my jaw, and my heart skipped at the feel of his skin on mine. "Every day I think about how you felt, how good you'd feel now that I know you. How badly I want to kiss you. Remi, I am in *agony* not being able to touch you."

I cannot want Archer Evans.

Loving someone like him would tear apart the fabric of my carefully-held-together world. He'd eclipse everything. The stage was too big, the risk of disappointment and heartache too great. Not just for me but for Gavin too.

"I can't," I begged, insides quaking. "Please don't make me push you away right now. I couldn't bear it."

For a moment, he let his forehead drop against the top of my head, his hands falling to the desk on either side of my hips. His chest was heaving. So was mine.

"Okay." He dropped a whisper of a kiss to my forehead, then said it again, almost to himself. "Okay."

As requested, he stepped back. Then stepped back again.

My senses cleared with each inch gained between us. Hopefully, his did too.

For a moment, we simply stared at each other. The anguish in his face was as clear as his ferocious desire. Mine probably looked similar.

My life—the tentative, chaotic nature of it—was the only thing holding me back from taking that one last step over the line.

"So is that a no to our date?" he asked.

I couldn't help it. I laughed. Laughed long and hard, clutching my stomach while he smiled fondly.

"Maybe we could be friends," I said once I'd regained control.

Archer tilted his head, dragging his gaze from the top of my head to the tips of my toes and back up. "Do you want my honest answer or a pretty lie?"

I sucked in a sharp breath. "I think I'll take a pretty lie right now."

Archer smiled sadly. "Then yeah, I can be just friends."

I cannot want Archer Evans.

So why did it feel like my heart cracked clean in half when he turned and left my office?

Chapter Eighteen

Remi

"Let's mark that one for donation."

"Like hell. That's my favorite couch."

I pinched the bridge of my nose. "Pops, we do not have space for that couch, which you knew. We're going to let someone else love it as much as you have."

He snatched the green Post-its from Gavin's hands, the ones used to flag items that would be picked up by the donation center.

Gavin gave me a wide-eyed look.

I leaned forward, snatching the stack of papers back. "We talked about this."

Pops glared. "I don't remember agreeing to this."

"See, I knew this would happen." As I pulled my phone from my back pocket, I gave Pops an indulgent smile. "This is why we made video proof."

"Shit."

"Language," I admonished without any heat. "Ahh, there it is."

I handed him the phone and pressed play. His entire face filled the screen, a lovely close-up of his nose coming into the frame.

"Where am I looking?" he said in the video.

"Back up, Pops. Not so close," I said in the background. *"We don't need to see your nose hairs."*

The shot was pulled back, and Pops peered over the rim of his glasses into the camera. *"What do you want me to say?"*

"Repeat what we just agreed to."

He let out a disgruntled sigh. *"I, Harold Sinclair, do solemnly swear that I've agreed to get rid of all my furniture, except my dresser, the leather chair in my bedroom, and the bench on the patio."*

"And . . . ?" I prompted.

Pops rolled his eyes. *"And I will not guilt my granddaughter into making me think I've forgotten this simply because I love that couch."*

"See? Was that so hard?"

"Yes."

The video cut off, and I sent him a smug grin.

"Rude," he muttered. "Who raised you?"

"You."

Gavin waited for my nod, then smacked a green Post-it on the back of the couch. Pops glared at that too. "Perfectly good couch."

"So is mine," I reminded him. "It's bigger than yours and doesn't have springs that poke you in the ass if you sit wrong."

He harrumphed. "Just keeps you from getting too comfortable. Kids these days watch too much TV anyway, so I think it's a good thing."

Gavin moved behind Pops and fiddled with the edge of his shirt collar. No matter the weather, no matter the occasion, my grandfather always wore a short-sleeved dress shirt and a bow tie, with a white undershirt beneath that was visible through the top layer. Today it was a light-blue shirt and a navy tie with white polka dots.

"Where'd you get this one?" Gavin asked, gently touching the bow tie.

"New York City," he answered. "I was twenty years old and wanted something nice for my first day on the job in the county clerk's office. Your grandma, God rest her soul, went into the city with me, even though she hated it, and we picked out this and about five others." He winked. "Best ties in the world."

"How many do you have in total?"

"Not sure."

"Too many," I answered. "But we won't donate those, I promise."

Pops motioned for one on the stack sitting on his dresser. Gavin picked up a red one with white pinstripes and held it out.

"No, you," Pops said, tapping the side of Gavin's neck. "Your turn, little bug."

His eyes widened. "Really? You'll teach me?"

"We'll have more time together now, won't we?"

While Pops drew Gavin closer and patiently walked him through the steps of how to tie a bow tie, I watched them from the corner of my eye as I folded a few of his favorite blankets, crocheted by my grandmother shortly after they'd gotten married. No matter the season, the blankets that covered his bed were hers—one in shades of red and maroon and pink. The other, green and white and orange.

I ran my hand over the woven strands and closed the box, slid the packing tape over the top, and then marked the contents with a Sharpie.

Gavin ran over and tipped up his chin. "Look!"

It was lopsided and far too loose. I touched the tip of his nose. "Perfect."

He ran into the bathroom to check his reflection, and Pops stood from his chair with a small groan. It was getting harder for him to get around, and he'd already fallen twice. The fact that he'd only ended up with bruises was a miracle, and the final straw in convincing him to move in with us.

"You sure about this, bug?"

I set the box of blankets on top of the others in the corner. "What do you think?"

He grimaced. "I just feel bad. I've always . . . I've always been able to take care of you. Feels wrong that you have to take care of me now."

I sat on the edge of the bed and quietly watched him take a section of hangers holding his dress shirts and hang them in one of the wardrobe boxes. His grizzled face—the one I'd loved before I knew what *love* meant—looked sad.

"Family takes care of each other. Someone very wise used to tell me that when I'd worry about the same thing."

He made a gruff, impatient noise. "That was different."

"How? I was no picnic in high school. And then I brought home a baby about a month after I got my diploma. You're telling me you're going to be more high maintenance than that?"

Pops's shoulders slumped. "I hate getting old, Remington."

My heart squeezed when he called me that. It wasn't my given name, but every once in a while, he said it was appropriate. His little pistol. The one that kept him young, he said.

I stood and slid my arm around his waist, laying my head on his stooped shoulder. "I know."

He kissed the top of my head, patting my hand where it lay on his stomach. "I'll be better about taking my meds, I promise. And maybe, hell . . . maybe I'll eat healthier too. Cut back on my red meat and french fries."

"Why do you think I'm giving up my guest room? It's so I can keep my eye on you all the time, old man." I dropped a quick kiss on his cheek and went back to packing more boxes. "I'll keep these out of your way for the next couple days. I can take a few of them tonight, but I need to find someone with a truck who'll help with your bed, the dresser, and the bench."

Gavin's head popped around the corner. "What about Archer? He's got a truck, and he's already helped Mom once."

Pops gave me a stern look. "Has he, now?"

"Oh yeah, he found me a babysitter and came over to the house and everything. He's so tall!"

Since when did my kid get so friggin' chatty?

"You told me it was just a few hours a week picking up dog shit."

Gavin rolled his eyes. "Language, Pops."

Pops waved him away. "I'm too old to stop swearing. You'll get over it, kiddo."

I slicked my tongue over my teeth and met Pops's unrelenting stare. "Gavin, can you go get my water out of the car? I think I left it in the front seat."

"Sure." He took off.

Pops pointed. "That water?"

"Yup." I picked it up off the floor, where it had been sitting out of Gavin's line of sight. "It's not how it sounds, okay? I needed a babysitter and his sister was available. She was amazing, actually. Gavin loved her."

Pops's mouth twisted into a frown. "I don't like it. He's a bad influence to have around Gavin. That boy might have been upset at first, but you get him around a man like that and he'll idolize him even more than he already did."

I rubbed my forehead. "I know."

Boy, did I know. I'd added that to an entirely new list, the one I'd started repeating as a mantra when lying awake the last two nights, unable to think about anything else but him as sleep remained frustratingly out of reach.

"A man who drinks and drives is the kind of man—"

"Pops, please."

"No, Remi, you have to listen. I know he's handsome and successful, but—"

I set my hands on his shoulders. *"Pops."*

At my firm tone, his head reared back. "What?"

Could I do it?

It would break my promise to Archer. But there were times when keeping a secret didn't benefit anyone, falling squarely in shades of gray on the scale of right or wrong.

Just like lying to cover for someone you loved.

Guilt and indecision fought for the top spot in my head, but when it came down to it, I didn't want Pops to hate him. I couldn't handle him looking at Archer and thinking he was a bad person.

"I have to tell you something, but you cannot tell another soul. Do you understand me?"

He blinked. "You're pretty serious, bug."

"I mean it." Then I held out my pinkie. "If you can't keep it a secret, I can't tell you."

After a disgruntled sigh that I knew was for show more than anything, Pops hooked his pinkie around mine and squeezed. He tilted his chin. "This better be good."

When I'd finished telling him Archer's secret, his mouth hung open, and he fumbled behind himself for the chair, lowering his body slowly. "My God."

"He's not a bad person. I misjudged him, but a lot of that is because of what he wanted people to believe."

Pops had a faraway look in his eye. "That's a big lie to tell, bug."

"I know." I sat on the bed again, bracing my elbows on the tops of my thighs, my chin resting on my fisted hands. "I wish he'd come clean, but damn if I don't respect him even more for not."

His cloudy gray eyes were far too knowing when they came to rest on me again. "How much do you *respect* him?" he asked.

I rolled my eyes. "We're . . . friends. Sort of. Trying to be."

"Friends. With the quarterback of the Buffalo Storm."

"Yup."

And I also knew the general size and shape of his dick, but I was not going to be sharing that with the class.

"Huh. Well, will your friend let you borrow his truck?"

I laughed. "Probably. You sure you'd want me to ask him for help?"

"Why the hell not? He's a lot stronger than both of us, and I can't lift that damn dresser." Pops stood again, smacking the arm of his chair as he did. "It'll make him feel good, doing something for a helpless old man."

I snorted. "'Helpless' my ass."

"Language," he said as he walked out of his bedroom.

With a sigh, I flopped back on the bed.

Gavin flew into the room, breathing heavily. "I looked everywhere. I don't know where your water is."

"It's okay, bud. I found it."

"Cool. Can I go mark those ugly dishes in the kitchen?"

"Whose dishes are ugly?" Pops bellowed.

Gavin giggled, disappearing from the room again.

For a moment, I closed my eyes. The need for a quick nap was so strong, but it was past dinnertime, and I really wanted to be able to sleep tonight.

Dinner. Shit. We hadn't eaten yet.

"Do you guys want me to make something for dinner?" I called, eyes still closed. "I could whip up some omelets."

"No," they said in unison. A curious beat of silence followed.

"No thanks," Gavin amended. "Pops said he'd order us some pizza."

My brow furrowed. "You're sure? That'll take longer."

"We're sure," Pops said. "You . . . you just text your friend about the truck. I'll take care of dinner."

"Fine." I rolled onto my side and pulled up Archer's contact information. A bright burst of nerves tipped my stomach sideways, then it righted almost immediately. This wasn't big. Just a friend asking a friend for a favor.

Lies.

Lies, lies, lies.

Every interaction with this man was loaded, and by this point, it had gotten so far out of my control, there was nothing to do but try to keep a level head.

I needed a truck and some strong hands.

He had both.

And . . . he looked at me like he wanted to devour me whole, so he'd probably say yes to anything I asked. Anything.

Any. Thing.

I set my jaw and started typing. No more nonsense. There was no need to spiral just because I was asking him for help. A grown-ass woman didn't spiral over such things.

Me: Hey, I hope I'm not interrupting anything, but can I ask you a huge favor?

Archer: You're interrupting a mighty battle with weeds along the side of my house. Ask away.

Me: You do your own weeding? I call bullshit.

Archer attached a picture—his face glistening with sweat, and next to his frowning, sweaty, glistening face was an angry-looking weed with clumps of dirt clinging to the roots. The picture cut off just below his collarbone, but he was shirtless. The rounded muscles of his shoulders made my mouth go dry. Those were all glisten-y too.

For *fuck's* sake. Those shoulders were borderline indecent. And looking like that while frowning? Ridiculous. Some decorum in this pseudo-friendship would not go unappreciated.

Me: I stand corrected.

Archer: Tell me what you need.

Me: You and your truck. If you're available.

Archer: I'm going to need more specifics, because I'm not sure we should trust my deductive abilities where you're concerned.

Me: Are you trying to flirt with me? We're friends now.

Archer: If I was flirting with you, you'd fucking know it.

Me: I guess I'll have to take your word on that.

Me: I was hoping you'd be willing to help move a couple pieces of furniture. My grandfather is moving in with me and Gavin, and he has a few things he's taking with him.

Archer: Of course. When do you need me?

Me: I think we're both at the shelter tomorrow, but the day after?

Archer: As long as it's after one, that works for me.

Archer: Just furniture?

Me: Yeah, I'm doing a couple trips today with boxes that I can fit in my car.

Archer: Don't. Just let me handle everything.

Me: Are you sure? I didn't mean for you to bring everything.

Archer: Haven't you figured out by now that if I'm offering, then I want to do it?

Me: Thank you. I can't tell you how much I appreciate it.

Archer: Feel free to thank me with a picture of what you're doing. If you happen to be shirtless, it would keep us on even ground.

Me: Archer . . .

Archer: That was also not flirting. It was a statement of fact.

I sent him a picture of me glaring at the camera.

Archer: Exactly what I was hoping for. That's one of my top five favorite facial expressions on you. Adding it to my list.

Archer: Must have the most beautiful glare I've ever seen.

Me: You're ridiculous.

Archer: Remi?

Me: Yes.

Archer: That was me flirting.

My face was beyond heated as I tucked my phone away.

"Mom, what are you smiling about?"

I wasn't. Was I?

Except I was. When my fingertips traced over my mouth, sure enough. Undeniable proof.

And when I looked over at Gavin, I was still smiling. "Nothing."

Chapter Nineteen

Archer

"You sure this is it?"

Remi's car was nowhere to be found, but the address matched the one she'd sent. It wasn't far from where she lived, and based on what I was seeing, it was a neighborhood meant solely for older people.

The homes were connected like condos, four per grouping. The aluminum siding was faded from time, and each unit had the same face—a single garage stall, a front door with a square stoop covered with an aluminum overhang, and a small window to the side of the front door.

Blocky, geometric hedges lined the front of a lot of the units, but some residents had seemed to have swapped those out for flowers. Remi's grandfather was one of those people. The front of his home was more open because of it, a neatly kept landscaping bed filled with red flowers.

Williams leaned in. "Where's Remi?"

"Not here, dumbass."

He grimaced. "So are we just hanging out in the street until she gets here?"

A face appeared in the front window, then disappeared again.

In the unit next door, a door opened with a loud squeak. The woman was wearing a bright-blue bathrobe over a printed muumuu, her hair wrapped in a scarf. "You two looking for someone? We don't allow solicitation here."

"No, ma'am, we're here to help him move," I said, gesturing at the home in front of us.

"Huh. Harold didn't tell me he hired movers." Her eyes narrowed, shifting between Williams and me. "Do I know you two?"

"Maybe?" Williams said. "We both—"

I reached up and pinched his side. Hard.

"Ouch, fuck. Why did you do that?"

"Shut *up*, Williams."

She crossed her arms, eyes still narrowed in suspicion, and I saw the moment she realized it. Her mouth fell open, eyes took up half her face. "You—"

"Maude, quit harassing these two. Go watch *Wheel of Fortune*."

The man who came out from the house in front of us was tall, with a proud bearing and thick white hair combed off his face. Dressed in a white, short-sleeved button-down and a purple bow tie, he looked more like he was about to officiate a wedding.

"Harold, do you know—"

"Maude," he interrupted, "I told you to keep your nose out of my business."

She pulled a disposal camera out of the pocket of her robe, brought it to her face, and snapped a picture, immediately cranking the little plastic wheel to take another one.

When I glanced over, Williams was giving her a big toothy grin.

Idiot.

"Maude, go inside," Remi's grandfather said more loudly. "And don't you go calling everyone to gossip."

She tightened the belt on her bathrobe with a haughty sniff. "You're not my boss, Harold."

"No, but you need one," he muttered. "Damn busybody."

When she disappeared into her house with an angry slam of the front door, he shook his head before giving me his full attention.

"Sir, I'm Archer." I held out my hand. He eyed it for a moment, his gaze sharp and knowing, then clasped it firmly. "It's a pleasure to meet you."

"Harold Sinclair. I've been a Buffalo fan my entire life, but I'll circle back later on whether it's a pleasure to meet you two." He brought himself up to his full height, trying as best he could to straighten his shoulders. "I like watching a game of football, especially with my great-grandson, but I won't blow smoke up your asses because you make more money than I do."

"Fair enough." I elbowed the rookie. "This is Grant Williams."

Harold's eyes widened. "The new receiver from Michigan? You had a hell of a senior year, kid."

"Thank you, sir."

"How'd he get you to come with?"

"Blackmail," Williams answered easily. "I embarrassed the hell out of him the other day with your granddaughter, sir. He's got quite a crush on her, and this is my punishment if I ever want to catch touchdowns this year."

Tongue slicking over my front teeth, I gave Williams an unamused look. "Thanks," I said tersely. "That's an excellent way to start off on the right foot."

The rookie shrugged. "It's the truth, isn't it? I believe in telling the truth whenever you can."

"Maybe not with this," I snapped.

Remi's grandfather's bewildered gaze bounced between the two of us. I sucked in a breath, waiting to see how he'd react.

He started laughing.

Big, deep, booming laughs, and I exhaled slowly, tension ebbing from my frame.

Harold wiped his eyes when tears gathered. "Oh goodness, that's the funniest shit I've heard in a long time."

The sound of two car doors preceded Remi's voice behind us. "Sorry we're late. I baked some muffins and they took a little longer than I thought."

The sight of Remi was a blow to my chest, and like a fool, I'd line up to take that hit over and over and over, until there was nothing left.

This woman had already wrecked me, and still I wanted more. I wanted nothing but for her to tear down whatever I was before I'd met her. Maybe what was left would be the good parts, the parts I'd never really tried to find until now.

Her eyes found mine, color creeping up her cheekbones. "Hey."

"Hey."

Friends, I thought. This woman, this exquisite creature, wanted me to be her fucking friend. Yeah, right. She wasn't looking at me like a friend, either, and my stomach twisted pleasantly when she fidgeted nervously with her hair. It was braided back today, but a few tendrils had escaped, fluttering around her face.

The way I wanted Remi Sinclair defied every law of logic in existence. And if she allowed me to stay in her orbit much longer, I'd fall in love with her.

Wasn't I already halfway there?

What else would you call this sickening feeling that gnawed ceaselessly at my insides? Even when I shouldn't be, I was thinking of her. Wondering where she was and what she was doing. How she'd react if I did something like buy her a new car or pay off the mortgage on her house. Something—anything—to bring a smile to her face, even if she didn't know it was me.

Remi blinked, severing the relentless build of energy as we stared at each other. I could breathe more easily now, but I wasn't sure that was a good thing. If I choked to death on my feelings for this woman, I'd probably do it with a smile on my face.

"Pops, did you meet Archer?" Gavin came tearing around the front of the car, stopping short when he saw the rookie. "Whoa," he breathed. "You're—you're Grant Williams."

Williams smiled easily, holding his hand out for a fist bump. "And you must be Gavin. Archer told me all about you."

"He *did*?"

The look Gavin gave me—full of awe—was a double-edged sword. No matter how much we didn't want it to be true, athletes and celebrities and musicians carried the weight of children like Gavin. None of us went into our respective fields wanting to be role models, but when you were good enough, popular enough, your platform stretching far enough across the globe, impressionable kids looked up to you.

I'd ignored that for a long time.

But I couldn't anymore.

"Of course I did," I told Gavin. "Listen, I felt really bad that I couldn't come in and see your room before, so I wanted to find a way to make it up to you."

He stared, wide-eyed, at Williams. "This works for me."

We all laughed.

I cleared my throat. "No, I brought him so we had an extra set of hands and another truck. But I'd still love to see your room, if you want to show me."

"Yeah, I can . . . I can do that." He puffed out his chest and looked at Williams. "Would you want to see it too?"

"Of course, dude. I bet your room is awesome."

Remi glanced at the second truck parked next to mine. "I thought you had the fancy sports car."

Williams shrugged. "What can I say? I have a weakness for vehicles."

She shook her head, a tiny smile playing around her lips. When she finally looked in my direction, what I saw there left me breathless with anticipation. With a plate of muffins clutched to her stomach, she met me halfway.

"Two football players for the price of one, huh?"

"Please don't slap Williams. I'd hate to think he gets the same treatment as me."

Remi laughed, and fuck, did I love what it did to her eyes.

Harold cleared his throat. "Come on now, we've got shit to do, and I'm not getting any younger."

"Pops," Gavin groaned.

"I know, I know. Language."

Remi smiled. "Anyone want a muffin before we start?"

Williams's hand shot up. "I love muffins."

"I hope you like banana," she said, pulling the clear wrap off the top.

Just as I went to reach for one, Harold caught my eye behind Remi's back. He shook his head frantically, mouthing *No*. Gavin covered his mouth to hide his smile. My brow furrowed, hand frozen mid-reach.

Remi glanced back, and her grandfather's face smoothed out. He patted his generous stomach. "I'm still full from my afternoon snack, bug, but thank you."

Remi shrugged.

"You know, I'm good, thank you," I answered carefully, giving her grandfather another curious look. He nodded like I'd made the right decision.

Williams popped half a muffin into his big mouth, took a few bites, and then froze. He tried to chew, his mouth moving even more slowly.

"It's a new recipe," Remi said, watching him closely. "I hope it's okay."

"Gweat," he said, mouth still stuffed full of muffin. "Reawy gweat."

She exhaled. "Good. Okay, let's get to work."

Harold motioned for us to hang back as Gavin and Remi walked into the house.

Williams was still trying to chew. Unsuccessfully, by the looks of it.

Harold pulled a napkin from his pocket and handed it to him. "Here you go, son."

The muffin came out as soon as the napkin was up to his mouth.

"That bad?" I asked.

"Like trying to eat glue," Williams answered gravely.

Harold sighed. "I love that girl, but she is the worst cook I've ever met in my life."

I laughed quietly. "Good to know she has a flaw somewhere."

Harold gave me a sharp look.

Williams whistled. "I'm gonna go help inside, I think." Then he nodded at Harold. "Thank you for the napkin, sir."

He patted his pocket. "I always carry some, just in case she springs something new on me."

After the rookie jogged into the house, Harold laid a hand on my arm to hold me back, and we were left alone.

Based on the scrutiny in his weathered face, there was a good chance I was in for a *what are your intentions toward my granddaughter* talk. My entire body braced for impact.

Harold pursed his lips before he spoke. "She told me your secret."

Okay then. Maybe not.

When my brow furrowed, he held up a hand. "Now, don't get mad at her."

I wasn't sure I was capable of that—not really—but there was a sharp pinch of betrayal over the fact that she hadn't even lasted a week without telling someone. "I'm not mad," I said carefully. "But I did ask her to keep it a secret. It's important that I protect my sister."

"Yeah, so she said." He adjusted his glasses. "I was in the middle of a phenomenal rant about why she should keep Gavin away from you, and *her* protective instincts kicked in too," he said pointedly. "She didn't much like what I was saying about you."

The way satisfaction seeped through my entire body was absolutely fucking pathetic. I should've been pissed. Should've been furious that she'd betrayed my trust. Except the only thing blaring through my head was *Tell me fucking everything.*

What did she look like?

What did she say?

How—and tell me in great detail—did she say it?

I couldn't remember a time anyone had been protective of me, and God, it felt like executing the perfect pass just before a sack, running in a touchdown when the defense doesn't see me coming, the winning moment that unfolded against all odds.

A skin-tingling high that you'd chase over and over and over.

I kept my expression even because he'd probably cuff me on the back of the head if I told him any of that. "Ah, please don't . . . please don't tell anyone."

"I'll agree to that," he said. "As long as you don't stare at my granddaughter's ass while I'm around. I might be a lot older and a lot slower, but I could still whip you, boy."

"Yes, sir." I winced. "I'll do my best."

He nodded. "See that you do."

Chapter Twenty

Remi

The amount of time it took me, Gavin, and the two strapping athletes to unload Pops's entire life was not indicative of how long it had taken us to pack, sort, and donate his entire life prior to move-in day.

All four of us had vehemently denied his request to help unload, so he was the traffic director instead, perched on the edge of his new bed, instructing us on where he'd like everything to go. While Archer and Grant (I refused to call him by his last name) moved the larger pieces into the house, Gavin and I started unpacking the wardrobe boxes.

We had already gone through two, and I shifted hangers around as Gavin passed them to me, keeping the colors grouped together the way Pops liked them.

"No, no, not that way. I want the dresser on the other wall instead."

Grant and Archer froze, as they'd almost set the heavy wooden dresser into place where I'd instructed.

"Are you sure?" I asked. "This is a bigger wall."

Pops nodded. "We can put my chair by that wall instead. Then I can see into the front yard when I come take my afternoon quiet time."

I snorted. "You mean when you snore for four hours, all the while pretending you don't ever nap?"

"I've never napped a day in my life," he said, utterly affronted. Archer turned his face into his arm, clearly hiding a growing smile. "I'm just resting my eyes." He tapped his cane on the floor. "Dresser over here, gentlemen."

Archer swung his end around, the two of them pivoting positions. Against my better judgment, my eyes took a lazy perusal over the way his muscles flexed as he carried that piece of furniture like it weighed absolutely nothing.

The curves of his biceps were obscene, like someone had wedged perfectly round boulders underneath the skin. It really was no wonder his ego was the size of a small nation. If I were a man walking around looking like him, I'd probably be full of myself too.

"Is there a bathroom I can use?" Grant asked.

I smiled. "Gavin, can you show him where it is?"

I was on a roll this week. A second NFL player waltzing through my home and I wasn't worried about scuffed trim or the fact that my end tables didn't match.

All that was left to be moved into the room was Pops's chair. While he waited for Grant to return, Archer picked up a dustcloth and wiped down the top of the dresser, then the face of each drawer, spending a little extra time around the aged brass handles. The veins along the tops of his hands shifted as he rubbed.

I swear to God, I felt it between my legs.

Pops cleared his throat, and I ignored the pointed look in his eyes, heat crawling along the back of my neck. So what if I was staring? Staring wasn't illegal. Not at veiny hands like that.

"I can unpack those," Pops said.

"I'm almost done with this box. Then it's just dresser stuff." I hung the last of the hangers and shifted the cumbersome box out of my way. "Don't worry, I'll let you do your own underwear."

Gavin shouted for Pops from the other room.

"What?" Pops shouted back.

"You've already got a bird at your feeder! It's one of those cute gray ones with the orange on it."

Pops pushed up from the bed. "A tufted titmouse? Don't scare him off, little bug, I want to see."

Archer and I traded an amused look as he left the room, and the heat from my neck climbed just a little bit higher.

"We get very excited about birds around here," I said.

"I do love a good titmouse."

I rolled my eyes, which made him laugh. God, what a laugh it was too. It wasn't loud or boisterous or meant to draw attention. It was quiet. Amused. Low enough that I had to strain to hear it. Deep enough that it sent a shiver down my spine.

Fortunately for me, he didn't notice, already looking for something else to do.

As I worked on the chunk of clothes, I watched from the corner of my eye as the edge of Archer's mouth lifted in a tiny smile. The box at his feet was pulled open, and a framed collage of pictures, just me and Pops, sat above a few others.

I set the burgundy sweater on top of a black one, allowing him a moment to look without interruption.

"When was this?" he asked.

Archer angled the frame so I could see it better, his pointer finger tapping at the bottom corner. I smiled. Pops had his arm around me, both of us younger and skinnier than we were now, and we were standing in front of the maroon Cadillac he used to drive. In my hand was a set of keys, the picture taken while I was mid-laugh. Pops was about to burst into tears.

"That was the summer I got my driver's license." I brushed a speck of dust off the glass. "He taught me how to drive in a church parking lot down the road from the house where we lived at the time. He was more stressed out for my driver's test than when I had to do testing at school."

"Why?"

"Because he had to drive me everywhere, and he kept talking about how he was so ready to hang up his chauffeur hat." I smiled softly. "And the day I got my license, he couldn't stop crying."

"How come?"

Even if lingering eye contact was a terrible idea in such close proximity, my eyes found his all the same. "Because we lost time together. Hours in the car every week, where he'd hear about my day. What I was stressed about. What made me happy. Until I got the keys, he didn't realize how precious all that time really was."

Archer tilted his head back, a small humming sound coming from the back of his throat. "I've never thought about it that way. But my mom was long gone back then, and my father never would've taken the time to talk about anything other than football, even if he did sit in the car with me."

There were deep-blue streaks in his eyes that I'd never noticed.

"How did you get around if it wasn't him?"

"I had a driver," he said, having the good sense to look slightly abashed.

"Of course you did," I murmured.

His face creased with a grin—a deeply, unfairly attractive grin—and while I tried to settle the burst of deeply, unfairly strong nerves at what that grin did to me, Archer shifted the slightest bit closer, his bicep brushing against my bare shoulder.

The air changed with that movement, small though it was. The simple addition of his skin on mine, no matter how innocent, made my mouth go dry.

"How old were you when your mom left?" I asked.

This was why I was single, ladies and gentlemen. A moment of ripe sexual tension and my first response was to ask about his childhood wound. Like a fucking *pro*.

To his credit, though, Archer didn't seem deterred.

"Eleven."

I rubbed at my heart. "I'm sorry. That's so young, but still old enough to remember."

"Not as young as Analise," he said lightly. "A couple years of trying to handle two kids, even with the help of nannies, and she was gone. Took a payout from my father and walked away."

"I will never understand," I whispered.

"That's because you're a good mom."

I turned to look up into his face. "Mine died when I was five. Heart attack that was likely caused by the drugs and the drinks she loved."

His face fell. "Remi, I—" Archer swallowed, giving his head a slight shake. "Fuck, I don't know what to say."

"It's all right. I don't usually give the full story because it's easier to say she had a heart attack and leave it at that. It's a more palatable tragedy, isn't it?"

We both had had mothers who chose something else over us, and I couldn't help but wonder how much of our worst impulses, the ones we'd flung at each other so early in this relationship, stemmed from the seeds they'd planted.

His gaze lingered on the side of my face as I set the picture down. "Thankfully, I had my grandparents. My grandma died about two years later—Pops always said it was from a broken heart."

Archer was quiet for a moment, letting out a sigh before he spoke.

"It's amazing, isn't it? How much destruction broken people can leave behind. And they move on without a second thought of what's trailing behind them as a result." Archer reached up and tucked some of my loose hair back, his thumb tracing the shell of my ear. My spine shook, but I kept still, stayed unmoving. "You turned out better than I did, though."

"Archer, your life is hardly a waste. Look at all you've accomplished."

"I'm not fishing for compliments." His eyes briefly glanced over my shoulder toward the other room, where the Pops and Gavin were watching the birds. When he seemed sure we still had privacy, his gaze locked on mine again, and he dragged his thumb down the edge of my jaw. "In every metric that matters, you're a better person than me. You burn so bright, and I'm not even sure you realize how powerful it is, being around the kind of light you generate."

He might not have fit a single criterion on my silly little list, meant to protect myself from exactly the kind of destruction he was talking about, but there was no mistaking it anymore: I'd have an Archer-size hole in my heart when he walked out of my life.

His features were blurry now, and I willed back the tears. When I opened my mouth to respond, he gently pressed his thumb to my lips. "Don't worry, I'm not flirting."

I had to blink a few times to clear my vision. "I'm not sure I believe you."

Archer took a step back, his gaze tracking over my face. "Just stating a fact, firefly."

A smile threatened before I could stop it. "Firefly?"

"Yeah. Pretty and bright. Everyone loves seeing them around because they make things a little bit more magical." He tugged gently on the end of my ponytail. "Am I allowed to use that one?"

There was no way I could speak over the emotions wedged tight in my throat, but I managed a shaky nod.

His eyes warmed. "Good."

Archer's hand slipped down my arm, the wall of his chest skimming my shoulder when he left the room. I speared my hands in my hair and blew out a slow breath through puffed cheeks.

"Holy shit, I am so out of my league," I whispered.

Luckily for my rapidly shredding sense of self-preservation, the rest of the items were moved quickly and without further incidents of rampant sexual tension, flirty not-flirting, or big trauma-sharing for either party.

Grant said his goodbyes—we learned he had dinner plans with someone he refused to talk about, but his cheeks turned flame red upon mentioning her—but made sure to take a couple pictures with Gavin, who proclaimed it to be "the best day of his entire life."

Archer could have left, but he didn't.

I could've questioned it, but I didn't.

Gavin disappeared to his room to play on his tablet, insisting over and over that he wasn't tired, despite the zombie-ish look in his eyes. Ten minutes later, I found him fast asleep on his bed.

He'd borrowed one of the blankets from Pops's bed—the green one he'd always said was his favorite—and it was bunched up over his feet. The tablet hung limply from his hands, and with his mouth open, he emitted a tiny snore.

I tiptoed in, much like I had when he was little, and settled myself on the floor so I could be at his height. When I pulled the blanket up over his body, I did it carefully, then eased the tablet out of his grip and laid it on the nightstand next to his bed. It was so tempting, in these moments of quiet, to run my hand through his hair or brush my fingers over his cheek. The boyish features were slowly melting away, and underneath were hints of what he'd look like as he grew.

Ten years had gone by in a blink. I set my chin on my forearm and watched him sleep, wondering if he was dreaming about football.

The floor behind me creaked, and I knew it was Archer. Both Pops and I knew to step over that spot when we were trying not to wake Gavin. I looked over my shoulder and smiled sheepishly. "You caught me."

"Doing what?"

"Doing cringey mom things."

Archer's mouth tipped up in a smile, and he leaned his shoulder against the doorframe while I pressed my burning cheek against my arm. "Like what?"

"Watching him breathe."

His eyes glinted with humor. "Just let me know if you want to watch me breathe in my sleep."

I stifled a laugh and kept my voice hushed. "You're so accommodating. I had no idea."

Archer's gaze swept over Gavin's room. It was small—just enough space for a twin bed and nightstand, his dresser, and a small bookshelf that held knickknacks and collectibles. Filling the shelves were a few LEGO sets he'd assembled with Pops, framed pictures, his favorite book series, and a miniature Buffalo helmet he'd bought with Christmas money.

"He's a good kid. You should be really proud."

"Thank you." I glanced back at Gavin, who let out another snore. Deciding it was worth the risk, I ran my fingers through the hair along the top of his head and leaned over to press a kiss to his forehead.

When I stood up, Archer was studying a LEGO car Gavin had finished a few weeks earlier.

"If you break a piece off, you'll be in so much trouble."

Archer smirked, carefully studying the bright-blue car. "He told me about every piece he's made."

"No wonder you were in here for a while." I'd take a bullet for my kid, but listening to him talk about one of his obsessions for thirty minutes nonstop required a supernatural level of patience. "I'm sorry."

"Don't be." His eyes shifted to mine. "He said this was his favorite."

"Yeah, he wanted that set for a long time. Every time we see a Porsche, he flips out."

Archer hummed, the timbre of his voice low and quiet. "He's got good taste."

"He better marry someone with money if he wants one of those."

The wide grin on Archer's face made my belly flip. I gestured behind him. "We should let him sleep," I said gently.

As Archer carefully set the car back down, there was a look of disappointment on his face that made me restless. Unsettled.

Wouldn't he want to leave?

If we played that dangerous comparison game, I knew who'd win by a landslide, at least if we were weighing the obvious metrics. No one would take my life over his.

And yet my house was where he lingered. Where he told my grandfather stories from playing college ball that made Pops laugh. Where he studied pictures and asked questions, like he genuinely wanted to know more.

Maybe it didn't matter to him that we had a small house and always drove used vehicles. Maybe it didn't matter that I had my entire life budgeted down to the last penny and hadn't flown on a plane since I was sixteen because vacations were for people with discretionary income and that was a category where I did not fit.

Maybe it really was the simple things that he craved, the things that were so easy to take for granted.

I had so many things that couldn't be quantified. A good man who'd raised me when he didn't have to, and fed my spirit when it could have been crushed on the path of someone else's destruction. A son who adored me. A job that nourished my soul and made me happy. And friends who would answer whenever I needed them.

The wealth in my possession was rooted in things that couldn't be bought.

When we left Gavin's room, Pops was outside on the back deck, trying to snap a picture of a bird at the feeder. The two of us returned to the bedroom and got back to work. Archer wordlessly pulled the empty boxes out of my way, using a knife to flatten them down.

He stayed.

He didn't have to, and I didn't ask. But still, he stayed.

It felt important that he did, and I wondered if that was because I was assigning meaning to things that were far simpler than I was making them.

If he noticed that I stayed quiet, he didn't say anything, simply let the silence be what it was.

Contemplative. Weighted. Anticipatory.

Once the last box was unpacked, Archer's fingers brushed mine as I handed it off to be flattened. I waited for some heavy eye contact, but his eyes were on the task at hand. His obvious lingering was so endearing, I could hardly stand it. I toyed with the idea of inviting him to stay for dinner.

There were leftovers in the fridge. It wasn't anything fancy.

Dinner with me and Archer and Pops. Oof. Talk about weighted. There was meaning behind that kind of invitation. Between the two of us, I was the one putting up a barrier, and it didn't seem fair to lead him on if I wasn't prepared to tear that barrier down.

My grandfather shook Archer's hand before he left. "I'm glad you're not a dick," he said.

I rubbed my face as Archer laughed. "Thank you, sir. I'm glad you're not either."

With Archer's back turned, I gave Pops an incredulous look.

He winked.

Archer lifted the stack of flattened cardboard with ease, maneuvering it out into the driveway, where he stacked it next to the recycle bin.

He was wiping his hands along the sides of his jeans when I joined him in front of the house.

"Thank you," I told him, shyly crossing my arms over my stomach. "I appreciate your help more than I can say."

His gaze lingered on my face. "What are friends for?"

I smiled, then rolled my lips together to hide it. "Right."

He tilted his head toward the house. "I should say goodbye to Gavin."

"Oh, he'll be out all night now."

Archer nodded. "Tell him I said goodbye." Then he smiled. It was small but genuine, and it tugged on something deep below my navel. "I had fun today."

"Me too."

An air of hesitancy hung around us like a dense fog. An unwillingness to walk away, but not ready to say things we shouldn't either. Anticipation for either option seemed to leave us both paralyzed.

"Good night, firefly."

It made no sense, the frantic urge to tug him closer when he turned to leave. But it was there, a wild buzzing through my veins.

Don't go.

Don't *go.*

I wanted to scream it. I wanted to see what would happen if I grabbed his hand as he walked away. But the words stayed locked in my throat. A decade of well-honed self-preservation was a ghastly weapon, one that had a hard time being set aside.

When he froze at the end of the driveway, my heart jolted in my chest.

Stay, I thought. *Turn around. Ask me . . . ask me if you can stay.*

"Shit."

"What?"

Archer sighed, then gestured to his truck. "Flat tire. I must have run over a nail or something." He rubbed the back of his neck. "And my truck doesn't have a spare."

The universe had a Machiavellian sense of humor.

The last thing we needed was to be cooped up together inside my dependable sedan.

The *last* fucking thing.

But this was me, and the urge to help someone I liked would always be greater than avoiding the things I was afraid of.

"I can bring you home."

His eyes snapped to mine. "Are you sure?"

No.

Yes.

Definitely not.

"What are friends for?"

Chapter Twenty-One

Archer

We walked to her car in silence, sharing a quick, loaded glance over the roof of her vehicle before she unlocked the doors. Remi's car was mostly clean, only some soccer cleats and an extra water bottle on the passenger side, which she tossed onto the floor behind her. In the back seat was a bag holding reusable grocery totes and a small stack of books that must have tipped over as she was driving.

The console held ChapStick, some spare change, a hair tie, and a bright-pink container of hand sanitizer. A large reusable water bottle covered with colorful stickers sat in one of the two cupholders.

Everything about her life was so heartbreakingly normal to me, in a way that almost hurt, and I fucking loved that she didn't apologize for having stuff in her car.

"You're probably gonna want to—"

My helpless grunt as I tried to fit into the passenger seat cut her off, because I was about seven inches too tall to fit. Her voice broke off into choked laughter.

"You'll want to slide that seat back before you get in," she finished around a wide smile.

"Thanks for the warning." I found the lever on the side of the seat and pushed it back as far as it could go. Better. Not perfect, but better.

"Your truck is probably immaculate on the inside, isn't it?"

"Afraid so. Growing up, I was convinced that if a single piece of garbage touched the interior of my father's car, the entire thing would self-destruct. Can't help but be influenced by that."

I pulled my seat belt over and clicked it into place as she sent her grandfather a text, letting him know what she was doing.

The dirt decorating the side of my truck caught her attention, and she gave me a quick look. "Not the outside, though. Even mine is cleaner than that."

I grinned. "I live on a dirt road. Just finished building the house a couple months ago, and I haven't gotten around to getting the drive out to the road done yet. Washing my truck regularly is an exercise in futility. The bonus is that it drives my old man fucking crazy."

My ribs squeezed tight as she handed me her phone so I could type in my address. What did she expect to find? I hadn't built my home thinking about anyone else's approval, but I found myself desperate for hers.

Remi wasn't thinking about my house. Her mind, apparently, was still on the last thing I'd said.

"Do you hate him?" Her eyes were big in her face when she turned them in my direction briefly. "It sounds like you might."

I allowed my head to rest and closed my eyes while I thought about how to answer.

"Sometimes." I turned to watch her, soaking in the details of her profile. "Not often enough."

Her brows bent in a thoughtful V. "What do you mean?"

"Friends don't judge each other, right?"

"They don't." Remi smiled. God, that smile made me fucking weak. "You should hear some of the things Ness tells me, and you'd know the answer to that."

It was a lighthearted comment that was meant to make me feel better, but it didn't. Turmoil over my relationship with my father had festered inside me for so long, it felt like lancing an infected wound to open up about it now.

On another night, I might not have answered. But after hours of watching her take care of people she loved, watching her smile and laugh and be a horrible cook and not know it, watching her extend herself over and over because her heart was as big as the entire world, I knew that giving her some truth was the only way to navigate what I was feeling.

What I was feeling for her.

If I put on a mask or tried to be perfect, she'd know. She'd see. And it would shatter whatever tentative truce we'd found ourselves in.

Swallowing that instinct to show her my good side, the perfect side, was like shoving the arm of a cactus straight down into my gut, but I did it all the same.

My voice was rough when I answered.

"Even when I do stupid shit, when I make decisions that are blatantly self-destructive, I still find myself wondering if he's paying attention." My hands curled into fists on my lap, and I forced them to relax. "Knowing I could make him angry, knowing I could disappoint him, felt better than his apathy. Fucked up, right?"

"*He* fucked you up," she corrected firmly. "That's on him, Archer. Not you."

"I'm closer to thirty than twenty-five, Remi. At some point, it *is* on me." I kept my eyes on her even though she was driving. "He's not standing over my shoulder, forcing me to make unhealthy decisions for the wrong fucking reasons. Like how I treated you. How I spoke to you. That's not my father's fault. *I* did that."

She sighed, her face looking so sad that I wanted to rewind everything that had gotten us to this point, undo every piece of conversation that made her mouth do that slight downturn like it was now.

"And you apologized." Her eyes cut to mine, a flash of temper there, like she was daring me to argue. "Would he have done the same thing?"

"No. Do you know what the first lesson was that he ever taught me? Evanses never humble themselves. *That* is what he drilled into me my entire life, and trying to dismantle the hold those words have on me is like tearing down a brick wall with my bare fucking hands." I laughed, dry and harsh. "That first week at the shelter? I wanted to keep you pissed off. I loved it. Your anger did something to me, Remi, and I know how fucked up that is. Don't give me too much credit here."

Her chest heaved on a deep breath, and I worried I'd gone too far.

Then she yanked on the wheel and steered the car into an empty parking lot. The church in front of us was brick walls and white columns, only one car parked close to the covered entrance. Great, a heavenly witness was just what I needed for this conversation. Might as well tell whoever was listening to add a couple check marks to my scorecard toward damnation.

With rough movements, she shoved the vehicle into park and turned, folding her leg into her seat so that it was resting on the console.

Too far.

Too much.

That would always be my problem, wouldn't it?

I could only come so far in trying to repair any of the relationships in my life before one stupid, rash decision knocked my progress off the rails and sent me spiraling in the opposite direction.

"Are you done sitting in the villain seat? You occupy it so easily in your own mind, I can't help but wonder if you like it."

"What? That's not what I'm doing."

"Yes, it is. And he put you there. Over and over, when you didn't act the way he wanted and when you didn't do exactly the thing that made *him* look best. The only lesson he's taught you is that acting out gets you attention from the people in your life who you should be learning from. He's just a really shitty teacher." She leaned in, her eyes blazing. "But guess what? It's still working, because he is not the only person giving you the attention you need. You respect your coach?"

"Yes."

"Have you learned anything from him? Has he been checking in on you more lately?"

"Yes," I said, more roughly than before.

"Your teammates. What about them?"

I couldn't speak now, so I nodded.

Her eyes. God, I could hardly meet her eyes because of how they burned. Ripped straight through all the pretense and all the bullshit and all the things I didn't want her to see.

Little by little, they softened. Her mouth did, too, shifting from a firm line into something else entirely. Remi Sinclair had the most kissable mouth I'd ever seen. The fact that I'd never kissed it was an absolute fucking tragedy.

"What about me?" she whispered.

My eyes snapped to hers. "You?"

"What about me? You wanted my attention and you got it, didn't you?"

The seat belt around my chest was strangling me, making it hard to breathe, so I tore at the latch, turning slightly to face her. "Did I?"

"Don't play dumb, Archer, it doesn't suit you." Her gaze was unrelenting. "You know you have it."

The moment got away from me, far too big to be contained in this small, unassuming car. But instead of running from it, I let the unknown settle in my chest and just tried to breathe.

In and out. Each breath was filled with Remi—clean and sweet and mouthwatering.

Before I'd even realized it, she was everywhere. Everything. And I had a desperate, clawing urge to rebuild my life with her at the center. Exactly the kind of grandiose statement that would send her screaming in the other direction.

"What do you want from me?" she asked, emotion making her voice shake.

She was asking me to hand over my heart on a platter, something I'd never done. Not for anyone.

Even if it was stupid and I'd torture myself over it later, I reached out and slid my hands under hers, dragging the tips of my fingers underneath Remi's until they curled up, a helpless response to the featherlight touch that I couldn't resist. She stared down at our hands as our fingers twined together, her chest rising and falling when I didn't pull away.

I held my answer until she finally raised her head and met my gaze.

"Would you believe me if I told you?"

At the gruffly stated question, torn straight from my chest, she sucked in a sharp breath, her exhale coming out in an equally harsh punch.

"I don't know." Carefully, she removed her hands from mine, covering her mouth with visibly trembling fingers. "I don't know."

It was so easy to think about what I wanted from Remi.

I wanted to take her out on a date.

I wanted to make her smile.

I wanted to kiss her in the morning when her hair was crazy and she hadn't had coffee yet.

I wanted to take her to bed and figure out all the things that made her moan.

I wanted to fuck her.

I wanted to make love to her.

I wanted to see her in the stands, wearing my jersey, and know she was mine.

I wanted to be someone her son could look up to.

I wanted to tell her that I was falling in love with her, and it scared me more than anything ever had.

And more than anything, I wanted a chance.

But right now, it wasn't about me, because what I wanted was more than she was ready for.

"Then I want you to tell me something," I said. "Tell me what *you* want."

Her hands fell away from her mouth, and she had to blink a few times as she gathered her thoughts. With the sun streaming into the car, the red of her hair was so vibrant, it almost didn't look real. My hands itched to touch it, but I kept them where they were.

"I want—I want to be *sure* when I go into any relationship," she said, forming the words slowly. "I want to be sure that my son and I will be safe with that person. Whoever that is will have to know that Gavin will always come first. He will always be the compass by which I make my decisions. I've tried dating in the past, and he gets attached so easily. That boy wants a father figure in his life, and that's why I cannot be flippant about who I let into my life in that capacity." She straightened her shoulders. "They'd have to know that sex is not a reason for me to pursue a relationship, because half the time I hardly have the energy to shave my legs. You combine that with everything else in my life, and—and I know . . . I know that's not what most men want to hear."

My brow furrowed. "You think I fucking care if your legs aren't smooth?" Her cheeks flushed, and it was so damn cute, I almost reached across the car and hauled her into my lap to kiss the embarrassment right off her face. "Remi, sex isn't the reason I'm here either. Even though I was being a dick when I said it, it was still true. If sex was all I wanted, that's not hard for me to seek out." Her gaze dropped into her lap, but I reached over and gently touched her chin, lifting her face back up to mine. "That is not why I'm here."

"So you don't want to have sex?" she asked lightly, the teasing glint in her eye almost severing the shaky grip on my restraint.

I leaned forward and allowed my forehead to rest on hers. "Yes, firefly, I want to have sex with you. God, it would be so good."

"That was unfair," she said quietly. "I shouldn't have asked that. I'm . . . I'm all over the place." She pulled back, her finger slowly inching across the console to drag along the knuckles on the back of my hand. "How do you know it would be good, Archer? We haven't even kissed. How do I know that that's not all this is? Sexual tension we haven't been able to act on? It might *not* be good." She grinned. "You might be selfish. And I might have forgotten what to do and I'd just lay there like a dead fish."

I sucked in a breath through clenched teeth. "Keep talking, firefly. You're just proving my point."

She laughed softly. "How?"

Knowing she might tell me to stop, I slowly reached up and cupped her face in both hands, allowing my fingers to tangle in the silky strands of her hair. "I don't need to kiss you to know. You and me, it would be magic," I whispered, leaning in to brush my nose along hers. "Because I've hardly touched you and I'm ready to fucking explode. Aren't you?"

Remi didn't answer, just exhaled against my mouth.

It was going too far and I knew it. She probably did too.

In her office, when we'd ended up just like this, she had begged me to back away first so she wouldn't have to ask, and even though it was one of the hardest things I've ever done, I backed away now too.

This last step had to be hers.

If I respected nothing else, I had to let Remi be the one to inch herself over the line she'd drawn in the sand.

Once she did, though, she was *mine*.

When I returned to my own seat, Remi skimmed a hand over the top of her hair, then rubbed it over her mouth as she blinked herself back into the present.

"Good. Good talk."

I laughed. I laughed long and hard. Then she did too.

This woman.

I didn't want to think about what my life would look like right now without her in it.

As the thought registered, I wanted to follow it, see here it would lead, but the angry buzz of my cell phone yanked me back.

Analise's name flashed on the screen when I pulled it out, so I tapped the button to answer it on speaker.

"Little A, how are you?"

She didn't answer right away. Then I heard a telltale sniffle. Remi gave me a concerned look.

I sat up straighter. "Analise, talk to me."

"Dad is so mad, Archer," she said, voice thick with tears. "He . . . he overheard me tell Rebecca I was driving, and he got so mad and he was yelling. He threw his glass across the dining room. Rebecca tried to get me out of the room and calm him down, and he told her to mind her own fucking business."

"Shit," I whispered. I gave Remi a pleading look. "I hate to ask you this . . ."

Her face was firm. "Give me the address."

"Analise, hold tight, okay? Remi and I will be there in about fifteen minutes. Don't leave your room."

"I won't." She sniffled. "Will you stay on the phone with me until you get here?"

"Of course."

I tapped the mute button and told Remi the address to my father's place in Orchard Park. She reached over and laid her hand on my forearm, the consoling squeeze feeling better than anything had the right to.

"Thank you," I told her.

She smiled. "What are friends for, right?"

I leaned my head back and groaned. "God, I'm starting to hate that phrase."

Chapter Twenty-Two

Remi

"My dad is a dick."

Normally, I would have responded to such a proclamation, but I was too busy trying not to gape at the house belonging to the dick in question.

"Yeah, you've mentioned this," I said absently.

We'd driven through a gate at the front of the property, the kind that needed a little code to permit entrance. The entirety of the home was light-colored brick—white columns and black shutters on countless windows. Turreted peaks flanked the stately front entrance, and a small balcony on the second floor—lined with thick, curved white railings—sat between those peaks. Off to the side of the house was a four-stall garage, and anchored in the middle of the circular drive was a fucking fountain.

"Who cleans all those windows?"

He gave me an amused look. "That's your first thought?"

"No, my first thought was, *Wow, this is exactly what I'd imagine a pompous prick's house would look like.*"

Archer laughed again, but there was still tightness around his eyes as I turned the car off and removed my seat belt.

"I'm reminding you that my dad is a dick because he will be awful," Archer said. "To you. To me. To my sister." He closed his eyes. "I hate that you're about to see any of this." I opened my mouth, but he set a gentle finger over my lips. "If you say that's what friends are for . . ."

I wrapped my fingers around his thick wrist and pulled his hand away from my mouth. "You'll what?"

His eyes opened, landing unerringly on my lips. "I'll be forced to kiss you as a distraction, and I promised myself I wouldn't do that."

"Oh."

My weak whisper made him smile. "Yeah. 'Oh.'"

Archer got out of the car first, and I took a quick moment to fix my ponytail, making sure there were no stray flyaways around my face.

"Are you fixing your hair for him?" he asked incredulously.

"No." I looped the hair tie one more time, tipping my chin up. "I'm fixing it for the moment. No one wants to look a mess during a dramatic family showdown."

"I'll take your word for it." His eyes skimmed over my face. "No matter why you're doing it, you look beautiful."

"Quit stalling," I teased, even as my stomach and heart did a quick little flip-flop.

Archer sighed, and I had to work to keep up with his much longer strides as he jogged up the stone steps leading to the double-door entrance.

The planters on either side of the porch were glossy black, filled with perfectly trimmed boxwoods cut to mimic a spiral pattern. On the black door was a gleaming knocker, heavy and ornate in a way that I'd never seen, EVANS etched into the gold surface.

Archer didn't use it, nor did he knock to signal our arrival.

He simply walked in and stared up the curved staircase that fanned out in two directions.

The entryway was two stories tall, everything inside the house black and white as well.

I expected to be impressed and awed, but in reality, the beauty of the house was only in its size and perfectly kept appearance. Everything else about it, as I should have expected, was cold.

"Analise?" he called. "Ready?"

"Coming," she yelled.

A short woman with ruddy cheeks bustled into the entryway, wearing a black-and-white uniform that matched the rest of the house. "He's in a foul mood tonight. If you take her without talking to him, it'll only get worse."

"Then leave at the same time we do," he told her. "I don't want you here alone with him."

She nodded, her eyes landing on me and widening incrementally. "Who is this?"

Archer and I traded a quick look, and when I didn't get the impression that this visit was one where I needed to keep my mouth shut, I held my hand out to the woman and smiled. "I'm Remi, a f-friend of Archer's."

"Are you?" she asked softly. "Mr. Archer doesn't have many friends, and certainly none as pretty as you."

"Rebecca," he warned.

"Nice to meet you, Rebecca. What do you do here?"

"I keep them fed and relatively happy," she said. "Most of them, at least."

Analise appeared at the top of the stairway, a backpack over one shoulder. Her eyes were red, the skin around them puffy from crying. At the sight of her, Rebecca looked so sad.

Once she'd neared the bottom of the stairs, she jumped off the last one and threw herself into her brother's arms, her tears starting again. "Please don't let him send me away," she sobbed.

"I won't." He kissed the top of her head. "Hey, look at me." Analise lifted her head, still so pretty even in her tears. "I won't, I promise."

Analise gave a shaky nod.

"That's not something you can promise, given you're not her parent. Not her guardian. And she's a minor."

My skin prickled at the sound of his voice, and when he appeared at the far end of the entryway, I took an unthinking step backward.

It was like looking at Archer in twenty-five years. They were *identical.* Older, of course, with salt-and-pepper hair and more wrinkles. But the height, the imposing presence, the jawline and the eyes, the proud, straight line of his nose—they could have been twins.

Archer shifted his sister behind him so that she was next to me, and he moved to the side, standing in front of both of us. Analise was crying quietly, and I grabbed her hand, clutching it tight with mine.

"She's coming with me tonight," Archer said firmly. "You need some time to cool down. She's spent the night at least once a week for the past year, and you've never complained."

"That was before the two of you lied to me and conspired to ruin your entire fucking career," he snapped.

"My career will be just fine. Many players do much worse than I did and we both know it."

"They weren't an Evans," he yelled. "It was bad enough that my son was taken in for a mug shot like a common criminal. But knowing you didn't even do it? What the fuck were you thinking?"

Archer kept his face even. "I was thinking about my sister—and I promise, you don't need to worry about my priorities, old man."

His father's eyes flickered dangerously, and I braced myself, expecting an outburst. But then his eyes landed on me and narrowed. "Well . . . it seems we have another uninvited guest." His gaze shifted to Archer. "Prettier than you, though, isn't she? Where'd you pick this one up?"

My heart stuttered, waiting for the flare of Archer's temper in response.

His jaw clenched. "Come on, let's go."

Analise and I started to turn, Rebecca right on our heels, when his father's voice rang out again.

"I could still have her arrested."

Analise let out a choked sob. When I glanced at Archer, his face was terrifying—harsh and unforgiving. "For what?" he ground out.

"She fled the scene of a crime. That destruction was caused by her."

Archer took a step forward. "It was an accident, and it's being fixed because *I'm* taking responsibility. There's no victims here. Nothing she needs to be punished for."

Rebecca wrapped her arm around Analise and whispered something in her ear. Analise nodded jerkily.

"Why would you do that to your daughter? She's a kid."

"I wouldn't be doing it to *her*," he said, cold as ice, slick as a snake. "I'd be doing it to you, son. These are the consequences of your actions. I thought it would be that you're stuck at that shithole for a few weeks with mongrels and martyrs." I sucked in a sharp breath, but he didn't hear, far too focused on spewing his venom at his own children. "But it turns out, there's a much more effective way to get this lesson through your head."

Archer shook his head. "What is wrong with you?"

"Me? Nothing. I have children acting out, and any good parent knows that discipline is required when that happens. She lied. You both did. She didn't take responsibility and allowed you to take the fall for her. And let's add theft to the list, given she used one of my credit cards without permission and charged eight thousand dollars for some fucking guilt gift for that fucking pound."

I gasped. Loudly. It was out before I could stop it.

Analise gave me a wide-eyed look.

"That was *you*?" I whispered. "You sent it?"

Tears continued to spill over her cheeks. "I had to do something. I'm so sorry I lied, Remi."

His father took a few steps closer, eyes narrowed, and the air seemed to drop twenty degrees as he connected missing pieces in his head. "You're from that shelter?" he said.

Archer stepped more fully in front of me. "Remi, Analise, let's go. Now."

Then his dad started smiling. Big and wide and toothy, his veneers white and blinding in his face. He was laughing in the next moment. "Oh, this is perfect." Then he clapped Archer on the shoulder so hard that the slap of his hand made me flinch.

Archer's chin rose, his eyes chips of ice in his face.

His father leaned in, lowering his voice. "Maybe you do have two brain cells left to rub together. Fucking your way through your community service might be a little cliché, but she looks like a pleasant enough way to spend the time."

The sound that left Archer was hardly anything more than a growl, but he had his dad's shirt fisted in his hands as he shoved forward, slamming his dad's back against the wall in the next heartbeat.

Mr. Evans made a choking sound, tearing at Archer's hands. "Get the fuck off me."

"One more word," Archer warned. "About either of them. One more word, old man."

His smile was sickly triumphant. "And you'll what? You can't do anything to me."

Archer's hands tightened, the muscles in his arms rock hard, the veins standing out in sharp relief. The damage he could inflict, should he choose, was enough to make my mouth go dry.

If he did, though . . .

If he did, things would get so much worse.

Even though my knees shook at the overwhelming display of strength and violence, I took a step forward. "Archer." He pinched his eyes shut, hands trembling where he held his father against the wall. "Please. Let's go."

Then he relaxed his jaw. His eyes opened. Hands fell away from his father's shirt. He stepped back.

His gaze found mine—exhausted and heartbroken, and more than anything, I wanted to wrap him in my arms.

"Let's go," he repeated.

Because he was looking at me, because Analise and Rebecca were already turning toward the door, I was the only one who saw his father ball up his fist and take the swing.

The angle was awkward, but he clipped Archer just underneath his eye.

Archer's head snapped back as I lurched forward, hand outstretched. There was a trickle of blood on his cheekbone when he touched his fingers to his face.

"Dad!" Analise cried. *"Stop."*

His father shook out his hand, studying the signet ring on his finger. "I've wanted to do that for years." He locked his eyes on me and smiled. "Thank you for giving me the perfect motivation."

Archer took a step forward, teeth bared, eyes blazing, arm raised, and I grabbed it with a shout. "*No,* Archer. Don't." I grabbed his face until he was forced to look at me. "He's not worth it."

After a moment, the anger fell from his features, tension bleeding from his frame. My thumb brushed at the blood. "Please," I whispered. "Don't let him win."

"Oh, it's too late for that, sweetheart," his father said behind us. "The moment he laid his hands on me, I already did. He likes fucking with his reputation? Let's see how good it feels when he's cuffed and taken in for assault from his childhood home."

He was already pulling out his phone, and Archer's eyes filled with resignation.

Analise sobbed behind us, Rebecca doing her best to calm her down.

My mind raced, and I didn't think, didn't process, simply turned and gave his dad a curious look. "Why would you call the cops?"

He stopped and gave me an incredulous look. "He pushed me. That's assault. I defended myself."

With a simple tilt of my head, I made sure to hold his gaze. I held it through the nerves and the second-guessing, and I held it through the tiny voice in my head wondering what the fuck I was about to do.

I held his gaze and spoke anyway. "But you hit him first. The push came second."

Shocked silence pulsed through the room, and I was sure they could all hear the thrash of my heart behind my ribs.

His eyes narrowed, then he let out an uncomfortable laugh. "Are you drunk?"

I smiled. "Sober as can be. And I know exactly what I saw."

Archer's hand found mine, his fingers sliding between my own and squeezing tight.

Behind us, Analise sniffed. "I saw it too."

"So did I," Rebecca said quietly.

Mr. Evans scoffed, but the color flooding his cheeks gave him away. "This is insane. You're all going to lie about what happened? You have no proof."

"Neither do you," Archer said in a dangerously low voice. "But by tomorrow morning, I'll have a black eye." He grinned. "Thanks for that, old man."

"Do you still want to call the cops?" I asked, giving him my sweetest smile.

He was breathing hard, jerkily smoothing out the rumpled front of his shirt.

"We'll take that as a no," Archer said. "Have a great night, Dad. I'll bring her back when she's ready."

He took a step forward, chin tilted arrogantly. "Yet," he said simply.

"What?" Archer asked.

"I'm not calling the cops *yet*." His gaze flicked to me, then the two women still holding each other by the door. "Rebecca, you're fired."

Archer stared at his father. "Rebecca, you ready to take me up on my job offer?"

"Yes, Mr. Archer," she said in a shaky voice. "I think I am."

"Good. Then let's go."

Analise was still crying as she waited for me to shift some items in the back seat so she had somewhere to sit. Archer walked Rebecca to her car, speaking quietly to the much shorter woman.

With a sigh, I pulled out my phone and called Pops.

"I'm going to be a bit longer yet."

"You're not doing any hanky-panky with the pretty football player, are ya?"

I rolled my eyes. "No. We had to go pick up his sister. She had an argument with their father."

He made a noise of understanding. "She okay?"

"She will be, I think. It wasn't pretty, though."

Across the driveway, Rebecca flung her arms around Archer's middle. His face went slack with shock, and I swallowed a laugh. When his hand tentatively landed on her back, I smiled. "I need to drive them back to his place, but I may not leave right away. In case Analise wants a female to talk to."

"You're a good kid, bug."

"I'm almost thirty, Pops."

"Still a kid to me."

I sighed. "I know."

"Going to his house, huh?" he asked slyly.

Archer closed Rebecca's car door and waited for her to pull away, his frame expanding on a deep breath before heading back toward where I was waiting. The slightly haunted, really pissed-off look in his eyes lifted the hairs on my arms.

"Yeah," I said absently. "Just for a little bit."

"Okay, bug."

His tone said he didn't believe me.

Which was problematic because I didn't believe me either.

Chapter Twenty-Three

Remi

Betty, the used Toyota that I'd bought from one of Pops's old neighbors, was one thing more than anything else: She was reliable. Deeply unsexy, of course, but she was mine. All 100,016 miles of her. I knew all her dings and scratches. I knew she struggled a bit to keep us cool on really hot, humid days. But I owned that car free and clear, and I loved her more for it.

Since the day I'd bought her, I was the only one who'd ever sat behind the wheel. Seeing a man drive Betty was odd under normal circumstances, but these were not normal. And it wasn't just a man driving my car—it was Archer Evans.

I didn't need to use his full name, of course. These past couple weeks, I'd learned exactly how human he was. But some situations required formality, you know?

This situation required all the emphasis I could obtain, because he looked massive in the seat that was mine, his legs spread to the sides and his wrist draped over the top of the wheel as he took us the rest of the way to his own home.

Analise stayed quiet, and when I glanced into the back seat, her eyes were closed, her mouth slightly open as if she was sleeping.

My heart and my head were on conflicting sides of the whole *Should I stay quiet* or *Should I talk to him about what I just witnessed* debate. My head was firmly camped on the side of *Shut up and stay out of it* because it was none of my business and would only risk deeper entanglement.

My heart, though, that was a different story. My heart felt all soft and squishy as I watched him drive with that stoic look on his face. Resignation looked really good on Archer, though I doubted he wanted to hear it, given what he'd clearly resigned himself to. My heart wanted to make him feel better. Wanted to help in any way I could.

"You were telling the truth, then," I started softly.

Looked like my heart was going to reign victorious, at least in this.

He glanced briefly in my direction. "About what?"

"You weren't the one who ordered all the donations for the shelter."

His mouth softened, eyes flicking to the rearview mirror as he checked on his sister. "Did you think I was lying?"

"Yes."

His smile faded, a troubled pinch appearing in his brow. "That's not good either."

"I assumed you didn't want the attention. Or for me to assume there were strings attached." I leaned my head back and watched the trees pass through the windshield. Fewer buildings now, more woods, and I prayed that his house wasn't an ugly rich person's house like his dad's. "But you did lie by omission," I pointed out. "You knew who ordered it."

"I did." Archer kept his gaze forward, like he felt too raw to look at me for an extended period of time. "But you didn't ask me that."

"That's true."

"She just felt so bad, you know? It was eating her up that I was the one there doing all the work." He shifted in his seat, or as much as he could in the small space. "I might have mentioned something about a wish list for the shelter."

Something warm unfolded under my skin, skimming my veins as it raced from the top of my head to the tips of my toes. "'Mentioned it'?" I said lightly.

His jaw clenched. "Okay, fine, I sent her the link."

I hid my smile behind my hand, turning to stare out the passenger window. "I see."

"I didn't think she'd use the credit card he gave her, though." He sighed. "She's got one from me for emergencies, and I guess I thought . . . I don't know what I thought. I don't always think things through," he admitted with a wry grin.

"So I've heard."

The car slowed near an opening in the trees. The single-lane road disappeared into the woods, and I found myself holding my breath as he followed the slight curve in the path that led to his house.

The road widened. So did the opening in the trees, and the warm skimmy thing turned into a full-fledged wave of *Holy shit, I might be in trouble*.

It wasn't ugly. It wasn't huge or ostentatious.

It was warm and welcoming, buttery-yellow light coming from fixtures on the deep-green siding that covered the porch area. The three garage stalls took up the majority of the front of the house, and I recognized the stacked-rock facade from the picture he'd sent me as he was weeding. It was only one story, and the raised porch was held up with beautiful stained-wood columns that arched off into the spaces between each one.

"It's gorgeous," I breathed.

He pulled the car into the driveway, parking it in front of the entrance. "You sound surprised."

"I am, I suppose." I scrunched my nose. "I expected something big and obnoxious."

His eyes were warm, and I was glad to see the haunted look disappear, even for a moment. "Like me, huh?"

"I haven't found you obnoxious for at least a week."

Archer laughed quietly. "Do you want to come in?"

"Yes." I sucked in a breath. "I fear my curiosity is overriding my better judgment."

"Won't get any arguments from me." He reached back and gently touched his sister's leg. "Wake up, sleepyhead."

Analise groaned, blinking sleepily as she sat up and then yawned. "Can I go to bed now?"

Archer and I traded a quick look.

"You sure you don't want to talk?" he asked.

She shook her head, eyes closing again. "We can talk tomorrow," she murmured. "Is that okay?"

"Of course."

Archer carried her bag, and I followed the two of them up the front steps that led into the house. There were planters in front of his door, too, but unlike mine, his weren't empty. They held white geraniums with some sweet potato vine draping over the side in a bright spring green.

It was hard to imagine him planting them himself, but there was a half-used bag of potting soil leaning against the door that led into the garage, so it must have been him.

With the press of a few buttons, the house was flooded with light as Archer ushered Analise toward a staircase that led to a basement. "I'll be right back," he told me.

Analise gave me a tired wave and a smile. "Thank you for coming, Remi."

"You're welcome, sweetie."

"I'm really glad you're here for my brother."

Archer ducked his head, keeping his expression hidden, and I chose not to respond to that one as they disappeared down the steps.

Loaded. Every part of every exchange tonight seemed to be loaded with a weight I wasn't entirely sure I was ready to carry. Like studying his house because I wanted to soak in the details that would help bring this man into focus.

As I wandered through the main floor, I shook my head. It was damn-near annoying how much I loved it. If someone plucked my home fantasies straight from the part of my brain that didn't think about things like budget or plausibility, it would be this one.

There was a mudroom with lockers off the three-stall garage, and a spacious guest room tucked away past the laundry. I wondered how many spare bedrooms he had in this place, if there was a full basement too.

This guest room held a few boxes and a queen-size bed with a deep-green comforter, but nothing else.

The kitchen was big and inviting, but not intimidating, everything done in warm wood tones and creamy whites. The island sat four, and the kitchen table in the area off to the side sat another six.

Next to the kitchen sink were a coffee mug and a small plate. On the island lay a stack of mail and a folded shirt in Buffalo's colors. Little signs of life that made it easy to picture him filling the space, returning here at the end of the day.

Off the kitchen was a smaller room with a couple overstuffed chairs and a floor-to-ceiling rock fireplace with windows on either side facing out into the woods. It would be a perfect place to read.

For . . . Archer. Not me. I didn't need to be reading anything in any of the very nice chairs in his house.

I swallowed roughly, then blew out a harsh breath as I wandered out of the kitchen and into the gathering area on the main floor.

Like the guest room, the family room was sparsely furnished, only a long oversize couch facing the television over the fireplace and a few pictures set inside the mostly empty bookshelves on either side.

It needed artwork on the walls and more furniture to make it feel like home, but every inch that I could see was warm. Cozy, even, despite its impressive ceilings and high-end finishes.

Past the stairs that went to the lower level, I could see the entrance to the primary bedroom suite. No amount of curiosity would convince me that it was wise to wander that way.

Seeing his bedroom was a bad, bad idea.

There'd be no bad ideas tonight. Only good, healthy adult choices that would keep my clothes right on my body, where they should be.

As soon as he came upstairs, I'd make sure he was all right, then head home.

I could do this.

If I closed my eyes, I could still hear the thwack of his father's fist on his face, picture the horrifying way his head snapped back from the force of it.

I'd touched him, and he'd stopped.

Touched him with my own very normal, average hands, and even through the haze of shock and betrayal and anger, he'd restrained himself on my request.

Power comes in different shapes and sizes, and I still wasn't sure how I felt about the power I seemed to hold over him. I glanced down at my hands, turning them until my palms faced the ceiling. Dried blood was on the edge of my thumb. Archer's blood.

In the kitchen, I washed my hands with brisk efficiency and found a drawer with a first-aid kit, selecting a small butterfly bandage and some ointment. I pulled open the freezer and quickly found a stack of flexible ice packs—a sure sign of an athlete who used them on a regular basis.

The sound of his feet coming up the stairs triggered a burst of nerves, but I kept my hands steady as I laid the ice pack on the island and busied myself finding a thin towel to wrap around it. Archer walked into the kitchen while my back was turned. I tore off a few squares of paper towel and got them wet with warm water from the sink, squeezing out the excess while the heat of his stare built on the back of my neck.

"Sit," I instructed gently.

"Yes, ma'am."

The amused tone made me smile, but I smothered it before I turned in his direction. The streak of blood had dried on his cheekbone, and the cut from his dad's ring was bigger than I'd realized.

Archer chose to sit on one of the stools at the island, which put us nearly eye to eye when I approached. His body language was relaxed despite the tension of the last hour, his legs spread to accommodate me. He kept his hands on his thighs, eyes tracking every move I made with sharp focus. This was power, too, in a very different way, and mishandled, it would cause ancillary damage I wasn't prepared for.

When I laid my hand on his jaw to angle his head, his skin was warm. As gently as I could, I dabbed the wet towel around the angry-looking skin, trying my best to clean off the blood without pulling at the wound.

"Does it hurt?" I asked.

His eyes stayed on mine. "Of the things that man has done, this doesn't even rate in the top ten."

My hand lowered. "Did he hit you when you were younger?"

"No." He lifted his chin, motioning me to continue. "Words were his preferred way to cause pain. I can guarantee this will heal faster."

With even, steady strokes, I got the last of the dried blood off his skin. My heart beat hard and fast at the way he watched me as I opened an antiseptic wipe, and Archer's eyes tracked my every move.

"This might sting," I warned him, but he didn't so much as flinch when I dabbed at the cut high on his cheekbone. As I finished wiping the area around it to make sure it was clean, I said, "I'm not sure I'd want to hear what's on the top ten list."

"No? What if it made you feel terribly sorry for me and you felt bad leaving me alone tonight?"

My hand paused, and I arched an eyebrow slowly. "You're not alone. Your sister is here."

His grin was quick and fierce, appearing like a lightning strike and fading just as fast. "Touché, firefly."

Oof. That was an entirely different sort of powerful, one I didn't particularly want him to know about.

"Tell me one," I said, quite against my better judgment. "Just for reference."

Archer's palms slid up and down the tops of his thighs, like the motion helped him think. His eyes were unfocused, no doubt riffling through memories that weren't so pleasant.

"I made my father the happiest when I was in college. Did everything he wanted of me. I played well enough to get drafted when I finished my undergrad, but he thought getting my master's would play well with the media, and I had the grades to warrant it. Plus, I'd gain more experience, get drafted higher, which was what he wanted. My entire life, all I heard was that he relied on me to bring pride to our name."

The blood was gone, but he didn't know that, so I picked up the damp paper towel again, gently gripped his chin, and tilted his face like I needed a different angle. The stubble along his jaw was prickly against my fingertips, and his eyes closed briefly when I let them drag over it as I dropped my hand from his face.

"Did you?"

His eyes opened, and again, I was struck speechless by the intensity of that blue.

"I was a finalist for the Heisman my last year. Broke school records for passing yards and touchdowns in a single season. Went to Buffalo in the first round as a hometown boy who'd return glory to the franchise. Thirteenth pick."

My hands lowered, but I didn't move back. He shifted on his stool, the insides of his knees brushing along the outside of my thighs. Carefully, his fingers reached forward to play with the strings dangling from my denim shorts.

The air between us pulsed with unspent electricity, only made worse by the almost-touches of his hands a fraction of an inch away from my skin.

"I remember walking off the stage with my first NFL jersey in my hands, and the sight of *Evans* on the back made me feel ten feet tall." A wrinkle formed in his brow, and I wanted to smooth it out with my fingertips. "I'd fucking done it. All the practices and drills and studying and years of my life that I sacrificed to make *our name* proud, all culminated in this. And I thought . . . he's going to be so proud of me."

A sick foreboding twisted my stomach as I continued to listen quietly.

"When I came offstage, he was waiting for me." His eyes were hypnotic, and I found it hard to breathe. "The first thing he said was, 'You should've been drafted higher. I expected top ten.'"

I didn't want my heart to break for this man. He probably didn't want that either.

But it broke all the same.

For years, as long as I could remember, I'd denied myself the things I wanted because money was tight, or Gavin needed something more, or the devil on my shoulder wasn't quite persuasive enough.

But I wanted to show him that his pain mattered. That he mattered to me.

The minutes and hours and days I'd spent resisting Archer—resisting his hold on me—were dust. Rubble.

Nothing outside this mattered.

I stepped closer in the space between his legs and wound my arms around his neck, wrapping him in a tight embrace. In the next breath, his arms banded around my back, anchored around my waist as his frame sank against mine.

I was hugging the past version of Archer, the one I couldn't be there for. And I was hugging the man I knew now, who was *trying* to be better, no matter how his upbringing was stacked against him.

He let out a deep exhale, burying his face into my hair. I did something similar against the side of his neck, breathing through the wave of panic that I'd done something stupid. That I'd done something irreversible.

No. It wasn't stupid. I refused to believe that.

Showing compassion to someone who'd just allowed you to see their pain was never an action that would end in regret. Archer wasn't someone on a pedestal, cold and untouchable, impossible to hurt. He was so very human, and as I knew from tonight, he bled just as easily as the rest of us, no matter how much money was in his bank account.

It's easy to dismiss people's pain when their lives seem less difficult than ours. But pain doesn't discriminate, and there's no concrete scale for whose wounds caused more damage. No barometer that labeled someone's grief or loss or hardship as worse or easier or better.

It was still grief and loss and hardship. Archer had to grieve something he'd never had—parents who loved and supported him unconditionally.

Without Pops, I would've had to grieve that too.

"He's wrong," I said firmly, keeping a tight hold on the wide expanse of his shoulders, my fingers curling into the material of his shirt. "You did something he could never do."

His fingers spread wide on my back, moving up and down, the heat of his palm seeping through the thin layer of cotton. The intention behind it, no doubt, was meant to be soothing. But I was not soothed.

"I like having you in my house," he said, voice muffled because of how tightly he held me.

I smiled, turning my face toward his neck. The edge of my mouth brushed his skin, and his arms tightened, the thick bands of muscles stealing my breath.

"I like that room off the kitchen," I told him. It was a much safer admission than *I like being in your arms*.

"Why are you whispering?"

I laughed under my breath. "I don't know. It feels like a secret I shouldn't be saying out loud."

"You can tell me."

I set my chin on his shoulder, leaning my head against his, and stared at the room in question as I felt a bittersweet tug down the center line of my chest. "It's a perfect place to read. Even in the summer, I'd want a fire in the fireplace. A big fuzzy blanket over my lap."

"Yeah?" His voice was rough, and I shivered, burrowing deeper into his embrace. "What else would you want?"

I licked my lips, shifting on my feet enough that it brought my hips closer to his. His hands tightened over my ribs. "I'd put a Christmas tree in the corner during the holidays. That way, when you're in the kitchen, you can see it. Family ornaments, maybe. The homemade ones that don't match and aren't perfect, but you keep them anyway because they're the favorites."

"I don't have any of those," he admitted in a gruff whisper.

Wisdom was shoved into the back of my mind because it was the last thing I needed as I pulled away just far enough to look into his perfectly handsome, perfectly rugged face. I cradled his jaw with my palm, heart expanding as his eyes closed and he leaned into the touch.

"I don't know what to do with you, Archer Evans."

He didn't open his eyes right away. His response came after a few moments, and only after he'd pressed his palm over the top of my hand, silently begging to keep my touch just for a little bit longer.

When he did open his eyes, there was a twinkle of humor there. "I have a feeling you won't like any of my suggestions."

"Try me," I whispered.

His chest rose and fell. "No, I need to let you decide what happens next, firefly."

Power.

There was no doubting that in this moment, with this man, it was entirely mine.

The question was, what did I want to do with it?

"You have been a mystery since the night I met you."

He turned his face, pressing a kiss into the center of my palm. My fingers curled helplessly against his cheek. "I'm easy to figure out."

"No, you're not. Knowing what you want isn't the same as knowing you." My gaze lingered over his face. "The first is very simple. The second? Not simple at all."

Archer's hands slid along my waist, down along my hips, and I let my hand rest on the side of his neck, my thumb over the skin where his pulse raced.

"You've come as close as anyone has," he admitted with a dazed shake of his head, like he couldn't believe we were here, we were having this conversation.

"Does that scare you?"

"Not anymore." His gaze was direct and unflinching. "Does it scare *you*?"

I couldn't hold the eye contact because my heart constricted with a dangerous tightening, so I focused on his mouth instead. "Yes," I admitted in a whisper.

Power.

It rolled through my veins as I leaned forward, ignoring my own response to the question, ignoring the logic telling me to back away, and gently kissed him.

Once.

He held perfectly still, not even seeming to breathe, but his eyes were open and locked on me.

Twice. A little longer, lingering over his bottom lip. His eyes closed. So did mine.

His lips were soft and dry, and his restraint to let me have this moment was the sexiest thing a man had ever done for me. That was probably why I did it. Not the only reason why—I wanted it too badly to pretend that was true.

I kissed him because my heart was screaming that if I didn't, I'd regret it for the rest of my life.

I kissed him a third time, lingering longer now, my fingers twining into his thick hair.

His hands tightened on my waist, firmly enough to make it difficult to breathe, and when my tongue slipped out to brush along the inside of his top lip, Archer groaned, standing from the stool in a sudden movement to take my face in his hands.

My power was gone. It was his now.

I gave it over gladly as he slanted his mouth over mine.

Chapter Twenty-Four

Archer

More.

I needed more.

More of her kisses.

More of her lips.

More of the sweet hint of her tongue.

More of her hair tangled around my fingers and her skin underneath my hands.

And with the pliant arch of her body into mine, the soft press of her stomach against my aching hardness, I knew she was willing to give it.

My hands curved around the back of her head, and I slid my tongue into her waiting mouth, the wet lick of her tongue on mine lifting the hairs on the back of my neck as we groaned in tandem.

Hers was relief.

Mine sounded dirtier, lower. This was from just a kiss. What sound would she make when I slid inside her body? What sound would I?

The need to know set my entire being on edge.

Having waited for this moment didn't make me rush through frantic kisses or groping hands. No, it had given me time to think.

Think about what I'd do to her, given the chance.

Kiss her everywhere, memorize all her sounds, taste every inch of her skin.

Take her past the edge again and again until she was spent and sated and sleepy. Then I'd take her one more time, wring every last ounce of pleasure from her body. Make up for all the days and hours I'd thought of her just like this.

I banded an arm around her lower back, my fingers splayed over the curve of her waist as I held her tight to my body. As our kiss deepened, the only thing I could hear was the furious pounding rhythm of my heart. Her hands skimmed my chest and shoulders as I dipped my knees to use my other arm under her ass to boost her up onto the island.

Her legs wrapped immediately around my waist as my hands wandered along her back and up behind her neck. The band holding all that red hair back had disappeared, and I hoped she never fucking found it again.

All that thick, silky hair. Fire in my hands. I wanted to see it tangled and messy all over my pillows in the morning, absolutely wrecked from what we'd done to each other.

Remi kissed like she did everything else—like the weight of her entire soul was behind it. Would she carry the weight of mine as I stumbled through this?

I wanted her.

I wanted her so fucking bad that my hands shook.

Kissing her might be my new religion. Her lips would bring me to my knees. Her tongue and her scent and her little sounds would have me worshipping her for the rest of my life.

When I skimmed my teeth over the tip of her tongue as it pulled away from mine, she whimpered, and it was like she tugged on a rope around my waist, my hips rolling into hers unconsciously.

At the feel of me hard between her legs, she made another sweet, helpless sound.

Her hands tightened on the back of my head when I did it, our kisses taking on a fierce, serrated edge. We'd excised the need for sweet and slow, for tentative kisses that felt like a question.

The only thing left behind was the raw desire we'd felt since the very beginning.

I pulled back and nipped along the edge of her jaw, sucking at the soft patch of skin underneath her ear. Remi tilted her head back and gasped.

"Right there?" I asked, my lips brushing against the spot I'd just found. Her hands fisted in my shirt, and she nodded like she was drunk. "Let me hear you, firefly," I whispered into her skin. "Don't keep those sounds to yourself. They're mine."

I dragged my teeth over her earlobe and sucked hard. She jerked me closer, her hips moving restlessly.

"Here?" I asked, sliding my hand between us and rubbing on the seam of her shorts.

She moaned my name, her head tipped back. She gripped my wrist, hips rocking back and forth as she worked herself on my hand.

"God, I want those shorts gone," I moaned into her neck. "Wanna feel you."

Could I lay her down here on the island and break her apart into a million pieces? I'd do it with my tongue and fingers first, and my mouth watered at the thought.

I wanted to see her dazed and limp. Wanted to make her scream.

Wanted to wrap her in my arms as she came down from the peak.

I wanted to love her.

The words threatened, but something in my gut whispered, *Caution. Not yet. Not yet.*

But I didn't want caution either.

Caution meant *slow*. Slow might pull us from this place, and that was the last fucking thing I wanted now that we were finally here.

Her mouth found mine again, our tongues winding around each other, slick and wet and dirty. My hands moved to her waist, pushing up to the sides of her breasts under her shirt. My thumbs found the hard tips through the thin layer of her bra, and I rubbed back and forth as she arched her back.

"Dreamed about these," I murmured. "It wasn't enough. I want to see them, kiss them, suck them."

When I pushed her bra out of the way, my fingers dragging over a nipple, she shivered.

Then I pulled back, studying the flush of color in her cheeks and down into her chest. With my finger working in tight, light circles, I wanted to see what that did to her. She kept her eyes closed, quick, panting breaths making her chest heave.

"So fucking beautiful," I whispered. "Look at you."

We'd hardly touched each other and I knew if I got her into my bed, I'd have her.

She'd let me do whatever I wanted right now.

God, I'd do so many things. I'd make it so good for her, she'd never leave.

Never leave me.

Remi's hands found the waistband of my pants, and she curled her fingers there, dragging her knuckles over the V of my lower abdominals. Her eyes were hazy when she opened them.

"Archer, what are we doing?" she moaned.

I stole another kiss, and she gave it willingly. When I pulled back, we were both breathing hard.

"What we've wanted since that first fucking night," I said, before finding that spot underneath her ear again and sucking. Hard.

She gasped, her hands fisting in my shirt. I grinned, nipping at her lips, then angling my mouth over hers for something deeper, wetter, a luxurious kiss that I had no right to take from this woman.

Remi made a plaintive noise as I gripped her breast, dragging my thumb over her, harder this time.

Her hand pushed at my shoulder.

Pushed.

Not pulled.

I broke the kiss, a harsh exhale leaving my mouth before I could stop it.

"Hang on," she panted. "Just . . . hang on a second."

"Fuck," I muttered, dropping my head against hers as I tried to catch my breath.

All the blood flow had diverted to my very angry hard-on, and at the moment, he could've broken through a brick fucking wall.

She kissed the edge of my jaw and breathed out an "I'm sorry."

"No, it's fine." I pinched my eyes shut. "It's okay."

"I just . . . I keep hearing his voice." Remi lifted her head, and her eyes weren't hazy with lust anymore. They were filled with apology. "What he said about us."

God, I didn't want it there, didn't want him anywhere near this, but as soon as she said it, his voice was in my head too.

Fucking your way through your community service might be a little cliché, but she looks like a pleasant enough way to spend the time.

"I could lose my job for sleeping with you right now. If anyone finds out . . ." She rubbed her face, and I took an unsteady step back. "Your dad could tell someone. The press, social media . . ." Her voice trailed off, hopelessness filling her gaze.

"I know," I admitted in a rough voice.

She searched my expression like she was waiting for me to say something else.

But I didn't.

I *couldn't.*

I wanted to tell her that sleeping with her now meant I was in. That she was it for me. That I wanted her reading in my chair and putting up Christmas trees with ugly ornaments. That I wanted to pick up Gavin from practice and help him with soccer in her tiny backyard. I wanted her in my life. Wanted to be in hers as much as she'd let me. And I still wasn't sure she was ready to hear it. That same voice that whispered *caution* told me that, even worse, she might not believe me.

"You have a lot more at stake than I do," I said in a dull voice.

Reality had a nasty way of elbowing into the best moments, and it absolutely devastated this one. The pretty pink color ebbed from her cheeks as we stared at each other.

Remi sighed, staring down at her hands where they were clasped in her lap. "I wish I knew how to make our lives make sense together, Archer."

"Me too, firefly. Me too."

She gave me a sad smile as I helped her down from the counter. I handed her the hair tie that had fallen to the ground, and watched in fascination as a few loops of her hands twisted all her hair up off her neck.

Everything she did seemed to fascinate me, though. Wasn't that part of the problem?

Remi was my addiction. And it didn't help either of us for me to replace one unhealthy behavior pattern with another.

Before she walked out the door, I tugged on her hand and pulled her back into my arms, sighing when she returned the embrace and rested her head on my chest.

"I've never had anyone fight for me like that," I admitted, pressing my nose into the crown of her head. "Thank you."

Remi didn't pull out of my arms right away, and knowing that this was hard for her helped, just a little. Even though I wanted her to be sure, and I wanted her to choose whatever was happening between us, I couldn't fault her reasons for holding back.

The stakes for her were much higher, and I knew it.

When she pulled back, I saw the indecision in her eyes, the slight pucker to her brow. I smoothed my thumb over the lines there and smiled. "Drive safe, okay?"

There was a moment where I thought she might say something, might kiss me again as her gaze flickered to my mouth. But she didn't.

Remi nodded and pulled out of my arms.

When she left, I stood on the front porch, leaning against one of the columns and watching her drive away. I did so knowing that she'd changed something fundamental inside me.

Or maybe I'd changed it, and she'd been the catalyst I needed. Allowing Remi to see more of me than anyone else ever had was upending my life as I knew it.

Carefully, I touched my cheekbone and winced.

Some things would heal on their own, and others . . . well, they required a little bit more intentional action.

I pulled my phone out of my back pocket and dialed a number I'd never called.

"Hey, it's Archer Evans. I know it's late, but I have a huge favor to ask, and you might be the only one who can pull it off."

Chapter Twenty-Five

Archer

It was a well-known fact that the two most intimidating people in the front offices were the team owner, Pearl—a stern octogenarian who took no shit from anyone and had outlived multiple husbands—and Coach's executive assistant, Bridget. Everyone knew she held the real power in the building.

Lucky for me, I was facing both of them.

I approached with a polite expression on my face and clasped my hands in front of my body, in case I needed to protect my balls.

Pearl stood behind Bridget's desk, wearing a pink tweed dress and a diamond necklace that probably cost more than my house. Anytime I was near, her facial expression resembled a faintly annoyed parent who still loved their kid but also fantasized about smacking the shit out of the back of their head.

"You want something from me?" she barked. "If you're trying to ask for a raise, I haven't had enough sleep or coffee to laugh you out of this office."

"No, ma'am," I said. "I'm here for Bridget."

Pearl sighed. "Lucky her. You gonna earn your paycheck this season?"

My neck felt hot. "Yes, ma'am. I hope so."

She grumbled something under her breath, snapping the binder in her hands shut. I thought she'd go back to her office, but both women merely waited for me to speak with faintly amused expressions.

"Sorry to interrupt," I said. "Bridget, I came to get that . . . thing."

She arched an eyebrow. "Yes, this *thing* cost me about seven favors in order to get it done in thirty-six hours, so you owe me, Evans." From behind her desk, she produced a sleek white box with the Buffalo logo on the top. "Don't worry, though. I'll call it in at a very inopportune moment when you least expect it."

The box was light in my hands, and I held it carefully. "Can't wait."

She smirked. "Who's it for?"

"A friend."

Bridget and Pearl traded a look, but Pearl was the one to speak next. "If it's a female friend, the kind that you'd like to play naked Twister with," she said pointedly, "I suggest flowers and jewelry. Not merch."

The ground could swallow me up at any point.

"Yes, ma'am. I'll, uh, keep that in mind."

Bridget snorted quietly.

"Thank you," I told Bridget, lifting the box slightly.

Her eyes warmed imperceptibly. "I hope it achieves the desired result."

"Me too."

Since Remi had walked out of my house not even forty-eight hours ago, time had slowed to a sluggish crawl. My entire body vibrated with the need to seek her out. She hadn't asked for space, per se, but she was off the day before. Therefore, I had no reason to be at the shelter.

Missing her was the best I'd ever felt in my entire life. It was an ache that felt good, like the healing of a bone, or the stretch of an unused muscle flaring back to life.

That being said, I didn't really know what to do either.

There was no protocol for this. No game plan I could take home and study.

Remi wasn't like reading a defense, who had a clear, definable objective, lining up against me while I tried to execute my own. Nor was she an opponent, even though it felt at times like we were always in opposition.

Wanting the same thing, going about it in entirely different ways.

Left up to me, we'd have spent the entire night in bed, and the next day doing clothed activities that I wanted just as badly. I could've taken her out to breakfast. Her and Gavin. There was this place not far from my house that served the best cinnamon rolls I'd ever had in my life, and I wanted to see their faces when they tried one. We could have watched a movie or played *Mario Kart* in their small living room, and I would have been the happiest guy in the entire fucking world.

Even if she couldn't see a clear path there, Remi wanted that too. All that was left was to find a compromise, if there was one to be found.

The sun was bright as I exited the building, and I whistled quietly as I walked to my truck. Just as I hooked my seat belt over my chest and lap, my phone buzzed in the console, the shelter's name appearing on the home screen.

A smile spread over my face before I could stop it.

God, I was a sap for this woman and couldn't dredge up a single fucking ounce of shame over it.

"Good morning, firefly," I said.

There was silence on the other end of the phone.

"Remi?"

"Yeah, no, this is Vanessa, I'm just . . . stroking out over here about the nickname."

I rubbed the back of my neck. "Good morning, Ness," I amended.

"*Firefly?* That little shit, she did not share that with her friends." Then she muttered something under her breath that I couldn't catch.

"What was that?"

"Oh, just that the giant hickey on the side of her neck makes a lot more sense now."

I slicked my tongue over my teeth, resting my head back as I slammed my eyes shut, thankful Vanessa couldn't see the heat climbing up my cheeks. "What can I do for you?"

"Right." She cleared her throat. "Remi won't call you because she's been handling her own shit for ten years, and while I'm all about being an independent woman, I'm also not a huge fan of arriving at work to see my friend being harassed by paparazzi."

My head snapped up. "She was what?"

"Maybe *harassed* is a strong word, but she was unloading some stuff from the parking lot, and those nosy little fuckers were snapping pics and asking her questions about you, and it was a whole thing. Had her pretty flustered, and I told her to call you, but she insisted on not bothering you because it wasn't your fault."

The silence that came after this statement very clearly pointed to the fact that it was, in fact, my fault, and we both knew it.

"They still there?"

She hummed. "Hanging just past the property line. I think they're waiting for you, pretty boy."

I clenched my jaw and turned the truck on, the roar of the engine ratcheting up the pulse racing in my ears to an unhealthy level. "Give me fifteen minutes and they'll get what they want."

"Glad to hear it. I may go entertain myself in the meantime, but it's good to know you're so responsive."

The drive over wasn't just tense—I thought I'd snap the steering wheel in half from the pressure of my clenched fists.

This was my dad. It had to have been.

The cavern inside my chest was brittle, like if I breathed in too deeply, hairline cracks would appear. This was Remi's nightmare, playing out on her metaphorical front yard. It was so much more pleasant to spend my morning obsessing over the way she tasted, over the feel of her soft skin under my hands, the noises she made when my tongue touched hers. Even though she'd pulled back, our parting hadn't felt like a rejection. It hadn't felt like defeat.

But now defeat was the thing knocking at the door, an ominous tapping with cruel, bony fingers.

If my dad was behind it, he'd picked a hell of a weapon. The irony, of course, was that prior to this, I was always more than capable of detonating my own kind of destruction. Now that I'd started making better decisions—decisions meant to inject distance between us—he was snapping at my heels, trying to light fire to the entire thing.

When I was tiptoeing toward something good, something pure in my life, something untainted by him, he had to do this.

By the time I arrived at the shelter, I was well and truly pissed off, anger rolling off me in waves.

Except they were gone.

There were no guys with cameras. Only two cars were in the parking lot—Remi's Toyota and the white Jeep that belonged to Ness.

I hopped out of my seat, slamming the door behind me so hard that the entire truck rocked from the force. The fact that they'd left was good, and yet I couldn't help but feel disappointed that I didn't get to smash someone's camera.

And the moment I did, they would have another headline. Another piece of ammunition. I sank against the side of my truck and scrubbed my face with my hands.

"Ness is in so much trouble."

The sound of Remi's voice made me drop my hands and straighten. She approached, her arms crossed over her stomach. Her hair was down, covering the thin straps of a royal-blue tank that made her eyes bright like jewels.

Those eyes could hardly meet mine, and the realization slid like a knife into my gut, quick and sharp and soundless.

"What'd they say to you?"

Remi sighed, glancing over her shoulder at the shelter. "I told her it wasn't a big deal."

"Remi . . ."

She shook her head. "They snapped pictures of me when I was unloading a crate of puppies from another rescue. Once I got the dogs inside, I came back out to ask if they needed something." Finally, her gaze locked on mine. "They knew my name. Asked when you'd be getting here. Asked if we'd been spending a lot of time together because of your community service," she said pointedly.

I ground my teeth together, my hands clenching at my sides. "Anything else?"

"I asked them to leave," she said with a helpless shrug. "They reminded me they were just outside the property line, so even if I called the cops, there was nothing I could do."

"And then?"

Her eyes dropped down to the pavement and she leaned against the truck next to me but stayed far enough away that there was no risk of her skin brushing mine. Those few inches felt like a fucking mile.

How was it just last night that I'd thought I finally had her? That she would finally be mine? In the harsh light of day, and with reality intruding like a storm tearing the roof off my fucking house, the space she was keeping between us felt like a death knell.

"Then I went back inside and ignored their questions." She tipped her head up, like the warmth of the sun on her face made her feel better. I might have tried it, too, but there was no tearing my eyes away from her. "I freaked out to Vanessa a little bit, and she called you."

"When did they leave?"

Her mouth softened into a smile. "When Ness came outside with a bucket of dog shit and said she had really good aim."

"Holy fuck." I let out a sharp exhale and tried the face-up-to-the-sun thing. Not surprisingly, it didn't have the slightest effect on my blood pressure or my mood. "Why didn't you?"

"Why didn't I what?" She attempted a small smile, but it didn't reach her eyes. "Throw dog shit?"

I stared hard at her profile. "Why didn't you call me?"

Remi turned to the side, leveling me with her knowing gaze. "You know why. I'm not trying to send you any more mixed signals after the other night, and asking you to come save me at the slightest inconvenience seems pretty mixed to me."

I pushed off the truck and shoved my hands through my hair. "Fucking hell, Remi, do you think I care about signals? You had assholes here with cameras in your face, likely tipped off by my father because he's trying to remind me that he's not going away quietly. You've never had to deal with that before, and even when you're used to it, it's not easy."

"It wasn't easy. It was horrible," she said, unflinchingly honest. "My hands were shaking so bad, I could hardly pull open the door when I tried to go back into the lobby. I could feel them staring at me the entire way, and I don't know how anyone ever gets used to that level of invasion of their privacy."

"You don't," I said gruffly. "You don't. But when you love the thing you do, it's a trade-off that you accept."

When you love someone who does what I do, it's a trade-off you accept.

I couldn't say it, because we weren't there. *She* wasn't there. But God, I wanted her to be. I wanted to press Remi against the side of the truck and kiss her the way I'd kissed her the night at my house. Wanted to feel her curves against my body and swallow those sweet little sounds she made. More than that, though, I wanted to absorb the pieces of this situation that caused her stress and worry, that she couldn't see a way past. Everything inside me was screaming to do something, to take something, to find an outlet for everything I was feeling but couldn't speak out loud.

The unspent tension made the blood pump furiously through my veins, seeking an outlet that was no longer there. My emotions were sharp and focused, so bright that they hurt, like trying to stare directly at the sun.

"I wanted to call you," she admitted quietly in a defeated tone. Her shoulders were slumped, her demeanor sad. "I went into my office and picked up my phone. And just before I hit the button, I thought, *This isn't fair. I can't do this to him.*"

"Do what?"

Her eyes were glossy with unshed tears. "Tell you one thing and then do another." She shook her head, staring down at the ground again for a moment. "Even before I got here, and even though I shouldn't have been, I couldn't stop thinking about our kiss and how it felt being with you."

"God, me too," I said, desire giving my voice a rough edge. "I can't get it out of my fucking head." I let out a short laugh. "I was a little sad I didn't have to come do hours today."

Remi sucked in a quick breath, then pulled a folded-up piece of paper out of her back pocket, holding it out to me with a decisive set to her jaw. "About that . . ."

"What's this?"

She waited quietly while I unfolded the paper and skimmed the lines, until I got to the bottom and saw her signature next to the tally of hours. "I didn't finish yet. Why does this say I did?"

"I decided to count the hours you helped me move Pops. You did it at my request, and even though it wasn't at the shelter, you were helping me, so I made an executive decision." She smiled, but it was bittersweet, and the sight of it tore through my fucking ribs. "Congratulations. You're officially done with your community service."

Not trusting myself to speak right away, I stared down at the paper for a few more moments while someone tore my sternum open to the size of the Grand Canyon.

I shouldn't have been surprised. Nothing I did was ever good enough. For anyone.

No matter how hard I tried, no matter how much my decisions improved, I couldn't break through that last barrier.

"You trying to get rid of me, firefly?" Remi's sharp inhale was enough of an answer, and I let out a bitter laugh. "Yeah, I guess so."

She stepped forward, resting her hand on my arm. "No. I'm giving you credit for time spent helping, and—" Her voice wobbled. "And I'm taking this out from over our heads."

My gaze locked on hers. "What?"

"This." She pointed back to the shelter. "I cannot process any clear way forward while we're in this position."

"Do you regret kissing me?" I asked. Her eyes flashed with something, and I didn't like whatever it was. Because after that flash was a pause. "Do you?"

Remi sucked in a shaky breath. "Archer, I—"

"Do you regret it?" I asked again. My voice tore through each syllable like someone ripped them from my throat.

She licked her lips, closing her eyes and sucking in a fortifying breath. "Your dad was right. It looks like the worst kind of cliché if something happens between us right now."

"I don't give a fuck what it looks like to other people."

"I do," she yelled. When my head reared back, she closed her eyes and softened her tone. "*I* do. I have a job that I depend on, and I have a son who is looking to me to learn lessons about how a person conducts themselves with integrity. I have already messed up in so many ways when it comes to you, Archer. I told him not to judge people by their mistakes, and that's exactly what I did. I punished you when it wasn't my job. I let you in when I kept reminding myself that I needed to keep you at arm's length." Her voice dropped to a whisper. "I kissed you. I kissed you knowing that it meant something, and knowing that I shouldn't."

A fat tear slid down her cheek, and my chest caved in at the sight of it.

"I have to draw a line somewhere around . . . whatever this is. And I care how it looks to the world when I will be the one at their mercy, without a multimillion-dollar paycheck to get me through, and a *son* who will have to live with the consequences of their judgment. Who will have to live with the consequences of a choice he had no part in making."

Rage—useless, cold, helpless rage—coursed through me, and I tipped my head back and gritted my teeth. I wanted to scream obscenities at the sky, just to let something out, but I didn't.

I hated every fucking word, but I couldn't argue with a single one.

Knowing she was right spun a tight web of anger deep in my belly, the intricate strings tangled up in everything so thoroughly that instead of trying to tear them out, I let myself get stuck dead center.

That anger loosened my tongue.

"But you can't tell me you don't want me." The words landed like a blow, and Remi sucked in a shocked breath. "Can you tell me that?"

Her bottom lip trembled. "Don't. Don't do this."

"Why? Because you can't give me a clear answer?" I stepped forward, frustration heating my skin, clawing just under the surface and desperate for air. "You can't even tell me what you feel right now, Remi, and it's not that fucking hard."

"Yes, it is." Her eyes blazed, and it made me realize I might not be the only one on the cusp of boiling over. What would she be like in her anger? I'd seen it once. And fuck if I didn't want to see it again. "The second we start doing that, it ups the stakes, and they are already high enough."

I took a step closer. "Tell me you don't want me."

"Archer, please," she whispered.

"I want *you.*" I held her gaze, even though my ribs squeezed against my lungs and I could hardly take in a breath. Even though it was the scariest thing I'd ever done in my entire life. "I want you, more than all the complications and the doubts. And I want to know if you feel the same."

It didn't have the intended result. This wasn't a movie where I could push and push and push until her only course of action was to submit to a kiss that would change nothing, would heal nothing, only serving to make us feel good for a fleeting moment.

Of the two of us, Remi had a better handle on what all this meant in the bigger picture.

No, her anger didn't flare like mine. She didn't match me step for step. All I could see was a broken heart.

She cried quietly, closing her eyes and pressing her hand to her chest. The anger had drained out of her and, with the sound of her tears, out of me too. This roller coaster we'd built, out of stolen moments and untapped tension, finally seemed to have taken the fight out of both of us.

Taken the fight out of me.

"What if I was normal?" I said raggedly.

"What?" she whispered.

"What if I was normal?" I held her gaze and took a step closer. "What if I was average and worked at a fucking . . . bank or something? Could I walk away from this and have a chance with you?"

"Archer." Another tear fell. "Stop."

"What if I was just . . . Archer?" I stepped closer again, my heart hammering wildly in my chest. As gently as I could manage with the screaming emotions I could hardly control, I cupped her face in my hands, wiping her tears away with the edges of my thumbs. "What if I walked away from all of it? Would you have me then?"

Remi let out a choked sob, eyes falling closed as I held her face. "I don't want you to be something you're not," she said. "I *like* who you are. I—"

I stepped back, my hands falling limply by my sides. "Stop, God, please don't say anything else."

She respected the terse request, covering her mouth with trembling fingers.

"Of all the ways he has fucked me up, this . . . this right here is why I hate him the most." I hung my hands off the back of my neck and stared forlornly at the woman I'd fallen in love with. The woman I couldn't have. "I don't know how people do this, and I have no compass to work my way through. I don't have a model. All I want to do right now is let my disappointment turn into absolute ugly fucking rage and say something to light a match between us right now."

Remi shook her head, closing the distance between us, her eyes holding mine. "Don't. Don't do that."

The temptation reared high and impossibly loud, sliding through my mind because I felt so fucking helpless.

"I could make you hate me," I said quietly. She lifted her hands and cupped my face. I held on to her wrists and exhaled heavily. "I could make you hate me so easily."

"No, you couldn't," she said, tears making her voice thick and wet.

I didn't want her crying for me.

The sight of her—beautiful even in tears—made me so fucking weak. Weak like I would walk away from the career I'd built. Weak like I would let my poisonous tongue take over and sever this connection so thoroughly, until the only thing left in her eyes was disgust.

An insidious voice, the one that cracked a curling whip over the nastiest of my self-sabotaging tendencies, whispered that she'd be able to move on easier if I did.

Be able to move on from me.

Before I could do either, I pushed her hands off my face and took a step back. "Yes, Remi, I could."

"Mom?"

My stomach bottomed out.

Gavin was standing in the doorway to the shelter, gaze bouncing between us.

Remi's eyes widened, her hands dashing furiously over her cheeks. "Gavin, I'll be right in. Go find Aunt Ness."

Gavin's brow furrowed at the sound of her voice, and he swung his gaze to me.

Confused.

Angry.

Heartbroken.

"What are you doing to her?" He took a step closer, his chest heaving on short, panting breaths. "Why are you making her cry?"

Remi reached for him. "No, Gavin, baby, let me take you inside."

He shook her arm off and marched over to me. "Go away!" he yelled, tears filling his eyes.

"Gavin," Remi begged, tears flowing unchecked down her face again as she tried to pull him back with one hand on his arm. "Stop. He's not doing—"

"I am," I said hoarsely. "I *am* making her cry." They both stopped. Remi stared up at me, wide-eyed. Gavin's chin wobbled. "I'm so sorry, buddy."

Twin tears fell down his face, and he jerked his chin up, marching forward until he set his hands on my stomach and shoved. I fell back a step, my chest severed in two. "Go away!" he repeated through his tears. "Get away from her."

I wanted to die before ever feeling that again. It was too thick to breathe through, too big to swallow.

He turned and flung himself at Remi. She fell to her knees and hugged him, whispering something in his ear while he wept.

A tear dripped from my chin before I even knew I was crying.

Vanessa ran out of the shelter, mouth falling open at the scene. "What the—"

Remi looked over her shoulder. "Ness, can you take him in, please?"

She gave me a stunned look and then blinked, doing as she'd been asked, gently removing Gavin from his mother's arms and taking his hand while she led him back into the building. The fire had drained from his little body, and his pitiful sniffles felt like barbed hooks lodged in every bone of my rib cage, pulled tight and ready to snap me in half.

Remi stayed on her knees for a moment longer, getting her bearings.

I sank back against the truck and swiped a hand over my mouth, letting it stay there until she finally lifted her head and met my gaze.

My hand fell back to my side. "I'm so fucking sorry, Remi."

I hardly even recognized my own voice—shredded with emotion, torn up with guilt and self-loathing.

"I'll talk to him," she said slowly. "He's never . . . he's never seen me with anyone, so he's not used to some of the ups and—"

"Stop." I lowered my voice. "Don't make excuses for me. Not to him. I deserved that."

Remi started to stand, and I held my hand out. She stared at it for a second, then slid her palm over mine.

What a wreck I was, that the touch of her hand almost took me to my knees. Maybe it felt better because I knew what I had to do, felt more perfect because I'd made peace with it.

"I get it," I told her. She stood in front of me now, her eyes red and her skin pale. "I get why you can't do this. I should've listened. Fuck, I should've listened."

"Archer, I'm not asking you to walk away forever. I'm just asking for time."

Remi's heart was bigger than mine, more generous in just about every way, and she'd never say it if she didn't mean it.

"I can handle a lot of things," I told her, cradling her jaw with one hand. "But I can't handle hurting you. Hurting Gavin. I'd never forgive myself. You deserve someone who won't make you cry."

She closed her eyes, more tears spilling down her face.

I brushed one away. "Will you do something for me?"

Remi sucked in a shaky breath and nodded.

I walked over to the truck, my body aching like I'd been worked over by a wrecking ball. I stared down at the box in the passenger seat, swallowing the hot press of tears at the back of my throat.

"Give this to him." I held out the box. "If you don't think he'd want it from me, just . . . say it's from you."

"Archer, please," she whispered.

Before she could say anything, I leaned down and pressed a kiss to her forehead, lingering longer than I should have.

"It's not supposed to be this hard, firefly." I filled my lungs with her scent, heartsick that it might be the last time. "Not for someone like you. You're too easy to love."

She didn't move.

Not when I got in the truck and reversed out of the spot. Not when I drove away.

I could still see her in the rearview mirror, holding the box in her hand, and the pain was so big, so great, that it felt like I'd left my heart behind.

Chapter Twenty-Six

Remi

We didn't stay long at the shelter. It was never meant to be a full shift anyway—only facilitating the puppies' arrival and coordinating the fosters since Ness was working by herself. Bringing Gavin hadn't seemed like such a big deal because it would only be a couple hours, and I didn't want Pops to cancel lunch with his friends.

Mistakes.

Mistakes had been made, and there was nothing I could do about it now.

There was enough left in my haywire brain to put the box from Archer in the passenger seat of my car before I went in search of my son.

I found him in the kennel room, helping Ness feed the puppies.

His eyes were clear, so there'd been no more crying, but his face was drawn, his skin pale.

"Ready to go?" I asked.

Gavin nodded.

"Or do you want to talk first? We can go in my office."

"Mom," he sighed. "You know how you said it's okay to take a little space from something that you don't understand?"

Screw my past self and her therapy-driven advice. Apparently, I'd taken that advice to heart, and it had landed me right in the middle of drama city. I didn't understand what I was feeling for Archer, and space felt like the only real option. Genius, Remi. Fucking genius. I'd spaced myself right into a breakup from a non-relationship and eviscerated my heart into pulp.

I rolled my lips together and nodded. "Yeah, I remember that."

"Is it okay if we talk about it later?"

Literally no greater weapon had been forged than a child giving their parent eyes like that. Big and pleading and sweet. I was helpless. Helpless to say no.

"Yeah, bud. It's okay."

Ness gave me a sad smile, and with her thumb and pointer finger extended out to mimic a phone, she held her hand up to her ear and mouthed, *Call me?*

I nodded, blowing her a kiss.

Gavin was quiet on the drive home, and even though I was too wrung out to attempt an emotionally appropriate conversation about what he'd just witnessed, I couldn't let him stew in it for too long. After asking permission to play Nintendo, he disappeared into his room.

It was too quiet. There was nothing to distract me. And in that stillness, I heard Archer's voice. Recalled the feel of his lips on my forehead. This was the messy side of love I'd avoided at all costs. Dangerous and tempestuous, a feeling that would never come close to average.

He'd never come close to average, and the fact that he wished it—for me—made my head spin like a top. What had I done?

How had I ended up here? Heartbroken over someone who'd never given their heart away before, and even though he'd never said the words, I felt like he'd given his to me.

I sank into a chair and speared my hands into my hair, trying to figure out what would make me feel better.

Archer.

Archer would make me feel better.

There was no distraction in existence that would replace him, not right now, and that was terrifying. The wildly selfish thought sent me spiraling, because I couldn't pinpoint when that had happened. *Terrifying* didn't even really cover it. Like standing with my toes over the edge of a waterfall. There was no seeing the bottom through the billowing mist. No way of knowing what waited for me when I jumped.

I could break every bone in my body.

Or it could be paradise.

If I stayed still much longer, I'd think myself right into a panic attack, and I was not trying to add that to my list of fun experiences for the day. I'd had plenty, thank you very much.

Pops wasn't home from lunch with his buddies yet, and when he came into the house about forty minutes later, it looked like the kitchen cabinets had puked all their contents onto the counters.

I was standing on a stepladder, furiously wiping down the top shelf, but his gaze bored into my back.

"Bug . . ."

"Hey, Pops." I couldn't look at him. If I looked at him, he'd know. Was I bottling feelings? Hell yes. I'd bottle the shit out of them for the foreseeable future. "How was lunch?"

"Fine."

Silence stretched between us, the only sound in the room the *squeak, squeak, squeak* of my scrubbing.

"What in God's name is happening here?"

"I'm just doing a little reorganizing. The shelves needed to be wiped down, and half of the stuff in here is expired." I kept my face forward, heart hammering in my ears. "It could make you sick, right? Making cookies with expired baking soda or something."

"Is that why they taste like that?" he muttered.

I turned around unthinkingly. "What?"

Once he'd gotten a good look at my face, his eyes sharpened. "Were you crying?"

I whipped around again. "No."

"Don't you lie to me, Remi."

Was it too much to ask for one of those faces that hid all the things? I couldn't lie for shit, and sometimes you just wanted the ability to deceive the people around you when your heart had been broken.

I set my arm on the shelf in front of me and laid my forehead on my arm. "I had a bad morning, and I don't know if I can talk about it yet, because apparently now we take space from big feelings in this house and I give terrible advice to everyone. I panicked and emptied all the cabinets because I felt like I needed to do something, otherwise I'd fall apart, and I really don't want to fall apart right now."

"Okaaay," he replied, drawing out the word. "Should I expect Gavin to be stress-cleaning too?"

Reluctantly, I smiled. "No, he's playing Nintendo."

"Something happen at the shelter?"

I gave him a pleading look over my shoulder. "Pops . . ."

He held a hand up. "Why don't you come down from there? If I keep staring up at you, I'm gonna get dizzy and fall and break a hip, and then where would we be?"

"Hopefully, in a place where you don't blackmail me with fictional scenarios." I took his hand and stepped down.

He patted it but didn't let go. "Come on. Come sit down."

"I'm not talking about it."

"All right. We can just sit and stare at each other, it'll be fun."

The man all but dragged me to the couch and sat me down in my favorite corner, then walked back into the kitchen and got a perfectly cold Diet Coke from the fridge, handing it to me with a knowing look in his eyes.

"This is emotional warfare," I muttered, but cracked open the can all the same. The first sip was always the best, and the burn down my throat grounded me amid the knotted mess of my thoughts. As I swallowed, I pressed the cold can to my temples, closing my eyes at how good it felt.

I probably had bags the size of a lemon under my eyes.

"Did you have to put a dog down?"

I shook my head.

Pops studied my face and took a deep breath. "Was it him?"

I chewed on my bottom lip for a second. "You know, your generation of parenting doesn't believe in allowing one space to process emotions, and I find that utter bullshit at the moment."

"Sweetheart, you could have a week and it wouldn't help you." It was said kindly, with the very best of intent, and I wanted to rage at him for saying it, but God, he wasn't wrong. "You'll just keep tangling yourself up until there's no fixing it other than to cut the knot out. Talk to me, bug."

This was what he did for me. What he'd always done.

It was impossible not to have flashbacks from when I'd told him I was pregnant with Gavin. I'd held on to that little bombshell for a while, until he could see the weight of the secret on my face. It wasn't until I processed it with him that I could see a way out that worked for me.

And much like he had so many years ago, Pops sat quietly, my hand in his, and just listened. I didn't cry when I told him—about meeting Archer at the bar, about the fight at his dad's, the kiss—but his eyes closed when I got to the part about Gavin interrupting us and the drama that followed.

"Shit."

"Yeah."

"Pops, I've never been more confused." I tucked myself into the couch, folding my legs up to my chest and laying my chin on my knees. "And that's saying something, because being pregnant at seventeen was awfully confusing."

"What's confusing to you?"

I blinked. "Well . . . all of it. He's doing the self-sacrificing thing and walking away. Shouldn't I be relieved? I told him I wasn't sure I could do this. But I'm not relieved. I feel like—" I set my hand on my chest and rubbed the dull ache that had taken up residence there. "Like he broke my heart. I have feelings for him, and it didn't feel fair to say it out loud. Like I would make it worse if I told him."

"Mm-hmm. Anyone with eyes could see that. But you've been attracted to people before and I didn't come home to . . . whatever that is in the kitchen."

"Big feelings," I whispered.

"Nothing wrong with those either."

I dropped my head into my hands and sighed. "But it feels impossible when I look at my life and then I look at his."

"'Impossible.'" His eyes stayed steady on mine. "That's a strong word."

"*Feels* impossible. I'm not saying it is," I amended. "But . . . think about Gavin. How am I supposed to ask him to navigate me dating someone like Archer? Today was hard enough, and that wasn't even a real argument. A real breakup. Can you imagine what it would do to Gavin if those things happened? At school and with his friends, and . . . I'd feel like . . ." My voice trailed off because something big and thorny swelled in my throat, and I couldn't force it out.

"Feel like what?" he asked, so patient and unrattled by everything I'd told him that it was almost unnerving. That was *my* role. I was the one who couldn't be shaken. But here I was. Thoroughly and completely shook.

I was the one people came to when they needed advice or help or a steady listening presence. Being on the other end, for the first time in a very long time, was disconcerting.

"Selfish," I admitted in a thick voice. "Like the most selfish thing I could possibly do. I want him so badly, it terrifies me that I'll let it take over." My voice faded to a whisper. "That everything will come second to what he makes me feel."

The words slipped through a crack in my chest—hairline thin, invisible to the naked eye. Until they rolled so easily off my tongue, I hadn't even known they were there. Wasn't that how it worked, though? There was something different about being in a safe place, with a safe person. We found ourselves admitting things out loud that we hardly dared to think inside our own minds.

I'd been running in terror from that feeling from the moment I met Archer, from that white-knuckled grip of attraction that felt wild and big and . . . destructive.

Like we'd lay waste to everything around us if we so much as tiptoed into the banked heat that framed every single interaction.

Pops sat back on the couch and folded his hands over his stomach, peering at my face so intently that I started fidgeting.

"What?" I asked.

He lowered his voice even though Gavin's door was closed. "It feels selfish to find happiness with someone?"

Something about his question made me feel a sharp edge of panic on my next inhale. It was too simplified. Too stripped down to encompass what this really was.

"Remi," he prodded gently. "Does it?"

"No." I picked at my fingernails, a wave of sadness crashing against my sternum. "But his job—"

"That's not what I asked." He refused to look away. I wanted to hide from what I saw in his eyes. "Did you know about his job the night you met him?"

I rolled my lips together and shook my head. I'd run that night, too, fled like my life depended on it because what he made me feel eclipsed all my better sense.

"So it's not just about what he does and the eyes that might be watching. It's not about your past and the douchebags you've dated before, and I think you know that. Those are excuses. But they're not the reason."

I didn't like this conversation.

I didn't like these questions.

I didn't like that this was so hard for me and that I couldn't just say *Fuck what everyone thinks* and take what I wanted.

That girl was still simmering underneath the surface, carefree and desperate for the kind of love that Archer would give me. It would be passionate and fierce. Nothing with us would be average or safe or normal. We'd argue, and it would feel like foreplay. We'd push and challenge and bicker, and it would be like sparks on a dry pile of tinder.

But I was so afraid of those flames. Was so afraid of who'd get burned in the process.

"I'm scared," I told him.

His eyes glistened. "I know, bug. But you don't need to be."

"How do you know that? How could you possibly know that?"

Then Pops did something I hadn't seen since the day Gavin was born. He cried.

It wasn't much, just a single tear escaping from the corner of his eye. "You're not her."

My heart stopped. "What?"

Another tear slipped down his cheek, but he didn't wipe it away. "You're not her, Remi."

I didn't need to ask who. I didn't need to ask what he meant. Goose bumps pulled at the hair on my arms. "I know."

He leaned forward. "You're *not* her."

I was crying too. Hell, I'd never stopped. "I *know*."

"No, I don't think you do." Pops sat forward and gripped my hands in his. "You're *not her*. You made one mistake, and I don't even want to call it that because we love that boy so much—but something changed in you when he was born. I have watched you work yourself to the bone to prove that you're not like her, over and over for the last ten years, but sometimes I worry you don't actually believe it."

The intensity of his gaze was a boot to my chest, a relentless crushing sensation, as was the unchecked emotion he usually never showed. "Pops, I know I'm not."

We never talked about my mom because *he* remembered. He held those memories alone, and I couldn't talk to him about the way she used to be when she was healthy and good and alive. I didn't remember. But her shadow . . . it was everywhere.

I'd told myself her story so many times that it inked a blueprint in my brain, one that I followed dutifully. It was a cautionary tale. A map with giant red X's to avoid. And I'd sidestepped all of them, a decade-long effort to keep Pops from any more heartbreak. To make sure Gavin knew that there was nothing more important than him.

But I'd never pulled my perspective into a different direction. I'd never thought about what it might look like to the man who'd raised me. How he viewed all these choices, the safety net I stitched together day by day, month by month, year by year.

The ache I felt for Gavin and what he was missing, it was the ache Pops felt for me.

"You give up everything for everyone else," he said, his voice cracking on the tears that flowed more freely now. "For me and Gavin, and your friends. For the shelter. God, Remi, you took a job that most wouldn't, because it's such hard work and it never ends, and I don't think you've ever even stopped to ask yourself why. You have built your entire life, brick by brick by brick, to be the exact opposite of her. And that selflessness is ingrained in you, Remi. It's not faked and it's not forced. But sometimes I wonder if you hold on to it so tightly because the thing you're really afraid of is turning out like her."

It was the emotional equivalent of someone dropping an atomic bomb on my chest. The plume went sky-high, blotting out everything else in my field of vision. And the fallout . . . the fallout was pure devastation.

I dropped my head to my knees and wept so hard that my frame shook. Pops slid an arm around my shoulders and cried with me.

We cried for the little girl who was scared and confused and didn't understand what was happening. For the parents who had to bury their daughter because she was sick and nothing they did made her want to get better. For the man who lost his wife to that heartbreak too.

Destructive choices by someone helpless against this addictive thing running their life.

We were the fallout. And I would never let Gavin feel that way. Not for a second.

"You could never do to your family what she did to you," he said next to my ear. "Not for anyone or anything in the world, Remi."

I clutched his arm as he held me, until the tears ebbed and the truth of what he was saying finally settled into something I could look at with clearer vision.

"I've never—" I stopped, trying to swallow against an aching throat. "I've never thought about it that way before."

"I know, sweetheart. You were so young, and I'm thankful you don't remember her, because it was hard." His chin wobbled. "It's hard to love someone when all they care about is destroying their life in pursuit of the thing that's killing them. But you still love 'em. You never stop." He cupped my face. "But that's not what you're doing. I'd tell you if you were. You have to stop chasing average and safe and small because you think that's the opposite of what she did. All you're doing is sacrificing the chance at a damn good life, sweetheart."

"I *have* a good life, Pops." I took a handkerchief from his outstretched hand and blew my nose. "I love our life."

His eyes were sad. "You don't know what you're missing, though. I do. I had that with your grandmother, God rest her soul. I wish I'd had eighty more years with her by my side, but even when they were hard, I'd never trade a single day for something less. For something easier."

"What do you miss most about her?" I whispered.

He sighed heavily but didn't need to think long before he answered. "I miss everything, bug. I miss telling her about my day and hearing about hers. I miss the look in her eye when she was fixing to argue. Holding her hand at the end of the day." He brushed a knuckle under his eye. "God, I miss holding her hand more than anything," he said, voice rough and quiet. "I want a love like that for you. Where something simple is the best part of your world, all because you've found the right person."

A carousel of seemingly simple moments flashed through my mind. Some not-so-simple ones too. I missed Archer. I missed him, and he'd hardly been mine long enough for the feeling to be so monstrously big.

I tried to imagine decades with him, and what it would feel like to have to keep going even after he was gone.

"I wish I'd had more time with her." I leaned my head on his shoulder and sighed. "It doesn't seem fair, does it?"

Pops hummed. "Life isn't fair, bug. Never has been. Never will be. Even the people we think have it easy, they've all got a little bit of unfairness about their life too. But that's the part that gives us hope. We can make different choices, we can do something about how our life turns out, no matter what hand we're dealt."

I thought about Archer and the selfishness of his parents. Analise too.

Everyone had their own story. Their own reasons for why they did what they did. All it took was knowing those stories, and you realized how resilient humans are. I wasn't crushed under the weight of my story, and neither was Archer. Pops had lost a daughter, and lost his wife shortly after, and he was still the best man I'd ever met.

"You did," I said to him, lifting my head and smiling. "You helped me do the same."

"I'm trying. Nobody breaks cycles on their own, kiddo. It's usually with a lot of help from the people they love, the people who give them something to be better for."

I extricated myself from his arms and sat forward, spearing my hands through my hair with a deep sigh.

"Oh my gosh, *more* crying?"

My head lifted, and at the sight of Gavin, wide-eyed at the edge of the family room, I let out a watery laugh. "A little bit."

His shoulders deflated. "Does this mean we have to talk about what happened now?"

Pops patted me on the back. "I got this one. Come here, kiddo."

Gavin let out a dramatic exhale as he trudged toward the couch. "Is this gonna be one of those adult talks that I just want to be over?"

"Probably," Pops answered.

I held open my arms, and Gavin snuggled into my lap. He was almost too big for this. But *almost* still fit, and I'd hold him close for as long as he'd let me.

"Your mom told me about what happened. It upset you, huh?"

He nodded. "I don't like it when she's sad."

Pops pursed his lips, giving my son a thoughtful nod. "I just made her cry too."

Gavin's body went still. "You did?"

"Yup. Said something important, something that needed to be said, and it made us both cry a bit." He furrowed his brow and studied Gavin's expression. "Sometimes when you're having an important conversation with someone you love, the tears just mean you're feeling something really big."

Gavin thought about that for a moment. "My teacher said we shouldn't bottle up our emotions. It's unhealthy or something."

Oh good, I'd had the healthiest fucking day of my entire life, then. Yay me.

Gavin tilted his head, then glanced up at me. "Does that mean you . . . you love Archer? Is he your boyfriend?"

My throat went bone dry. "He's not my boyfriend, honey. But I do care for him. A lot. And today we had a hard conversation about whether we can stay friends, because our lives are so different."

His little brow furrowed. "Just because someone's life is different doesn't mean you can't be around them. Isn't that what you always say? That it's good to be around people who are different than you? It's how we learn."

Innocence had a way of cutting so effectively through all the bullshit. "You're right. I do say that." I smiled. "I think maybe I need to take my own advice a little bit more."

"Yeah," he sighed. "You're pretty smart. For a mom."

Pops laughed. I rolled my eyes but kissed Gavin on the cheek. "Thanks. I think."

"So what are you gonna do?" Gavin asked.

"About what?"

He gave me a *duh* look. "About Archer."

"You'd want me to talk to him again?" I asked carefully. "Even after today?"

Gavin dropped his gaze. "Yeah. I think maybe I should apologize for pushing him. That wasn't nice." He raised his eyes. "Do you like him? Like, *like him* like him?"

Turned out, it wasn't as hard as I thought to say what I was feeling. Not now, after I'd peeled back something I didn't know I'd been hiding behind.

I was still raw. Stripped down to the bone. If I had the ability, I'd sleep for a week after what I'd just experienced. But it wasn't hard to look back and see why I'd fled, why I'd warred so mightily with myself, without even knowing the reason why.

It wasn't about Archer. It wasn't about his job.

Not really.

It was about me. About finding a balancing act between the life that I knew and a life that seemed like a fantasy. A life he'd thoroughly anchored himself at the center of. A life that would always remain just out of reach.

"Yeah. I do." I exhaled. "I like him a lot."

"Good." He smiled. "He likes you too. He always stares at you when you're in the room."

My heart rolled unsteadily in my chest, and to my surprise, the ache wasn't nearly as bad as before. "Does he?"

"Yeah. He's not very good at hiding it. I should probably give him some tips."

I arched an eyebrow. "And how do you know about all this?"

"Mom," he groaned. "I'm not talking about my crush with you—but trust me, I'm way better at it than he is."

Chapter Twenty-Seven

Archer

"You okay, QB?"

I paused as I reracked my weights, meeting Williams's concerned gaze. I'd been quieter than normal for two days before someone finally asked. Even Analise gave me a wide berth at home.

"No, Grant, I'm not." I laid my hand on his shoulder and squeezed. "Thank you for asking."

"D-do you want to talk about it?"

My entire body felt heavy with grief, and if I tried to explain a single bit of it to anyone, I'd end up crying in the middle of the fucking weight room.

"Not yet, kid. Not yet."

◆ ◆ ◆

"Archer, hello?"

The question hardly registered because I was staring at my phone, wondering what would happen if I just called her, texted her, anything.

Analise called my name again.

I turned my phone over so she'd know I was fully paying attention. "Sorry. What?"

"Could you give me a job?" she asked with a hopeful smile. "As much as I love lounging on your couch after school, I need something to do. And I just don't know if I want to go to college or not."

"Doing what?"

"I could be your assistant? Or . . . *Oh!* I could manage your social media. You never do anything. The last post you made was eighteen months ago, and it was a picture of *dirt*."

"It was breaking ground on my house, Analise. I was excited."

"No one else was," she muttered. "Did you ever read the comment section?"

"No."

Analise gestured like I'd just proven her point.

I laid my head back on the couch. "Fine. Social media manager. How much will that cost me a month?"

"I don't know. What did your first job pay?"

"Eleven million a year," I answered dryly.

Her shoulders deflated. "Oh. Well . . . maybe a bit less than that, plus room and board?" she asked hopefully.

"Seventy-five grand. Half of it goes into a savings account, and you have to take some online classes to figure out what you want to do."

Her eyes lit up. "A month?"

"A year, you punk. Give me a break."

"I'm kidding." She leaned forward and hugged me tightly around the neck. "Thank you."

"You're welcome," I said gruffly.

Why did every small act of kindness make me want to have a fucking breakdown?

Three days since I'd driven away from the shelter and I was ready to crawl out of my skin. I'd never felt so uncomfortable in my own body before, like I'd pulled my clothes on backward. Or I was wearing my shoes on the opposite feet.

Something didn't fit right.

"Archer," Analise said haltingly.

"Yeah?"

"You can talk to me, you know." She twisted her fingers around the fuzzy blanket in her lap. "I don't have much relationship experience—"

"You don't have any," I pointed out.

"I don't have any. But I read a lot of books," she said with an imperious tilt of her chin. "And I watch a lot of romance movies. I know how this works."

"Do you?"

"Yes. You screwed up, didn't you?"

"Why do you assume it was me?"

Analise arched an eyebrow.

I rolled my eyes. "It was both of us." I scrubbed my face and sighed. "It was mostly me, though. I'm too fucking impatient."

My sister set her hands in her lap and gave me a look. "Tell me what happened. No sex details, please. I don't want emotional scarring."

"No details to give you there, kid."

Her eyes narrowed. "You haven't slept with her yet? I figured you would've been, like, *right* in bed with her, based on the moony-eyed looks you were giving her."

I contemplated inducing a voluntary concussion just to get out of this conversation. "You told me you didn't want details," I hissed. "And I was not moony eyed."

She snorted. "Okay."

"This isn't helping." I was getting a migraine. I'd never had one in my life, but I was getting one now. "Where's the sage advice, oh wise one?"

"Tell me what happened."

The CliffsNotes version was all I was capable of, because when my mind replayed it, I'd get stuck on the details and fucking spiral. In hindsight, I could see Remi's discomfort, could see her gearing up to admit what was going on in her head. And it was in that hindsight that I felt that familiar self-loathing when my worst instincts ran right the fuck away with my mouth.

After my somewhat-matter-of-fact retelling, Analise's brow pinched. "So you hear her fears as rejection because Father has twisted your perception of how you engage with the world. That if something isn't going perfectly, you're failing."

My stomach twisted like a knot, cold sweat forming along my hairline. "That's . . . that's not exactly right. She can't even tell me what she feels for me, Analise. But even that is a moot point because I was so fucking impatient that her kid probably thinks I'm a monster."

"There is no way he does."

It still felt like breathing through thick mud when I recalled Gavin's face. "You didn't see him."

"No, but I know Remi. She'd never let him think something of you that's untrue."

"I felt like a monster," I said wearily. "Isn't this always my problem? Something happens that I'm not expecting, and I just . . . don't fucking think."

"Your intent is always good, though," she added in a gentle tone. At the expression on my face, she held up her hands. "I know, I know. That doesn't make you feel better, but it's the truth. Every time you've gotten yourself stuck in a corner like this, you're headed in the right direction. You just . . . go about it the long way. Like you're climbing up the side of a mountain barefoot when you could just take the sidewalk around the base. You'll get there eventually, but God, you make it harder than it needs to be."

"This is a really flattering analogy."

"Yeah, well, you're kinda bad at this."

"I'm ten years old than you," I snapped. "Let's cut the condescension by about fifty percent, please."

"Relationally, you're a *toddler*."

"Hey. I'm trying here."

Her eyes were fierce. "I know you are. And he's made you think you have to do everything exactly right all the time, and you *don't*. It's okay to tell her that you're feeling a little lost and confused, which is what *she* was doing, by the way. You just swung way too far in the other direction. You don't have to walk away because something got you all up in your man feels. That's what you do. You shut down when it gets hard, with everyone."

I rubbed a hand over my mouth, glaring at her just a little as I did.

"I'm aware," I managed through a tight jaw. "I just don't—I don't know how to stop myself before I get to that point."

"I don't know. Maybe put yourself in time-out?"

I gave her a dry look.

"I'm not kidding. Tell her you need five minutes. Chances are, you won't even need it. By the time you walk away and get his voice out of your head, you'll be fine."

"Time-out," I grumbled. "I'm almost thirty fucking years old and I need to be put in time-out."

"We all do sometimes."

"I need *her*," I said, only a little petulantly.

"No, you don't," Analise pointed out gently. "You want her. The two of you could go your separate ways and you could still live a really fulfilling life."

Tell that to my heart, I wanted to say. My bruised, battered, self-sabotaging heart that said her name with every weak, sickly beat.

I lowered my voice and closed my eyes. "What's a fulfilling life, then? Is it making more money than I can spend and coming home to a dark house with no one to share it with? You and I both know what it's like to live that way, chasing that as your only goal, and it's so fucking empty." I opened my eyes, chest heavy with longing as I conjured an image of her face. The shape of her smile. The bright sound of her laughter. "I didn't feel empty when I was with her. I felt whole."

"No, it's not about money." Analise chewed on her bottom lip. "But every part of our life needs tending if we want to build something good. It isn't fair for Remi to be the sole carrier of that responsibility. You have friends, if you'd let them be there for you. A team, if you'd let them support you. And me," she said with a tiny shrug. "You've never asked me for advice before. It's nice to feel like we can help each other, you know?"

A decade more life lived than her and I was cowed into silence by my teenage sister, whose sole relationship experience was watching it play out with fictional people.

I tugged her toward me and wrapped her in a hug. Analise sighed, laying her head on my chest. "How'd you end up with such a good heart, kid? I was not nearly this smart or thoughtful when I was your age."

Analise lifted her head, an incredulous laugh coming out on a short puff of air. "Because I had you."

"What?"

"You are such an idiot." Sympathy filled her gaze, but love was there too. "I turned out this way because I had *you*, Archer. You had no one for a really long time, and it shows. But I had a big brother who loved me exactly the way I was, who listened to me when I was hurting and did everything in his power to make it better. Our father failed at the most important job he's ever had, but you still gave me that relationship. I know what a good dad should look like, because that's how you've always loved me."

Evanses *did* humble themselves. And it turned out, as the sneaking burn of tears pressed at the back of my eyes and my chest pinched with unnamed feelings, they humbled each other.

Analise grabbed my face. "He made you think that you need to be perfect all the time, but you don't. I have never needed that from you, and neither does Remi. Stop acting like that's your only option—that you do it perfectly or you have no choice but to tear it all down."

"So what do I do now?" I closed my eyes. "I miss her, Analise. I miss her so much."

"Then tell her that. Tell her you miss her and you want to talk."

Slowly, I nodded. "I never . . . I never told her how I really felt. That I was falling for her. That I fell in love with her," I amended. "I fell in love with her and she doesn't know."

She grinned. "Don't drop that on her the moment she answers. Lead into it naturally."

For the first time all week, I felt something other than sick, heavy dread. The hope that took its place was tentative, but it was there.

"Thank you." I kissed the top of her head. "Maybe I'll hire you for pep talks instead."

"Yeah, right. You couldn't afford me for that." She gave me a once-over. "You have your meeting with the judge the day after tomorrow, right?"

I nodded. "I had to write out a statement about what I learned. What the experience meant to me."

Analise's eyes glowed. "Sounds like a great thing to invite a friend to, huh? A public forum where you can talk about how and why you've changed. Women love a display of personal growth."

I ruffled her hair, laughing when she smacked at my hand. "She probably knows. I think the shelter has to send a copy of the paperwork to the judge before we meet."

Analise smiled. "Well. That's convenient."

I shook my head and smiled, then told her I needed to get to sleep.

When the sky was black and the house was quiet, I sat in bed and thought about Remi. I was always thinking about Remi, it seemed, and I couldn't help but wonder when that might change, even if I never saw her again.

I tapped out a few text message options. Just to see how they looked.

I can't sleep. I keep thinking about you. (*Pathetic, vetoed immediately.*)

I fucked up. I didn't want to get hurt and handled it wrong. (*Better, but too attention-seeking.*)

I miss you. I miss you. I miss you. (*No, no, no.*)

I tilted my chin up to the ceiling and took a few deep breaths. Immediately, my brain went to *it shouldn't be this hard.* But that was a cop-out. And I didn't want to do that anymore.

My entire body ached like I'd been worked over with steel bats. Personal growth was fucking exhausting. But maybe this was the kind of fulfillment Analise meant. The kind separate from Remi.

It took hours for sleep to find me, but when it did, I imagined the edge of a sidewalk curving around the base of a mountain, and knew that the first few steps would probably be the hardest.

Chapter Twenty-Eight

Archer

There were too many fucking people around for step one.

I stood outside the door to the training fields and watched the commotion with glass separating me and my teammates. Watched their faces as they talked and laughed, as they ran sprints and did conditioning in groups of two and three and four, coaches milling around with clipboards and tablets in hand.

This was the important stuff before the whistle blew.

It wasn't where the world watched, but it was where we put the work in to make us strong. Fast. Capable of inhuman bouts of athleticism. It wasn't hard to draw the comparisons between days like this and what I'd talked about with Analise.

We put in the work, day in and day out, for months before the fans filled the stadium, because if we didn't, we'd come up short when it mattered most.

With Remi, I'd tried to skip all those steps. The thought of taking time and space to feel things out felt like a punishment, felt like rejection, but what she was talking about was effort. Not when it was easy or sexy or fun. But putting in the time, dissecting what worked, strengthening what didn't.

I'd done that with my body in the weight room until I could trust it to do the things I asked it to and push myself past the limits of what was considered normal. I'd done it with my mind, watching hours and hours and hours of film, memorizing plays until random words came together in X's and O's that I could visualize perfectly. I'd done it after my injury, pushing through pain and discomfort to reset my own capabilities.

I needed to do it with her.

But first, I needed to do it in other places too. For me.

And it started here.

Coach King stood on the sidelines, his arms crossed over his chest, watching everything with a stern expression on his face. I hadn't seen him in a few days, and I sucked in a deep breath as I walked in his direction.

He lifted his chin as I approached, and as soon as I came close enough, his gaze sharpened when he clocked the bruise spreading across my cheekbone and underneath my eye.

I stood by his side and watched the other players, exhaling slowly when neither of us spoke right away. Some teammates glanced in our direction, mainly the veteran players who were still trying to decide if I was someone they could trust under center once the season began.

"You gonna tell me what happened, or should I guess?"

"Not sure you'd be able to guess this one, Coach."

He nodded, finally cutting his gaze to the side to study my profile. "You probably don't want to talk about it."

"Not really." I scrubbed a hand over my jaw. "But I'm going to, all the same. I think you'll want to know in case I get arrested again."

"For fuck's sake," he muttered. "What happened, Evans?"

I exhaled heavily and turned to face him head-on. "I got into an argument with my father over something to do with my sister. It got physical, and he punched me."

Coach's face went slack with shock, and he blinked a few times. "Okay."

"I didn't punch him back, but I did shove him up against a wall. And I'd do it again, given the chance, because he's threatening to send her away, and I will not let him do that." My throat tightened around all this honesty, but I didn't let it stem the words either. "I lied about something big to protect her, and he found out about it."

His eyes were hard as steel. "Lied about what?"

I licked my lips and stared down at the field.

Could I do this?

He might not believe me. He might berate me for being stupid and rash. Tell me I'd disappointed him.

Or he might not do any of those things.

It might work out just fine.

"About the DUI," I told him. "I wasn't the one driving. She was. She can't afford an accident, not with the way my father treats her, so I took the fall."

Coach's mouth fell open, but he didn't speak. He blinked repeatedly, his brow lowering as he let out a stunned exhale.

"I'd do that again too," I told him with a challenging lift of my chin. "But I'm telling you now because my father may press assault charges. I'm telling you because I want to earn my place on this team again. I want to do better. And I don't want to lose your respect or the respect of my teammates anymore." I shook my head. "It's too late explaining all of this to you, but the biggest reason I acted the way I did when you first came to Buffalo was because of him. It had nothing to do with you or anyone else. When I gave you shit about always wanting to be perfect? That's because I had his voice in my head, telling me that's what I needed to be. What he expected of me. And I never fulfilled that expectation. But I can handle it. The more he keeps his focus on me, the less he pays attention to my sister—and believe me, that's the best gift I can give her."

"Fucking hell, Evans," he breathed. "You're just telling me this now? Why didn't you come to me right away? I could've *helped* you. I could've helped her."

There'd been so many times that I wondered how he'd react. If I was honest. If I let down the armor and allowed him in. Every time I did, I told myself that I couldn't. That it looked weak. That I didn't need him. Didn't need anyone.

Turned out, I was really fucking wrong.

"Because I don't trust easily," I admitted. "When people react negatively to the things I've done, my brain immediately tells me it's rejection. That I'm too much to handle and no one will ever be able to do that. And I've never known how to ask for help." I swallowed. "He didn't teach me how to do that. But I'm telling you now. And I'm . . . I'm asking for help."

Coach ripped his hat off and ran a hand through his hair, a sure sign that I'd flustered him thoroughly. The man had ice in his veins, so this felt like a strange win. "Okay." He stared hard across the field, his gaze unfocused as my teammates worked around us. Then he gave me a long look. "You trust me?"

"Yes."

God, it felt good to answer so easily. The weight of the last two years melted off my frame when he gave me an encouraging nod.

Coach set his hand on my shoulder and squeezed. "You're part of this team, Archer. Part of this family. And we will have your back—but you have to trust them, too, okay?"

He was asking me to set aside my pride. To humble myself in front of guys who might never do the same in return. Some of them would, of course, but most still looked at me with an edge of distrust, and I couldn't blame them.

Wasn't that part of the lesson I needed to learn anyway?

If I stayed, if I let this be uncomfortable, it didn't mean something was wrong. It didn't mean I was failing. It meant I was fucking trying. I was doing the kind of work that was necessary to have the kind of fulfilling life that my sister talked about.

With my eyes on Coach, I nodded, feeling better than I had in days. "Okay."

His mouth edged up with a smile, something that didn't happen very often. "Good."

He placed the whistle in his mouth and blew two short bursts. Activity on the field stopped, all eyes swinging in our direction.

"Everyone," Coach called, "meeting in thirty minutes. Grab the rest of the guys and meet us in the team auditorium. There's something Evans and I want to talk to you about."

There were only two people needed for step two.

On the front door of my father's house was an ornate brass knocker in the shape of a lion, its gaping mouth holding a heavy handle that had probably never been used in all the years he'd lived here.

EVANS was etched into a plate underneath the handle, the markings of the letters still pristine after all these years.

It was just after sunrise, and even though I could have marched into the house, I raised my hand and used that ugly-ass knocker simply to prove a point.

Nothing happened at first. It felt like I waited for an hour, but in reality it was only a couple minutes, so I knocked again, a bit harder this time.

When the door opened, it was clear he hadn't been expecting me. He wasn't in his suit and tie yet—just a black robe and cotton sleep pants, his silver hair slightly unkempt.

His voice was rough with disuse. "It's six in the fucking morning, Archer. What are you doing here?"

"You're not coming to the courthouse this afternoon. Just wanted to make that clear."

Father narrowed his eyes. "I'm still your lawyer on this case."

"You're fired," I said easily. "But that's not why I'm here."

"Is your sister ever coming back?"

"Doubtful." I lowered my voice. "And you won't ask her to."

His eyebrows rose slowly. "I won't? It's amazing how sure you sound."

"Because she's almost eighteen, and if you press this, I'll help her file for legal emancipation." Despite the shocked huff he let out, I held his gaze. "She has a job working for me, and you've given us plenty of ammunition to tell a judge why she disagrees with your parenting choices."

The color faded slowly from his face, but I didn't take much pleasure in it.

Instead of waiting for him to respond, I kept my voice pleasant. "She said something to me yesterday that got me thinking. About how, when I don't know how to react, I lash out. So do you." Even though his eyes flickered, he didn't respond, so I continued. "My mother didn't, though. She fled. And I lay awake last night, wondering why I've never thought to ask you why she left. I never worried about it as a child, and I think it's because I knew I could never, ever ask a question like that."

"Your mother left because she couldn't handle—"

"You," I interrupted. "She couldn't handle you. I was a kid who never stepped out of line. Analise was practically a baby. And you were the only adult she had around her. So who's to blame for that? It's not us."

He started to speak, but I held up my hand and took a step closer into his space. "You've cost me so much more than you realize. You've cost Analise too. And maybe when you're alone in this big, ugly house and the only people who are willing to be around you are on your payroll, maybe you'll feel regret someday."

"Do the dramatic pronouncements make you feel better, son?"

"Shockingly, yes. I should've tried them earlier." I leaned in like I was sharing a secret. "No matter how many times you said it to me, I never once considered saying it back to you."

"Said what?" he snapped.

"*You* are a disappointment. You failed us. The man who expects perfection out of everyone around him is an *utter* failure at the thing that matters most, and I needed you to hear that. Not because I hate you, but because hearing it might be the only thing that makes you feel an iota of contrition."

"You'll both come back eventually," he said, voice chillingly calm, but I saw the flicker of doubt in his eyes.

"No, we won't. You're not allowed around me anymore. You're not allowed at games. At events. At anything to do with my life after today. And as soon as I can help Analise get her paperwork filed, you won't be around her either." As I looked at his face, I didn't feel sad. I didn't feel angry. In truth, I didn't feel much of anything. "We're ready to move on, and I hope you do too."

"Move on?" He laughed under his breath. "I can still send her away. I can still press assault charges. You'll be ruined."

"You won't do any of those things. You were never going to." His eyes flickered, and I knew I was right. "I couldn't sleep last night, thinking about all the things I need to undo about myself and how ready I am to make changes. And then it hit me. You won't send her anywhere, just like you never would have pressed charges. If you did either of those things, it would make *you* look bad, and that's the one thing I've always been able to rely on when it comes to you."

His voice was tight and uncomfortable. "You've got it all figured out, don't you?"

"No," I said. "Not even close. I've got so much to fix." When I exhaled a quiet laugh, my entire frame felt lighter, like I'd released a thousand pounds of weight. "I don't know if I'll be able to, but I'm going to try. If it works, I'll have the kind of life I never thought I'd get. Someone to love me, someone to build a family with." I shook my head. "Not that you'll be a part of it. But maybe you'll get to a point where you're happy that *I'm* happy."

Father snorted, a red wash over his cheekbones that gave him away. "Would you even believe me if I told you I was?"

For a beat, I simply stared at him. Slowly, a smile grew.

Then I laughed. I laughed hard. He didn't understand it, of course, but I didn't need him to. When the laughter finally faded, I set my hand on my chest and let out a deep, relieved breath. "No. No, I wouldn't." Then I tipped my chin. "I'll send someone for Analise's things in a few days. See that they're ready."

The door slammed shut, and I whistled as I walked back to my truck.

Step two had felt really fucking good.

Chapter Twenty-Nine

Remi

"Babe, we just got a really good volunteer application. I think you should meet this one."

I didn't take my eyes off the email I was typing. "Just set it on my desk. I'll look in a little bit."

Ness chuckled, like she was thoroughly amused that I thought she'd disappear simply because I was busy. "No, I think you should meet them now."

I finished the last sentence, did a quick skim, and then hit send. Ness was lounging against the doorway to my office with a smirk on her face. She'd been walking around on cloud nine ever since she and Christian had finally taken their relationship from theoretical to full-on Kama Sutra. That bitch was wearing the smug grin of a woman getting off multiple times a day, and I for one was ready to smack her. Just once. Just a little.

I wasn't jealous, per se. But I was also so jealous that it was a miracle I hadn't turned green.

"That good, huh?"

"Oh yeah. Total winner." She perused my outfit with a slight purse of her lips. "That's a . . . choice."

"What's wrong with this?" I tugged at my Backstreet Boys T-shirt. "It's vintage. I've had it since high school."

"Yeah. I know." She patted my shoulder as I pushed her out of the doorway. "You have time to change. Don't worry."

"I don't think I should go, Ness. He hasn't reached out, and I don't want to distract him from something this important. I'm . . . thinking about how I want to handle this."

"You should definitely go. God, imagine if you show up and he cries in the courtroom or something. Wouldn't that be *epic*?" Ness didn't wait for me to answer. "I made Christian cry yesterday. For different reasons, of course."

"Yeah, you told me about seven times. Gold star for you," I answered. "You still can't convince me it's a good idea to go to that courtroom," I said, just as we cleared the hallway and walked into the lobby.

"Maybe I can convince you, then."

At the sight of Analise Evans in the lobby, her pink sunglasses perched on top of her head, I stopped short, my mouth falling open. "What are you doing here?"

Ness snickered, then handed me the papers in her hand. "I told you. You just never listen to me."

Analise was clasping her hands in front of her, a hopeful smile on her face. "I just filled out my application. I'd really like to help out, if that's okay."

I skimmed the paperwork, my eyes snagging on her home address. Archer's address.

"Are you meddling, Analise?" I asked gently.

She shook her head. "This is an honest attempt to make amends." Her eyes were wide and serious, her tone genuine. "My brother came for fifty hours for something he didn't do. I don't plan to leave when I've hit that number, but it's a good start, don't you think?"

Good Lord, these Evanses were going to be the death of me.

"Yeah," I said slowly. "I think so. We'd love to have you, and I promise I won't stick you on poop duty like I did your brother."

She laughed. "That was a valuable lesson for Archer."

Why had I brought him up? At the sound of his name, my body throbbed painfully.

"Good." I didn't really know what else to say. "Is he . . . is he ready for court? I'm sure he'll do great."

Or, you know, I could ask that. Analise's eyes gleamed when I did, like she'd gotten exactly what she hoped for.

"He won't call and ask you to come," she said. "And you won't show up because you're thinking of him for the exact same reasons. You're both so worried about each other that you're still not talking yet, and I've decided that's stupid."

It wasn't a surprise that he was worried about me. After all, it was the whole reason he'd walked away. But confirmation that I wasn't alone in it . . . felt good. It felt really good.

It was comforting to know that the impulsive, emotionally driven behavior wasn't just an Archer trait. Something warm settled in my chest, and I reached for Analise, giving her a brief, hard hug. She melted into me, setting her chin on my shoulder.

"Did you want to come?" she asked quietly. "Even if you'd talked yourself out of it?"

I sighed, pulling back, leaving my hands on her arms. Then I smiled. "You're relentless, just like him."

She grinned. "Is that a yes?"

I wanted to see his face.

I wanted to kiss him.

I wanted to tell him that we could do this, even if I didn't know what that looked like.

I wanted this reunion to go perfectly, and maybe that had been my problem from the start.

Nothing we'd done was perfect. Nothing had gone the way I'd imagined. And maybe . . . maybe that was how it was meant to be all along. The most imperfect parts of us, laid bare. Archer never hid who he was, and neither did I.

We'd shown each other our worst, and still . . . still my heart ached to be near him.

Yes, I wanted to see him. Wanted to support him, no matter who was watching.

I sucked in a quick breath and met her eyes. "Yes. Yes, I want to go."

"For the love of God, please go change," Ness yelled from around the corner.

The clock on the wall showed a time that made my brows pop high. "I don't even know if I have time, at this point."

Analise was courtroom ready in a knee-length summer dress with cap sleeves and subtle makeup. We both looked down at my Backstreet Boys T-shirt and winced.

Ness popped her head out, a wide grin on her face. "I have a shirt you can borrow."

I narrowed my eyes. "I'm quite done borrowing your clothes, thank you very much."

Chapter Thirty

Archer

"Analise, we're going to be late."

"No, we're not."

"Where were you? You didn't tell me you were running an errand."

She rolled her eyes. "I was home in plenty of time, calm down."

"I am. I'm so fucking calm."

"Is that why your face is turning red?"

I yanked at the neck of my collared shirt. "Probably because I can't breathe. It's too tight."

"I told you not to wear a tie. You're just handing in some paperwork and showing her your letter, it's not like you're going on trial."

It felt like I *was* going on trial. The calm I'd felt leaving Dad's was long fucking gone. My entire life, there'd been a plan laid out for me on how to proceed. Eat these foods. Run this many miles. Do this many reps. Lift weights. Go to practice. Go to class. Do your homework. Get better. Get better. Get better.

Be the best.

But you hit a certain point when there was no one forcing you to do anything.

Life became yours to mess up. And yours to change, should you realize that staying the same wasn't an option.

Analise and I jogged into the courthouse, and at the sight of *multiple* paparazzi in the parking lot, I fought the urge to break into a run, just to get this over with. Clutched in my hand were two envelopes.

One was for the judge, something I'd practiced all night.

One was for Remi, if by some miracle she decided to come.

If she didn't, I'd call her. I'd ask her out on a date. I'd give it to her then.

I wasn't done with this woman. Not by a fucking long shot.

I'd never felt so vulnerable, rushing into the courthouse not knowing whether she'd be waiting for me or not. We were on the second floor, and instead of waiting in line for the elevator, Analise and I opted for the stairs.

The door at the end of the corridor opened with a sharp snap, echoing loudly through the hallway of gleaming tile floor. Three minutes until my appointed time with the judge.

The bailiff at the correct door gave me a look of consternation when we rushed toward where he was waiting.

"Sorry," I told him. "We got held up."

Analise smiled prettily. "It was my fault." She held up her phone. "You know how us young kids can be. I got distracted. We *really* appreciate your patience."

The bailiff softened, nodding his chin toward the heavy wooden door. "Head on in. They're all waiting for you."

I blinked. "Who is?"

Before he could answer, Analise stopped, straightening the collar on my shirt and smoothing my perfectly smooth tie. "You'll do great. Just . . . just do what you practiced. You have both of your letters?"

As I batted her away with one hand, I held up the other, showing the slightly squished letters.

"One for the judge," she said. "And one—"

"We don't even know if she's here," I answered gruffly, fighting the knot of nerves at the base of my throat. "But if she is, yes, I know what to do. I think. As long as I can find a private moment with her and she's willing to hear me out."

Analise nodded, her eyes lingering on the door.

"Why do *you* look nervous?"

"I'm not," she said. Nervously.

There was no time for this. I shook my head as I pushed into the courtroom, expecting a bunch of empty rows and the stern expression of the judge, just like last time.

Except it wasn't empty, and the judge's expression wasn't stern. She was peering over her glasses, smiling.

And the room . . . the room was *full.*

Almost every head turned in my direction, and my lungs ceased functioning.

In the back row, team captains and some of the defense.

In front of them were Coach King and his wife. Assistant coaches. Mitch, my quarterback coach. Even Coach King's scary assistant, Bridget, sat next to the team's owner, who was dripping with diamonds and whispering to Coach's wife.

Brooks, Williams, Smith, and half of the Buffalo offense sat in the middle two rows.

"How?" I whispered.

Analise gently gripped my hand and squeezed. "I told you I was busy this morning," she whispered back. "You needed to see people who are proud of you, and there's so many more than you realize."

My eyes jumped from face to face, humbled beyond words at what I saw but still looking, looking, looking for the one face I really wanted to see.

In the front row, I saw her, and I couldn't breathe.

Remi.

Pops was to her right, Ness on her left, and a silver-haired woman I recognized from my first day at the shelter. Remi's boss, if I remembered correctly. Everyone was looking at me, smiling or nodding or showing some variation of support. Except Remi. All I saw was red hair, straight and smooth down her back, as she faced the judge.

She was here. She was here. She was *here*.

Maybe I'd still have to climb Mount Everest to overcome the damage I'd done, but God, I'd do it. I'd do it a thousand times if I had to.

Finally, she turned.

When her eyes met mine, my heart pitched erratically in my chest, wondering what she might be thinking. And then she smiled.

It wasn't big and it wasn't showy. Closed lips, no teeth, and I felt like I was a hundred feet tall. I needed that smile to keep breathing, for my blood to keep pumping, my legs to hold me upright when I felt really fucking unsteady. My nervous system lit the fuck up like she'd clipped it to a live wire. That smile staked a claim in the corner of my mind that hadn't stopped thinking of her for the last four days.

Unthinkingly, I raised a hand and settled it over my heart, the thrashing beneath my palm a strange comfort when I'd felt disconnected from my own life for so long.

Remi saw the gesture for what it was, read the relief behind it, and her smile softened even further.

"Mr. Evans, welcome back."

The judge was happier to see me today, and I pulled in a deep breath before laying my hand on Analise's arm. "Thank you," I told her, then lifted my chin toward the bench seats. She leaned up on the balls of her feet and laid a quick kiss on my cheek, then took a seat next to Pops.

The envelopes in my hand were crumpled to hell as I made my way to the table where I'd sit to face the judge. The same seat where I'd sat next to my father and kept my eyes down and my mouth shut, just waiting for it to be over.

There was no point in letting shame boil over, because that feeling only held power when you continued to define yourself by your worst choices.

Shame had no place here because I wasn't ever going back.

As I took my seat, someone else joined me. When Williams stood behind the chair at my side, I blinked up at him. "Rookie, what the fuck are you doing?" I hissed.

He ignored me. "I'd like to stand in as his legal representation today. He has no one to act in that capacity, and, um, I don't want him to feel alone up here."

I pinched the bridge of my nose. "Grant, go sit down."

He ignored that too.

The judge eyed him warily. "And you are . . . ?"

"Grant Williams, sir."

A low swell of laughter worked through the room, and the judge arched a brow very, *very* slowly.

He blanched. "Ma'am. I'm sorry, ma'am."

She sighed. "*Your Honor* works just fine, Mr. Williams."

"Of course, Your Honor. I'm a teammate of Archer's. I'm . . . I'm his friend. I think. He intimidates me a little, but I still like him."

Slowly, my hand dropped, and I finally glanced up at his face. He was nervous, yes, but determined.

This fucking kid would be the death of me, and now I'd never want to get rid of him.

The judge gave me an amused look, then shifted her attention back to Grant. "Do you have a license to practice law, young man?"

"No?"

"I didn't think so." She sighed. "It's illegal to practice law without a license, but I'm feeling unexpectedly generous today by this display of goodwill and support for Mr. Evans. You may sit with him—but first, why don't you bring me the signed paperwork from his community service hours."

"Yes, ma'am. Your Honor," he corrected on a rush.

I handed him the paper bearing Remi's signature, and Williams walked it up to the judge's bench like it was the most important thing he'd ever done in his life. While she studied it, I laid both envelopes on the table. One was void of any writing, and the second held the judge's name.

The adrenaline rush from Remi's smile had ebbed a bit now that I wasn't facing her, and nerves quickly eclipsed anything else I was feeling.

This wasn't a trial, I reminded myself.

Williams took his seat and smoothed his hands down the front of his dress shirt. "How'd I do, QB?"

"You're a natural, Williams," I answered dryly.

He grinned.

"Fucking rookie," I heard someone mumble behind me, followed by the sounds of a few teammates laughing.

"Quiet, please," the judge murmured, peering over her glasses briefly before she set the paperwork down. "This isn't a football game, and I don't appreciate vulgarity in my courtroom, gentlemen."

"Yes, Your Honor," they all said in unison.

I tipped up my chin and stared at the ceiling for a moment.

"You finished your community service incredibly quickly, Mr. Evans," the judge said, folding her hands on top of each other on the surface of her desk.

I stood up. Was I supposed to stand up?

"Yes, Your Honor. I enjoyed my time at the rescue very much."

"And what sort of duties filled your time?"

It was on the paper, so she damn well knew what I'd done, and the gleam in her eye gave her away.

I exhaled a quiet laugh. "I was on poop duty, Your Honor. Cleaning up the yard. Litter boxes. Mopping the kennel floors when they got messy."

"Were they trying to teach you a lesson?"

"Yes, Your Honor."

"And did it work?"

My smile faded, and I gave her a serious nod. "Yes, Your Honor."

She made a small humming noise. "I'm told you have a statement you'd like to make for the court?"

"Yes, Your Honor."

"Hopefully, it includes more than those three words," she said pointedly.

I grinned. "Yes, Your Honor."

"All right, would your nonlegal legal representation please bring a copy forward?"

Grant was drumming his thumb on the surface of the desk.

I kicked the side of his foot. "The letter," I hissed.

"Oh." He scrambled to his feet and grabbed the envelope, rushing it to the judge's bench.

Her facial expression was the kind of patience you'd usually reserve for a wayward child. "Why don't you take a seat now?"

"Yes, ma'am—Your Honor." He gave me an apologetic look, and I shook my head as he did as she'd asked.

As she pulled the paper out of the envelope, she asked, "Mr. Evans, did this give you the kind of experience I'd hoped for when we discussed your sentence?"

I kept my eyes forward as she skimmed the letter in her hands. "Yes, Your Honor. I found it to be life changing. It's all in there."

Her mouth fell open, a shocking burst of pink washing over her cheeks. Her dark eyes darted up to mine. "Mr. Evans, this is . . . unexpected."

"It is?"

She let out a shocked exhale. "I had no idea I'd made such an impact on you," she said, tone wondrous.

My brow pinched. "I . . . Yes? You did?"

"Almost inappropriate, but I'll let it slide."

Inappropriate?

My eyes flew down to the desk, and the entire fucking floor could've given way underneath me and I wouldn't have noticed.

The only envelope sitting on the table in front of me was the one with the judge's name on it. Which meant . . .

My eyes snapped back up to the judge as she skimmed the rest of the letter with a shocked smile on her face. Fuck. *Fuuuuuuck*.

I kicked Williams again.

"Ouch, what?"

I leaned down. "You gave her the wrong fucking letter," I hissed.

His eyes widened. "I thought it was a copy. You didn't tell me which one to give her."

"Give her the one with her name on it, you twit."

The judge cleared her throat. "Is everything all right?"

"Yes, Your Honor," we said in unison.

"Good. I haven't even finished it yet, but I'm going to read a section of this, if you don't mind," she said, a regal tilt to her jaw. "This is *lovely*, Mr. Evans."

I was going to fucking kill the rookie.

"Your Honor," I started haltingly, "if you don't mind, I—"

"Sit, Mr. Evans," she instructed, not taking her eyes off the words in front of her. She held the letter out so she could see it clearly and began to read. "The moment I saw you, I knew my life had changed. I should have known that it would, because looking in your eyes made everything clearer and sharper than it ever had been."

I covered my mouth with one hand and pinched my eyes shut.

Please, I prayed fervently. A natural disaster. Fire in the building. Anything.

The rookie groaned under his breath and braced his elbows on the table, covering his face with his hands.

"When you walked away," she read, "I should have trusted life would find a way to put you in my path again, because that's where we're meant to be. We're meant to be in each other's lives. You bring a light and warmth to everyone who knows you, but what you brought me wasn't just about those things, though I experienced that too." She paused and gave me a delighted look. "This is just incredible, Mr. Evans, I had no idea our first meeting meant so much to you."

I gave her a weak smile. "Your Honor, please—"

"Yes, yes of course, I'll keep going, my apologies." She cleared her throat. The court reporter kept typing, and I was so very glad there'd be a record of this for all eternity. "But I needed more than just light and warmth. I needed change. And while you've kick-started mine, I won't only be changing for you. I'll change for me. For my sister. For a family I hope to have someday, the family I pray you're a part of, where I can teach my own children how to be imperfect and mess up and love each other. Trusting me will be difficult. If that takes time, I understand. I'll never be a poet, and I don't know how to say pretty things that put into words what my time with you has meant, but I've realized something in the time we've spent apart.

"It feels better to work really fucking hard to be the best version of myself, and not allow myself to be the worst simply because it's what everyone expected. I'd let them—let you—form those expectations, but it's also in my power to try to break apart the notions people held of me. I want to do that with you. For you. But for me too."

If it was possible to feel the weight of a dozen or more shocked gazes on the back of my head, then I was feeling them, and I sucked in a fortifying breath and turned slightly, hoping I was right and just one of them was hers.

I was.

Her eyes were big, her cheeks flushed. Her mouth hung open.

I smiled and shook my head, giving her a helpless shrug. *For you,* I mouthed, tilting my head back toward the judge.

A shocked laugh burst out of her mouth, and in the stunned silence of the courtroom after, Remi slapped a hand over her lips, eyes widening in horror.

The judge stopped. "Is everything all right?"

Slowly, I stood and held up my hands. "Your Honor, please, if I can finish what I was saying. You have the wrong letter."

Her head reared back. "What do you mean?" Her eyes scanned, mouth moving as she neared the bottom. "Oh. *Oh.*" With careful movements and color flooding her cheeks, she folded the letter back up and slid it back into the envelope, eyeing the rookie over her glasses. "Why don't you come get this?" she asked politely.

Among the quiet tittering in the room, he kept his head down and retrieved the letter, ignoring her pointed glare as he set it back down in front of me.

"You can rejoin your teammates, Mr. Williams. I think we've had enough of your help."

"Yes, Your Honor."

I let out a slow exhale. "Sorry," I told her. "Really, *really* sorry."

"Mm-hmm. And who was that letter meant for?" Her eyes skimmed the faces behind me. "Someone here, I'm assuming."

The thought of outing Remi in front of her boss, in front of my teammates, made my lungs squeeze. "Your Honor, with all due respect, that was meant for a private moment."

"And yet it's become so very public."

I picked up the second letter and held it up. "This was meant for you. If you'll allow me to approach?"

She continued, undeterred, as if I hadn't spoken, "In my many years on this side of the courtroom, I've found something to be almost universally true, Mr. Evans. Do you want to know what that is?"

Given I didn't really think I had a choice, I found myself nodding. "Yes, Your Honor."

"Every person in the world is born with the ability to change. To better themselves. But we fail to dig deep enough when it's only our own happiness and satisfaction on the line. What I've found is that the love of others, what we give and receive, is the most powerful motivator for change." Carefully, she removed her glasses and set them down on the desk in front of her. "I hope the intended recipient of that letter is aware of what your love for them has done, because it's a wonderful sight to behold."

Anxiety had a fucking choke hold on my ability to breathe properly. I'd practiced. I'd practiced how I was going to say it, when, the intonation—everything. We'd be alone with no eyes on us, and this was not how I'd intended it to go.

I'd get her fired.

She'd hate me.

She didn't want attention ruining her life and Gavin's life and—

"I *am* aware, Your Honor." Remi's voice was clear. No hesitation.

I whipped around, eyes finding hers. "Remi—"

"May I approach?" she asked, gaze locked on mine.

The judge made an amused sound. "I think you better."

She was standing. Why was she standing? God, I couldn't fucking breathe.

Then she was moving.

Then she was running.

It only took one stride and I had her in my arms, holding her as closely as I dared. Arms tight around my neck, Remi buried her face against the side of my neck and exhaled shakily.

I pressed my nose into her hair and filled my lungs with the clean, sweet scent of whatever crack shampoo she used. The courtroom filled with claps and whistles, and I couldn't even pretend to be embarrassed.

"What are you doing?" I whispered.

She pulled back, eyes watery, and she cupped the side of my face. "I'm making a change too," she said. "No more holding back because I'm scared."

I set my forehead against hers and exhaled a shocked laugh. "I've missed you so—"

She kissed me before I could finish my sentence. In front of the entire fucking room, in front of every person in the world who mattered to me, Remi Sinclair staked her claim.

The applause was raucous—loud and obnoxious and perfect—as I kissed her deeply, tightening my hold on her body. I was never letting her go again.

We broke apart, and Remi smiled.

In the space of a heartbeat, my entire world shrank down, with that smile dead center.

"We did this all wrong, didn't we?"

She laughed. "I don't know. It feels pretty right to me."

Ignoring the eyes on us, I leaned closer and let my lips brush hers. "Are you gonna get fired if I tell you I love you right now?"

"Probably not, since I told Muriel about an hour ago that I was in love with you too."

My head reared back. "You did? You do?"

Her gaze was filled with adoration. "You gonna believe me when I tell you?"

I kissed her again, my chest filling with something warm and soft and perfect. Love, probably. Whatever it was, it was hers.

"Yeah, firefly, I think I will."

The judge allowed Remi to take Williams's seat—an upgrade in just about every way that mattered for me—and with her by my side, I read my actual statement for the court. Remi cried. So did Williams. And I held her hand when the judge gave me a fond smile and told me she never wanted to see me again outside of her TV on Sundays.

The entire group filtered out of the courtroom, and the amount of hugs and backslaps and congratulations I received made my head spin, all of it with Remi's fingers wound through mine.

We took the elevator downstairs, and I dropped a kiss on Remi's head, then leaned down to whisper in her ear. "There's journalists outside," I told her. "Just a heads-up."

She wound her arm around my waist and hummed in acknowledgment. The thought of letting her go, even for a moment, sounded like fucking torture, but this was the kind of patience I was ready for.

My teammates left the courthouse first, and before we walked out behind them, I took a deep breath and dropped her hand, even though we were still walking side by side.

I hated it. I *hated* it.

Hated pretending like she wasn't my entire fucking world.

Eventually, I'd be able to. Small steps. Building to the thing we wanted. And for her, I could handle the waiting.

As we left the building and moved into the harsh sunlight, I pulled out my sunglasses and slid them on my face. Remi paused, glancing up at me.

"What are you doing?" she asked with a tilt of her head.

The click of camera shutters came closer, and I ignored them.

Archer, how did court go?

Archer, tell me who's with you?

Archer, give us a picture!

I kept my eyes on her. "I'm . . . going to my truck. You're coming over, right?"

Remi smiled again, then stepped forward, sliding her hands up my chest. "Not just yet."

Then she tugged my face down for a deep kiss, and I wound my arms around her waist, clutching her as close as I could. Could she feel the hammering of my heart? There was no way she couldn't.

I was breathless when she pulled back. Lightheaded from the kiss. From the statement it made.

From her.

"What are *you* doing?" I asked against her lips, my hands still anchored tight around her ribs.

"Setting the record straight," she whispered.

Chapter Thirty-One

Archer

My house was full. Of people. Laughter. Music. Food.

Sitting in one of the dining room chairs, an iced tea in hand, I couldn't help but marvel at the bizarre scene taking place in my home.

Pops sat between Coach and Pearl. He was telling a story that made them both laugh. Ness was in the family room with four of the offensive players, talking them into adopting dogs, and her animated hand gestures brought a smile to my face.

Gavin, who'd gotten picked up early from school because Remi didn't want him to miss this, was outside with William, Brooks, Smith, and my QB coach, teaching them the sounds of different birds. At the moment, he was perched on Smith's broad shoulders, pointing frantically at a grove of trees behind my house.

In the kitchen, Lily King was dishing up pieces of pizza for anyone who hadn't eaten enough already. Not two minutes earlier, Remi had been by her side. The two had met last year when Coach brought his family by to adopt a dog.

Analise was holding court with the rest of the players, discussing their social media strategies.

For the moment, at least, I was separate from what was happening. Not because I was punishing myself, but because I needed to sit back and soak this all in.

For two hours, I'd watched Remi circling around. She always found herself back by my side, checking in to see if I needed anything, tucking herself under my arm for a hug. Or she'd walk past when I was in conversation with Pops and Coach, and do nothing but lay her hand on the back of my neck and squeeze.

This moment of separation, the first for me since everyone had arrived, was necessary because the enormity of it short-circuited my brain. Not simply because of all the teammates, the coaches, and her family.

It was her.

Remi in my home set my entire fucking soul at ease.

I wanted to keep her here. Wanted to keep her, period.

Lily moved away from the island to find her husband, perching herself in his lap and winding her fingers through the hair at the nape of his neck. But Remi didn't follow her in from the kitchen.

I looked around but didn't see her anywhere on the main level, so I set my drink down and wandered off to find my girl.

She wasn't in my bedroom or bathroom, or the fireplace room off the kitchen, where I'd thought I'd find her.

When Williams had walked into the house earlier, he'd stared at the roaring fire there. "It's eighty degrees outside," he said slowly. "You have the fireplace on."

I merely glared at him. "So?"

From where she was tucked underneath my arm, Remi turned her face into my shoulder and laughed.

His eyes widened, his brows shooting up like I'd lost my mind. "It's . . . nice."

I kissed the top of her head and squeezed her waist. "Don't touch it, rookie. She likes it."

"Right." His throat worked on a nervous swallow. "It's perfect. I love a hot, cozy fire at the end of May."

Once I'd looked through all the rooms on the main level, I made my way downstairs, smiling as I reached the bottom. She was in the middle of the second family room, her hands on her hips.

"There you are."

It was my first chance to be alone with her, and while the caveman part of me wanted to drag her into the closest room and lock the door, I'd happily settle for just having her in my arms again.

My hands eased around her hips, tugging her back against my chest, and when she tilted her head to the side, I brushed her hair out of the way and kissed the soft skin on her neck. Remi slid her fingers over mine and settled into my embrace.

"You have a whole other house down here."

"Do I?" I kissed the edge of her jaw. "You like it?"

"It's terrible," she said breathily. "Who needs a home gym and a comfortable place to watch movies or three extra bedrooms with their own bathrooms?"

With our hands joined, I gently raised the hem of her shirt, teasing the soft skin on her belly. "Analise has the room to the left." I kissed her shoulder while my pointer finger traced around her belly button. "The other two are guest rooms."

She dropped her head back on my shoulder, arching her back slightly when I started toying with the button of her jeans. "Don't you already have a guest room upstairs?"

"Yes."

"Show-off."

I chuckled, mouth brushing over her skin. "I do try."

Remi turned in my arms, coasting her hands over my stomach and chest while I clasped mine on her lower back. "What did the rest of your letter say?" Her smile was mischievous, tightening my stomach with heady anticipation. "Was it terribly inappropriate for her to see?"

"No." I grinned. "I wasn't writing it to seduce you. I just wanted to tell you the truth."

"And what was that?"

I dragged the back of my knuckles over the line of her cheek. "That I wanted another chance. That I'd wait for you to be ready. That I wanted this to work, no matter what that looks like right now."

Her eyes fluttered closed as my thumb dragged along the line of her bottom lip. "I would've liked to hear that."

"Eight dates or eighteen or eighty-four," I repeated, picturing the words on the paper. "It doesn't matter, because any amount of time is worth it if the time is spent with you. When I told you it shouldn't be this hard, I was wrong. Fighting myself was hard. Falling in love with you was easy. So easy, it happened before I could even put a name to it." I ducked my head and ghosted a kiss over her upturned lips, pulling away before it could deepen. "Give us a chance, firefly. I want to know what life looks like with you in it. You and Gavin and Pops—and Ness, probably, because I don't think I'm ever getting rid of her either."

Eyes full of tears, Remi shook her head. "I don't need eighteen dates."

"No?"

She came closer, her fingers inching underneath my shirt. "I don't need eight dates."

My voice lowered to a desperate rasp. "I'd take you on however many you want."

Remi hummed, sidling her hips closer to mine, her eyes fluttering shut when she felt my aching hard-on between us. "The bar was number one." She dragged her fingernails down my abs, eliciting a shocked hiss from my mouth. "Number two was definitely when I slapped you in the parking lot."

"Fuck, Remi, that does not count as our second date."

Her eyes were devilish as she stared at me. "Are you going to argue right now?" Her palm slid down to the front of my pants, and she rubbed back and forth.

"No, fuck no." I cupped the back of her neck. "But our entire family is here and you're about to make me come in my pants, you little devil."

Remi rolled onto the balls of her feet and sucked my bottom lip into her mouth, releasing it with a dirty pop. "Good. I vividly remember someone whispering in my ear when there were dozens of people around that you'd bend me over and take me right there."

Her fingers curled around my length, and I groaned. "Remi, have mercy."

She grinned. "Need a time-out?"

"Yes. Yes." I plucked her hand away and nibbled at her fingers. "Later. Everyone will leave and we can do whatever you want. Or you can go home and I'll plan our next date and we'll have phone sex and I'll listen to all those sweet little sounds you make, and I'll be just as happy. God, whatever you want to do will make me happy."

Her eyes were glowing, and she bit down on her bottom lip. "I don't want phone sex."

"No?" I gripped her ass with my hands, leaning down to bite along the edge of her jaw. "Great. Neither do I."

"Phone sex is bullshit," she sighed. "When can we kick everyone out?"

As I wrapped her tight in my arms again, I laughed. "Soon, firefly. Soon."

Soon ended up being about forty-five minutes later, when I spied Vanessa and Remi whispering in the kitchen. Most of my teammates had already left, as had the coaches. The only people left were Remi's family and Analise. And somehow, quite inexplicably, Williams.

He was talking about World War II with Pops, and I was pretty certain I'd have to physically throw him out the front door and lock it in order to get him to leave.

Remi said something to her friend, and Ness nodded vigorously, then hopped off the island. "Analise, how do you feel about epic blanket forts that fill an entire room?"

My sister blinked. "I can't say that I have an opinion on them one way or another. I've never been in a blanket fort. Why?"

"Oh, honey, we need to fix that immediately. Blanket forts are awesome." Ness dragged Gavin in front of her. "My godson here loves them, and I've been promising him a blanket-fort campout at my house, which we're going to do tonight."

Gavin's face transformed. "We are?"

"Yup." Ness looked at Remi and winked. "I had to work pretty hard to convince your mom, but she always gives in to me."

Remi snorted.

Ness shifted her smile back to my bewildered sister. "Would you like to join us?"

"She would love that," I said. Analise gave me a look, and I grinned. "You didn't answer quickly enough, and you would *love that*," I said.

"I would?"

"Yup."

When I glanced pointedly over at Remi, Analise's mouth fell open. "*Oh*, yes. I would love that. I'll, um, go pack my bag?" She looked at me again. "Now?"

"Right now would be perfect," I told her.

Remi covered her mouth with one hand to hide her laughter. Ness whispered something to Gavin and he nodded, then ran over to me. I crouched down in front of him.

"It's okay if you're going to hang out with my mom tonight." His eyes were wide and serious. "I know you're friends, and friends spend time together."

"You sure you're all right with that?" I asked.

Gavin nodded. "As long as you hang out with her at our place, too, sometimes."

Remi and I locked eyes over his head, then I smiled at Gavin. "You'd be okay with that too?"

He smiled. "Yeah. But if you marry her, I'd probably want to move in here. It's nicer."

"Gavin," Remi hissed.

I laughed, holding my hand out in a fist. Gavin bumped it with his own. I set my hand on his back, leaned closer, and dropped my voice to a whisper. "I tell you what, when I'm ready to ask your mom that question, I'll make sure to talk to you first, okay?"

Not *if.*

When.

Was next week too soon?

Gavin, smart little kid that he was, picked up on that difference, and his face filled with awe. "Okay," he breathed. "If you're dating my mom, does that mean we can go to a game?"

Everyone laughed.

"I think we can make that happen."

Remi shared a look with her best friend, who silently mouthed, *Holy fuck.*

Within ten minutes, we'd said our goodbyes, Ness loaded down with kids for the night. Pops and Williams were the last to leave.

Williams lingered by the door, and I used both hands to steer him outside. "You're leaving," I stated.

"I am?"

"Yes."

"Pops is leaving too?"

The man in question held up the keys. "Kid, if you think I want to see what's about to happen here once they're alone, you're cracked in the head." He kissed Remi on the cheek. "Please use a condom, okay?"

Her cheeks were pink. "Got it. Thanks, Pops."

His smile fell when he glanced over at me. "You. Don't fuck it up."

"I don't plan to, sir."

Williams glanced between us, and the moment understanding hit, he turned beet red. "*Oh.* You want to be *alone.*"

"You think?" I shoved him toward his showy fucking car with no hint at propriety. "Leave."

Remi buried her face in my chest as her body shook with laughter, and Pops gave me a tiny salute over the hood of her car. "Bring her back sometime tomorrow."

"Yes, sir."

The Toyota left first because Williams hit the wrong button trying to shut the door of his sports car. "This fucking kid," I muttered.

"You love him."

When I glanced at Remi, she raised an eyebrow, daring me to disagree. I couldn't. So I didn't, giving a small, annoyed grunt when he finally got the door shut and the car started with an obnoxious roar.

Then we were alone.

I took a deep breath, goose bumps popping along my arms as I thought about an entire night with her.

"When was our third date?" I asked.

She didn't miss a fucking beat. "When the truck delivered all that stuff."

With firm hands, I gripped her hips and walked her toward the house. She almost stumbled on the steps, and we both laughed.

"Did we have a fourth?" I asked, sliding my hands underneath the hem of her shirt, relishing the curve of her ribs under my palms.

"You don't remember?" Remi turned, backing up against the front door, tugging on my hands until I was pressed tight against her. The coquettish tilt of her head and the heated look in her eye made my mouth water. "Four was when you dropped off Analise."

"That was a good one." I stared at her parted lips. "What else?"

"You don't have neighbors, right?"

"Are you kidding? I bought ten fucking acres just for this moment."

She smiled. "What a forward thinker you are."

"Fucking psychic." My thumbs brushed the soft skin over the waistband of her jeans. "Why do you ask?"

Remi rolled up on the balls of her feet and kissed me. Hard. Before I could sweep my tongue into her delicious mouth, she pulled back, then used both hands and tugged her shirt off.

"Fuck," I groaned. Her bra was a black lace thing that propped her glorious tits up, just waiting to be touched and sucked. Behind the sheer fabric, her nipples were hard. I brushed the hard tips with my knuckles and she dropped her head back, a delicate shiver racking her frame. "Six," I said in a desperate, rasping voice.

"I . . . I can't think when you do that."

"Want me to stop?"

"No," she moaned. "Six was . . . it was when you brought your friends to the shelter."

I ducked down and licked along the generous swell of warm, delicious flesh, and groaned when she gripped the back of my head to keep me there. While I licked at the nipple through the bra, I wedged a thigh in between her legs, and she whimpered, instantly seeking the friction she needed.

"That's it," I praised. "Show me what you need."

I encouraged her hips to roll forward, slanting my mouth over hers in a slick, dirty kiss that left us both gasping. "Seven," I commanded, fingers plucking at the button and zipper on her jeans.

She was trying to climb me, and I had to fight through the clawing, screaming urge to fuck her through the front door.

"S-seven," she gasped when I slipped my hand down the front of her jeans. Remi gripped my wrist, letting out a sweet keening sound when I pushed aside her lace underwear with two fingers and found her slick and wet and perfect. There wasn't much room to move, and the frustration made my hands tremble.

"Seven was when I helped you move Pops," I said against her mouth, then kissed her again.

"Yes." Even though I didn't have enough space to work her over the way I wanted, Remi was riding my hand like it was all *she* wanted in life. "*Yes.*"

"God, I need these fucking jeans off," I growled. "I need to see you, pretty girl."

Our kisses were frantic and deep as I fumbled with the door, tongue against tongue in decadent, slow strokes.

We almost fell into the house. I kicked the door shut behind me, and the walls fucking shook from the force. We made it as far as the family room, tearing off our clothes with greedy hands and greedier kisses.

Carpet. Carpet was good for sex, right? Thank God I got the expensive rug that was soft and easier on the knees, because I was about to take her right there.

I wanted her so badly, I could hardly think, and my bedroom was too fucking far away.

"Here," she begged. "Please."

I tore at the clasp of Remi's bra as she lay back on the floor, kissing her so deep, we could hardly breathe. When I flung it away, I sat back between her spread legs and ran my hands up and down her toned thighs, dragging my thumb along the black lace I found there, eyes locked on the trembling breaths that made her breasts heave.

"You are so damn pretty," I said reverently, ghosting my fingertips over her pebbled skin, down the line of her ribs, up over her sternum and tracing circles over her nipples again, watching the helpless arch of her back with a slight smile on my face. I was still in my boxer briefs, but she stared down between my legs with her bottom lip trapped between her teeth.

"Eight," she whispered in a shaky voice.

I prowled over her, ducking down to drag my tongue over her right breast. Then her left. I used my teeth in a gentle tug, and she keened.

"Right fucking now," I said, then sucked her breast into my mouth.

Remi tugged my face up to hers, and we kissed deeply. My free hand yanked at her underwear, and she wiggled her hips to help, shifting her legs back around my waist when she'd kicked it free of her right leg.

We did the same movements to rid me of my boxer briefs, and when she wrapped her hand around me, working her wrist in a way that made it hard to breathe, I set my forehead on hers and moaned her name.

"Now," she begged.

"I didn't get to taste you, firefly." I kissed her, sliding my tongue against hers in the same way I'd use it between her legs. She whimpered into my mouth. "I bet you're so sweet."

"Later," she promised. "We'll have date number nine in about . . . an hour. Mouths for date nine."

My shoulders shook as I laughed. "I love the way you do math."

"You'll love the other things I do even more," she promised, then bit down on my bottom lip as we kissed.

Even though it felt like a crime to pull away, I refused to rush this, so I sat back, committing the sight of her to memory, flushed and pink-lipped, her skin marked from my tongue and teeth and lips, her fiery hair spread wide on my floor. Her eyes softened the longer I stared.

"I love you," I told her, my hands coasting up and down the impossibly soft skin of her inner thighs.

Remi pushed herself to a seated position and tugged my head down for a lingering kiss that made my head spin. "I love you too," she said against my lips. Something set itself to rights inside me, snapped in place from an off-kilter position that I'd never really noticed. I loved her and she loved me. "Now, show me how much."

I'd show her for the rest of my life.

And that life started right now.

"Yes, ma'am."

I reached over to grab my pants, pulling my wallet from the back pocket. She watched with a heated expression, her hands trailing lightly over her breasts while I tore open the condom packet with my teeth.

I rolled it on, eyes locked on hers, and I knew, with every fiber in my wrecked soul, that she was it for me.

Remi's legs hitched against my sides as I lay over her again, bracing my weight on my forearms next to her head. We kissed again and again as I worked my hips between her legs, small, rolling teases meant to make her crazy.

She was no passive participant—arching her back, clutching at mine, sucking at my jaw, biting down on the meat of my shoulder, sucking my tongue into her mouth, begging with her body when I still didn't press inside.

When I gave her an inch, then retreated, doing it again, going a bit deeper, then deeper still with another rock of my hips, she tossed her head back and moaned my name.

It was the best fucking thing I'd ever heard in my life. As I moved, I watched her facial expressions, the furrow of her brow and the gentle O of her mouth showing me when something felt really good.

I pressed her leg high against my side, opening her up a bit more, then took her mouth in a wet, dirty kiss as I rolled my hips forward in a long, deep thrust that made her gasp.

Fuck.

Fuck.

She was tight. Hot and wet and the most incredible thing I'd ever felt.

"You're so good," I groaned. "I can't believe you're mine."

"Yes."

"Say it." I stayed still even though my body screamed to go hard and fast and chase the thing building in my bones. "Say it, firefly."

Remi opened her eyes, a slow blink heavy with pure lust, the green of her irises sharp with need. "I'm yours."

The pull back from her body was slow, so much slower than I thought I was capable of, but God, I wanted to feel every second, every breath, every fucking inch and sear it in my brain. Remi shifted underneath me when I didn't move right away, wiggling her hips in a way that made me clench my teeth.

My fingers dug into her skin as I held her in place, the breath snagging in her throat when I gave her a soft, teasing kiss. "Mine," I growled against her lips.

The next thrust was brutal—sharp and fast as I buried myself to the hilt. Remi's shocked gasp cut off on a whimper when I did it again.

And again.

It was better than good. Better than perfect. This woman was made for me, and by some miracle, I seemed to be made for her.

As I worked myself between her legs in long, rolling strokes that made her moan, sweat building at my hairline, I felt like I'd been waiting for this my entire life.

Home.

She was my home.

When I couldn't push hard enough, when I couldn't go deep enough, I sat back on my haunches between her spread legs and hitched her higher, my hands around her thighs to hold her in place, snapping my hips between hers, fucking her so hard that her breasts bounced on each decisive snap.

Remi was pulled taut, her entire body tight like a bowstring, and she gripped my hands where they held her thighs, her teeth clenched as she tossed her head back and moaned my name. I wanted to hear it every day. In every way she could say it.

Wanted to hear her say my name on a sigh when I took her sweet and slow in the dark.

Wanted to hear her moan it in frustration when I teased her until she broke.

Wanted to hear her beg until I gave us both what we needed.

Her. I needed her.

My hands trembled at the enormity of what we were doing, so I pressed them tighter against her soft skin.

Suddenly, I was too far away. I wanted her skin on mine, I wanted to suck the sweat from her chest and feel the quiver in her stomach when she exploded. I wanted her lips on mine. For the rest of my life.

I wanted to marry her.

Wanted to watch her walk down the aisle and thank my lucky stars that life had put this woman in my path, no matter how many mistakes had to be made on the way or what we'd had to endure to get there. It was worth it, just for this. Just for her.

I wanted to see her round with our child. Wanted to grow our family and see her belly lush and her breasts full.

A groan tore out of my chest, my body falling over hers at the thought.

One lifetime of loving Remi Sinclair might not be enough.

I'd beg the stars for more.

Remi clutched at my back, and I took her mouth in a ferocious kiss that sent my pulse sky-high. The pleasure was so high, so sharp, it felt like a razor blade dragging over my spine while I waited for her to go first.

I slid my hand between us and found the spot that made her shake. My thumb moved in tight circles, and on a particularly hard thrust, Remi broke on a choked gasp.

It rolled out, low and slow, gripping me with a brutal fist that made me half stupid. Remi orgasmed with her entire fucking body, and I kissed her through it while I chased my own.

It barreled down my legs first, a splitting sensation that bled warm through my body as I tipped my chin up and groaned her name.

I collapsed on top of her, gathering her close to my chest as we both caught our breath.

Remi cradled my jaw and kissed me again, her tongue brushing mine softly, and I smiled as she pulled back and gave me a dazed look. "We just had sex on your family room floor."

"Number eight, baby." I kissed her again. "It was always gonna be a good one."

Remi laughed, tucking herself against my chest. "I suppose it was."

"Can we move to the bed now?" I asked. "This is killing my knees."

She clucked her tongue in faux sympathy. "Rough life, Evans. I'm not sure I feel sorry for you."

I lifted her slightly so I could smack her on the ass. "You shouldn't. But if you want date number nine in the next hour, I need some hydration and a mattress."

Remi rolled over, giving me a glorious view of her backside as she got on her feet. I wedged my hands behind my head and watched her unabashedly. She picked up her underwear and stepped into it, smirking at whatever she saw on my face.

"Not a bad view from down here," I murmured, sliding my hand up her calf, circling her ankle with my fingers. "Maybe the bed is overrated."

She motioned for me to stand, and I did with a groan. When I stood over her, my hands skimming her hips, her chin tilted in invitation, and I obliged happily, sliding a soft kiss over her waiting lips.

"Please tell me you have a big bathtub back there."

I spoke against her lips. "The biggest."

She shivered. "God, I made such a good life choice with you."

"Want to get in? I'll wash your hair if you want."

Remi arched an eyebrow. "And go to bed with wet hair? You have no idea what you're asking for in the morning."

I slid my hands into all that glorious red hair, tipping her head back as I worked my fingers to the roots. "I'll dry it."

Her eyes heated. "Oh, keep talking, buddy."

I smoothed my hands down the lithe line of her back, ending with my palms on her backside. "Yeah? That do it for you?"

As I walked her backward toward the bedroom, toward the very big bedroom and very big bathtub, she hummed. "Let me show you how much in about three minutes."

I dipped, sweeping my arm under her legs and banding the other behind her back as I lifted her easily. "Three minutes?" I said with mock disapproval. "I need a little more time than that. Bath first."

Remi bit down on her bottom lip, a devious grin pulling at the edges of her mouth as she toyed with the hair on the back of my neck. "You're saying you don't want me on my knees showing you my gratitude?"

I snatched her mouth in a hot, fast kiss, growling as I pulled away. "Putting that image in my head when I'm trying to take care of you. What a naughty girl."

The bathroom was dark, but I stopped by the switch to flip on the lights over the vanity. Her eyes glazed over as they locked on the bathtub. I wasn't sure she'd sighed that decadently when my hand was between her legs. "Oh, I take it back. Everything can wait until after we use that."

I switched directions, heading toward the bedroom instead. "Never mind."

"What?" Remi kicked her feet, trying to get down with a laugh. "I want that bathtub."

I tossed her onto the middle of the bed, and she let out a breathless giggle that made my chest fucking twist. "I told you I was going to take care of you," I said, dragging her to the edge of the bed and then dropping to my knees. "Will you let me do that?"

Remi braced herself on her elbows and stared down at me with her heart in her eyes. "Yeah. Yeah, I think I will."

Chapter Thirty-Two

Remi

Archer's bathtub was as incredible as promised. If that thing had been in my home, I'd have used it every single day. We soaked until our skin was pruny and the water temperature had cooled, but I didn't find that I minded much with his big, warm body bracing mine. He kept his arms around me, unwilling to let me sit opposite of him in the obnoxiously large space while we talked.

As promised, he washed my hair and carefully dried it with a bit of instruction from me. The sight of him in the mirror, shirtless, brow furrowed in concentration as he brushed out my hair and moved the hair dryer evenly, would have obliterated even the most daunting reservations.

But there were none to be found. Throughout the evening, I waited for them to appear. For a voice in the back of my head to slither in and remind me that this might not last. That he'd get bored and move on. That I was a selfish creature for wanting him the way I did. But there was never an opportunity.

Archer refused to concede an inch of space to any thoughts like that with the way he loved me through that first night.

Even when we were quiet, his hands dragging over my skin because he couldn't stop touching me, I felt an ease that might have seemed too good to be true.

No. That phrase had no place here.

Too good implied that it wasn't deserved, that it required a transaction to be earned. That we hadn't fought to get here, when the fighting had begun long before we ever met.

The doubts stayed far away as we talked in the dark, facing each other in his bed. A small light on the nightstand allowed me to see his face, and him to see mine. Occasionally, he'd trace the line of my eyebrows and the slope of my cheek while I talked.

With his eyes steadfastly on mine, I told him about my conversation with Pops, and we traded confessions that becoming our parents was the thing we feared most. Then he kissed me. It wasn't the kind of kiss that you dream about when you're single and loneliness is threaded through your day-to-day to a point that you don't even really see it anymore.

It wasn't a passionate kiss, it wasn't dirty or fierce. It wasn't a prelude to something else, demanding that we be swept away into more. Those were the kisses I'd imagined for so long, when I'd lain in bed and told myself that a love like this was too complicated. That it was for someone else.

Archer kissed me soft and sweet and fleeting—a reminder that he was here. That he'd anchor me in place if those fears ever threatened to unmoor me again.

That was the irony. He'd already unmoored me so thoroughly that there was no going back. I didn't want to.

Loving him wasn't an act of rebellion or a selfish impulse to feed a fix. It was an acknowledgment that sometimes the universe gifted us the perfect person in the most imperfect way.

Sometime in the middle of the night, tucked against his chest with his arm around my back and my leg slung over his, we fell into a deep, uninterrupted sleep. This was a whole different kind of sleep.

An *oversexed, just had four orgasms in as many hours, my body has never registered these muscles before but they're sore* kind. Sleeping naked was a big no for me, because I didn't need to traumatize my child if he came into my room in the middle of the night, and I didn't like the idea of a cool breeze over my uncovered ass. But tangled up with Archer, too exhausted to dig something out of his very nice closet, there wasn't a stitch of clothing to be found.

When I woke, weak gray light filtered in through the windows. We'd moved to our own pillows at some point in the night, though they were pressed close together in the middle of the bed. That foggy half sleep didn't let go of my brain right away, and I lay there for a few minutes with my eyes closed and simply rested. There was no to-do list today. The shelter was covered, with someone else on call. Nothing screaming for my attention.

Just this.

Burying my face into the pillow that smelled like him, I pulled in a deep breath and then studied him while he slept. He looked younger like this. Less serious.

The line of his jaw was too tempting to be ignored, and the edge of my thumb found it, dragging over the stubble. If I looked, I'd have redness on the inside of my thighs from that stubble, and my cheeks warmed at the recollection. God, he was good. He was *so good* at everything.

To think I'd gone so many years not knowing this kind of physical compatibility existed, only to find it with someone who cared just as much about protecting my heart. It was a gift. Something I'd never take for granted.

Unable to resist, I leaned over and kissed the slope of his shoulder, then the notch at the base of his throat, where his delicious scent was concentrated. I dragged my nose over the skin there, my hands wandering down the tight muscles of his stomach until I found the trail of hair that I was looking for. I didn't move on just yet, tickling the skin with light brushes of my fingers.

Archer groaned low in his throat, his eyes still closed. "You're gonna kill me, woman."

I kissed his chest. "No, I won't."

His hands traveled along my waist and my back, coasting up and down my spine as I shifted over him and tugged the sheet down, dragging kisses along his sleep-warm skin as I did.

"Coach is gonna ask me why I'm slow as shit, and I'll have to explain that you literally fucked me into a coma."

I chuckled against his stomach, placing gentle sucking kisses between his abs. I loved his body. Hard, chiseled muscles for my own personal playground. Created for strength and speed, but I'd be the giddy recipient of all his other talents too.

Archer wound his fingers through my hair in a firm but gentle grip, tilting my face so that I looked up at him with my chin set on his stomach. I expected to find thinly veiled desire, with pupils blown wide, but what I found was something entirely different.

The way he looked at me was akin to adoration, almost worshipful. It wasn't sex in his bright-blue eyes, the heated looks that used to make me squirm. It was love.

I spread my hand over his chest, splaying my fingers wide over the firm, steady beat of his heart, and soaked up the charged intimacy of the moment. He dragged his thumb over my bottom lip, smiling faintly when I sighed.

"I'm going to be so pissed if I wake up and this isn't real," he murmured.

My heart gave a warm, contented beat before a smile ever formed on my lips. "I bet if this was a dream, my hair would be perfect and you would've woken up with my mouth on your—"

He growled slightly, pressing his thumb against my lips to cut me off. "No."

I raised an eyebrow, nipping at his thumb as he pulled it away. "No?"

Archer shook his head. "I don't want the fantasy of you, Remi. I want the real thing."

Wasn't the idea of reality the thing I'd donned like a shield? That the combination of his and mine was fundamentally incompatible, or so I'd told myself over and over. Remembering how thoroughly I'd believed that lie conjured a band of tension tight around my ribs, and as it snapped in place, I kept my gaze locked on his. What I saw there made it easier to breathe, and the tightness dissolved in the space of a heartbeat.

We could do this.

It wouldn't be easy, and we'd stumble more than once, but it wasn't impossible. How sweet it felt to believe that with every ounce of my being.

"Even when we hardly see each other because of work?" I whispered.

He nodded.

"And when Gavin gets sick and I can't come here on your day off?"

"I'll come over and help take care of you both."

My eyes fluttered shut as he traced a finger down my spine. "O-or when we have something planned and I need to go pick up a dog?"

"Dates in the car are sexy, didn't you know?"

I pried my eyes open, and he was watching me with a content smile tugging at the edge of his lips. "Are they?"

"So I hear," he answered easily.

Slowly, I shifted higher on the bed so his mouth was within kissing distance. Just in case.

"I could give you a hundred examples like this," I told him, tracing the edges of his lips with my fingertip. "Even if I did, we'll figure it out, won't we?"

His voice was rough. "Even then." His hand settled, big and warm, on the back of my neck. "Even when I'm exhausted and beat up and grumpy because we lose, and I'm still working twelve hours a day during the season."

I adopted a serious expression. "You won't lose now. I'm your good luck charm."

"That so?" He dipped his chin and gave me a lingering kiss, humming as he pulled back. "I'll let Coach know he's got nothing to worry about."

I laughed against his mouth, nuzzling into his touch as he slid his blunt fingertips down the line of my jaw. "Good."

Archer's gaze searched my face. "Can I make a request for today?"

"Me on top this time?" I teased. "You did say you were tired."

"Not that." His eyes heated. "But bookmark it for later."

My fingers drummed on his chest, and I bit down on my bottom lip to keep the laughter at bay. "If not that, what do you want to do?"

Archer's eyes dipped to my mouth, and he gave me a soft kiss before speaking. "Can we go hang out at your place?"

My heart stopped. "You'd want to?"

"Yeah." The shy smile tugging at his lips absolutely unraveled me. "I didn't get much time with Gavin yesterday, and, I don't know, I forgot to ask him what he thought of my present. If he opened it yet," he added. "It's fine if he didn't."

Melted.

I completely melted.

If I hadn't been in love with him before, that would have done it. I had a feeling that I'd fall in love with Archer Evans a million times for a million different reasons before my life was over.

"Yeah, I think we can arrange that."

"Well, look who showed up while the sun is still shining. Didn't think we'd see you before dark, bug."

Archer laughed, and over my shoulder, I gave him a narrow-eyed look. "Don't encourage him."

He gave me a crooked grin. "Sorry."

Yeah. He looked really sorry, especially when he paired that unrepentant smile with a quick squeeze of my ass since Pops couldn't see him yet.

Pops was in his recliner, reading a book about the Cold War, and he set it down on his stomach as we rounded the corner into the family room. His gaze tracked over me, then Archer right behind me, and down to where he held my hand in his. Pops smiled, then lifted his book back up to cover the bottom half of his face.

"Good to see you, Evans."

"Likewise, sir."

"You gonna be here every day now?"

His hand squeezed mine. "As long as she's not sick of me."

"Already looking for compliments?" I clucked my tongue. "What an unfortunate personality trait."

Archer's eyes glinted, and he dipped his head closer to my ear, lowering his voice so Pops couldn't hear him. "I'm pretty sure you came so hard, you saw stars about an hour ago. I'm not looking for shit, sweetheart."

Cheeks hot, I rolled my lips together and cleared my throat. "Right."

He straightened, looking like the cat who ate the fucking canary, and if it weren't so stupid attractive, I would've smacked him just for being cheeky.

Except it *was* attractive. And now my very well-used lady bits were throbbing.

I blew out a short breath and refocused. "Where's my kid?"

Pops tilted his head toward the bedroom. "He disappeared in there after Ness dropped him off."

"Gavin?" I called.

The door to his room flew open and he barreled out, almost knocking me over with his enthusiastic hug. "I had *so* much fun last night. Did Auntie Ness send you pictures of the blanket fort? It was huge."

She had. But I'd been too busy getting banged until my eyes crossed, so I hadn't seen them until we ventured back into the kitchen in search of food. I'd offered to whip up a couple omelets, but Archer started making out with me against the kitchen counter, and it proved too great of a distraction when I started thinking about hot stovetops and wandering hands, so we settled on leftover pizza from the night before, simply from a safety standpoint.

"I saw them a little bit ago. Pretty epic."

Gavin batted my hand away when I tried to fix his hair, his eyes darting over to Archer. "H-hey, Archer."

Even though he'd just seen him the day before, there was still a shy quality to his greeting, like he wasn't exactly sure how this was supposed to go.

"Hey, bud. Did Analise survive her first blanket fort?"

He grinned. "Yeah, she said it was awesome. We ate popcorn and M&M's and watched a movie in our sleeping bags."

Archer's smile was small, but so genuine that it made my chest ache. "That's good. I'm glad you invited her."

Gavin sucked in a sharp breath. "Can I open that present from you now?"

Archer glanced in my direction, and I smiled encouragingly. He turned his gaze back toward Gavin, his hand holding mine even more tightly. "You didn't open it yet?"

Gavin shook his head. He ran off to his room, returning with the box in his hands and his cheeks flushed with excitement. "I told Mom I wanted to wait until you were here again."

That hit him hard. I'd expected it would. Archer blinked a few times, then attempted a swallow. "You were pretty sure that would happen, huh?"

Gavin shrugged. "Yeah. I knew you liked her. And she wouldn't have been so sad if she didn't like you too. You guys just took a really long time to get back together." His eyes widened. "Like, *really* long."

"It was four days," I answered dryly.

"I know," he sighed. "Do you know how long four days is at my age? An eternity. I thought I'd have to help you out if it took much longer."

Archer laughed. "Yeah? Give me your best advice. I might need it, because you know her a lot better than I do."

Gavin plopped onto the couch, and Archer joined him, spreading his legs out wide as he settled into the middle cushion.

Pops watched the two of them from over the edge of his book.

"First, you have to know she cries a lot. Even when she's happy."

Archer nodded. "Noted. What else?"

"She said it's okay for boys to cry too. But I don't really understand half the stuff that makes her weepy. And I've never had happy tears, so I think that's just a mom thing." Archer managed to keep a straight face as he listened intently. "She loves chocolate. And she reads every night before bed, but she drops her Kindle on her face all the time."

"Twice. I've done it twice," I said.

Archer swiped a hand over his mouth to cover his smile. Based on the crinkles next to Pops's eyes, he was doing the same behind his book.

Gavin pursed his lips and tried to think of other things he could share.

"She says she doesn't take naps, but she falls asleep putting away laundry if she does it in the afternoon." His expression turned serious. "And if she offers to make you eggs, just say no."

I clapped my hands. "Okay, this has been fun."

Gavin and Archer shared a look. "You can tell me more later," Archer whispered loudly.

"Oh Lord." I rolled my eyes. "Just what he needs, a coconspirator."

The grin on Archer's face was devastating, dimpling his cheek in a way that made my heart flip, even more because he was aiming that grin at my son. He motioned me closer with a crook of his fingers. I curled up on the cushion next to him, sighing contentedly when his arm draped over my legs where they were bent next to his thigh.

Present clutched in his hand, Gavin watched us, the wheels turning behind his eyes.

He'd never seen me with a boyfriend. There was a slight catch in my throat, a blossoming worry that I'd sprung this on him too fast.

Yesterday at Archer's house had been different, busy enough with dozens of other people there to distract him. But here, in our home, it was a very different story.

His expression didn't look upset. Just thoughtful. But he'd stayed quiet so long, I couldn't help but worry.

"Is this okay?" I asked him. "I know we didn't, like, talk about it."

For a second, he stared down at his lap, then he nodded slowly. When he raised his head, his eyes were glossy. "I feel like someone is squeezing my heart and all the good stuff just can't stay stuck inside, so it's coming out my eyeballs."

I leaned my head against Archer's shoulder and smiled, so impossibly, blissfully happy that it didn't even seem real. His fingers twined through mine and squeezed.

Gavin sniffed. "Is this why you always cry during that commercial?"

"Yup. Heart squeezing out of my eyeballs, for sure."

Archer laughed under his breath, turning his head to press a soft kiss to my temple.

Pops caught my eye and winked as Gavin carefully slid his fingers underneath the beautiful red ribbon holding the box closed.

"Did you wrap that?" I asked quietly.

Archer shook his head. "No way, I'm the king of gift bags."

"Good," I exhaled. "If you were that talented at wrapping presents, too, I'd have to worry you were too perfect."

He grinned, his hand sliding over my thigh.

Gavin pulled the ribbon off and carefully set it on the floor next to the couch. The box on his lap was white with silver edges, a Buffalo logo gleaming in the middle. It wasn't even a gift I'd purchased, but I found myself nervous as Gavin used both hands to slide the top off. Black tissue paper covered the contents, held together by a Storm sticker.

I gave Archer a quick look, and he was holding his breath, uncharacteristic nerves stamped on his face.

Gavin tucked his tongue between his teeth and peeled back the sticker, then the tissue paper.

It was folded neatly into the box so that the name and number were visible first.

Gavin's mouth fell open, his eyes flying up to Archer's. "How did you . . ."

From my angle, I couldn't see it clearly, but when Gavin slowly lifted the jersey out of the box, my mouth fell open too.

It wasn't EVANS on the back, like I'd assumed.

It was SINCLAIR.

My gaze flew to Archer, but he didn't look away from my son.

"It's real," Gavin whispered in a trembling voice, his fingers tracing over the stitched letters, the patches on the shoulder.

"Exactly like the ones we wear on the field," Archer explained. "Let's see how it fits. I had to guess on the size, so I hope it's not too big."

Gavin's cheeks were flushed pink, and he pressed his lips together like he was trying to keep from crying, but he did as Archer asked. He tugged his T-shirt off and unfolded the jersey like it was a precious material that might rip or snag or tear at the slightest mishandling.

Archer motioned him closer and carefully eased the jersey over Gavin's head, holding it so that he could slide his arms through. It was a little big, unfolding down to Gavin's thighs, but based on the rapt expression on my son's face, he really didn't care.

"Whoa," he whispered, voice shaking slightly. "Why did you get me this?"

Archer set his hands on Gavin's shoulders, expression serious. "I understand why you got rid of my jersey," he explained slowly. "Until I earn the right to have you wear mine again someday, I still wanted you to have one." He paused, throat working on a thick swallow. "But you should wear a name that's worthy of respect." He tapped Gavin's chest. "I couldn't think of any name that was better than yours."

A tear spilled over Gavin's cheek.

My vision was already blurry and my cheeks wet, to the surprise of no one.

I'd lost the battle as soon as he pulled the jersey on, but kept my tears quiet so I could let them have this moment. Pops didn't have the same qualms, because he pulled out a handkerchief and blew his nose with a noisy honk.

We all laughed, and Gavin ran his fist under his nose as he stared down at the crisp lines of the number one stitched onto the front of the jersey. "I think this is the best gift I've ever gotten." He lifted his watery eyes to Archer. "Thank you."

Archer's voice was rough when he answered, his eyes slightly red. "You're welcome."

Gavin didn't hesitate, launching himself at Archer, who caught him with a startled laugh.

He'd given him so much more than a scrap of fabric, more than team colors or a number on his back. Archer was giving Gavin the kind of love and acceptance that Archer himself had never been given at this age.

Healing had a ripple effect, something that could be felt by more than just me and Archer. Not just in gifts or unscripted acts of benevolence. It was the feelings that spread as a result.

It was becoming abundantly clear that I'd need to reframe my inability to be surprised, because this one would've knocked me on my ass. Appropriate, I thought, considering that was exactly what Archer had done since the very first night.

Pops caught my eye and winked again.

Archer stayed at the house for the rest of the day and well into the evening, hanging out, watching TV, he and I sneaking kisses when no one was looking.

We made Archer watch *The Sandlot* because he'd never seen it. A tragedy, in the Sinclair house.

Gavin won a series in *Mario Kart*, and I came in second, despite Archer's claims that I was cheating. Pops beat them soundly in a couple games of Clue, while Archer cleaned house on an intense game of Monopoly that lasted well through dinner (which I had delivered, because all three of them put up a ridiculous protest when I said I'd grill some chicken and veggies).

"You've never even tried my cooking," I said to Archer when he insisted on paying for the food, handing a generous tip to a wide-eyed delivery person, who took it with her mouth hanging open.

As he eased the bags of Chinese food from out of my hands, he gave me a sweet kiss. "I've heard about it, and I think that might be enough for me."

"From *who*?"

Gavin hid his giggles behind his hand, and Pops covered his smile with an obnoxious cough.

"Hey, I'm good at other things," I protested.

Archer served up some beef and broccoli and handed me a bowl. "Lots of things," he said quietly, eyes glinting with double meaning.

I narrowed my gaze, and he gave me a wicked smile and walked off to enjoy his food.

Payback came later, after Pops and Gavin went to bed, and I forced Archer to watch me strip in my bedroom without allowing him to touch.

His heated gaze tracked over every inch of my body from where he sat with his back against the headboard of my bed. He absolutely dwarfed the space, and I smiled, imagining us trying to keep quiet with people sleeping on either side of the house.

"Come here," he commanded in a low voice.

I ran my hands over my breasts and down my stomach, watching with delight as his expression glazed over when my hands hooked into my lace underwear and tugged them off. "I thought you didn't want to enjoy my offerings," I said lightly.

"Remi," he growled, palming his hard-on through his shorts, giving himself a slow tug that made my stomach flip, "get over here."

"Take off your shirt."

He complied instantly, and the stacked muscles on his stomach pulled a whimper from my mouth. There was just enough hair on his chest and running down his stomach, like an exclamation point to just how fucking masculine he was.

It was my turn to wonder if I was dreaming. If my subconscious hadn't conjured the perfect man and was teasing me with what life could be like.

Not that it would always be like this—hours of relaxing and laughing and kissing when no one was watching, holding hands under the table and counting down to when we could be alone. It would get harder. We'd miss each other.

That was a strange sort of privilege, though, wasn't it? To miss someone and know they'd come back as soon as possible. To bicker and know that there was love underneath. To walk through the everyday stress of life and know they had your back, even if the fantasy faded in the face of the mundane.

But that fantasy wasn't fading today.

Today we could bask in how good this felt, and how right it was.

With his attention fixed solely on me, I climbed up onto the bed and swung my legs over his hips, settling on his lap while his palms skimmed my waist, his fingers ghosting over my nipples as he gave me a tongue-heavy kiss that lifted the hair on my arms.

I pulled back, biting down on my bottom lip. "You were so tired this morning. Maybe we—"

He gripped the back of my neck and gently bit down on the slope of my shoulder. "Unless you finish that sentence with *maybe we should keep this quiet*, I don't want to fucking hear it."

I smiled, running my hands over his chest. "You know what I was thinking about earlier?"

He kissed along my collarbone. "What?"

It was hard to speak through whatever he was doing with his mouth, but I wanted him to hear this. We'd both need reassurance as we moved forward into our new normal. Mine looked different from his, but they held equal weight. As much as I loved the feeling that he'd protect my heart, I wanted him to feel the same.

That I'd take care of him. That he was safe with me.

When Archer kissed underneath my jaw, I cupped his face in my hand and held his gaze.

I spoke quietly. "You're going to be an amazing father someday."

His eyes stayed locked on mine, his chest rising on a sharp inhale. "You sound very sure about that."

"I am." I ran my fingers through the hair at the back of his neck. "I've worked very hard to be both parents for Gavin. Some days I do better than others, but I've always worried—" My voice cut off when tears threatened. His hands moved in soothing motions on my back. "I've always worried that he'd be missing something by not having a father. You gave him something today, and I'm not sure it would have meant the same if it had come from me." Archer's eyes were bright with unshed tears, his hands tightening on my back as he listened intently. "You gave him what was never given to you."

It took him a moment to speak, and when he did, his voice was rough. "When he hugged me, God, it felt like . . . like it healed a scar I couldn't see or reach."

I leaned forward and kissed him just by the corner of his eye. Then the slight wrinkle in his brow. The tip of his nose. His cheek. Between each kiss, I whispered how much I loved him.

Archer gathered me close to his chest with a deep sigh as our mouths met in a long, slow kiss.

"I can't wait to see it," I whispered against his mouth.

He pulled back, gaze full of heat and love and breath-stealing certainty. "I'm going to be insufferable when you're pregnant."

My lips curled in a delighted smile. "Are you?"

Archer kissed me. "The worst. Won't be able to keep my hands off you. I'll worry endlessly. Get you everything you want."

"Keep talking," I moaned.

He nibbled along the line of my neck. "It'll be almost as bad when I get a ring on your finger."

I rubbed my chest against his and let out a stuttered exhale. "And when we get married?"

"Fucking obnoxious." He sucked the spot beneath my ear. "Like a caveman."

Our mouths clashed in a messy, heated kiss, and I rocked my hips back and forth over the tantalizing hardness beneath me.

Archer reached between us, teasing between my legs with his knuckles as he pushed his shorts down just enough.

I moaned, and he quieted me with another slick, tongue-heavy kiss.

"Quiet," he commanded against my lips. "I don't fancy getting in trouble with Pops."

I was giggling helplessly as he nudged me up with a firm grip on my waist. But when he teased me with a shift of his hips, the laughter turned into a soft whimper. His skin was impossibly hot, and I knew the stretch would be just past too much, especially after last night. We'd had the birth control talk sometime after the second round. I'd been on the pill since Gavin and hadn't slept with anyone in years, and to my shock, it had been well over a year for him too.

He watched with heavy-lidded eyes, his palms coasting up and down my thighs. "We're going to need a lot of practice before I get to call you my wife, aren't we?"

"Practice?" I grinned, biting down on my bottom lip. "Oh, you were so concerned with your stamina this morning. Maybe I should go get some cookies or something." I started to move off him, and his hands clamped hard on my hips, locking me in place.

"I'm having you for dessert," he whispered, nudging me up with an arrogant tilt of chin. His voice was rough and desperate as I reached between us to line myself up. "Now, fuck me, firefly."

That's exactly what I did.

Chapter Thirty-Three

Archer

"Is it too soon to propose?"

Remi handled my question remarkably well. With a thoughtful expression on her face, she set down her mint–chocolate chip ice cream and swiveled to face me. The place was almost empty, considering most of our dates happened later in the evening, when her work was done and Gavin was almost in bed.

"Well, it's our second official date," she said, her eyes glinting with humor.

"That's not a no."

She motioned for some of my ice cream by opening her mouth. I raised the spoon, loaded with chocolate chip–cookie dough topped with brownie pieces, and watched raptly as she closed her lips around it. Remi hummed, licking at the corner of her mouth.

"Tease," I whispered, tugging her closer for a sugary kiss.

"Maybe a little too soon."

It didn't feel like rejection because we were so fucking happy. Beyond the once-a-week dates, we'd seen each other every day for the last two weeks. Sometimes Analise came to their house with me—she and Pops had discovered a mutual love for Clue—and sometimes Remi and Gavin came over to mine. She hadn't spent the night again, but we'd gotten very good at quiet sex in her bedroom after the other occupants of her house were asleep. Or loud sex in my truck before I brought her back home and knew Analise wouldn't hear.

After another bite of ice cream, an idea occurred to me. "Eight dates," I told her.

Her brows furrowed. "What about them?"

"That sounds like a perfect amount of time, doesn't it?"

"To propose," she clarified. I could tell by the look on her face that she wasn't sure if she should believe me.

"Marriage." I motioned with my hand, making a circular motion over my ring finger. "You and me. Big ring."

Her eyes widened. "Not that big, please."

I chuckled, pulling her close for another kiss. The sweet old lady behind the counter smiled, then disappeared through a swinging door to give us some privacy. We'd enjoyed a decent amount of that since the pictures outside the courtroom went public. The buzz had faded quickly because there wasn't enough of a story to make it juicy.

We met in an unconventional way and fell in love. The end.

Not for us, of course. For us, it was the beginning.

"Sorta big," I whispered, then kissed her again. "I told you I'd be obnoxious."

"Fine. Big ring, small wedding," she said, brow arched in a challenge.

Even though my heart thundered in my chest at the ease with which we talked about it, I kept my face even. "I can handle that."

As long as she was the one walking down the aisle in my direction, I could handle fucking anything.

It didn't come up again. Not on date three, only a few days after date two—when I rented out a Michelin-star restaurant and watched her eat the most decadent meal either of us had ever experienced. Not on date four, when we went to a drive-in movie and cuddled under the stars in the bed of my truck.

We didn't talk about it in between our dates either. Not when I picked up Gavin from the last day of school in a blue Porsche that looked exactly like his LEGO set and watched with satisfaction as his classmates high-fived him on his way to where I was waiting in the parking lot. Not when we took Analise to the courthouse to finalize the paperwork for her legal emancipation, which went off without a hitch.

We didn't talk about it when Analise and I snuck into the shelter and filled out paperwork to adopt Bandit while Remi was in a meeting. She found us in the outdoor space, fitting him with his new red collar and a Buffalo Storm bandanna around his neck. She cried, of course, and even if it still didn't come up, we were both thinking it.

When dates six and seven rolled around—a picnic dinner at midfield, where we talked about football and what the season would look like when training camp started in just a few days, and then when I cooked dinner at my place, after which she spent the night again—I woke with her in my arms and wondered how the fuck I was supposed to wait to make her mine.

Every single day, every single action, big or small, was another building block in the kind of life we wanted together.

Remi was sound asleep when I snuck into the kitchen to start the coffee. Bandit lifted his head from where he slept on the couch. I'd bought the dog five beds of various shapes and sizes, and the only place he'd sleep was in the corner of the couch where I preferred to stretch out when I watched film.

"What do you think, bud? Stick to the program or wing it?" I asked, leaning down to scratch behind his ears. He leaned into my touch and groaned happily. "Yeah, I think I should wing it too. She'll forgive me."

While the coffee brewed, I opened the tallest cabinet and reached around until I felt the small velvet box. It had been up there for three weeks. I opened it, studying the way the ring caught the light.

Nothing had felt more right than this. Than her.

I fixed her coffee and started walking back to the bedroom, then froze, remembering a promise I'd made. One I'd never forgive myself for breaking.

I set the coffee down and skipped down the steps, carefully opening the door to the guest room we'd designated as Gavin's. He was sprawled out in the middle of the queen-size bed, snoring lightly. I crouched next to the side of the bed and gently rubbed his back.

He snapped up, hair crazy and face creased from heavy sleep. He was sleeping in his Sinclair jersey. "Wha— What happened?"

"Sorry to wake you up early, buddy."

Gavin's eyes stayed closed, but he nodded. "It's okay."

"Can I ask you something?" I whispered.

"Sure," he answered around a yawn. "Can we go out to breakfast to that cinnamon roll place?"

I smiled. "Yeah. I'm about to bring your mom some coffee. But I wanted to ask you something else. Something I promised to talk to you about first."

Gavin scrubbed at his face, finally awake enough that the small box in my hand registered. His eyes widened. "Whoa. Is that for Mom?"

I nodded. "I'd like to give it to her, yeah. But only if you're okay with that."

Gavin reached for the ring box and held it carefully in both hands, prying open the top. He didn't say anything as he stared at the ring, then closed it on a quiet snap. Then he handed it back and leveled a serious look in my direction. "You love her?"

There were no words for how much. Every day, I tried to think of a different way to say it, a different way to show it, but in the end, I knew it was in the simplest ways that she'd feel it the most.

"I do," I answered. "And you know what else?"

He shook his head.

"I love you too," I told him in an emotion-thick voice. "And one of the best parts of marrying your mom, if she says yes, is that I'll get to be with you every day too."

Gavin's chin trembled, but a tear spilled down his cheek before he could brush it away. "I love you too," he said in a shaky voice. "I really want you to marry her."

My vision had blurred dangerously, and when he leaned forward, throwing his arms around my neck, I didn't try to stop the tears that fell. "So I have your permission?"

He pulled back, eyes bright. "Do you need my help asking her?"

I grinned, ruffling his hair. "You got a good idea?"

Gavin paused, then glanced over my shoulder. "Well, maybe you could just do it now," he whispered.

I froze. "She's in the room, isn't she?"

He nodded.

"Right." My chest was too tight, my heart pounding too hard. I hadn't practiced what I was going to say. Not really. But I tucked the box in my hand and looked behind me. Remi had donned one of my college shirts and some cotton sleep pants that were way too big on her, a tiny smile curling her lips.

"Hi."

"Firefly. Didn't expect to see you down here."

Her eyes were glowing. "Apparently."

I stood from the side of the bed and approached, my eyes drinking in every inch of this woman I loved so much. When her gaze flicked down to the box in my hand and stayed there for a breathless moment, her chest rose and fell on a deep inhale and a long exhale.

I took her hand in mine, dragging my thumb over the soft skin on her knuckles.

"There are a million different ways I could try to say this," I started, "but there's only one thing I need you to know, and if you believe in that, then we don't need a million ways. We just need ours."

Remi's eyes sparkled with unshed tears as I slowly lowered to one knee, keeping her hand in mine. Then I opened the box and pulled out the ring, staring down at it for a moment. When I looked back up, she wasn't looking at the jewel. She was looking at me.

"I love you, Remi Sinclair. I will always love you. Always take care of you. Take care of our family. The one we have now and the one we build together. And if you'd do me the honor of marrying me, showing you that will be the greatest thing I've ever done in my life."

She closed her eyes, tears coursing down her cheeks. My face was wet, and when she sank down to the floor with me, wrapping her arms around my neck and finding my mouth for a tear-salted kiss, I exhaled an incredulous laugh.

"Yes," she whispered. "Yes, yes, *yes*."

Gavin jumped up on the bed and whooped loudly. Bandit ran down the stairs to investigate, hopping up onto Gavin's bed before he let out an excited bark. The dog had no idea what was happening, but damn if he didn't look happy. From across the basement, the sound of Analise's door opening made me grin as I buried my face in Remi's neck.

"It's so early," my sister groaned. "What is going on down here?"

I pulled back and slid the ring onto Remi's finger. She let out a shocked exhale when she finally saw it—two carats of a cushion-cut yellow diamond. A bright, warm light for my bright, warm girl.

"Archer," she breathed. "It's beautiful."

Analise gasped. "Is that—"

Gavin thrust his fist into the air. "We're getting married!"

Remi and I traded a look and burst into laughter.

Epilogue

Archer

Six months later

"God, you guys are messy."

"You're supposed to make a mess on Christmas morning," Gavin informed me, tearing into another present. The floor was littered with wrapping paper and bows and boxes and packaging. Pops was in his favorite chair—the one we'd bought him just before they moved in—studying the binoculars Analise had given him. She was leaning over his shoulder, pointing out the knobs to dial in the clarity.

Bird-watching was busier out at my place, so he needed to step up his game.

Our place, I corrected. Gavin, Pops, and Remi had moved in the weekend before Gavin went back to school. Same weekend the season kicked off. We'd talked it over and decided not to wait until we got married.

Being apart for training camp was hard enough. I hardly saw her during those six weeks. Even though my body and mind were sharp and ready for the regular season, there was an undeniable twinge of pain every time I came home at the end of a long day and she wasn't there.

Not only was she here now, but she was also my wife.

My *wife.*

Remi was sitting at my side on the floor, flipping through a hardcover book about cooking for beginners (a present Gavin had insisted would not offend her in the slightest), and every time I saw the glint of her ring, a proprietary thump echoed through my chest.

The chaos of our home was the kind of happiness I never could've dreamed up. Between Gavin and Analise and their school activities and homework, that would've kept us busy enough. Add in Pops, how busy Remi was at the shelter, and the grind of a regular season, and it was a miracle we got through every week with our sanity intact.

Our wedding, a small, intimate affair in our backyard, took place on a Friday night during our bye week in October. There were no big, flashy displays. Just us and our family, a few of our closest friends, and Bandit—with a bow tie around his neck.

We could've waited until the season was done, but it felt like we'd waited so damn long as it was. Adding a couple months for something bigger, grander, was a waste of time.

Our honeymoon, on the other hand, was the carrot dangling over my head as the season came to a close. Ten days in a private villa in the Maldives. Just me and Remi and the bikinis I'd be peeling off her behind closed doors. We had two games left—a few more, if we made the playoffs.

Expectations were high for the Buffalo Storm, and we were more than ready to meet them. The energy in the locker room was electric, day in and day out. We'd proved who we were as a team, not just to the fans but to each other too.

Nothing was ever a guarantee in my job, but this one was close as we looked ahead into the postseason. We had a two-game lead in our division and the easiest stretch of games in front of us, starting with the Christmas Day game later that day.

We opened presents early, woken up by Gavin and Bandit jumping into our bed at six thirty. I didn't have to leave for the game until noon, and even that felt too soon. Rebecca had left us with homemade cinnamon rolls that were just as good as the ones at the restaurant near my house. Better, probably, because we could have them anytime we wanted.

These were the moments I never thought I'd have, and man, they were good.

We'd spoiled the kids this year, and even though I'd promised Remi we wouldn't do presents with each other because of our honeymoon, I found a loophole by giving the shelter a half-million-dollar check so they could expand into a bigger building and hire more staff.

When she'd found out, she thanked me with sex in the bathtub, which was quickly becoming one of my favorite traditions—climbing in with her after she'd soaked away all her tension, only to wind her up again with my hands all over her wet, soapy body.

Not that I donated all that money so my wife would sleep with me. I did it because they needed it, and seeing her happy was the best part of any one of my days.

Remi loved her job, but with the way our life was now, she asked Muriel if she could share the director duties with Ness and pull back to part-time. It still let her stay involved, but now she had the kind of time she'd always wanted to volunteer at Gavin's school and be with Pops more.

Not just that, but the way she'd bonded with Analise was one of the best things I'd ever seen. Giving my sister someone like Remi, who could mother her in a way that I couldn't, was fucking incredible.

"Did we open everything?" Analise asked, joining Gavin on the floor as he studied the back of his new LEGO box. At his side, Bandit was on his back, completely oblivious to the holiday carnage around him, snoring lightly while Gavin scratched his stomach.

Gavin lifted his head like he'd just remembered something. "Oh! No, I forgot one."

"I think you opened everything, dude."

Remi slid her hand over my stomach, and I settled my fingers between hers. "I don't know," she said. "I think there's one more under there."

Gavin glanced at Remi, his eyebrows high on his forehead. "Should I . . . ?"

She nodded, then stole a glance at me when she could feel my curious look. Her smile was downright mischievous. "What? You just said *I* couldn't get you a present."

"I don't need anything," I said in a low voice while Gavin waded through veritable oceans of wrapping paper to find a small box at the base of the tree. "I have everything I need."

My wife smiled. "You can handle one more."

"Does it come with you wearing that lace thing I saw in the closet?" I whispered close to her ear. Pops cleared his throat loudly, giving me a sharp-eyed look that made me sit up straight. "Sorry," I told him. "It's her fault."

Remi laughed, elbowing me in the side.

Even though Pops loved the upstairs guest room, the three of us had decided that having his own space would be nice, too, and we'd begun construction on an "in-law suite" for him off the back of the garage. It wasn't huge—a spacious studio bedroom with a kitchenette and gathering area—but it was still part of the house when he needed us, and that was the most important thing.

Gavin stood up, hopping over the mess until he was standing in front of me.

"It was my idea," he said, shoving the box in my direction. He looked nervous.

Because it felt unbalanced to be on the floor while he was standing, I gave Remi an absent kiss and then shifted up onto the couch, my legs spread while I took the box from Gavin. It was light, almost like there was nothing in it.

I made a big production of weighing it in my hand, shaking it close to my ear. Gavin laughed.

Analise rolled her eyes. "Oh my *gosh*, just open it."

Remi shifted to the side so she was facing me, and she shared a quick glance with Gavin. Pops had set down his binoculars, and Analise moved onto her knees, her phone in one hand as she started filming. The weight of their attention made me nervous. The air in the room was charged, heavy with expectation, and my throat tightened inexplicably.

I slid my finger underneath the tape holding the gold paper down, then tugged the slim box out through the opening.

When I took the top off, there was a piece of paper inside, folded in thirds. My fingers trembled slightly as I lifted it from the box and held it in my hands. Gavin's handwriting appeared as I lifted the top fold and began reading.

"Dear Archer, I never thought too hard about what it would be like if my mom married someone. Sometimes I would see a dad with one of my friends and wonder what it was like, but we were happy, and I was okay. But now we're more than okay, and that's because of you." My voice cracked slightly, and I paused to let the wild pulse of my emotions settle. "I thought it was fun when I used to watch you on TV, but knowing you is even better. You make my mom really happy, and even though you're my stepdad now, I think it's even cooler that you're my best friend." I swiped my hand over my mouth and stared at Gavin. His eyes were wide and bright, and I could hardly see him through my tears. I inhaled deeply, and kept reading. "But I want you to be more than that." Remi's hand came up and her thumb brushed over my cheek, wiping away the trail of tears. "All I want for Christmas is for you to adopt me," I read in a trembling voice. "I don't just want you to be my stepdad or my best friend. I want you to be my dad."

With my chest cracked open, I pulled Gavin into my arms and held him as we both cried.

"Nothing would make me happier," I told him in a thick voice, pressing a kiss to the top of his head.

Then I wrapped my arm around Remi and held her close. Analise cried quietly as she filmed, and Pops wiped his cheeks unashamedly.

Later, when the mess was cleared up and Remi was tucked against my chest on the couch, I looked around the room—the fire in the fireplace, the tree full of homemade ornaments, and the woman I loved in my arms—and promised myself that I'd never take this for granted.

"Everything okay?" she asked quietly, her chin on my chest and her eyes soft.

I tucked her hair behind her ear and brushed my fingers over her cheek.

"Perfect, firefly. Everything's perfect."

ACKNOWLEDGMENTS

To start off, please forgive any legal discrepancies that arose in the writing of Archer's story. While I did my research on DUIs, I'm not a lawyer, y'all, and sometimes we need a good courtroom-gesture scene to really cap off a story. Blame Amy Daws, because it was her idea and it was too good not to use.

As per usual, Remi and Archer pushed me to the brink of my sanity as I got to know them well enough to tell their story, and trudging through those hard days where words don't come easily made it really clear how fortunate I am with the people in my corner.

My family, for the endless support.

Amy Daws, Devney Perry, and Kathryn Andrews were the head of the pep talk squad for this book, so the fact that I finished writing it at all is a testament to their ability to put up with me.

Kelli Collins and M. E. Carter for helping me polish the story. Maria Gomez and my agent, Georgana Grinstead, for being the very best cheerleaders.

Team Sorensen (a.k.a. Tina Stokes and Colby Robbins) for understanding why I had to ghost for an entire month, and keeping things running while I did.

"And hope does not put us to shame, because God's love has been poured into our hearts."

—Romans 5:5

ABOUT THE AUTHOR

Photo © 2018 Perrywinkle Photography

Karla Sorensen is a #1 Amazon bestselling author who refuses to read or write anything without a happily ever after. When she's not reading or avoiding laundry, you can find her watching football (British and American), HGTV, or listening to Enneagram podcasts so she can psychoanalyze everyone in her life, in no particular order of importance. With a degree in advertising and public relations from Grand Valley State University, she made her living in senior health care prior to writing full-time. Karla lives in Michigan with her husband, two boys, and a big, shaggy rescue dog named Bear. For more information, visit www.karlasorensen.com.

CONNECT WITH KARLA ONLINE

Instagram

www.instagram.com/karla_sorensen

Facebook Reader Group

www.facebook.com/groups/thesorensensorority

Website

www.karlasorensen.com

Newsletter

www.karlasorensen.com/subscribe